REUNITED WITH THE HEART SURGEON

JANICE LYNN

THE PAEDIATRICIAN'S TWIN BOMBSHELL

JULIETTE HYLAND

MILLS & BOON

Published in Great Britain 2021
by Mills & Boon, an imprint of HarperCollins*Publishers* Ltd,
1 London Bridge Street, London, SE1 9GF

www.harpercollins.co.uk

HarperCollins*Publishers*
1st Floor, Watermarque Building,
Ringsend Road, Dublin 4, Ireland

Reunited with the Heart Surgeon © 2021 by Janice Lynn

The Paediatrician's Twin Bombshell © 2021 by Juliette Hyland

ISBN: 978-0-263-29765-2

05/21

MIX
Paper from
responsible sources
FSC™ C007454

This book is produced from independently certified FSC™ paper
to ensure responsible forest management.
For more information visit www.harpercollins.co.uk/green.

Printed and bound in Spain
by CPI, Barcelona

REUNITED
WITH THE
HEART SURGEON

JANICE LYNN

MILLS & BOON

This book is dedicated to
medical professionals around the world.
Thank you for all you do.

PROLOGUE

Nurse Natalie Gifford unlocked Dr. Will Forrest's door and let herself into the luxurious New York City penthouse. She'd never known money had a scent, but the condominium they'd shared the past six months reeked of it. Money. Wealth. Extravagance. The finest of everything.

Just like Will.

But not her. How had she ever thought a girl who'd grown up in a poor North Jersey neighborhood could fit into his life? That they could be a couple and function as equals in their relationship? If nothing else, her birthday party had proved to her that she'd just been fooling herself.

"Rough night?"

Startled, Natalie jumped. She'd expected Will to have left to make early-morning hospital rounds and she hadn't noticed where he stood by a row of windows overlooking Central Park.

As usual, he'd dressed his six-foot frame impeccably, wearing dark gray pants and a crisp white shirt with the top couple of buttons undone. Perhaps it was because he had grown up as the only child of one of America's wealthiest blue-blooded families that he had such an air of power and allure. Or it could be his rich dark brown hair and vivid green Harroway eyes which graced the most handsome face she'd ever looked upon that made him so appealing. Even after spending a tearful night at Callie's, asking herself why she'd had to fall for someone so beyond her world, seeing him made her pulse pound so fast her breath could hardly keep up.

That's why she'd fallen for him. Despite their many differences, her silly heart had led her to believe they could have a happy-ever-after. That dreams really did come true, and although not quite a Cinderella story, she could have the fairy tale with a real-life Prince Charming.

Despite his silverspoon upbringing, Will worked hard, genuinely cared about others and had completely wowed her when they'd met. Watching the kindness and compassion he showed while interacting with others had stolen her heart from the beginning and still gave her aww moments.

Watching Will stirred her no matter what he was doing. Quite simply, the man took her breath away.

He'd yet to turn toward her, but didn't question that it was her. The building's doorman had probably called to let him know she was on her way up before she'd even stepped foot into the elevator. Usually friendly, the doorman had given her messy bun, the ill-fitting jeans borrowed from her best friend, sandals, T-shirt, and the paper bag containing her party dress and heels a disapproving shake of his head. Yes, she had stayed out all night, but not because she'd been up to no good. She'd been nursing a broken heart. How horrible that her surprise twenty-fifth birthday party had ended with her crying on her best friend's sofa.

"You might say that," she admitted, pushing a stray auburn hair behind her ear as she stared at his stiff back. Did he regret their fight as much as she did? Was he ready to admit that his mother had intentionally used

Natalie's birthday party to drive home the differences in their socioeconomic backgrounds? Not that Natalie needed any help in recognizing the stark contrast. These days, she felt it more often than not. To put the icing on the cake, Rebecca Harroway Forrest had invited Will's "perfect for him" ex-girlfriend and kept throwing them together. When Will had given in to his mother's urging and danced with the woman, Natalie had had enough.

"How about you?" she quipped. "Rough night or did your mother send Stella over to comfort you?" She wouldn't have put it past Rebecca.

What had Natalie ever done other than love Will? But Rebecca's issues with her had nothing to do with how Natalie felt about Will and everything to do with the fact Natalie wasn't good enough for her precious son. Natalie didn't have the right pedigree or back account.

Will turned and the coolness in his eyes just about undid Natalie. She knew he was mad that she'd left her party without telling him. He'd made that clear during their brief phone exchange which she'd ended by hanging up on him. But she'd been mad, too. Livid. How dare he be so blind to Rebecca's meddling in their relationship, so tolerant of how she took every opportunity to let Natalie know she wasn't a welcome part of Will's life or their upper-crust family?

"Then you agree I was wronged and needed comforting?" His tone matched his gaze. She couldn't recall having ever seen that particular hue to his eyes before. Who knew green could look so cold?

"Not at all," she corrected. He'd been the one dancing with Stella Von Bosche. Yes, it had only been after Rebecca's urging, but *he should have said no*. "It was my night that was ruined."

His gaze narrowed. "Was something at your birthday party not up to your expectations?"

"A lot. For example, I expected my family and real friends there." She didn't attempt to hide her anger at the poor choices he'd made. For such a brilliant man, when it came to his family, he could be so clueless. "Not a bunch of strangers invited to purposely make me feel as if I didn't belong. And, you dancing with your ex-girlfriend absolutely wasn't something I expected."

Guilt flashed across his face, momentarily replacing the ice.

"If I'd realized it would bother you, I wouldn't have danced with Stella," he admitted.

Relief rushed through Natalie. His admission was a start in the right direction to soothing the unease she'd been experiencing more and more over the past few weeks. They never fought. Her gut twisted that they were now. Natalie's nature was to keep the peace, even to her own detriment. But not this time.

"You should have talked to me, not left without a word."

He wasn't wrong. She should have talked with him. At the time logic had been beaten down by her own emotions, and her self-doubts worsened by Rebecca's cooing over how wonderful it was that Stella was back in her son's life, how much they had in common and how no couple had ever been more perfect for each other. Natalie had had to leave. Either that or she'd have done something she would have regretted—like tell Rebecca what she thought of her.

"Do you know how I felt when I realized you were gone?" Raw emotion harshened Will's words. "That I had to make excuses at your own party for why you were no longer there?"

Nausea churned the few bites of breakfast she'd forced down at Callie's insistence. The entire night had been such a mess.

"I dare say you didn't feel nearly as upset as I did that leaving appealed more than staying at my birthday celebration. Then again, that party wasn't about me."

"If you'd stuck around, you'd have realized it was." Any semblance of calm was gone as he stepped away from the window. "I wanted to spend my night with you, and you left. *You left me.*"

His reactive, accusatory words both hurt and soothed her inner ache, but not enough to sway her sharp, defensive reply.

"You were barely with me when I was at the party." She lifted her chin, daring him to say otherwise.

"My father is up for reelection for his Senate seat. Spending a few minutes talking with his supporters shouldn't have been a problem." His brow arched. "Mother said you didn't appreciate—"

"That she invited your ex-girlfriend? That she planned my birthday party that you said was a surprise from you?" Natalie's anger surged. "Or that while I was listening to her go on and on about how perfect you and Stella were together and she just knew wedding bells were in your future, you were on the dance floor with said ex-girlfriend hanging all over you?"

"Natalie—"

"You seriously think I'm wrong to be upset?" she interrupted, gripping the sack she held tighter and crinkling the paper as her hand fisted. Part of her wanted to whack him with the bag to knock some sense into him.

Stopping to stand just in front of her, Will's gaze narrowed. "Stella's family are longtime friends of my family and she's Mother's goddaughter. I'll be cordial to her for that reason, if no other. Have I ever given you reason not to trust me, Natalie?"

He hadn't. That is, until she'd seen him laughing with Stella and felt the sharpest stab of pain she'd ever known, and all her doubts about their compatibility had exploded within her. After seeing him with Stella and Rebecca's words ringing in her ear, she'd felt so emotionally defeated she'd begged her only actual friends present, Callie and Brent, to get her out of the pretentious party.

"I don't appreciate not being trusted," he continued.

She jutted her chin upward. "I don't appreciate that your ex-girlfriend was at my birthday party."

"My mother—"

"Don't get me started about what I don't appreciate where that woman is concerned," she huffed, glaring at him.

Warning flashed in Will's eyes. "Stop right there, Natalie. You're treading on thin ice."

No doubt. Which was why she'd let Rebecca get away with her jabs time and again. Because Will would defend his mother to his dying breath. Why was Natalie bothering? They were so close that Will couldn't imagine his mother as anything other than Saint Rebecca. If Natalie told him everything the woman said and did, he wouldn't believe that Rebecca continually insinuated he was just passing the time until Stella returned.

And now, much to Rebecca's joy, Stella was back.

Natalie's stomach lurched. Her belly had been on edge the past few weeks as she'd felt Will's distraction, knowing he was keeping something from her and had grown withdrawn. Had Stella's return triggered the change in him, or had he just grown bored with Natalie?

The writing was on the wall. She could cut her losses or she could continue to live on edge, waiting to be tossed aside when Rebecca succeeded in driving a wedge so deep between them that they couldn't recover. Was that what the night before had been about? His mother smiling so happily as she'd surprised him with Stella's appearance?

No doubt anyone who'd looked their way would have thought Natalie and Rebecca were having a pleasant conversation as Rebecca smiled at the dancing couple while verbally inserting a knife into Natalie's heart and twisting it. For all Rebecca's gouging at her happiness, Natalie blamed Will as much, if not more, than she blamed his mother.

"Fine. I'm on thin ice, but guess what?" she spat back, months of biting her tongue unleashing. "So are you for being blind to the way your mother treats me. Thin, *cracked* ice."

"You're wrong," he defended, his brows furrowing. "Mother tries to reach out to you, but you're so biased you don't see that you push her away. That you let your insecurities about your background be a barrier to your relationship with her."

"Seriously?" Natalie rolled her eyes. "Is that what she tells you?"

"She asked to help me with your party because she wanted to do something special for you, to introduce you to our friends, and welcome you to the fold to let you know you're welcome."

"Of course she did." Natalie snorted. "And lucky for her that Stella came home to make the night even more welcoming."

Hands trembling, she turned to go. She really had had enough. If he'd loved her, she'd have been invincible to anything Rebecca tossed her way and would stay forever, but Will had never said he loved her. The one time she'd braved saying those three words out loud to him, he'd feigned being asleep. She should have known right then that they weren't meant to be.

Maybe she had, because wasn't that around the time she'd started feeling him pull away from her? Becoming more and more distant the weeks that followed?

She'd been such a fool. Love really was blind.

"Natalie!" Her name came out a bit ragged as he reached for her arm, stopping her from leaving. "You're behaving childishly."

Probably. The tears in her eyes certainly made her feel less adultlike.

"I can't believe you've allowed your bias about my mother to ruin your birthday party and lead us to spend a night apart." He sounded incredulous as he gently turned her to face him. "Nor can I believe we're fighting over my mother and Stella when there's no need."

Battling her tears, Natalie's heart thundered against her ribcage as he traced his finger over her cheek. Every nerve ending within her sparked to life like a Fourth of July show finale. Lord help her. It was no wonder she was putty in the man's talented hands. He touched her and she turned to mush. Only, she didn't want to be mush.

Not anymore. She wanted…

"Surely you know you have nothing to worry about where any woman is concerned?" he continued, his touch gentle as he cradled her face, forcing her to look up at him. He looked sincere, looked upset that they were at odds. Good. It upset her, too.

"How do I know that, Will?" she pressed even as tingles of awareness shot over her body just as they always did when he touched her. One little touch and she instantly wanted to kiss him until they were both breathless. Their chemistry was intense and had been from the moment they'd first met at the hospital when she'd dropped off lunch and a drink for Callie.

Will studied her, seeming surprised by her continued antagonism. "Because I want you."

Want. She needed more than want. Their explosive attraction was what had gotten her into this mess. One sexy I-want-you smile and conservative, play-it-safe, gonna-have-a-better-life-than-my-parents Natalie had been his for the taking. To be fair, all she'd had to do was give him a flirty look and he'd been hers for the taking, too. That Will had been so smitten had stunned her. When the good-natured cardiac surgeon, who also happened to be the only son of Senator William Forrest Sr. and business icon Rebecca Harroway Forrest, could have anyone, why Natalie?

Maybe that's why it was so easy for Rebecca's barbs to dig in.

Most days Natalie barely believed one of the city's most eligible bachelors wanted ordinary her.

"I'm tired of doubting myself, feeling as if I don't belong here, in your apartment, and in your life. I'm not willing to live like this, questioning myself all the time, questioning us, anymore. I deserve better."

"Questioning us?" He frowned. "I'm sorry you misunderstood about Stella, but if you'd stayed, you and I would have had an amazing night celebrating your birthday rather than a miserable one."

Natalie's insides shook. She might have misunderstood his dance with Stella, but there was nothing to misunderstand about what Rebecca had bluntly said. Nor the fact that Will refused to acknowledge that his mother had never approved of their relationship.

"I was miserable long before your dance with Stella," she admitted, realizing it was true and wondering how a person who made her so happy could also leave her feeling so unsure of herself. "It just took seeing you with her for me to admit to myself that I'd had enough."

To say he looked stunned was an understatement, and Natalie just stared as he asked, "You were miserable with me?"

Natalie put her hands on her hips as anger, frustration and so many emotions batted for pole position within her. Disgusted with herself, she flipped her hair back and spoke with more bravado than she actually felt.

"In case your memory is foggy, I wasn't with you," she pointed out, refusing to back down as all the things she'd been holding in poured from her. "I haven't been with you in weeks. Longer. You've been so busy and distracted that, other than at the hospital or at the Cancer Society for Children committee meetings, we've barely seen each other. You come home tired and distracted and won't talk to me about what's bothering you, even though I know something is. I feel the change in you and want to help and yet, you shut me out. Do you think I'm incapable of understanding? Or that I haven't felt the changes in our relationship? You and me—" she gestured to his chest, then her own "—we don't fit. I thought we did, but I was wrong."

The words gushed from her and, deep down, maybe she'd always known they were true. Maybe that's why she hadn't interrupted his dance or rebutted Rebecca's barbs, but had retreated to lick her wounds. Because part of her had always acknowledged Will would never be hers long term.

His face losing color, he took a step back. When his mouth opened, likely to remind her just how well they did fit together physically, she continued.

"At least, not outside the bedroom, we don't." Because

there was no denying how perfectly their bodies melded. Maybe that's all it had ever been, phenomenal sexual attraction and she'd been too naive to see the truth. "I thought we did—" oh, how she'd believed that "—but your mother was right and I was only fooling myself that we ever could. Whatever was between us is over. I'm done with trying to fit into your world and pretending that I ever could."

The skin on his face pulled tight, his cheeks flushing to an angry red.

Before he could tell her to get out, she said, "I'll pack a bag to take to Callie's and be back for the rest of my things."

Tell me not to go. Tell me you want me to stay. Tell me your mother will eventually approve of me despite my lack of pedigree and hefty bank account and that someday we can be a family. Tell me you love me.

He said none of those things.

What did she say to the man she loved when she didn't want to go, but when even on the verge of goodbye, he couldn't find words to convince her to stay?

Natalie sighed as she battled with the surrealness of what was happening. She was leaving Will. He was letting her go. They were ending. How could her fairy-tale romance have turned into a nightmare heartache?

"I'll have your other things delivered to Callie's later today."

"Okay," she choked out. "Thank you."

Heart breaking, she headed to the door.

"Natalie?"

Thank you, God.

She turned back, hoping he was going to tell her not to leave, that he'd make his mother understand how important she was, that he couldn't imagine his life without her, and then she'd run into his arms, they'd kiss and figure this out. They couldn't be ending.

They just couldn't.

Her gaze connected to his. His usual polished persona faltered and she got a brief glimpse that he wasn't as calm about her leaving as he'd appeared, but his next words shattered that illusion.

"Goodbye, Natalie. Have a nice life."

CHAPTER ONE

"IF POSSIBLE, I need you to swap my patient assignments," Natalie pleaded with the Cardiovascular Intensive Care Unit's nurse manager. "As in immediately, please. I can't work as Will's nurse."

Early that morning when she'd agreed to cover for another nurse who'd unexpectedly called in sick, she'd never imagined she'd be assigned Will's patients or she'd have refused to come in on her day off. Yes, she'd known it possible she'd see him, but thought she could mostly avoid him by staying busy in a patient room. Not that they traveled in the same circles, but having lived with him for six months, she knew his routine and the places he frequented.

Knew and had avoided them for the past month.

She'd not heard a peep from him since she'd walked out of his apartment on the morning after her birthday party. He'd had a moving company bring her boxed-up belongings that were, with a few unpacked exceptions, now stacked in the corner of Callie and Brent's spare bedroom, awaiting her decision on what she planned to do next. Her friends had set up a cot in the room they'd been using as an office, telling her to stay, and that they appreciated the rent money she'd insisted they take. She tried to make sure they had plenty of private time, but she knew it couldn't be any fun for the newlyweds to have her crashing in their space. She'd been volunteering a lot at the Cancer Society for Children to work on the gala and anything else Katrina had for her to do. She'd also signed on to work as many extra shifts as the hospital would let her. She'd been staying busy so she didn't have time to dwell on Will.

She'd like to say it was working, but unfortunately, she wasn't sure that level of busy existed.

"You have a problem working with Dr. Forrest?" the nurse manager asked, barely looking up from initialing papers on her desk.

Natalie stared at the older, stern woman. She'd seen her around the hospital a few times and always had a healthy respect for Callie's boss. Her bestie both admired and feared no-nonsense Gretchen and Natalie felt the same.

"I'd prefer not to work with him." Oh, how the tides had turned. Once upon a time she'd thought about putting in for a transfer to CVICU just so she could spend more time with Will. Thank goodness she'd decided against doing so or she'd be stuck seeing him over and over.

"Do you feel you can't professionally perform your job duties, Miss Gifford?"

Now, there was a loaded question. If she said she could, then there was no need of a patient assignment change. If she said she couldn't, then it made her look incompetent.

Staring the woman in the eyes, Natalie chose her words carefully. "I would have much higher job satisfaction if I wasn't Will—er… Dr. Forrest's nurse today or at any point in the future that I agree to fill in at the CVICU."

To put it mildly.

"You expect me to completely shuffle the schedule because of your personal relationship with Dr. Forrest?"

"Past personal relationship," Natalie clarified, her face heating. "And, yes, I would be appreciative if I didn't have to work directly with him." Why was the woman giving her a hard time? After all, she'd agreed to come in to help and in some ways was doing the lady a favor by ensuring the floor had enough nursing staff. "Surely, you understand my request given the circumstances?"

The thought of seeing Will made her head spin and her heart hurt. How was she supposed to focus on her patients when he was near and no longer hers? When there would be no more special smiles or winks when their eyes met? When he wouldn't go out of his way to make her laugh or to brush his hand against hers or whisper sweet nothings in her ear? Or…or refuse to believe his mother was out to destroy their relationship? Refuse to treat Natalie as his equal and someone he was proud to have at his side when attending his father's political fundraising events or the Harroway Foundation business dinners he'd gone to without her?

"Can you professionally perform your job duties?" the nurse manager repeated, her tone brooking no argument and suggesting that Natalie had best answer correctly.

It appeared she was going to have to see him. Her relationship with Will had already cost her heart and countless hours of sleep. She wouldn't allow it to affect a job she'd always loved.

"Yes."

"Then go do them."

Frustrated, Natalie reentered the CVICU unit, and signed in to her patient's chart, trying to focus on the orders even though her mind raced. Before the day was over, she'd see Will, have to interact with him, have to pretend they'd never meant anything to each other. Was she really that good an actress?

Was it possible that maybe her heart had grown immune to his many charms in the weeks since she'd last seen him?

Spotting her, Callie joined her at the nurses' station. Correctly reading her expression, her friend asked, "She wouldn't change your assignments?"

The words on the screen blurring, Natalie sighed. "She wouldn't even consider it. It's my own fault. I should have put that stipulation in when I agreed to cover for Connie this morning. I just never thought, well, you know."

"Oh, Nat. I'm glad you're here, getting to work with me just like back in nursing school, but I'm sorry she wouldn't swap your patient assignments." Callie made a face, then brightened. "Problem solved. I'll take care of your patients and you take care of mine. Both of my patients are admitted to Dr. Kumar. No big deal on the swap."

No big deal prior to her conversation with her nurse manager, perhaps.

Natalie shook her head. "Thank you, but after how adamant she was about her schedule not being disrupted I have a feeling I'd be fired if we swapped, or at the minimum, written up. Which would be bad enough on my end, but I'd never forgive myself if you got in trouble, too."

Callie's eyes widened. "You think? Why would they do that? Why should they give a flying flip how our patients are divvied up so long as we provide excellent care to them all?"

"Who knows? Maybe it's because a wealthy doctor whose family pours a ton of charity money into the hospital is involved." Natalie shrugged. "There's a wing named after his great-grandfather. They'd think nothing of letting me go if there's the slightest tension."

Callie frowned. "Why would they care if you're assigned to his patients or not? Looks like they'd want to make things easier by avoiding potential conflict."

So one would think. Natalie sure hadn't expected to get a no when she'd asked to swap. "Who knows? Maybe Will will take one look at me being on the unit and let it be known that he doesn't want me assigned to his patients today, and that'll be that."

No way would the nurse manager deny *his* request. Not when his family was so generous to the hospital.

While working in the CVICU, she wouldn't be able to avoid seeing him, but if she wasn't assigned to his patients, it would help. No doubt he'd be doing his best to avoid her, as well. Maybe things wouldn't be as bad as she feared. Maybe she'd be over him and the mere sight of him wouldn't send her heart into palpitations.

"I'm being paranoid." Wanting to bang her head against the fuzzy computer screen, Natalie sighed. "Don't listen to me. I'm just aggravated that I'm being forced to work with him when the last thing I want is to lay eyes on Will Forrest ever again."

"I'll keep that in mind."

Natalie and Callie spun at the sharp words.

"Will!" Natalie gasped, her heart slamming against her ribcage as her gaze ate up the sight of him. So much for hoping a month had left her immune to him. If anything, all time had done was make her that much more aware of how every fiber of her being yearned for him.

His deep green eyes regarded her, his expression terse, reminiscent of the coolness with which he'd looked at her that last morning at his apartment. Time didn't seem to have made his heart grow fonder, because any fool could see that he wasn't happy she was there, in the CVICU, on his turf. How long had he been standing there? Had he heard her talking about his mother? Ugh. She should have known better. She did know better.

"I mean, Dr. Forrest," she corrected, not willing to let him be the one to tell her to address him more formally as she no longer had the right to call him by his first name.

All she had left was her dignity and she wouldn't let him take that, too. His expression didn't change, other than his eyes darkening further before turning to address Callie.

"Which nurse is assigned to Mattie Johnson?"

"Natalie, but I'll be happy to round with you," Callie offered despite their previous conversation about the nurse manager refusing to switch patient assignments. No doubt her friend was trying to save her.

His lips tightened. "Is there a reason why Natalie can't provide care for her patients?"

"No reason," Natalie jumped in before Callie felt further obligated to rescue her from this awkward situation. How many times had she wondered what it would be like to see Will again? Now she knew.

"Let me get logged out of this chart, and I'll be right with you," she said to buy herself a few seconds to collect her wits. After not seeing him for a month, she was face-to-face with the man she'd once thought she'd spend the rest of her life with. How could she have been so naive? Men like him didn't marry social nobodies like her.

Now, at least for the day, they'd be coworkers. Her nurse to his doctor because both of her patients belonged to Will.

"By all means take your time." His sarcasm wasn't lost on her. "It's not as if our patients in CVICU are critical."

Will's judgmental tone irked. How dare he stare down

his snooty nose at her as if she'd done something wrong in saying she was going to log out of the chart she was in. She hadn't, and he knew good and well that she couldn't walk away from a computer that had a logged-in patient on the screen.

All she'd ever wanted to be was a registered nurse and she strove to be a good one. Today, taking care of his patients, was no exception. Other than for the remainder of her shift she'd be pretending that he hadn't broken her heart.

Darn him for making her question herself. For making her pulse pound, for making her nerves jittery, and shattering her dreams of a happy-ever-after. Just...darn him.

Clicking to log out on the chart her fuzzy brain had failed to decipher anyway, Natalie narrowed her gaze in feigned disgust—or maybe it was real. She'd given him her heart. Shouldn't he have had her back? Even when it came to his mother? Regardless, she glared long enough she hoped he got the point. She didn't plan to pine away for him—or, at least, not let him know she was.

She'd do her best to concentrate on her patients. It was only for a day. She could do this.

Mattie Johnson was a sixty-year-old African American woman who'd gone to the emergency room via ambulance with chest pain and ended up admitted with a "widow-maker" early that morning. Thank goodness the woman hadn't delayed in activating the emergency system or she likely would have died from the significant blockage of the main artery supplying her heart with oxygenated blood. Will had just arrived at the hospital to prep for a routine procedure, which had gotten pushed back while he stented the woman's left anterior descending artery, restoring oxygenated blood flow to her heart and saving her life. After she was stable enough, she'd been transferred to the CVICU, which had occurred just prior to shift change.

And she'd been assigned to Natalie.

Will's gaze narrowed slightly at her scowl, then without another word, he walked away, leaving Natalie and Callie to watch him leave.

Natalie's heart squeezed and she fought to keep from saying his name to call him back. She wouldn't.

What would it matter if she did? He'd been hers and she'd chosen to leave, a little voice reminded. Only, he hadn't been hers. Not really. If he had, he still would be. She'd decided in the past few weeks that his mother had been right. He'd been Stella's all along and Natalie had just been a fun way to pass the time until his true love came home. She had been convenient, and the sex had been great, so why not? Otherwise, he'd have come after her, right? Or he would have at least called or texted or reached out in some way to let her know that he was sorry, that he missed her, that absence really had made his heart grow fonder.

"You okay?"

Not meeting Callie's eyes, Natalie nodded. She needed to do her job and to not let her personal life seep into her workday. She couldn't afford to lose her job.

"I know seeing him wasn't easy."

Ha. That was the understatement of the year. Who wanted to see their superhot cardiac surgeon gazillionaire ex-boyfriend after the breakup? After the he's-the-one-I'm-going-to-marry euphoria had morphed into heartbreak and tears? Why couldn't his hold over her heart have loosened over the weeks apart?

"It'll get easier."

Natalie couldn't fathom how. She'd not been willing to live the rest of her life as things had been, with his not valuing her role in his life and his refusing to see the truth about his mother. But maybe she hadn't thought out the whole living-without-Will bit as thoroughly as she should have.

Still, if she had to have Will as an ex, then at least she could hold her head high knowing she'd been the one to walk away rather than waiting for him to kick her to the curb. Yes, everyone probably thought her crazy, but at least she could cling to that small tidbit as she was bombarded with sympathy from her well-meaning coworkers.

"You're right. Things will get better." She smiled at Callie and thanked God she had such a great best friend. She needed to keep her thoughts trained on the good in life. A month had passed. She'd survived. She had this. "I'm going to check on Mrs. Johnson. Thanks for everything, Cal."

Right before Natalie had spoken with the nurse manager, Mrs. Johnson's readings had essentially been the same the night nurse had reported at shift change.

Will must have gone to a different patient room since Mrs. Johnson was still alone in her room. At first glance Natalie knew something had changed during the short time lapse between checks. She listened to the woman's chest and didn't like the raspy breath sounds she heard. Nor that the woman's oxygen saturation level had dropped some despite her being on oxygen via a nasal cannula. Not enough that her monitor alarm had sounded, but a few percentage points.

"Mrs. Johnson?" she said, hoping the woman responded and her vitals improved with some deep breathing exercises. Perhaps she was just in a deep sleep and that's why her vitals had declined.

Mrs. Johnson opened her eyes, but never fully focused

on Natalie before closing them again. She'd been sleeping when Natalie had been in the room earlier, too.

"Mrs. Johnson, I need you to take a few deep breaths for me." Some big ones in the hope it would help clear her noisy chest and increase her oxygen saturation.

The woman's eyelids flickered, but that was the only response to Natalie's request.

"Mrs. Johnson, it's time to wake up. You need to use your incentive spirometer." She attempted to rouse her patient with a gentle shake of her shoulder, again to no avail. So much for gently trying to wake the woman. Natalie clenched her fist and rubbed her knuckles across the woman's chest in a sternal rub meant to elicit a pain response. She got a flinch from the lethargic woman, but nothing more.

She glanced at the monitor screens. Nothing was so out of line that she should be alarmed, but something more was going on. Sometimes it happened that a patient just needed rest and didn't wake much post-surgery, especially one as critical as Mrs. Johnson's early morning procedure. But Natalie didn't like the fact that she couldn't get the woman to wake.

Was Will still with his other patients? Whether she wanted to interact with him or not, she was going to have to call him to the room.

Will paused outside Mattie Johnson's room when he realized Natalie was with his patient. Since she'd not been at the nurses' station, he'd known he'd likely see Natalie in Mattie's room.

Like a glutton for punishment, he'd practically ordered her there.

To check his patient, he assured himself. Because he'd operated on Mattie and was making rounds. Of course he'd check the woman prior to leaving the CVICU and would want to discuss how she was doing and her care with her nurse. It's what he did.

His reasons didn't have anything to do with seeing Natalie and how his gaze had immediately latched onto her when he'd entered the CVICU. Thanks to an early-morning call saying Natalie was covering in the unit, he'd known she'd be there. Was it wrong that when a friend in human resources had asked, he'd told them it was fine for her to care for his patients if that's how the assignments naturally fell? That she was an excellent nurse, and he didn't want his patients deprived of her nursing skills? Probably. He'd not wanted to risk the hospital dinging Natalie's career in any way if he'd said he'd rather her not be on the unit. Plus, he had wanted the best for his patients. Natalie was.

The best at a lot of things.

Part of him still couldn't wrap his brain around the past month. How he'd gone from feeling as if she completely adored him to—her words from earlier popped into his head—to her not wanting to see him at all.

How was that even possible?

He'd felt powerless when she'd walked out of their apartment with her suitcase. Completely gutted. Something he wasn't used to feeling and didn't know quite how to deal with. She'd left him. If she cared for him, how could she have done that over what he considered nothing more than a misunderstanding?

Knowing he was going to come face-to-face with her for the first time in a month had kept him hyperaware of every breath, every beat of his heart as he'd made his way to the unit. Would their eyes meet just as they had the first time he saw her and would his world shift again? Or had her abandoning their relationship killed his feelings for her?

How could she have just walked away without fighting for what they shared? If she'd loved him as she claimed, she wouldn't have left.

Yet, she had.

Which told him all he needed to know. Just as well that he'd choked up when she'd whispered those three words to him one night after they'd made love. After his failed relationship with Stella, and then with Natalie, Will didn't know what love was, but he had a lot of experience with what it wasn't.

Still, overhearing Natalie's conversation with Callie first thing had knocked him hard, again. Not only did she not regret leaving, but she didn't want to see him, period. That shouldn't matter. It didn't matter, right? She'd left. A month had passed. Of course, she didn't want to see him. Only a fool would have thought otherwise.

Will was no fool.

But when he'd heard she'd agreed to work on his floor, he'd wondered if maybe she wanted to see him, maybe she…never mind what he'd felt when he'd gotten that call. It didn't matter.

He'd been devoted to their relationship and she hadn't. Why had she gotten so upset? Because his overwhelmed mother had wanted to help with her party, and he'd been thrilled that even with as much as she had going on, she wanted to do that for Natalie? He'd hoped maybe for once Natalie would see that his mother wasn't the enemy? Or was she mad because he'd danced with Stella?

That Natalie had jumped to conclusions and walked away spoke volumes. She hadn't trusted him. That cut deep. He'd dealt with jealousy in the past, even with Stella. Relationships were doomed to fail when there was no trust, and to pretend otherwise was a waste of a couple's time.

Not that he'd given Natalie any reason not to trust him. Admittedly he had been distracted by his mother finding a lump in her breast and trying to keep it hush-hush when she went for testing, because she'd insisted no one know. Which included Natalie. Harroway Industries was in billion-dollar negotiations to buy out a tech company that held the patent on a revolutionary 3D-printed two-sided circuit board. His mother refused to risk anything—including her health—affecting the deal. Obtaining the patent was huge for Harroway's future growth and they'd been just one of many companies wooing the firm.

In his efforts to be there for his mother and lighten her load at the foundation, had Will been so preoccupied he'd missed seeing that Natalie had become disenchanted with their relationship, and was thus taken by surprise at her leaving when he should have seen it coming? Or had his concern over his mother's health crisis been the catalyst that had pushed Natalie away?

Where his mother was concerned, Natalie had never thought rationally, always assuming his mother didn't like her and wanted them apart. He'd talked to his mother about how Natalie felt, urging her to reach out, to make her feel more welcome. He'd been thrilled when she offered to help with Natalie's party. He'd wanted Natalie to learn to feel comfortable around his mother so she'd want to go with him to dinners and business functions. Instead, the party had been a disaster. Natalie had left upset. His mother's feelings had been hurt.

His mother had always been invincible. As if his breakup with Natalie wasn't enough, watching his mother struggle to keep up her public facade was tearing him to bits. Tough as nails, she insisted she could beat her cancer without the world being privy to her private hell. God, Will hoped so. He couldn't imagine the alternative. He'd wanted to share his fears with Natalie, to hold her tight and have her tell him it was going to be okay. But the one time he'd tried, she'd become so prickly at the mention of his mother, he'd held his worries inside, instead.

Seeing her at the hospital shouldn't have been a big deal, but it still left him unsettled. To the degree that he decided he'd finish with all his other patients prior to checking on Mattie in hopes of avoiding direct interaction with Natalie.

But she was still there.

He'd wait, come back later, at lunch maybe, and hopefully avoid bumping into Natalie again.

Just as he started to walk away without her having known he'd been outside the patient room he noted the rising concern in her movements as she shook Mattie's shoulder and insisted the woman wake up.

Something was wrong.

He rushed into the room. "What's going on?"

Natalie's only reaction to him was to briefly flick her gaze his way before returning her attention to her patient. "She doesn't want to wake. Her oxygen is dipping into the mid-eighties, and her lungs sound junky when they didn't earlier. I don't like what I'm seeing or hearing. I was just about to call you."

"Mattie?" He attempted to get a response from his patient. Her eyelids fluttered, but she never opened them. "Mrs. Johnson," he said more brusquely, shaking her shoulder as he did so. "Open your eyes and look at me."

One eye peeped open just enough for Will to know she was at least somewhat aware of what was happening around her.

"Mattie," he purposely repeated her name. "Are you hurting anywhere?"

His patient's hand moved a little, but she never pointed out any particular spot.

A machine dinged, sounding its alarm.

"Her oxygen saturation dropped to 83 percent," Natalie warned as she adjusted the woman's airway tubing, making sure flow was unimpeded.

Mattie had been breathing normally on her own earlier when Will had removed her intubation after her surgery. She'd looked good when he'd checked on her in recovery.

"Increase her liter per minute flow rate," Will ordered as he examined his patient. Her lungs were crackling. She was prophylactically anticoagulated, but had she thrown a clot? Or was she coming down with pneumonia or in fluid overload? Either could explain what they were hearing. "If that doesn't increase her saturation, then mask her. Also, let's get a CT scan on her chest."

Assuming they got her stable and he didn't have to put her back on a ventilator. As if Mrs. Johnson had read his mind and was preempting him, her blood oxygen saturation dropped further. Her heart rate sped up, then drastically dipped. Another warning alarm sounded.

"Mattie?" Natalie tried to stir her in hopes of rallying her vitals as she changed her nasal cannula over to a face mask in an attempt to increase the woman's blood oxygen concentration.

It didn't work and another alarm dinged, causing Will's gaze to go to the significantly decreased oxygen ratio.

"Do you want me to start bi-pap therapy to try to regulate her breathing?" Natalie asked.

Will nodded. Maybe it would be enough, and they wouldn't have to put her on a vent. Only, before Natalie could even get the woman hooked up to the respirator machine, her breathing worsened.

Mattie was spiraling into a complete crash right before their eyes.

He needed to put her back on the ventilator.

Without his saying a word, Natalie went into action, immediately changing course. They worked together seamlessly, Natalie knowing what to do without his ever having to ask. She'd always been great at anticipating his needs, filling them.

Once he had the tube inserted down Mattie's airway, his gaze cut to the monitor and he gave a sigh of relief. Her numbers had instantly improved. Taking his stethoscope, he listened over her lung fields, pleased at the air movement the ventilation machine was providing.

"Placement sounds good, but her chest CT will double-check it," he said, planning to enter in the order for the test, but Natalie was a step ahead and was already punching the order into Mattie's computerized chart.

Once Mattie's heart rate had calmed and her chest was rising and falling rhythmically from the machine breathing for her, Will checked her over one last time, assessing for any external clue of what was going on to cause her crash and finding nothing unexpected.

"Did she say anything prior to my coming into the room?"

Natalie shook her head. "She opened her eyes when I tried to wake her, the same as she attempted to do with you, but she never seemed aware of where she was or who I was."

Pulling off his gloves and tossing them into a waste bin, Will accidentally brushed up against Natalie. At the same moment he registered they were touching, she jumped back as if scalded, crossing the room to stand far away from him and Mattie's bed.

"Don't," he couldn't keep from saying, even though he immediately regretted having revealed how her reaction had gotten to him.

Natalie's gaze lifted at his ground-out word.

"Don't act as if my touch offends you," he elaborated, moving to stand near her so they could keep their voices down, and thinking for a moment that she was going to relent, apologize for her lack of faith in him and their relationship, and tell him she'd missed him. He'd swear that was what the emotions in her eyes were conveying, but rather than agreeing, she lowered her gaze to hide whatever shone there.

"Let's not have this conversation here, Will."

"Then where?" he demanded, wondering what it mattered at this point. They were over. He didn't want her back. So, what did any of this matter?

"I…" She hesitated, then keeping her gaze averted, asked, "Is there a need to have a conversation at all?"

His breathing halted. Thank God no monitors were attached to alert her to his body's response to the thought she no longer cared about him, that seeing him didn't affect her the way seeing her affected him.

"You tell me. You're the one who left." He hadn't meant to sound so accusing.

"You're right. I did." Her gaze narrowed and she tossed out an accusation of her own. One that stung Will to the core. "But you're the one who left me at home night after night. No wonder you encouraged me to take a more active role on the Children's Cancer Gala committee. That way I wouldn't be home to notice you never were."

"Of course I wanted you on the committee. I'm on it, too, remember?" He'd known she'd give the gala her all and do a great job for an important charity, ensuring its success. It was a cause he believed in and thought she had, too. That had been before he'd known of his mother's cancer diagnosis and how pulled into a dozen directions he'd be. As much as he'd hated to, he'd missed the last meeting. "You knew I was a cardiac surgeon when we got together. I'm going to get called into the hospital—"

"It's not the hospital calling that was the issue," she cut in, ungloved hands on her hips.

"My mother—"

"Was a big problem in our relationship," she interrupted again, keeping her voice at barely above a whisper. Although unconscious, neither of them wanted to risk Mattie being aware of their conversation in whatever realm her mind currently functioned.

"Be careful what you say," he warned, his jaw tightening. Natalie was so sweet and kind with everyone except the other woman who mattered most in his life. Why couldn't they have gotten along?

"Because we're talking about your mother and that's a big no-no topic?" she scoffed, her eyes glinting. "We should have talked about how she undermined our relationship from the moment she met me, months ago, and was appalled that you were dating a nobody. She must be over the moon that I'm gone."

Natalie's defiant tone startled him. She'd never talked this way. He'd thought she understood his role as an only child. He might have gone into medicine, but he still had family obligations to his late grandfather's company, to the charity foundation that had grown out of the corporation—the Harroway Foundation, that his mother ran—and to his parents. Ever since his mother's biopsy on the breast mass had come back as invasive carcinoma, she had needed him more than ever. Things would be simpler if Natalie knew the reason he'd been so tied up with his mother, but she should trust there was a good reason why he wasn't at home. Shouldn't she have had his back when times were tough without his having to ask her to?

Is there anything wrong with Natalie? his mother had questioned him as to why she'd left her birthday party.

Not that she's said. His mother had been genuinely worried Natalie hadn't liked her party. Not wanting to add to her stress, he'd merely responded that he and Natalie had realized their relationship wasn't working and gone their separate ways. His mother was dealing with enough, with her radiation treatments and hiding her illness, without worrying about the demise of his relationship or why Natalie didn't like her.

He didn't need to worry about it, either.

Too bad his body was still pro-Natalie. No woman had ever affected him the way she did. Still, he hadn't expected to feel so tightly wound at seeing her again. Crazy as it was, her eyes sparking fire, her chin high and her hands on her hips sent a surge of testosterone through his system. He shouldn't want her. Not under these circumstances. Not at all since she'd so easily turned her back on him. But his body reacted to Natalie like gasoline tossed on fire. It's how it had always been physically between them. Did she feel it, too? Did she see him and have a thousand regrets the way he did?

"Let's go somewhere after work and talk."

The light in her eyes flickered, dimming a little, indecision emanating from her.

"I can meet you here at the end of your shift and we'll get dinner," he offered, seeing the softening on her face and seizing the opening she was giving him, although he wasn't sure why. They'd been apart a month. Would saying he was sorry even matter at this point?

"I…are you sure you want to do that?"

Was he? Staring down into her eyes, seeing the indecision and wariness, he felt gutted. They'd been so close, and now…they weren't. That couldn't be right.

"We need peace between us, don't you think?"

She looked away, again. "Do we?"

"We work in the same hospital. Our paths will cross. It would make things easier if we didn't have animosity between us."

She sighed. "Okay. We'll go to dinner. Will, I—" Her lashes fluttered. But rather than finish her comment, she gazed beyond him and her cheeks pinkened. "Um, thank you, Dr. Forrest," she said in her most formal tone as she pulled away from him. "I've got that chest CT and labs entered into the system and will have Radiology and the lab call you directly with the results."

Face still flaming, she rushed from the room.

Frowning at the interruption, Will turned to see what had caught her eye. Her nurse manager stood outside the doorway. Disapproval shone in the woman's dark eyes.

Will gave her a curt nod, then went to document Mattie's incident. Part of him was disappointed they'd been interrupted before Natalie could finish her sentence. Even more, he was disappointed in himself, for his desire to follow her and ask.

His pulse pounded in anticipation of an evening spent with Natalie, even if it was only an hour or so spent talking about things he'd thought over and done with.

Would he and Natalie ever truly be over and done with?

CHAPTER TWO

ALL DAY NATALIE'S stomach had been a tight mess. All week, really. No wonder with her nerves on edge. Would Will come by at the end of her shift as he'd said prior to her spotting Gretchen and making a run for it? Why had she agreed to go to dinner with him? Not that she didn't know. He'd crooked that finger and she'd instantly wanted to say yes to anything he asked for, just like always.

Weak. Weak. Weak, she scolded herself. Had she learned nothing over the past month?

Why was she questioning whether he'd come by? Physically, he wanted her. She'd seen it in his eyes when he'd accidentally brushed against her. Emotionally, well, despite his lack of verbalizing those words she longed to hear him say, once upon a time, she'd believed he cared about her. Wasn't that why she'd been so willing to fall into his life? Because she'd believed that and hoped that eventually their worlds would meld together? She'd been so wrong.

The real question was whether she should go anywhere with him or cancel completely so they didn't end up between his fancy high-count Egyptian cotton sheets.

What was she saying? She had fallen head over heels for him, but what woman privileged enough to be a part of his life hadn't? She wasn't happy with the way things had become between them, but hadn't her ultimate wish been for them to work things out? For them to find some happy medium where his mother was concerned? Where the disparities in their relationship could be overlooked so they were on equal ground with each other? If he was willing to make concessions, to see her point of view and make changes in how he handled their relationship, especially regarding his mother, wouldn't she want to hear what he had to say?

If nothing else, her birthday party had taught her how fragile their relationship really was and even more so, how fragile her confidence in his feelings toward her were.

Natalie had no option but to meet Will, but she was determined not to let the sexual sparks between them lull her brain.

She was going to have to be careful not to get distracted by him while at work, too. Her nurse manager had been watching her with hawklike eyes all day, as if waiting for some misstep so she could call her into the office for reprimanding.

"That must be one interesting chart you're documenting."

Natalie glanced up at her bestie's comment. "Nothing like a patient throwing a pulmonary embolism and a thrombosis in her left lower extremity gastrocnemius vein despite being anticoagulated to keep life from being boring."

"Better you than me." Callie gave a dramatic quiver. "Stable now, though?"

Natalie nodded. "Yes, Mrs. Johnson is stable. Will… I mean, Dr. Forrest…" She stopped, met Callie's eyes, then shrugged. "Never mind."

Her friend gave her an empathetic look. "I think it's a

good thing you're going to dinner tonight. You still have feelings for him." Ugh. Was she that obvious? "Talk and maybe you will get things patched up."

Natalie didn't fool herself that their issues could be patched up over a single dinner. She wasn't convinced their issues could be patched up period. Will was who he was. Dr. William Harroway Forrest, heir of Harroway Industries and cochair of the Harroway Foundation, a duty shared with his mother. He was a talented heart surgeon, generous with his time and money to so many. She imagined she'd only been privy to a fraction of the good Will did as it wasn't something he talked about, but Natalie knew enough to know he had a big heart. Natalie was who she was. Nurse Natalie Jane Gifford, a woman who had lived her twenty-five years leading a hardworking life to be proud of, for the most part, even if her accomplishments were simple compared to Will's world. She was a woman who deserved to be loved, cherished, proudly shown off and treated as having equal weight in the relationship. All women deserved that and shouldn't settle for less.

Why had she?

Because when she'd brought Callie's forgotten lunch to her and bumped into the most gorgeous man she'd ever met, he'd smiled at her in a way that had made her heart race and her body glad to be alive. While she had waited on Callie to come out of a patient room, they'd chatted a few minutes. Her breathless and him all teasing and sexy grins. When she'd handed over Callie's lunch and started to walk away, he'd surprised her by asking if she was busy that evening. Her heart had cleared its schedule indefinitely.

Only, she hadn't known who he was. When he'd introduced himself as Will Forrest, she hadn't known anything of his wealthy, blue-blooded background. If only he could have just been the man she'd met that day forever, without the trappings of being the Harroway heir encroaching on their happiness, or their backgrounds having ever been a big deal.

He'd kept saying their differences didn't matter, but he hadn't been the one thrown into a world he'd not been accustomed to and had felt overwhelmed by. The only times she'd even come close to his glitzy world had been when she'd accompanied her housekeeper mother to some of the upscale apartments she'd cleaned and those had been nothing compared to Will's world. A memory of a particular family's kids laughing at her ill-fitting hand-me-down clothes hit her. She'd barely been school-age but recalled the moment vividly.

Rebecca Harroway Forrest had looked at her with the same disregard as her mother's employers had and, standing in the grandeur of the Harroway penthouse, Natalie had reverted to that ridiculed poor little girl rather than the young woman she was proud to have become.

Looking back, meeting Rebecca had been the turning point in her relationship with Will. He'd gone from an exciting man she was falling in love with to being a part of an elite club she wasn't a member of, could never really belong to, but might be allowed to play so long as she didn't cause any problems and stayed in the background. She'd been so caught up in their whirlwind romance that she'd not even realized what she was doing as she strove to make their relationship easy for him at all costs.

Deep down she'd been waiting for him to realize he'd made a mistake in thinking he wanted to be with her, and she hadn't wanted to make the end happen sooner by causing resistance of any kind.

Just like with the rich kids she'd encountered through

her mother's housekeeping, she only got to play if she went along with everything they wanted. So, she had. As a child. And, once she'd met Rebecca, she'd fallen into those ingrained habits with Will without realizing what she'd done until he'd started becoming emotionally distant and distracted when they were together.

Their issues lay as much with herself as with Will. She should have addressed how she felt the moment she realized, talked with him about the way his mother made her feel. She shouldn't have let it reach the point of complete resentment and emotional breakdown it had at her birthday party when she'd looked around at the glamourous party, realized none of her family and real friends were there, and known that this wasn't the life she wanted.

Did she really want that? To have to constantly prove her worth to Will's high-society friends and family who seemed to only value bank accounts and social status and not what was on a person's inside?

She'd tried talking to him about his mother a few times, but he refused to see anything except what Rebecca wanted him to see. As entangled as her heart was with Will, nothing had changed. What purpose would it serve for them to go to dinner? She wouldn't go back to being a yes girl. Not even for Will.

Callie motioned to the hallway leading to the CVICU. "He's here, but don't look because his eyes are trained right on you and aren't budging as he heads this way."

Natalie's heart somersaulted. To Will's credit, he'd returned to the unit fifteen minutes before the end of her shift and not left her to awkwardly wait to see if he showed.

"Callie, Natalie," he greeted when he reached the nurses' station. Rather than linger, with a quick meeting of their eyes that acknowledged his main purpose for being there, he headed to Mattie Johnson's room.

Since Natalie had finished her charting and the night nurse taking her place hadn't shown yet for report, she went to check on her patients, saving Mrs. Johnson for last so that odds were higher that Will would have already left the CVICU room.

But he hadn't.

"Dr. Forrest," she acknowledged where he stood by Mattie's bed. "I thought I'd do one last check before giving report at shift change. Do you want me to come back later?"

His gaze colliding with hers, he shook his head. "There's no need for that, Natalie."

Heart pounding so loudly she worried the reverberations might alter Mattie's telemetry, Natalie checked her patient while her doctor watched her sleep.

Still on the ventilator and unconscious, Mattie's vitals were holding steady.

"She's been stable since you intubated her," Natalie said, although she wasn't telling him anything he wasn't well aware of. He'd kept close tabs on the woman all day.

Watching her examine Mattie, he nodded. "Thanks to your quick actions this morning in realizing something wasn't right she should be fine. We'll let her rest and watch her extra close over the next twenty-four hours."

Natalie's face heated at his praise. She'd done nothing more than what any nurse would have done.

"I got lucky that I was in here when she started crashing." Natalie kept her gaze trained on the rise and fall of Mattie's chest rather than look toward Will. Looking toward him, meeting those amazing eyes trained on her, tied her stomach into knots. "Anything in particular you want me to convey to her night nurse?"

"Just what you normally would, and the morning lab orders that I put into her chart earlier. I'd like them drawn and back by the time I round in the morning."

"I'll note it." Natalie finished assessing her patient, with Will at the bedside. When she was done, she hesitated. How could being near him feel so right where she wanted to be, and so awkward and nerve-racking and not okay at the same time?

Because when it was just the two of them, everything had felt perfect. Those moments of going for a walk in Central Park or sitting out on his balcony for hours just talking had melded her heart to him. A memory popped into her head of the time he packed a picnic and they spent an afternoon flying a kite of all things. How they'd laughed at their silliness, at how good it felt to be together.

Oh, how her heart ached at that loss.

She missed him. A month hadn't lessened how she yearned for his smile, his laughter, his simply telling her good morning. If they could have shut the world out forever, they'd have been just fine. But that wasn't reality. Nor would she have wanted it to be that way. Not really. If they had any chance of working things out, they had to accept who the other was. The good. The bad. The ugly. She had to keep her voice and get over her hesitancy, her self-doubts and her willingness to settle for anything less than being his partner in every sense of the word. And, then there was his mother. She wouldn't put up with her interfering in their relationship forever, either.

Although, if he'd loved her, she'd have waited indefinitely.

Glancing at her watch, she saw it was past time for the night nurse to have arrived. She needed to get back to give report.

"I'll wait here with Mattie," he said, reading her well. In many ways, he'd always read her well. She shouldn't have worked so hard hiding her insecurities. If she had let him see her struggles more, how unsure she felt in his world, would it have made a difference? If she'd stressed to him how his mother made her feel? Or would they just have ended sooner?

"When you're off the clock, let me know, and we'll head out," he told her, his gaze never leaving hers.

Natalie swallowed. Hard. Because so many memories of his waiting on her shift to end, of their leaving the hospital together, hand in hand, to go on some adventure around the city or just straight home for an adventure all their own.

"Yes. We'll go talk." She wanted to talk, wanted to hear what he had to say, couldn't not hear what he had to say, and maybe she'd say things she'd held in too long. Doing that would be good for her. Good for him to hear, too, because he needed to know what was in her heart. Still, what she didn't want was to get caught up in the same mind fog she experienced when he was near. She glanced toward their unconscious patient, then walked out into the hallway, not really surprised when he followed her.

She paused, took a deep breath. "Promise me something?"

His brow lifted.

"No touching," she said low enough that only he'd be able to hear. Not that anyone seemed to be paying them the slightest attention, but she didn't want to risk it.

He frowned. "What kind of promise is that?"

"The one I need you to make," she reiterated, knowing his agreeing was vital to her sticking to her goals. His touch held too much control over her willpower. "We're going to talk," she whispered, "not get distracted by sexual attraction. Please, promise me."

"No touching?" He regarded her a moment, then nodded. "If that's what you want, then no touching it is."

"Thank you."

He shrugged as if it were no big deal, then added, "Your loss, though."

Yeah, she was well aware of that. Unfortunately.

No touching. What had Natalie thought? That he was going to drag her back to his place for— He shook his head to clear it as he walked back over to Mattie Johnson's hospital bed.

Staring down at the unconscious woman, he wondered what she was thinking or if she was in a peaceful rest. The rise and fall of her chest was rhythmic, lulling one into a false sense of calm.

Will didn't feel calm.

He felt…torn. What was he doing asking Natalie to go to dinner with him? After all, he'd decided that with his mother's breast cancer his being single was probably for the best. Best for his mother. But for Will, despite the month apart, he longed to tell Natalie everything. On every subject other than his mother, she was the best listener. If he told her his mother might be dying, she'd understand why he'd been so distracted. Will had trusted Natalie completely, but his mother had reminded him of the fallout to the company if word got out of her illness and it affected their acquisition, and following that how many of their loyal employees and stockholders were in jeopardy. They couldn't risk the consequences if he was wrong about Natalie. He'd never thought he was, but he'd not anticipated Natalie leaving him, either.

Sighing, Will reached down, placed his hand over

Mattie's still one, saying a silent prayer for the woman's speedy recovery, then, "I'll be back in the morning. Have a good night's rest and wish me luck."

Wish him luck? Luck for what exactly? What was it he hoped to gain by taking Natalie to dinner?

To get his friend back because he missed her.

To get his girl back because he missed her.

To get his lover back because he missed her.

Will sucked in a deep breath and reminded himself that Natalie had walked away from him when he'd needed her. She'd judged him wrongly at her birthday party, condemning him without cause, and let her own insecurities poison their relationship. No trust and no commitment to what they'd shared.

Taking her to dinner just meant he was a glutton for punishment.

Promise not to touch, she'd requested. Yes, that definitely was for the best. But his last remark to her had been wrong.

Not being able to clasp her hand with his and feel the connection he'd imagined they shared was his loss, not hers.

Will's choice of the small coffeehouse where they'd had their first date both surprised and pleased Natalie. The family-run business was off the beaten path, earthy, with great food and amazing coffee. It was one of those hole-in-the-wall places where you were just as likely to see a sport's star or other celebrity as you were to see your grocer or beautician.

The perfect eclectic blending of two worlds where everyone fit.

If he'd taken her somewhere else on that first date, somewhere where she'd have been expected to know what fork went where or had to interact with the rich and famous, would she have let herself fall so madly in love with him?

Let herself? Ha. As if she'd had a choice. Will had stepped into her life, and she'd tumbled. There had been no letting or conscious decision. Will had just happened.

As always, he was the perfect gentleman, opening doors, pulling out her chair. But beneath the polished exterior most wouldn't see past, she sensed his tension. Tension that was perhaps caused by his care in making sure he kept his promise to not touch.

She'd caught him pulling away twice during their walk to the restaurant and wanted to cry both times. He'd often put his hand at the small of her back or held her hand when they'd walked together, and she'd sorely missed that gesture.

He'd been right that his not touching her was her loss.

But she'd been just as right to insist that he keep his hands to himself. She only had so much strength.

Unlike the present, that first dinner together had been filled with excitement, anticipation and fun conversation as they'd sat across from each other and gotten to know one other. He'd taken her breath away when his hand had covered hers on the table. That had been the first time they'd skin-to-skin touched. Her hand stung from the memory and she rubbed the area as if her flesh truly burned. She should have known from the bold signet ring he wore that he came from wealth. He'd not told her his father was a senator, nor that his mother was worth millions, if not billions. What was it he'd said? That his father worked in government and his mother managed a family business? What he had told her was that his favorite food was lasagna, he had a secret obsession with watching old late-night sitcoms, that his mother had made him learn to play the piano and that he'd done so to please her even though he'd been dreaming of kicking a ball into a net the whole time because he loved playing soccer. He'd recounted numerous tales of doing so, and admitted he'd continued to play during university and still played in the occasional friendly rivalry pickup game.

They'd talked about her parents, four older brothers, their wives and her numerous nieces and nephews. She'd told him how she'd worked from the moment she was old enough to get a job, kept her grades high enough to get a full scholarship, and proudly told him that she'd been the first person in her family to graduate from college. Sitting across from him, smiling at him, she'd felt as if they were having the most important conversation of their lives.

How ironic that they now sat across from each other in the same restaurant.

Oh, Will. Why did you bring me here, where it all started?

"Ninety-four!" Their order number was called.

"I'll get it," Will assured her when she started to rise, motioning for her to sit back down.

Leaning back in her chair, Natalie watched him go to the counter and smile at the attendant as he gathered their tray. When he turned, their gazes met and every emotion she'd ever felt for him zinged through her. Every desire. Every smile. Every bit of joy. Every hope and dream. Her heart broke from the loss of it, from the loss of him, and she had to look away before she lost her composure.

She understood how she could have just gone along with everything he wanted for so long. Even now she was tempted.

Setting the tray on their table, he settled back into his seat, but seemed more interested in watching her than in the food.

Natalie had forgone lunch because she'd been too nervous to eat, her stomach was protesting as it had been doing a lot lately, and her food smelled delicious, so she took a bite of her panini. The warm gooey cheese made her mouth water. Hopefully, eating would settle the uneasiness in her belly. Either way, the last thing she needed was a lack-of-food hypoglycemic episode leaving her fuzzy-headed. No telling what she'd do. Like beg him to forgive her stupidity in moving out of his apartment and zipping her lips on how she truly felt about so many things in their relationship, such as his mother, and how he'd chosen to go to so many family events alone, and how being here with him filled her heart with such remorse for what they'd lost.

Trying to make sure she didn't choke on her food, she chewed the bite thoroughly, self-conscious of every movement of her mouth. When she'd swallowed it and he'd yet to pick up his food, she asked, "What?"

"Just wondering how we reached this point."

Natalie paused, her panini midway to her mouth. "I guess the way any couple's relationship fails, lack of communication and growing apart."

"What happened around your birthday felt more of a ripping apart." Watching her, he took a bite of his Cajun spiced sandwich, taking his time as he slowly chewed. "I didn't see it coming, so I felt blindsided."

Trying to figure out what to say, she toyed with her food. Another wave of nausea hit hard. She set her sandwich down on her plate. A hypoglycemic episode would be way preferable to throwing up.

"My leaving was the culmination of the issues in our relationship that were there from the beginning, but had festered and poisoned everything," she told him, pushing her plate back as now she couldn't stand the smell of her food.

He arched a brow. "We lived together for half a year and you never said a word about relationship issues, other than my mother. These issues hit you at your birthday party to the point you left without so much as a word to me, without our discussing them as two adults should. Instead, you moved out of our home?"

She flinched at his accusatory tone. She should have spoken up sooner. She should have talked with him about how she felt. How did she explain that she'd been afraid of losing him if she spoke up and made demands on their relationship? Pathetic.

"Your apartment is beautiful, Will, but it was never *my* home."

Progress. She'd made an admission, that being in the pristine apartment overlooking Central Park had often left her feeling as if she was checked into a sterile luxury suite rather than any sense of her belonging.

She'd felt like the poor little girl from Jersey, wearing hand-me-downs from the children her mother was paid to pick up after, and was there to play nice, or not allowed to play at all.

Will furrowed his forehead. "You lived there for six months. What was that? An extended vacation?"

His question echoed her thoughts, her feelings. Being with him had been like being on a dream vacation, an escape to a fantasy theme park where she ignored unpleasantries because she knew she had to eventually go back to reality. That feeling had kept her from ever relaxing enough to feel at home in his apartment or his life.

"It was my being at your beck and call for however long you were interested in me," she admitted, not quite believing she'd found the nerve to be so honest. "My living with you made our relationship convenient for you."

His face twisted with confusion. "But was somehow an inconvenience for you? Is that what you're saying? That living with me was a problem? That you didn't want to be there, and I coerced you into moving in with me?"

"No," she denied. When she'd first moved in with him she'd been wearing rose-colored glasses and everything had seemed wonderful with the exception of Rebecca's disapproval. "Not an inconvenience, but, looking back, it happened too soon and there were a lot of things we should have discussed first. We should have spent more time together before we took that step. We weren't ready to live together."

Her claim had doubt spreading across his handsome face. "Apparently, but not having to go back and forth between two places cut down on travel time so we could spend more time together. We were both ready for that."

"True." They'd been desperate for every precious second together.

"But you're saying the relationship issue that occurred to you at your birthday party is that you think things would have been better had we continued to travel between two residencies rather than having lived together?"

"Better?" She shrugged. "The obvious answer is no. But if I think back to the time we lived apart, then I recall you hungry to spend every spare moment with me and that's been gone from our relationship. At times over those past few weeks, you were so distracted it was as if you didn't even see me."

A flicker of guilt flashed on his face. A flicker that made her wonder what he wasn't telling her. He'd glossed over his dance with Stella, but was the woman's return the reason Natalie had felt he was keeping something from her?

"Besides all the things going on at the hospital and Harroway Industries and the foundation, it's an election year for my father," he pointed out, but his gaze didn't quite meet hers. "I'm expected to make an appearance at certain family and press functions. As an only child, it's important that I be there."

All true but none of the things he listed were the real cause of their problems. Or the cause of that guilty flash.

Her stomach growled. Lowering her gaze to her sandwich, she forced herself to take another bite and slowly chewed, hoping it stayed put. "The problem, since you seem oblivious to it, is that I'm not welcome to come with you."

His forehead furrowed. "There's nothing to be oblivious to because, for the most part, that's not true."

"Isn't it? How often was I included in those invites? How often did you bring me to those fancy Harroway dinners and campaign parties? To your mother's when she called and needed you to come running for her latest emergency on yet another of the few nights we had alone those last few weeks?"

The skin pulled tight over his cheekbones as his gaze narrowed. "I was under the impression you didn't want to go to my father's campaign events, to my mother's business dinners, that you didn't like the attention, and that you preferred I go as Mother's escort while you spent time with Callie or visiting with your family."

She couldn't deny his claim, but only because she'd been made to feel so unwelcome by Rebecca. She'd wanted to be with him, to be included and for him to be proud to have her at his side rather than worried that she

was a cause of embarrassment as his mother had insinuated on more than one occasion.

"With the exception of private meetings with Mother,
you were always welcome to attend, Natalie."

Natalie rolled her eyes. "You think your mother would
have allowed that? That had you started showing up with
me in tow that she wouldn't have let her displeasure be
known?"

"I don't understand why you're always so negative
about her." He genuinely looked confused. "She sensed
how you felt, of course, but still reached out, like helping
with your party because she wants me happy."

Natalie fought rolling her eyes, again. Rebecca wanted
Will happy with someone of his own social status and
any negativity Rebecca had sensed was her own. At least,
initially. But, even at the end, Natalie had never said anything back to Rebecca out of respect for Will as she'd
known it would upset him. She'd just silently suffered the
woman's obvious disapproval, just as she'd stood there,
watching Will and Stella, listening to Rebecca go on and
on about them as if Natalie wasn't Will's live-in girlfriend
right up until she'd realized she'd had enough.

And, rightly or wrongly, she'd ditched her own birthday party.

"You'd have to ask your mother on my reasons why
I was so negative regarding her," Natalie suggested be-
cause she suspected nothing she said would convince
Will.

"I'd rather you tell me." Will's phone began to ring.
Pulling the sleek gadget from his pocket, he glanced at
the screen. "It's my mother."

Of course it was. She probably had his phone tapped,
listening in to their conversation the entire time, and had
decided enough was enough.

Enough is enough, Natalie's insides screamed.

"Great. You can ask her what possible reason I could have for feeling negative toward her, but we both know she'll act as if she has no idea." Because Natalie knew the woman presented her feelings toward Natalie very differently to Will than she did directly to Natalie.

"Natalie." His tone held warning.

"Don't you dare tell me not to express my feelings, Will Forrest," she interrupted, anger filling her at just how long she'd let Rebecca play mind games with both her and Will. "You asked me here tonight for a reason. For us to talk. If it was to prove that I was wrong to leave—" leaning forward, chin high, she held his gaze and gestured to the phone he now held and was about to swipe "—then, don't answer that, and we can finish our conversation."

Why it was suddenly so important he not answer the phone at that particular moment wasn't exactly clear, but Natalie felt adamant in insisting he not answer.

Frowning, he glanced down at the lit-up screen. He looked torn, but rather than swipe to answer, he hesitated.

With bated breath, she waited to see what he'd do.

Eyes glittering, expression stern, he stared back, then set his phone down on the tabletop. "She's my mother, Natalie. I'm her only child. She's going to call, sometimes at inopportune times. She is a part of who I am. Is this what you want? What will make you happy? For me to ignore her, or push her out of my life because you don't like her?"

Stunned by his question, she fought to keep her jaw off the coffee shop floor. "When have I ever said I didn't like your mother because I know I've never said that?"

He harrumphed. "Some things are obvious."

How dare he act like she'd been the one to shun his

mother? To put the wedge between them? Rebecca had taken one look, turned up her snooty nose and not hidden her displeasure of their relationship to Natalie.

"She probably knows we're talking right now and that's why she called to interrupt." His gaze darkened. But now that the filter was off, her hurt was mingled with anger and pent-up frustrations poured from her. "She did a great job keeping you away from me the past month of our relationship. Why stop now?"

"You're wrong about her." His expression had grown terse, his lips pulling into a tight line. "But even if what you claim was true, what reason does she have to interrupt us at this point? You moved out weeks ago. Besides, if you weren't so prickly around her—"

"Prickly?" Natalie interrupted, her head starting to hurt. "The woman can't stand me and you're implying that's my fault? I met her with my arms wide-open and from the beginning she rejected me as being part of your life. She may have smiled and talked nice to you, but her teeth were bared when she looked my way. Why are we even here?"

Will took a deep breath, then quietly said, "Because once upon a time we had something special between us and now we don't even talk and that doesn't feel right."

Natalie's mouth opened, then she closed it as his sincerity defused her anger.

As frustrating as she found their situation, Will was a good man. Maybe he wanted to be "just friends," and that was what had prompted him to ask her to dinner. How could Natalie be "just friends" with someone who put her hormones into high gear and her heart into a vice?

Regardless, she didn't want to argue. Not because of a need to try to keep the peace, although that was there, too, but because being upset with him made her insides hurt. She didn't want to fight with Will.

"You're right. It doesn't feel right that we no longer talk." Understatement of the year. "You know how I feel about you," she said, determined that no matter what his reasons for being there were, that her reasons for coming were to be open and honest with him. "But my caring about you isn't enough. That's why I left. I want more."

She wanted him. As her partner. Her lover. Her everything. She wanted to not question her place in his life when other women flirted with him. When other women danced with him. She didn't want to feel the tug-of-war for his time and attention from his mother or wonder if someday he'd give in to Rebecca's desire for him to replace Natalie with someone "more fitting." Someone like Stella.

His phone started ringing again.

Sighing, Natalie's eyes dropped to where the offensive device sat on the table, then rose back up to Will. For once, he completely ignored his phone, his gaze intent on her instead.

"What more are you talking about, Natalie?" His eyes darkened to a deep green that cut into her. "Tell me how much it's going to cost me to get you back in my bed. We'll negotiate from there."

Cost him? Negotiate? He sounded so much like his mother that Natalie cringed. And *back in his bed*? Was that why he was there? Because of *sex*? She wanted his heart and he just wanted sex.

Fighting disappointment, she shook her head. "Nothing, Will. Our relationship—former relationship—isn't going to cost you anything." She lifted her napkin from her lap and placed it on the table. "Answer your mother."

His gaze narrowed. "Why are you being so stubborn?"

"Is that what you call my wanting to be treated with respect? As an equal in our relationship?" she countered.

"You're saying that I've treated you poorly? Or inferior in some way?" he scoffed, clearly not seeing her point.

"Not poorly, but not as your partner, either," she clarified, fighting to keep her voice from breaking as she spoke. She wished her head and emotions weren't such a jumbled mess. What was wrong with her? It was as if she couldn't think straight or keep her feelings in line for anything these days.

"My partner?" He leaned back, staring at her for long moments before he spoke again. "Is this some get-a-ring ploy? Is that what this past month has really been about? I won't be manipulated."

Realizing what he meant, Natalie gasped in horror. "Are you serious? Get-a-ring ploy? As if." Okay, so she had dreamed he'd someday want to marry her, but not because of a desire to manipulate him or anything other than to love him and share his life. The nerve. "Perhaps you've forgotten, but you're who asked for us to go to dinner. Not me," she reminded. "I've not asked for anything from you, *ever*," she also reminded. "And I never will. You must have me confused with one of your other ex-girlfriends."

His facial muscles tightened with displeasure. "There you go with more Stella accusations. Your lack of faith in my fidelity to you is disturbing."

His phone quit ringing but immediately started again. The sound grated on her nerves to the point Natalie could stand no more.

On the verge of spilling the tears rapidly accumulating in her eyes, or possibly taking his phone and flinging it across the café, Natalie gestured to the offending technology. "My 'lack of faith in your fidelity,' as you put it, no longer holds relevance. We're through with our relationship and this conversation, so answer your mother. She won't quit until you do."

With that, she rose from her chair to leave.

"Natalie!" He stood, reached out to stay her, his fingers firm around her wrist.

Her gaze dropped to where he held her, not hard, but with enough force that she'd have to jerk free to walk away.

The phone's blaring rang through her like an annoying reminder of why their relationship hadn't worked, would never work, and why no matter how much her heart and body said otherwise, she had to heed logic. Will cared for her. Natalie knew his feelings for her had been real. Although perhaps his back-in-his-bed comment hinted at where his feelings toward her really lay. She deserved to be loved, to be in a relationship where she stood on even ground with her partner. She'd never be that with Will. Not when his mother continuously interfered, fanning the flames of Natalie's insecurities, and Will was oblivious to how his mother affected Natalie and their relationship. He didn't even want to see but seemed to prefer being in denial.

They really were over.

She lifted her gaze to his.

"Don't touch me," she reminded.

His expression tightened, his eyes searching hers a brief moment, then his face became an unreadable cold mask that would make his mother proud.

"As you wish." Then he let her go.

CHAPTER THREE

"BUT I'M AN ICU nurse," Natalie insisted the next morning when she arrived at the hospital for her regular shift to find that she'd been scheduled to work in the cardiovascular intensive care unit.

"Our census is down," her ICU nurse manager pointed out, not looking overly concerned that Natalie was in a near panic. "Theirs is up, and Connie is going to be out for a couple of weeks. You're already familiar with the patients from yesterday. It makes sense you'd be who we shifted to the unit for continuity of care."

"But…"

"No buts, Natalie. For the foreseeable future, you're covering for Connie."

Which is how Natalie ended up in the CVICU again that morning with two of Will's patients, Mattie Johnson and Donald Eastland, who was a new admit that morning after Will had performed an emergency coronary artery bypass graft on him in the wee morning hours. Mattie she could understand, but Natalie would have thought after the eagle eyes from the day before that Gretchen would have intentionally kept her away from any of Will's newly admitted patients. No such luck.

"You could check with some of the other ICU nurses to see if any of them wanted to trade. If you had someone lined up, wanting to be in CVICU, maybe they'd let you transfer out," Callie suggested, giving a look of commiseration as Natalie unlocked the medicine cart to get her morning medications for Mr. Eastland.

Natalie shook her head.

"I'm fine." If she said the words often enough, maybe she'd start believing them and feeling them, because stress was taking its toll. During the long restless night, she'd resigned herself to possibly never being fine again. Or at least not whole, because Will would always have a piece of her heart. "I am just going to have to toughen up and get over seeing him here. It sucks, but what choice do I have unless I want to change jobs?"

Callie gave a sympathetic look.

"Besides, whether I work with him, or not, I'm not going to escape seeing him." She didn't need the media for that, either. Every time she closed her eyes he was there. In her mind. In her heart. "We're both on the Children's Cancer Charity Gala committee, and unless he chooses not to come—" a distinct possibility as he'd already missed a few of the meetings "—then I'm going to have to learn to let my feelings for him go."

"The woes of dating someone like Dr. Forrest, I suppose," Callie mused, then cut her gaze to Natalie's and she lowered her voice conspiratorially. "He's coming up the hallway."

Natalie's heart skipped a beat as she steeled herself to the prospect of seeing Will. A Will that wasn't hers. That qualifier made all the difference. She'd held out a sliver of hope until he'd asked what it was going to cost him to get her back in his bed. Money. When had she ever asked him for anything? She wanted him. Not his money or his status. And she wasn't for sale. Her heart had been his for the taking, free of charge, but apparently all he'd really wanted was her body.

She wanted *him*. His time. His attention. His heart. All things she'd never have. The sooner she accepted that, the better. She couldn't start healing until she completely abandoned that hope.

Bracing herself, she turned, faced him and was shocked to see that he didn't look quite as well put together as Dr. William Harroway Forrest generally presented himself to the world. Although it was slight, there was a fatigue around his eyes that wasn't usually there, as if he'd had a rough night.

There she went again. Wanting to hope when none existed. He'd been called in to stent Donald Eastland in the early morning hours. Of course he looked tired. His weariness had nothing to do with her or how their dinner had ended.

"Here again, I see. Who's Mattie's nurse?" His tone was brusque, conveying his irritation that she was one of the first people he bumped into upon entering the CVICU.

She took a deep breath and steadied herself for their required interaction. She could do this. She had to do this. Unlike him, she needed her job.

"I am."

He nodded as if he'd expected that. Her own annoyance grew. It wasn't as if she wanted to be in the CVICU or that she'd arranged to be his patients' nurse. Besides, he should have known when he saw her that she'd been assigned to provide Mattie's care. If he didn't like it, maybe he should talk to management. They'd listen to him.

"The night nurse said Mattie had an uneventful night," she kept her tone level, professional. "Her vitals are consistent with how they were when I clocked out yesterday and she was stable when I was in her room just a few minutes ago."

"If she stays stable, I'll cut back on her medications in hopes of weaning her off the vent today. The sooner we get her back to breathing unassisted, the better."

Natalie nodded. She'd expected that as soon as Mattie was strong enough to breathe on her own he'd remove her intubation tube.

"I'll let you know if anything changes."

"You do that."

Natalie's gaze cut to his. Had his comment been laced with sarcasm? It was hard to fathom that it had been as Will wasn't one to make snide remarks. But that's what he'd just done.

Sensing the growing tension in their exchange and probably wanting to remind them that there were others around, Callie nudged her arm. "I'm off to check on my aortic aneurysm repair patient in room two. Yell if you need me or need to know where to find something."

Natalie smiled at her bestie. Thank goodness for her friend. Everything would be so much more difficult without her love, support and spare room to crash in while she figured out her next step.

Callie walked away, leaving Will and Natalie alone near the medication cart and he just stood there, staring at her as if he didn't know what to say. Natalie sighed. "Callie's not the only one who needs to check on her patients. It's time for Mr. Eastland's meds. Have a good day, Dr. Forrest."

Fighting a busting headache that throbbed at his temples, Will watched Natalie dart into Mr. Eastland's CVICU room. As if she sensed his gaze followed her, she drew the curtain, blocking his view through the glass wall that faced the nurses' station so the nurses could more easily keep a check on their critically ill patients.

He struggled to keep from marching into the room and pointing out that what he needed was for her to stop this nonsense. Nonsense such as calling him Dr. Forrest.

Her comments from the night before raced through his mind for what seemed like the millionth time. Not once had she previously said anything about not feeling at home in his condominium. He'd known she worried about the differences in the background, but he hadn't realized she didn't like their home. If she'd disliked their place, they could have looked for something more to her taste. The layout and the view had appealed to him, plus he'd been able to jog in Central Park, but he would have been fine with giving her carte blanche.

As far as his mother went, yes, he'd made a mistake in letting her put Natalie's party together, but he'd been thrilled she'd wanted to help, that yet again she was trying to reach out to Natalie. He suspected she'd called her event planner and had her invite the "usual" guest list, not thinking to add Natalie's friends and family. No wonder, with everything she had going on with her health and the company. It seemed the more his mother tried to build their relationship the more Natalie backed away from it.

It had been the only area of real contention in their relationship as far as he'd known, and he'd believed she'd eventually realize their financial differences didn't matter to him. Even with his mother, he'd thought their relationship would eventually improve. How could it not when they were the best women he'd ever known?

He'd thought Natalie didn't like going to his father's political events or his mother's business ones, so he'd purposely not pushed for her to when he always felt her discomfort, trying to shield her from the press and whatever it was she feared so much. How was he to know she'd take that as his not wanting her there?

He'd wanted her there.

But he needed to get his head on straight. If Natalie cared so little that she could leave, be upset over his mother, over Stella when there was no longer anything between them, not even rationally talk things over before just disappearing from her birthday party and their home, then so be it. He needed to focus on helping his mother get well, anyway. That she refused surgery until after contracts were signed frustrated him. He understood her desire to do what was right by the company and their employees, but, selfishly, the company meant nothing to him if it cost him her. At least she'd agreed to go for localized radiation treatments in hopes of shrinking the mass, or at least keep it from growing while she delayed the mastectomy her specialist had recommended.

His mother beating her cancer was what he needed to focus on.

He was just finishing in Mattie's room when Natalie popped her head out of Donald Eastland's CVICU room.

"Good. I was hoping you were still here."

She actually did look relieved to see him. Her big brown eyes were filled with concern. He didn't fool himself that it was because of anything personal, and hadn't he just decided that was fine by him? They were through.

"I know you probably planned to, anyway, but do you mind listening to Mr. Eastland's chest before you go?" she asked. "I don't like what I'm hearing in his lower lobes."

He might question her good senses on moving out, but Natalie's nursing skills were top-notch. He trusted her patient assessments implicitly. She had a good ear and her nursing instincts were on the money. They'd only worked together a handful of times prior to the day before, but she'd always impressed him with her quick mind and healing touch.

"What's up?" he asked as he stepped just inside the room, disinfected his hands, his stethoscope, then donned gloves and a mask before moving closer to his patient's bed.

"Soft rales heard anteriorly and posteriorly in the lower lobes bilaterally," she told him, pulling the sheet back to uncover the patient's chest, exposing the heart monitor lead dotting his chest. "I wasn't sure if you planned to round on him prior to heading to clinic, but believed you'd want to listen for yourself and order a chest X-ray."

Will placed his stethoscope diaphragm to Mr. Eastland's chest and listened for the soft crackle in the man's lower lung lobes. He immediately heard the abnormal noises and frowned.

"It's quick for post-op pneumonia to have set in," he mused, doing a quick assessment for fluid retention. His patient's left leg had plus two non-pitting edema. His right leg had plus one swelling. Neither side was necessarily unexpected following the removal of a femoral vein on his left leg to graft in his heart to bypass the blockage, but Will appreciated Natalie's quick assessment. The sooner a problem was caught the less damage it was likely to cause. "Good call. I definitely want that chest X-ray. Draw labs on him, too, including a BNP, complete blood count, comprehensive metabolic profile and a D-dimer, just in case. I may end up ordering a CT of his chest, but I'll see what these show and go from there."

Concern flickered in her eyes. "Surely, you won't have two patients throw clots on back-to-back days."

"I hope not." His patient statistics were better than average, but when dealing with the human body anything could, and often did, happen. "Make all his tests STAT and let me know the minute they're available."

Already logging into the computer system to enter the orders, Natalie nodded. "I'll keep a close check on him and will keep you updated."

Taking another listen to his patient's chest, Will watched Natalie type and hated the ache that settled into the pit of his stomach. They were through. How could he look at her and miss that she was no longer there when he got home when he knew she didn't want to be there? Perhaps if he had told Natalie what was going on with his mother, it would have made a difference. That despite the strong front she put on, he was terrified he was going to lose her and wished she'd step away from the company she loved and focus on her health.

His heart squeezed. He'd been so caught up in worrying about his mother he probably had taken Natalie for granted those last few weeks they'd been together. But shouldn't he have been able to count on her to be there for him even when he was distracted?

Perhaps sensing his gaze, she glanced up, their eyes meeting as she caught him watching her. But rather than say anything, she swallowed a bit nervously, then returned her attention to the computer screen without comment.

Best thing he could do was forget her and move on with his life. It's what he'd done when Stella had left. She'd betrayed his faith in her by taking off to Paris when he'd thought they were serious. He'd been fine. He'd be fine again. Only, this time felt different. His insides felt more raw, more betrayed, more panicked to undo whatever had made Natalie leave him so she'd return to their life together. Probably because of what was going on with his mother and how that already had his personal life on edge.

Getting over Natalie might take a long time, he thought later that morning when his phone pinged with a text message from her while he was seeing patients in clinic for follow-up. It was probably a Pavlovian response, but when he glanced at his smart watch and saw her name, his heart sped up, pounding his pulse in his ears. It wasn't as if he thought the message was personal. Whatever her real reasons, she felt it necessary that their relationship end. So be it.

He glanced at the message on his watch. Donald Eastland's chest X-ray showed infiltrates in both lower lobes. His white blood cell count had been normal. His D-dimer was still pending.

"Get a CT of his chest. With and without contrast," Will said out loud, his phone taking the message and sending it at his voice command.

Yes, sir, came her immediate reply.

Will winced at her formal response, then berated himself for doing so. What did he expect? For her to still put smiley faces and hearts in her messages to him? He'd never been a mushy kind of guy, hadn't really thought much about her emojis, but the barren reply felt like another slap in the face in a long string of them over the past few days.

Maybe someday he'd get a text from Natalie and his body wouldn't react any differently than it would to a text from any other nurse taking care of his patients.

Maybe.

"Good morning, Mrs. Johnson," Natalie greeted her patient. She greeted every patient every morning as if she expected a response. Sometimes she got one. Sometimes she didn't.

"It's shaping up to be a beautiful day. A bit cold, though," she continued as she moved about the room.

Mattie's dark eyes watched her closely.

"I imagine you're ready for that ventilation tube to come out today."

Mattie's head nodded ever so slightly.

"Dr. Forrest was hoping he'd be able to remove it yesterday, but you never roused enough for him to feel he should. Maybe today will be the day. How are you this morning?" Natalie held out the nine-by-nine dry erase board and a marker to the woman.

Been better.

Natalie smiled. "True. You've been worse, too, but Dr. Forrest has you on the mend and hopefully you'll be ready to go home soon."

The woman gave another slight nod.

Natalie explained each medication as she administered it via Mattie's intravenous line.

Next, she gave her patient a sponge bath, taking care to be gentle as she cleaned her frail skin and then applied lotion. When Natalie was done, she made sure the sheet covered Maddie's freshly bathed body.

"I'll get someone to help me and be back in a bit to get you onto clean bedding," she promised, turning to leave the CVICU room.

She came to a quick stop just outside the privacy curtain.

"Will…er… Dr. Forrest," she corrected herself, cheeks heating. Would she ever be able to see him and not feel the personal connection between them? To not think of him as Will, the man who'd wooed her, and wowed her, and ended up breaking her heart? "Good morning."

She'd do her best to greet him with the same respect she showed every hospital employee. Just because Will was the most beautiful man she'd ever seen and she'd once kissed every inch of him didn't change the fact that he was her colleague.

Just because he used to be hers and her body didn't understand that he no long was didn't change that. Just because…

Natalie swallowed, then refocused her thoughts. "I was on my way to grab Callie or one of the other nurses to help me change Mattie's bedding."

"I'll help you," he surprised her by offering.

Natalie bit into her lower lip. Refusing his help would mean delaying getting Mattie onto fresh bedding. Maybe he was just as helpful with all his patients. She suspected that was the case. Just because he'd flunked out on being her Prince Charming didn't mean he wasn't a fantastic doctor, person and coworker.

"Okay."

Together they untucked the lift sheet, then slid Mattie to the far side of the bed, taking care to keep the loose top sheet over her for her privacy. When they'd accomplished that, Natalie undid the old sheet, then made up half the bed with the clean linens.

"If you'll raise her feet and hang on to the old sheet, I'll slide it back over the new," Will offered.

Together they got the soiled bedding all removed and Mattie situated. Natalie put on the woman's fresh hospital gown, then replaced the top sheet while Will talked to Mattie, explaining what her latest set of labs and vitals had revealed, while holding the woman's hand.

Fighting the aww moment his gesture of kindness and comfort sent through her, Natalie bagged up the soiled linens. She'd seen how he was with other patients in the past, with his mother. The man had a heart of gold. If only he could have given that heart to Natalie.

"Your oxygen saturations dipped some with all the moving around of getting clean," Will told his patient. "I'm not convinced that you're ready to go off the ventilator yet."

Mattie grunted, making her disapproval of his comment plain.

"Maybe later," he offered with an empathetic pat to her hand, reminding Natalie yet again that the reasons she'd fallen for him had gone far beyond their sexual chemistry. "I'll check back after I finish in clinic and will keep my fingers crossed that you're strong enough for it to happen soon."

Mattie wrote "Okay" on her board, and then, a disappointed look on her face, she closed her eyes. Within seconds, she was asleep, the exertion from being bathed having taken its toll.

"She looks better today," Natalie mused watching the rise and fall of the woman's chest as she tucked the covers around her.

"She does. I was hoping she'd be improved enough to come off the vent, though. Maybe I'll reconsider when I check on her this evening."

Natalie turned, expecting to see Will staring at his patient. Instead, his gaze was trained on her. Heat flooded her face and, self-conscious, she quickly glanced away and walked over to the curtain that provided the room with a bit of privacy through the heavy glass walls. She pulled the curtain back so she'd be able to see into the room from the nurses' station.

And then they were both just standing there.

"I should go check on my other patient."

Snapping out of whatever it was that had held his eyes to her, he nodded. "Me, too."

Which meant they were headed in the same direction.

"How is Mr. Eastland this morning? Urine output good? Oxygen saturation holding? His swelling any better?" Will asked in rapid-fire succession as he disposed of his used personal protective equipment then disinfected his hands and stethoscope.

"The night nurse reported that he remained stable with no episodes or evidence of reoccurring fluid overload. His vitals have been good this morning and he was asking if he'd be able to eat today," she. Wow. Her voice sounded normal. How was that even possible when being near Will made her insides ache so? When her heart was screaming in frustration?

"Good to hear," he answered, oblivious to her inner turmoil that they were carrying on a conversation as if they had never been anything more than coworkers. As if they'd never meant anything at all to each other. "If everything appears okay when I check him, I'll change his nothing-by-mouth orders to a liquid diet and we'll advance him as tolerated."

Trying to force her mind to focus on their patient, Natalie nodded. "He'll be glad to hear that."

"If his vitals remain good, he'll transfer to a step-down unit later today, and hopefully be home within a couple of days at most."

She'd suspected as much when the night nurse had given a good report on the CABG patient that morning. Good. That would be one less patient she and Will would have to communicate over. Maybe her manager would be kind and make sure her next assignment belonged to another physician.

While Will went to check on Mr. Eastland, Natalie

dropped off the dirty laundry. First peeping through the glass wall into the room to make sure Mattie was still resting okay, Natalie then disinfected herself and donned appropriate PPE prior to entering Mr. Eastland's room to see if Will needed her assistance.

The man was sitting up in his bed, smiling and talking with Will. Amazing what a few bypassed blocked arteries and some diuretics could do to improve a person's life outlook.

Hearing her enter the room, Will turned her way, his lips automatically curving in a smile. That is, until he seemed to remember all the reasons why he shouldn't, and his smile disappeared as quickly as it had happened.

His smile disappearing was like going from brilliant sunshine to being banned to the darkest dungeon. A chill prickling her skin, Natalie quivered at the drop in room temperature.

She could do this, she mentally prepped herself. She had to.

Natalie stepped in Mr. Eastland's CVICU room and Will's world immediately lightened. But that joy only lasted for a moment before it was replaced with the recall that Natalie wasn't his any longer.

He wavered between frustration and resignation that maybe he was meant to just remain single.

Being single didn't set one up for disappointment and betrayal.

But it did leave him lonely at night when he got into the bed he'd shared with Natalie. At times, he'd swear he could smell her favorite scented lotion, could hear her breathing next to him.

Yeah, he'd just stay single.

Not that his mother agreed. It was barely past 8:00 a.m.

and already she was texting to find out his dinner plans. No doubt any invitations issued would include Stella since he'd declined her invitation the prior day. Subtlety wasn't in his mother's nature and she was worried about him. Maybe he shouldn't have been so open with her about his breakup with Natalie. He should have known she'd try to patch up that part of his life by pushing him and Stella together, saying she'd rest easier knowing he had someone special in his life.

He'd had someone special in his life and look where that had gotten him.

Besides, even if he did decide to date again, it wouldn't be with a woman who'd proven she couldn't stick around any better than Natalie had. Losing Stella had never left him feeling gutted. When he saw her, he didn't fill with longing and have memories pulling him toward her.

Turning back to Mr. Eastland, Will fought to keep his sigh from escaping by retrieving his stethoscope from his pocket to listen to the man's chest. He went through his check, making sure pulses were good in all four extremities, that his swelling was decreased, his lungs cleared from the day before noises and that the man truly was as spry as he appeared.

"You going to send me home, Doc?"

"Not today."

"I feel a lot better," his patient pointed out, his dark gaze watching Will's every move.

"You look a lot better, too, and I intend to make sure it stays that way for at least another night. If you continue to do well today, I'll discharge you home tomorrow. For today, if there's a bed available, you'll be transferred to a regular hospital room, otherwise, you'll stay here for the duration of your stay."

The man nodded as if he'd had no true thoughts of going home that evening but had asked anyway.

Will and Natalie left Mr. Eastland's room together.

As they both reached up to disinfect, their hands touched, then immediately jerked away from each other, but not before Will felt the same shot of awareness touching Natalie always gave him. Apparently, his libido didn't care that their relationship had ended.

"Is this how it's going to be from now on?" he asked, fighting to keep his agitation under control. He'd cared about her, asked her to live with him. He'd dived in, opened his home to her, been crazy about her, and she'd turned her back on him. How could he have been so foolish?

Her gaze shot to him. "What do you mean?"

"This awkward silence and jerk-away reactions if we accidentally touch?"

Her brows drew together as she regarded him. "I can't imagine that we could ever be just friends, can you?"

He hadn't done anything deserving of her shutting him out of her life.

"No, I suppose not," he ground out, wondering how he could have been so wrong about her, about them. He walked away, gutted more than he should still be a month after she'd left him, but determined that he was done with Natalie Gifford.

CHAPTER FOUR

"OH! I WASN'T expecting to see you here."

Natalie's wide-eyed gaze had already clued Will in to that as they arrived at the conference room of the New York City Children's Cancer Charity office at the same time.

Will took a deep breath. Did she think he'd skip out because they were no longer together? Due to his mother's illness, he'd missed a few meetings, but he'd been a part of the organization for years. Now that cancer had personally touched his family he couldn't imagine not participating. If anything, he'd be pushing for the Harroway Foundation to increase their donations and involvement in organizations fighting cancer for these kids and their families, plus expanding what the foundation was doing for breast cancer research.

"I'm a board member representative on the committee," he reminded, aggravated at her accusatory tone. "The only times I miss a meeting are when it's unavoidable."

"Of course. It's just you've not been here the last few times, so I…" Her words died away and she sighed. "Never mind. The more the merrier, right?"

With that, she gave a tight smile, which might have been more of a grimace, then took off to find a seat.

Rather than follow, Will stood back, watching as she did a quick assessment of available seats. It wasn't lost to him that she chose one sandwiched between two places that appeared to be already occupied based upon the young mother sitting at one, and the pad of paper, pen and half-full water glass at the other.

The committee consisted of twenty people and were a diverse group from various walks of life. Some, like Will, were mostly there for their financial resources or board positions. Others like Natalie were doing the bulk of the organizing and legwork. And, then there were those who represented the group meant to be benefitted: children with cancer and their families.

Long before his mother's diagnosis, oncology had been a field dear to Will's heart. During residency he'd considered pediatric oncology as his focus after completing a short rotation, but cardiology had been his true love. One of his medical school buddies who had chosen to treat cancer in kids stopped him inside the doorway, a smile on his always friendly face.

"Will, good to see you." Lee shook his hand and they caught up on mutual acquaintances for a few minutes. "There's an empty seat on the other side of me. I'll slide over and you can sit next to Natalie."

Which meant his friend hadn't heard that he and Natalie were no longer together. What had Natalie told the man at past meetings when Will had been absent? Or had she just changed the subject anytime he was mentioned?

Glancing around the small meeting room, Will considered his seating options. There was only one other empty chair in the room and that one was next to Gregory Kendall. Will didn't have the patience for the man's stories about his greatness and prowess this evening. Or any evening, really, but Gregory's father was a longtime family acquaintance so Will had been enduring his over-flowing trust fund arrogance for years.

"Thanks, Lee." He wouldn't not sit by someone he liked so that he could sit by someone he barely tolerated just because Natalie happened to be in the opposite chair. He'd just ignore her. No big deal.

"Hello, Natalie," Lee greeted her, sliding his belongings over one seat before Will could stop him.

"Hi, Dr. Lewis," Natalie responded with a brief look upward before going back to staring down at the note-book she'd placed on the meeting table as if the blank pages had her in a trance. She didn't look up as Will pulled out his chair and sat next to her. How awkward to be so close physically and so distant emotionally to someone who'd so recently occupied such an important role in his life.

The entire office space was tiny, and the meeting room barely fit all the committee members. If Will wasn't care-ful he'd end up bumping again. Refusing to look her way, he turned toward Lee and asked how his practice was going.

Lee's forehead furrowed as he realized something had gone wrong in paradise. Will shook his head, indicating he didn't want to discuss it. Not ever, but definitely not with Natalie sitting next to him. Fortunately, Lee gave an understanding nod and most likely assumed they were having a lovers' quarrel. Lee would realize soon enough that they were done.

Something his body was struggling with as he caught a whiff of the scented lotion she used when not working at the hospital.

His insides knotted as flashbacks of rubbing the lotion onto her slender back, her thighs and calves as she lay naked on their bed filled him. She'd rolled over, looked up at him with eyes full of passion and adoration as she'd taken the lotion bottle from him, then pulled him to her and kissed him so thoroughly he'd trembled. Had that been two months ago? Three? Or longer?

Certainly, over the past few weeks of their relationship he'd been tired and torn emotionally with worry over his mother, wondering if her strong spirit would be enough to help her overcome her cancer, and if a son could love his mother through her treatments to see her ultimately cured. How many nights had he gone to bed those last few weeks and immediately drifted to sleep without making love to the beautiful woman next to him? He should have held her every night he'd had the chance. Made love to her until they'd both drifted to sleep sated and in each other's arms.

Unable not to, he glanced Natalie's way, his gaze colliding with hers. There was no way for her to know where his thoughts were, or that her scent was driving his desire through the roof with sensual memories. Her breath caught, her cheeks flushed and her eyes widened just a little before her long lashes swept down to hide anything that shone there.

The meeting started. Katrina Matthews, a full-time employee of the charity, stood and spoke for a few minutes, thanking everyone for coming as this was the last scheduled meeting prior to the gala. When Katrina finished the introduction to the night's agenda, as the cochair of the gala benefit, Natalie stood and handed out papers from a folder she'd had tucked beneath her notepad.

"The gala is fast approaching. For the most part, everything is coming together and running smoothly," she began, pushing a long red hair tendril behind her ear as she continued. "On the handout, I've listed where we stand on food, donations, etcetera, and included our planned timeline for the evening. If you will please take a moment to look it over and let me know of any corrections that need to be made, that would be wonderful."

They ran through the night's schedule, what they hoped to accomplish, and addressed a few last-minute concerns.

"Donations are lower than this time prior to last year's gala," the charity's other board member in attendance commented, glancing up over the rim of his reading glasses as he tapped a section on the handout. "Is that being looked into to ensure this year's event is viewed as a success?"

Natalie glanced toward Katrina, who gestured for her to continue. "We are aware donations are down. As with many charities, world events have strained corporate donations. We've reached out to several companies who've been generous in the past. Unfortunately, we've yet to hear back, but hopefully we will have prior to the gala and will have good news on those fronts."

"Times have been tough financially on a lot of places," a committee member pointed out. "We should be contacting more than just our same benefactors. Someone should generate a list of corporate charities and what their qualifications are, and if we fit, then apply for us to be considered. If we're lagging behind this year, we need to up what we're doing. Our cause is an important one."

"Good point," Natalie praised, then looked the man square in the eyes. "Would you like to volunteer for the position, Mr. Felix?"

The man quickly shot down that idea and everyone else in the room seemed too busy to take on the last-minute additional efforts to increase funds.

Will was willing to make a few calls to old family friends that should rally up their total by several thousand, but his time was too stretched already to take on heading the project. He'd work behind the scenes to help and, as in the past, would make a sizable donation. The more cancer research and support for families affected by it, the better.

When no one volunteered, Natalie said, "I agree that it's a worthy idea and I will do what I can to see it to fruition. Is anyone able to meet with me to do some research, fill out applications and possibly make some calls? We could meet here one day later this week or early next."

"I'll help."

Will's gaze shot to Gregory. Lee might not have heard about the breakup, but the man grinning at Natalie knew. Knew and was leering at her overtly. The man truly disgusted Will in ways that had nothing to do with the surge of fury hitting him in response to the way Gregory gobbled up Natalie with his eyes.

That was why Will's fingers had clenched, causing his grandfather's signet ring to dig into his flesh, not because Will felt any type of jealousy or protectiveness over Natalie. They'd been apart for a month. What she did was none of his business.

"Will and I want to help, too," Lee added, nudging him with his elbow as he spoke.

Will frowned at his friend. What was Lee saying? He'd thought Lee had figured out that he and Natalie were at odds. The last thing Will wanted was to interact with Natalie even more than necessary. With her scheduled indefinitely in the CVICU, work was difficult enough.

But as his gaze returned to Gregory eyeing her, Will corrected himself. The last thing he wanted was for Natalie to be stuck alone with that pompous Lothario.

Not that she couldn't handle herself or that Will had any say in how she spent her time. But Gregory was a smooth operator with a history of fooling even some of the city's most seasoned beauties. Regardless of what had happened between them, Natalie was a sweet, good person who'd had limited experience going into her relationship with Will. It was only natural that he wouldn't want her to be taken advantage of by the slick man.

He wanted to punch the man in the face, but maybe that was only natural, too, since a month didn't seem nearly long enough to be accustomed to the fact that Natalie was no longer his girlfriend.

Not that he'd ever had that problem in the past. Not even with Stella, who he'd once assumed he'd marry. When she'd broken his trust and taken off for Europe, he'd certainly not felt as if a hole had been torn in his chest.

"It's for a good cause," Lee declared, elbowing him again, not appearing bothered by Will's frown, as if Will wasn't catching the fact they were saving Natalie from Gregory. Apparently, Lee's vibes about the man were the same as Will's. But his friend was missing the point that it was no longer his place to rescue Natalie.

His gaze shifted to hers, and when they met, emotion sucker punched him.

She'd rather deal with Gregory's advances than spend time with him.

Her eyes instantly lowered, and, reeling from the realization of how different life could be in such a short amount of time, Will leaned back in his chair.

Not so long ago he'd seen himself growing old with Natalie, spending his life with her. Maybe he should have told her that. Maybe it was better, given the circumstances, that he hadn't.

Staying away from her was the best thing for him,

and her, too. He just needed to say he was already over-extended and to find someone else.

But there had always been something about Natalie that pulled him in. Sitting next to her, watching her take charge of the meeting and continue to grow with the confidence she seemed to exude in every aspect of her life—with the exception of him, apparently—he filled with pride at how far she'd come from when he'd first encouraged her to volunteer with the organization.

Looking at her, he knew that despite how their relationship had failed Natalie was a rare flower just waiting to blossom and stun the world with her inner and outer beauty.

He'd been damn lucky to have played even the tiniest role in her life, and even luckier to have gotten to so closely behold her magnificence.

And as much as logic said they'd never work, that he should stay away from her, he wasn't sure he could do that.

Or that he even wanted to.

One thing he was positive on, though, was that no way was he allowing Gregory Kendall alone time with Natalie.

Speak up and deny what Dr. Lewis just said, Natalie willed the silent man sitting next to where she stood.

Why wasn't Will vocalizing some great reason why he couldn't, or wouldn't, help with the mini project? Lord knew he could choose from a dozen excuses why he didn't have time to take on yet another endeavor. No one would judge a cardiac surgeon harshly for saying no to the volunteer project when he already did so much for so many personally and through the Harroway Foundation.

Surely, any moment he'd list one of the reasons he couldn't help.

But rather than wiggle off the hook Lee had put him upon, Will nodded. "Sure. Why not?"

As if he didn't know why not. She glared at him. She'd not wanted him to be the one to volunteer. Having to see him at the hospital each time she went in was enough to keep her stomach in tight knots, as it was. She didn't need extra time with him via the gala fundraising event.

"Between the three of us reaching out to those in our inner circles," he continued, his green gaze avoiding hers as he glared at Gregory Kendall, "I suspect pre-event donations will exceed last years and no one will question the event's success."

Was he trying to rescue her or torture her? Regardless, Natalie knew his increased involvement would be a good thing for the charity, and wasn't that her ultimate goal?

"No doubt," Lee agreed, grinning at Will. "Chump change to your inner circle. We got this."

Will ignored the comment, which didn't surprise Natalie. She'd never known him to make a big deal of his background. Sad that it had still played such a key role in driving a wedge between them.

Or his mother alone had done that. Had Rebecca pushed him to not include Natalie in social functions? Or had Will truly believed she'd not wanted to go and that he'd been doing her a favor by attending alone and leaving her to spend her time as she chose with friends and family? Or maybe Natalie's own insecurities about her background had caused the rift that had prevented her from ever truly trusting in their relationship. Most likely it had been a nasty combination that had knocked so many holes in her happiness and her ability to feel as if she belonged in Will's world.

Which was too bad because she missed him. The Will who would roll over and grin at her first thing in the morning. The Will who had kissed her and spun her around when she'd agreed to move in with him as if she'd made him the happiest man in the world. The Will who'd reach over and hold her hand as they drifted off to sleep. She missed that Will and couldn't help but wonder if they would still be together if he'd just been a cardiac surgeon meeting a nurse.

What was she doing?

Now was not the time for another round of twenty questions on why she and Will had failed as a couple. Time for that had come and gone. A month had passed. She needed to get over Will, although she suspected he would always hold a big chunk of her heart. How could any man ever take his place when Will was in so many ways the total package?

If only he'd loved her, been willing to take her side or at least acknowledge her concerns about his mother as legitimate.

If only she could quit thinking about him.

Forcing herself to refocus, Natalie thanked all three men, then moved on to the next question presented by a committee member. When they'd gone through everything on her portion of the agenda and the concerns raised, she thanked everyone for coming and turned the meeting over to her cochair.

Keeping her eyes on Katrina as the woman rose to speak, Natalie sat down, bumping against Will when she did. Although their clothes prevented skin-to-skin contact, the interaction had her knees wobbling and her head spinning. "Sorry," she mumbled, straightening her notebook to give her hands something to do to cover her discomfort. Once upon a time she'd sought any excuse to touch him, had thrilled that she'd had the right to run her hands over his body. Now she apologized for an accidental bump. Oh, how that made her heart grieve.

"No problem. Happens all the time."

Surprised at his light, almost teasing response, Natalie's gaze shifted to him.

"Women bumping into me accidentally," he clarified. His eyes were trained on Katrina, but she'd swear his lips had just twitched as if he found the incident humorous.

"It was an accident," she defended in a whisper, not sure why she felt the need, but not willing to let him imply she'd touched him on purpose.

"Sure. No problem." His tone suggested he didn't believe her.

Confused by his comment and determined she was going to just ignore him, she attempted to focus on what Katrina was saying.

To no avail, though, as her attention wandered back to the man sitting next to her. Did he realize his leg was close enough to hers that she could feel his body heat? That all she had to do was move her leg a hair's breadth and they'd be bumping against each other again?

His body heat enveloped her. As did his scent. It was all she could do not to breathe in the familiar spicy male fragrance that tempted her with memories of nuzzling against his neck in the early morning hours. She had lain awake so many nights, cradled against him, counting her lucky stars that she was there in his arms.

Why had she let the doubting demons inside her rob her joy? Why hadn't she felt she had a right to stand up to his mother and demand Will acknowledge her place in his life rather than watch their relationship erode because she'd been too afraid to fight for it? To fight for him?

Why? Because she'd grown up poor and his parents

were on a first-name basis with iconic American found-ing families. But ultimately, Will was still just a man to her woman. She'd worked so hard to overcome her poor beginnings, determined she wouldn't live just above pov-erty, but perhaps what she'd really needed to work on was how she mentally saw herself.

And how she saw him.

She inhaled and her senses filled further with Will, causing her to shift in her seat. Her knee brushed against his thigh and lightning shot through her. She reflexively jerked away. Her eardrums thrummed. The only thing she could hear was the pounding of her heartbeat, which seemed to be playing a tune devoted to him.

Will. Will. Will.

"Hmm?"

Natalie blinked. Good grief. Had she said his name out loud?

Noticing that all committee member eyes were on her, she realized she had. Her face caught fire as complete mortification hit.

"*Will* there be an opportunity for any of the special guest children and their family members to be recog-nized?" she asked, grasping at straws to cover her blun-der. A stupid question as she knew the answer, they all did, but less stupid than admitting the truth: she'd said the man's name out loud because he'd overpowered her senses.

"We've always recognized the children we invite and their families," Katrina reminded, her brow furrowing at the interruption. Her look clearly said Natalie's ques-tion made no sense.

"Oh, sorry," she apologized, knowing her cheeks were a bright ruddy color. "This is my first year being in-volved."

"No problem," Katrina commented, then moved on through the items she wanted to cover prior to the meeting ending.

Will leaned over and whispered, "Nice cover, but I recognized your tone and what you just did. Want to tell me what you were really thinking?"

Rather than answer, she narrowed her eyes, then turned away from him to write some notes on her legal pad. How dare he make fun of her for being so stupid as to say his name? For being so weak her brain turned to mush when she was near him? Then again, with a mistake that ridiculous maybe she deserved to be made fun of.

She ordered herself to not look at Will, not think about Will, and to definitely not say his name out loud during a meeting ever again.

No matter how devoted he was to the Children's Cancer Charity, any hope Will had of paying attention to Katrina was shot the moment Natalie said his name.

Not that he'd been having much luck prior to that.

Being near Natalie was a distraction under the best of times.

She might have fooled the others with her gala question, but the rosy color to her cheeks divulged it had been a cover. What had she been thinking when she'd said his name? That she wished she was anywhere but next to him because his nearness was affecting her the way her nearness was affecting him?

His body had instantly recognized her tone. Longing had been evident in how she'd said his name and he'd zinged to life.

Convincing his body that their chemistry should have fizzled out the moment she turned her back on their relationship seemed impossible. Especially when she was mere inches from him and everything in him had sensed her beckoning him long before her lips had murmured his name.

Just the memory of their bodies entwined had Will swallowing. He had to stop, or he'd be the one with rosy cheeks from embarrassing himself in front of the others. He'd never been one to embark in a relationship based solely on physical attraction. Never had. Couldn't imagine that he ever would. Sex with Natalie had never just been about physical attraction, anyway. She'd always made him glad he was a man, glad to be alive and the recipient of her smiles.

His gaze lowered to her notebook and, his breath catching, he tensed.

She'd written his name and doodled around it.

They were supposed to be over as a couple. They were over. So what was she doing? Toying with him? Flirting with him? Letting him know she was as torn about being near him as he was her?

It took him only a millisecond to realize she drew without conscious thought to what she was doing as her eyes were trained on her cochair. As he watched her continue to mindlessly trace her pen over his name, his brain raced, trying to decipher the past week's events. He'd gone from confident in their relationship to crushed at her lack of commitment. Had he learned nothing from his relationship with Stella? He'd gotten too caught up too quickly with Natalie and made some bad choices, like asking her to live with him. He'd surprised himself as much as her when his question had slipped out of his mouth. He'd never lived with a girlfriend, but once the seed had been planted in his mind, he'd acknowledged living with Natalie was the perfect solution.

He'd wanted her there when he closed his eyes at

night, when he woke up in the mornings, when he came home. What was it she'd said? That his apartment had never felt like home to her. It sure hadn't felt like home to him since she'd moved out. He could barely stand to be there, seeing her and some memory everywhere he looked, hearing the echo of something she'd said, her laughter. The less time he was there these days, the better.

Maybe the stress of the past few months was getting to him. His mother finding her lump, confiding in him before she'd told anyone, including Will's father. Her swearing him to secrecy to protect Harroway Industries. His taking her to multiple specialist appointments as testing was performed and treatment decisions made. Work had always been his passion but was busy, with more early-morning calls summoning him to the hospital. And going from thinking his relationship with Natalie was solid to having it ripped away from him.

You let her go, an inner voice reminded him. *You were so caught off guard that she'd leave you that you let her go without putting up a fight to keep her.*

Had he asked her to stay, for them to work on the things that bothered her, would she have reconsidered?

If he'd told her about his mother, explained why he'd let his attention to their relationship slip, would she have wrapped her arms around him and promised him everything was going to be okay?

Natalie would swear that Will's leg had just brushed against hers on purpose. Rather than jerk away, his leg had lingered, the warmth searing her flesh.

She turned to look at him, meaning to frown as she shifted her leg away from his. He stared straight ahead as if completely caught up in the remaining details of the gala that Katrina was laying out.

Surely, he saw her from his peripheral vision, but if so, he ignored her, and she was making a spectacle of herself continuing to look at him.

Sighing, she turned away, telling herself she needed to pay attention and take notes on what Katrina was saying so she could clarify anything she didn't feel was clear.

Although most of the committee members were alumni, Natalie really was a newbie with a lot to learn. Glancing down, her eyes lit on what she'd written so far. Her lips parted and her stomach fisted.

Oh. No.

Will's name with scribbles around it.

What was wrong with her? Had she reverted to a love-sick teenager?

Trying not to attract attention, she flipped over her notepad. Unfortunately, she dropped her pen onto the table with a loud clang that once again had everyone in the room looking her way. Great.

"Sorry," she mumbled, mortified that she was causing a disturbance during the meeting and because she'd drawn Will's name. Had he seen?

Please let him not have noticed.

This was difficult enough without embarrassing herself that way.

She fought to keep from looking his way. She just couldn't.

If he'd seen, was he laughing at her? Probably. Poor, silly Natalie who couldn't be near him without making a fool of herself. Would he make a joke about women accidentally writing his name, as well?

And why, dear heavens, was his thigh brushed up against hers again? Was he trying to torture her? Or just singe her skirt to her flesh from his heat?

When the meeting adjourned, Natalie longed to make

a beeline for the door, but as cochair, she had to stick around to answer questions.

Unfortunately, Gregory kept firing them off her way.

"Maybe we should go to dinner to discuss how I can best serve you," he offered, his tone leaving no doubt as to how he'd like to serve. He waggled his bushy dyed blond brows. "You'd be impressed at how handy I can be."

Gag. Was the tanning booth bronze guy serious? His handsy-ness was what concerned her. Concerned and repulsed. Currently, she couldn't imagine wanting to ever date again, but even if she could, Gregory wouldn't make the cut. The man seriously gave her the creeps. But his family did make huge contributions to the charity, so she'd choose her words wisely.

"I—"

"Ready to go?"

At Will's unexpected question, Natalie blinked at him. He joined them and placed his hand possessively on Natalie's back. His touch seared through her clothes, causing her to gulp. "Go where?"

"Whatever you feel like is fine. I've no real preference on where we dine this evening." Will's intense gaze connected with Gregory's, warning the other man to back away.

What was he doing? And even more importantly, why was he doing it? Surely he didn't think he had to protect her. But everything in the way he eyed the other man said that was exactly what he was doing.

"I ate prior to the meeting." Part of Natalie rebelled against his high-handedness. Another part was grateful he'd realized what was happening and was giving her an easy out to escape Gregory without offending and possibly causing detriment to the Children's Cancer Charity.

"But, if you don't mind waiting, I'll be ready to leave in a few minutes."

Will's green gaze not leaving Gregory's, he nodded. "I've never minded waiting on you, Natalie. When you're finished, I'll walk you home."

She'd swear his comment was directed at Gregory more than herself, reiterating that Natalie was off-limits. As Will had never shown jealousy in the past, had never had reason to, Natalie fought to keep her jaw from dropping. Had he really never minded waiting on her?

Insides shaking, she gathered up her notebook, then went to talk to Katrina and one of the parent volunteers. Only her gaze kept going back to where the two men still stood.

"I thought—" Gregory said loud enough anyone in the room could hear.

"You thought wrong," Will corrected, then in a voice that would have made Rebecca proud had Natalie not been the subject, he ordered, "Stay away from Natalie."

Will walked away from the red-faced man, going over to where Lee was chatting with a couple of the parent committee members. After a few minutes, the parents left them on their own.

Natalie's heart raced. She smiled at the right times as she chatted with her cochair and fellow committee member, but her mind was on the man talking to his medical school buddy. Their voices were too low for anyone to hear what they said, for which Natalie was both grateful and wished she could move close enough to overhear.

By the burning of her ears and the way Lee kept looking her way, she was the topic of conversation.

When Natalie had procrastinated as long as she could, she hugged her notebook to her like a shield and made her way to where Will and Lee laughed at something.

She'd thank him for saving her the trouble of dealing with Gregory, then head out on her own.

"Ready to go?" Will asked when she joined them.

Noting that Gregory was still in the meeting room and was watching them, she decided they could part ways on the street below. "Let me grab my bag."

Will said his farewell to Lee, as did Natalie after she'd gathered her things, then they headed toward the elevator bank. When the door slid open, there were already several people in the car, chatting away, saving Natalie from feeling as if she had to make conversation to avoid silence.

Once they stepped outside the building onto the still-busy sidewalk, Natalie prepped herself for saying goodbye. Polite. Professional. Grateful. She had this.

"Thank you for saving me from possibly having to make a scene in there. Gregory can be a bit much."

Will shrugged. "You're welcome. He's not someone you need to be alone with."

"I agree, and appreciate you giving me an easy out."

"No problem."

She hesitated, searching for the right words. "But I'd have handled it since it's really not your place to rescue me anymore."

His eyes glittered with the reflection of the street-lights.

"When we were a couple it was different," she clarified. "We're not now, so I need to, and can, handle things on my own."

"It's not a big deal, Natalie. I did what any gentleman would have done where Gregory is concerned."

Maybe. She didn't want to seem ungrateful, because he had simplified things. Under different circumstances it wouldn't have been a big deal. But this was Will and anything to do with him was a big deal.

Still, he was right. She was making a mountain out of a molehill over something he'd as much as said he'd have done to rescue any woman.

"Thank you, then," she said, then forced a polite smile. "I'll be on my way. There's no real need for you to walk me home."

His brow arched. "I said I would walk you home, so I'll walk you home, Natalie. Unless there's a reason you'd rather traipse the streets of Manhattan alone at night than be escorted by me?"

He made the route to Callie's sound dark and dangerous. It wasn't. But, rather than argue, she bit the inside of her lower lip, welcoming the pain as it kept her from admitting that she didn't want him to walk her home because putting Gregory in his place would have been easier than fighting her body's reaction to being near Will for the ten-plus blocks home. Knowing he was waiting for a response, she nodded then took off walking.

"Are you still at Callie's?"

"For the time being," she admitted, relieved that he'd changed the subject to something benign. "She and Brent have offered to let me have my old bedroom back permanently, but I'm still of the mindset that I shouldn't encroach on their newlywed time together. I'm scanning the roommate wanted ads daily in hopes of locating a place that works."

"It's a big city. Something should come up."

"You'd think," she agreed. "Finding something that's within a reasonable walking distance of the hospital and affordable seems to be almost impossible. I've given up and started looking at traveling back and forth by subway." Nervous, she kept talking. "I looked at a place earlier today, actually, that I thought was going to be perfect. But the ad was deceiving about the monthly rent and it ended up being way outside my budget."

Had the real monthly figures been put before her from the beginning she could have saved herself the trouble of viewing the place.

"Do you need money, Natalie?"

Confused, she looked his way. "For what?"

"An apartment of your own. The one you looked at today that you wanted, do you want me to arrange it for you? Say the word and I'll make it happen."

Were they back to that?

"No," she gasped, horrified that he'd thought she'd been hinting. "I'd never let you do that." She shook her head in denial, angry that he'd thought she would. "Besides, why would you be willing? We're no longer together. I'm not your responsibility, Will. Not where other men are concerned and not on where I live."

They paused at a street crossing and he took a deep breath. "In some ways I'm responsible for you not having a place to live."

The light changed and the waiting crowd started moving.

"Not really," she corrected, resuming walking in the direction of Callie's apartment. "You just delayed the inevitable. Callie and Brent had gotten engaged months prior to you asking me to move in with you. My moving out made their going ahead and marrying easy because they didn't have to worry about me and where I'd go. For that, I'm grateful because I wouldn't have wanted to stand in their way. So, I would have had to find another place and roommate, regardless of you and me."

Had the suspicion that Callie and Brent were delaying a trip to the justice of the peace because of Natalie living in the apartment played a role in her decision to move in with Will? She hadn't thought so, but she knew what she'd told him was true. Just as she knew it was true that she needed to find a place of her own and get out of their hair. But she'd stay put forever before she'd let Will set her up in an apartment.

They walked in silence for long enough that Natalie glanced his way, realized he was lost in deep thought.

"Whether you view me as responsible or not, I do feel responsible that currently you're essentially homeless. Give me the address of the place you looked at earlier. I'll set you up in it, help you get on your feet in your own place for however long you need. It's the least I can do."

She stopped walking and gawked at him.

"No," she said with enough force she hoped he got the message. "I wouldn't have allowed you to set me up in an apartment at any point in our relationship. I'm sure not willing to now. Listen to me carefully as I say this again, I'm not your responsibility and, in case you failed to notice, I never wanted your money."

His lips pursed and she could tell he was still plotting. "The money is nothing to me."

Exactly, she thought, and it was a big deal for her and most of the world.

"I don't need your money or your help."

She took off walking again, increasing her pace because she was ready for their walk to end. Well, part of her was. Another part was saying, *This is Will. Your Will. Walk slower so you can be near him longer.* Yeah, that part of her was crazy.

"I'll find the right place for me that's within my budget," she said, hoping to silence the voice in her head. "Until then, I'm fine at Callie's."

And hopefully she wasn't too much in the way. Her

friends were out on a date night to watch a new theater production. They'd invited her, but even if she hadn't had the gala meeting, no way would she have intruded on their date.

Focused on her thoughts, she stumbled, but didn't fall thanks to Will reaching out to steady her.

"You okay?"

All except where his hand burned into her flesh, melting her insides.

"Um…yeah, fine," she mumbled, not looking up at him. Could he tell how his touch affected her? That she hadn't wanted him to let go of her arm? That what she'd really have liked was him taking her hand into his and… No, she wouldn't have liked that. Their hand-holding days were long past.

Only…she snuck a glance his way and was struck by how handsome he was, by how safe she really had felt with him at her side during their walk. Her heart thundered so loudly in her chest he must have heard, because he turned toward her.

"Natalie?"

She swallowed. "Hmm?"

"Is everything okay?"

No. Nothing had been okay for months. Not from the point she'd started feeling as if he was hiding something from her. Was Stella's return to New York what had triggered his withdrawal from her? She'd not heard anything about him dating the blonde beauty, but she'd purposely avoided social media where photos might pop up of his after-work life.

"Just a long day," she answered, knowing he expected an answer and knowing she didn't want to tell him where her thoughts had gone. Her insides ached at what they'd once had and lost.

"Tired?"

She should be. She'd gotten up early, cleaned the apartment, then spent the biggest portion of her day volunteering with Katrina to prepare for the meeting. But looking into his green eyes, seeing something flickering there, as if he was asking something so much more than his single word, she just felt energized.

"No. I'm not."

"Because tonight's meeting went well?"

It had gone well, but she didn't credit that for the energy moving through her.

"I'm very proud of you, by the way."

Natalie missed her step but recovered without his help again. "For what?"

"For the amazing work you've done on getting the gala together and for how with each meeting you shine a little brighter. I recall how you weren't sure you were the right person for the job of cochair. I never doubted that you were."

Natalie looked toward him in a bit of awe.

"That shine was probably just me being embarrassed by one of my many blunders," she said, trying to damp down how good his praise made her feel. How hearing him say he was proud of her made her want to throw her arms around him and…

No, she couldn't do that. If her arms went around him, gratitude would soon morph into something so much more powerful.

"I doubt anyone noticed any mistakes you may have made," he assured, one corner of his mouth lifting.

"Except you?" she asked, knowing he'd been on to her when she'd said his name out loud. Had he also seen where she'd written his name? Known that he distracted her?

"I know you better than most, but like I said, I'm very proud of you. You're an amazing woman, Natalie."

Natalie couldn't hold back her smile. "Thank you. That means a lot to me."

Because he meant a lot to her.

"I think you're pretty amazing, too."

He smiled back and they walked the rest of the way to Callie's in silence.

When they arrived, Natalie paused outside the door. Unlike his apartment complex, there was no doorman, just a keypad code to get into the high-rise building.

"Thank you, Will. I really do appreciate your help with Gregory and for you walking me home."

He nodded. "You're welcome. I enjoyed stretching my legs and the company."

Natalie bit into her lower lip. "Callie and Brent are gone to a show."

Now, why had she told him that? She'd pretty much just hinted that she wanted him to come up. She didn't. Only…she did.

"Did you really already eat? We could go somewhere," he offered, his gaze searching hers.

"I did, but if you've not, then we could…" She paused. What was she doing?

"It's a long walk back to my car. Maybe just a glass of water before I head that way would be nice."

Realization dawned. "You drove to the meeting?"

His gaze locked with hers and he gave a wry grin. "I did."

"I'm confused. Why did you walk me here, then, knowing you'd have to make the walk back to get your car?"

"Because I said I would." He'd gone completely out of his way and had to backtrack now. Good grief. But she'd enjoyed their walk, too, and would forever treasure his having told her he was proud of her. "And, I wanted to walk with you, Natalie."

Natalie opened her mouth, then clamped it shut. What was she supposed to say to that? Feel at his admission? Because her insides had just gone into circuit overload.

"Fine. One drink of water, then you should be on your way before it gets any later."

But even as she punched in the keypad code that unlocked the double glass doors, Natalie's pulse raced, pounding in her ears. Thirst hadn't been what she'd seen in those brilliant green eyes. Which meant she shouldn't be letting him come upstairs and yet, she was.

Had she lost her mind? She needed to tell him she'd changed her mind, and if he needed water he could stop by a shop on his walk back. Only every nerve cell lit up and pulled her toward him as they waited for the elevator door to welcome them inside. And he was looking at her as if he knew her thighs were clenched beneath her skirt in response to the thought she was taking him up to Callie's apartment.

Callie's empty apartment.

Where they'd be alone.

Just the two of them. Her and the most beautiful man she'd ever set eyes on and who'd said he was proud of her. Did he have any idea how his words made her chest swell? How his smile had sent her stomach into cartwheels?

She was pretty sure she chattered some gibberish on the elevator ride up to Callie's floor, continued to blabber while she unlocked the apartment door, but for the life of her she had no clue what she said.

It must have been something amazing, though, because the moment they were inside the apartment and she turned to tell him she'd be right back with his water, he pulled her to him, and held her close, his eyes searching hers.

"It's not water I'm thirsty for, Natalie. You know it's not."

"I know," she admitted, heart racing, breath ragged, good sense nowhere to be found as her palms cupped his face and she stared up into the face she saw every time she closed her eyes and drifted into a dream world.

"I'm going to kiss you," he told her, his emerald gaze locked with hers and demanded she hide nothing from him. "If that's not what you want, tell me to leave now, because we both know a sip won't be enough to quench my need."

She knew what he was saying. Good Lord, she knew. They couldn't do that. They just couldn't. Not when they weren't together, and it wouldn't mean anything but just sex.

Only, this was Will and, on her part, being with him could never be just sex.

"Leave," she somehow managed to choke out. Then, as he immediately let go of her and took a step back, all her willpower drained. To her chagrin, she touched his arm. "No. Don't."

Rather than take her back in his arms, he studied her, waiting for her to say what she wanted him to do. If she told him to go, he would. Of that she had no doubt. He wouldn't seduce her and allow her to blame him for whatever happened between them. The choice was hers. All she had to do was say yes and he'd kiss her. Did kisses without love feel the same? Then again, she'd been the only one in love. If they had sex, to Will it would be nothing other than physical gratification. It's all it had ever been. Only, it had felt like so much more.

Natalie gulped back all the regret she knew she was going to have for what she was about to say, about to do. But Lord help her, this was Will and all she had to do was say the word and his lips would be against hers. How could she say no? No matter what tomorrow brought, she wasn't strong enough to deny herself the pleasure she knew he would give.

"I don't want you to go, Will," she admitted, somehow managing to keep her gaze locked with his.

His smile was lethal when he moved closer and his breath tempted her lips with his nearness. He was a man used to getting what he wanted and knew tonight was no exception. He wanted her and she was his. "You want me to kiss you?"

Or maybe *she* was getting what she wanted. Yet, *want* seemed such a tame word to describe the desire overtaking her.

"I need you to kiss me," she countered, knowing any semblance of pride was long gone. Will was here and for a brief moment in time, he'd be hers again. Logic told her that he wasn't, that he hadn't ever really been hers, but sanity was long gone. What was real was how her body sparked to life in anticipation of the magic he wielded. "Kiss me, Will. Please."

Her words snapped whatever held him back. With a growl from deep in his throat, his arms enveloped her, pulling her close, his hands molding her to him as his mouth covered hers in kiss after kiss.

Thirsty, he'd said. She felt it, too. Almost savagely so. Only, she wasn't sure who was devouring whom because she craved everything about him. His hands, his mouth, his body.

Against hers, his lips tasted sweet, triggering deep

aches. Aches that consumed her and grew hotter and hotter with each touch.

She hadn't meant for this to happen, that wasn't why she'd let him come up to the apartment. And yet, during that elevator ride hadn't she known exactly why Will was coming up with her? She shouldn't have put herself into that situation. But now that he was there, kissing her, she couldn't imagine not kissing him, not having her every breath filled with his. She'd never been able to resist this wonderful man who'd once filled her thoughts every waking moment. Who was she kidding? He still did.

She kissed him with the desperation of a woman who'd been deprived of oxygen and he was her air. She kissed him with the desperation of a woman who had loved and lost but was being given a short reprieve from her broken heart.

Which was why when he tugged her shirt from her skirt, she not only let him, she helped him and returned the favor, sliding her hands beneath the crisp material of his button-down.

Mine, she thought, as her palms skimmed over his abs and around to his muscled back. Mine. Mine. Mine. Only, he wasn't.

The thought that this might be the last time she ever touched him, kissed him, spurred her on, making her want to put every caress to memory, to imprint his taste upon her lips. She clasped his broad shoulders, holding on to him as tightly as she could as he shimmied her skirt up her thighs so he could cup her bottom.

"Will," she whispered, loving his name on her lips.

"Yes, my sweet Natalie," he replied, his fingers looping around the lace of her panties and sliding them down her legs to pool at her feet.

His eyes met hers, dark with desire, but with just

enough hesitancy that she knew he was making sure she was still with him before they went any further, that this was what she wanted.

Could he have any doubts? She couldn't imagine so as she lifted one foot, then the other, and stepped out of her underwear and nudged them away with her toes.

"Natalie," he moaned, but otherwise he didn't talk and for that she was grateful.

She didn't want words or reason. She wanted him. She felt as if she'd always wanted him. Maybe she had because he was the man of her dreams in so many ways.

Soon, she was pressed to the door, her skirt bunched at her waist, and her legs wrapped around his hips. His mouth feasted on her throat, her lips.

When he positioned himself against her, her breath caught and, gaze meeting his, she imagined everything she'd ever felt for him shone in her eyes. Part of her believed that's what she saw looking back at her in those beautiful green eyes of his, too. No doubt lust blurred her vision.

"Will," she gasped as, eyes still locked with hers, he thrust deep inside, claiming her and sending her body into spasms of pleasure. "I—I like that."

She'd almost said *I love you*. She'd stopped just in time, reminding herself that this wasn't about love, just physical chemistry.

If only she could believe that was completely true.

Will's breath ragged, he dropped his damp forehead against Natalie's and tried to make sense of what just happened. They were over so how had he ended up walking her home and taking what her sweet body so generously gave to his?

Of course he knew the answer.

There had always been something about Natalie that drew him to her in ways he'd never experienced, making him long to see her smile, hear her voice, give her pleasure.

He'd meant to kiss her, to slowly make love to her and pull orgasm after orgasm from her lush body. Instead, all power of reason had left him long before he'd pushed into her velvet. He'd been so in awe that he was touching her, kissing her, and that he got to feel her heat, there'd been no room for sanity. He'd looked into her eyes that were dazed with pleasure, lost himself in the big brown depths and just marveled that he once again held this special woman. His Natalie, who he'd missed so much.

And he'd rushed the whole thing.

"I shouldn't have done that," he murmured. He should have made love to her slowly, not taken her as if she meant nothing to him. They should have at least made it to the sofa rather than barely inside the door. She deserved better than that.

Natalie's eyes opened and filled with regret.

"Right," she murmured, wiggling free to stand on her own two feet. "You just wanted a glass of water and I… never mind. Sorry."

Will's stomach twisted at her instant tension. He didn't want to let her go but had no right to hold her to him, not when she wanted to be free, so he dropped his arms. Seeing the embarrassment in her cheeks, he cursed at his bumbling the moment yet again. "That's not what I meant, Natalie. You know that's not what I meant. What we just shared—"

"Was a mistake." Not looking at him, she smoothed her skirt down over her hips. "No worries. You just said what we both already knew. Neither of us should have done that. We have great physical chemistry, but we're wrong together."

Her words were burning arrows striking deep in his chest. When his gaze had been locked with hers, their bodies one, he'd have sworn nothing could be more right than Natalie being in his arms.

And not just because of physical chemistry.

"I wanted you but should have had more finesse than to take you against the living room door as if…" As if she weren't special, he finished in his head.

Natalie had always been different from any other woman he'd ever known. Not just because the sexual chemistry but because she made him feel more alive, more aware of every breath he took, more appreciative of his life's blessings. He'd not told her how much he appreciated her nearly as often as he should have. He'd not held her as tightly as he should have. He'd gotten so distracted by life and lost her.

"I wasn't complaining," she surprised him by saying with a bit of a whimsical smile that tugged at something deep within him and had him wanting to wrap his arms around her and hold on forever.

Which was a problem since she was no longer his. They'd had their shot and it hadn't worked. So why, even knowing that, did he suddenly wish they could start over? He wished he could scoop her up into his arms, carry her to wherever she was sleeping, and spend the night worshiping her body and convincing her that they were worth a second chance.

"I'd like to see you again, Natalie."

Her gaze cut to his. "You see me right now."

"True, but yet again you're purposely misunderstanding me."

She hesitated. "Then tell me, Will. When you say you want to see me again, what do you mean?"

She was looking at him, listening to him, giving credence to what he was saying, and it thrilled Will, made him think maybe they could figure out something for their future. Something where they could see each other and decipher exactly what it was they felt for the other. Somewhere where they could shut out the world and it could just be the two of them. Somewhere Natalie chose where she could be happy and feel comfortable. Somewhere they could laugh and smile together and see if the bonds they shared could be weaved into something unbreakable.

"Let me set you up in an apartment, Natalie," he urged, his mind racing ahead, wanting her to know he'd listen to her this time, that if she hadn't been happy in his home, they didn't have to stay there. "Just pick one, whatever makes you happy, and it's yours."

Which was apparently the completely wrong thing to say because her smile disappeared and she clammed up, moving away from him.

"No."

In frustration, Will ran his fingers through his hair. "What just happened between us—"

"What just happened between us shouldn't have happened," she interrupted as she looked around until she spotted her panties against a wall where she'd kicked them.

"I disagree," he said. "What just happened between us is what we do best."

"It's everything else we have issues with," she murmured, picking up her underwear.

He wanted to argue. They hadn't had issues with everything else. They'd been just fine until he'd messed up her birthday party and she'd walked away. At least, as far as he'd known, they'd been just fine. He'd thought their relationship solid. They could start over, take things slower this time, work through their issues—his mother, her insecurities, his not having appreciated her the way he should have and whatever else had driven them apart.

"We don't have to live together," he attempted to explain, doing up his pants. "You were right about that." Apparently, since living together had led to their no longer being together. "Let me help you."

Her gaze darkened to the point her chocolate eyes appeared black. "By setting me up in an apartment so you can stop by anytime you feel like a repeat of what just happened?"

Heat stung his cheeks. "It wouldn't be like that."

"That's exactly what it would be like and my answer is no. No. No. No!" Her tone grew angrier with each word and with the last she threw her underwear at his chest. "Go away, Will."

Frustrated, Will caught the scrap of lace and clenched it in his fist.

"I'm trying to help you, Natalie. I want to help you. Why are you making things more difficult on yourself than they have to be?" Why was he doing such a terrible job of conveying that he wanted to make things better for her, that there was no need for her to be crashing at Callie's when he would gladly help her get into a place of her own? A place where they could start over.

Her breath huffed out. "I'll move back to New Jersey with my parents and commute into the city every morning before saying yes to being your paid sex toy."

Will grimaced. Was that how she thought he viewed her? Yes, he'd gotten caught up in what they'd just done, but he cared about her, didn't want her struggling when making things easier for her would be so simple. "That's not what I'm asking you to do."

Rather than relax, her fists went to her hips and she glared at him as if she wished she could make him disappear forever. "You're saying you want to set me up in an apartment and that we wouldn't ever be having sex?"

"You still want me," he reminded, hurt that she was pushing him away yet again despite what they'd just done. She'd proven that her body craved his as much as his did hers, and she wouldn't have shared her body with him if she didn't still care.

"At no point have I said that I didn't want you," she immediately flung back, then marched over to snatch her underwear out of his hand.

Her answer had him pausing. She'd never stopped wanting him. He sure hadn't stopped wanting her. And yet they hadn't worked.

"But I sure don't like you very much at the moment," she told him as she stepped into her panties. "It's been a long day. I'm not very happy with myself at what just happened between us. I'd really prefer it if you leave now, Will."

CHAPTER FIVE

WHETHER OF HIS own accord, because of prior commitments, or because of Will's warnings two evenings previously, Gregory was a no-show for the fundraiser meeting Natalie arranged at the hospital on her next day off work. She'd figured meeting at the hospital for a quick lunch would be easiest on Will and Dr. Lewis and would be a safe, neutral location.

After the way she'd practically thrown herself at Will, inviting him up to Callie's apartment and embarrassing herself, Natalie was completely mortified, and needed safe and neutral. How could she have been so foolish as to have sex with Will?

As usual, Dr. Lewis treated her with the kindness that no doubt made him an excellent pediatric oncologist. The man had heart.

Whereas the other man sitting at the table acted as if he didn't want to be there but had felt obliged to attend. That made two of them. She'd wondered if he wouldn't show, but since the gala was important, he'd been right on time. Natalie would do everything she could to make it a success. Which was why she'd distracted herself most of the previous day by researching corporate charities, making lists and consulting with Katrina.

Mostly, she'd just been trying to avoid Callie and

Brent's apartment because every time she went through the apartment doorway, she had flashbacks. Plus, with her nerves so torn up, they must hate sharing a bathroom with her. Nothing wanted to stay in her stomach since prior to her birthday party. A broken heart could really work a number on a person. At least at the Children's Cancer Charity office, it was just her and Katrina there most of the time to share the bathroom.

"I made some calls after our meeting the other night. Several of my peers plan to purchase tickets to attend the gala, including their staff. Plus, they've committed to making donations." Lee gave a low laugh. "The board should be all smiles at this year's fundraiser and the amazing things we'll be able to accomplish with the funds raised." He nudged Will's shoulder. "Because I have faith that this guy's going to top everything I've done. Knowing him, he already has."

Natalie had been avoiding looking directly at Will, but at Lee's comment her gaze shifted to him. He'd not made eye contact with her, either, but kept glancing at his watch as if he had to be somewhere soon or was bored by the conversation. He was a busy heart surgeon and it was the middle of his workday. Of course he had other things he needed to be doing.

"I'll keep this short," she began, making sure he knew she didn't want to be there any more than he did. Seeing him only reminded her how weak she was where he was concerned. "I've done an online search of the companies we should qualify for. I've printed my list and their donation application process. Several aren't taking new charity applications currently, but for the ones that are, we need to apply. I also plan to send out a batch of email invites to the gala, again. Katrina is helping."

"Good idea," Lee praised, looking impressed. "Do we need to divvy up the application list?"

Natalie hesitated. She'd planned to ask them, but both men were busy doctors. She had the rest of the day off and could get most of the applications done if she worked on them. But when she realized that she was yet again valuing others' time more than her own, she nodded. She had to start placing value upon herself and her time.

"That would be great."

There, that wasn't so difficult.

"I met with Katrina this morning and we went through my list. I've printed a couple of the applications that, with her help, I've done as a guide to know the correct answers on the forms. Anything you need to know should be on one of the examples, but if you run into problems don't hesitate to reach out to myself or Katrina. I think it'll make going through the list much simpler as they all seem to need similar information."

They continued with the brief meeting until Lee's phone pinged. Glancing at his message, he frowned.

"Sorry, guys, but I've got to run." He grabbed the file folder Natalie had handed him. "I'll get this taken care of." He paused, then grinned. "To be fair, it'll likely be by one of my staff, but I'll make sure it's done within the next twenty-four hours."

When he was gone, Will opened his file to peruse the names on the list. When he'd skimmed over the top page, he lifted his gaze. "If that's everything, I've a busy schedule."

"That's everything." She went to pick up Greg's file folder, figuring she'd take care of his list after she did her own. Much simpler to do that than to reach out to the man and open herself up to having to interact with him.

"I'll take that." Will gestured to the folder she held.

"You want Gregory's list?"

He nodded. "I'll see that it gets addressed by myself, or my staff."

She gave him the file, feeling a bit guilty for doing so, then reminded herself that he'd probably hand it off to a staff member like Lee was planning to do.

Instead of immediately leaving, he flipped it open and scanned over the names on the list. "You gave Stella Fashion to Gregory?"

Natalie's face heated. Had she?

"Not intentionally," she defended, hating how she could feel the heat rising in her face. "I just randomly cut the list and placed them in the folders. She just happened to be in the folder that was left for Gregory."

"Right."

"You think I intentionally didn't give Stella to you?" She snorted, shaking her head at him. "Wrong. Had I given it any thought, I'd have purposely given her to you since you are such *close* friends. How could she say no if you ask her to donate?" She smiled sweetly. "Plus, now that Gregory's not here to do his part and you're taking his list, what does it matter? You have your excuse to contact Stella."

He glared at her. "I don't need an excuse."

Ouch. Natalie's heart tanked somewhere in the vicinity of her big toes. She swallowed. Was he purposely trying to make her jealous? If so, he was doing a good job, because the blood flowing through her arteries had turned as vividly green as his eyes. "You're seeing her, then?"

Oh, how she hated that she'd not been able to resist asking.

"She's Mother's goddaughter," he reminded her, "and had dinner with my family last evening."

Two nights ago he'd taken Natalie against the door.

Last night he'd had dinner with Stella. Had he…? No. She was not letting her mind go there. Not happening. What Will did was his business. Only…

She could feel him studying her, could feel how his gaze on her was speeding up her pulse.

Not quite meeting his eye, she tried to sound nonchalant as she said, "That's great."

Great for Stella. Or Rebecca. But for Natalie—yeah, not so much.

Not thrilled with himself for testing Natalie to see if she was jealous, Will watched as red splotched across Natalie's throat. He shouldn't have mentioned Stella. She meant nothing to him, and he hadn't been pleased to see her at his parents' the evening before. He'd thought he'd been called over for a quick dinner with them, and instead he'd walked into a setup. To say he'd not been happy with the arrangement was an understatement and he'd reminded his mother that relationship was dead and couldn't be revived.

Was that an accurate description of his relationship with Natalie? Perhaps their relationship couldn't be revived, but their feelings for each other weren't dead. Far from it. Not on his part and not on hers based upon the way her lower lip had just disappeared between her teeth and her pulse hammered at her throat.

"You don't have an issue with that, do you, Natalie?"

"Of course not."

What had he expected her to say? That she wanted him to remain faithful to her for all time?

If she'd wanted that, would he have been willing?

He started to ask, to admit he hadn't so much as thought of another woman that way since meeting her, but she spoke before he could.

"I've no right to have issues with whatever you do outside the hospital." She swallowed, then straightened her shoulders as if steadying herself for impact. "It's not as if I expected you to stay celibate when I moved out."

Memories hit of his being very much not celibate with Natalie just a few nights ago. They probably hit her, too, judging by her reddened cheeks.

"Just as you don't expect me to stay celibate," she continued.

Will couldn't prevent his sharp intake of breath or the heat that flooded his face as her words sank in.

"You've found an apartment, then?" he asked, trying to buy himself a moment to steady his nerves, and think of something to say that conveyed his sense of betrayal that she would allow someone else to touch her. Her comment had yet again caught him off guard to the reality that they were no longer a couple. "A place to start this new not-celibate life you want?"

He had no rights, yet the thought of her with someone else shredded his insides, causing his defenses to kick in and the voice inside his head to remind him that she'd left him, betrayed his trust and that some things were better left undone.

Her gaze didn't quite meet his as she shrugged. "Perhaps. I'm going to view another place this afternoon. A friend from nursing school called yesterday to say she was looking for a roommate and had heard I might be interested. We got along well together and have loosely kept in touch. It's a three-bedroom unit, so there's another roommate who I don't know, though. Hopefully, if everything is as I was told and, after seeing the apartment and if it seems a tolerable living situation, then I can get moved in soon."

Soon, so she could start her new life without him in it.

Panic hit. Natalie was moving on with her life and, despite whatever emotions lingered between them, she didn't want him in it.

Will's phone buzzed, causing him to glance at his watch. His lips tightened, then he picked up the file folders. His life was crazy enough without exposing his heart.

"I'll do as Lee promised and make sure these are addressed within twenty-four hours." His gaze met hers and, ignoring the tightening in his chest, he said, "Good luck on finding that tolerable living situation."

Natalie changed out an on-its-last-drops intravenous fluid bag for a fresh one, chatting to her nonresponsive patient as she did so. Jim Holland had been admitted for an acute cerebrovascular ischemic attack triggered by uncontrolled atrial fibrillation. While still in the emergency department he'd started having chest pain and when checked, his troponin levels had been elevated. He'd ended up in emergency cardiac surgery.

Will had put several stents in the man's heart, restoring blood flow to his ischemic myocardial tissue. But with the atrial fibrillation–induced stroke topped by the man's heart attack, the next twenty-four hours were crucial and, although his surgery had been a success, he'd suffered so much body trauma that no one was confident he'd pull through.

Both of Natalie's previous patients had been transferred out of the CVICU so it made logical sense that she'd been given Mr. Holland. Knowing she'd have to interact with Will before the end of the day made her heart heavy. Their interactions over the past two weeks since their lunch meeting had been professional, but terse. Hopefully, the intensive care unit's census would change soon so she would be needed there more than in the CVICU and she could go back to not having to see Will at the hospital.

Was there a procedure that healed a broken heart?

If so, sign her up. She'd had about all the moping, tears and nausea she could stand over the past few weeks. Every time she saw him was like a fresh wound into her already bleeding heart.

Glancing at her watch, she double-checked to make sure her patient was clean, then tucked his sheet in around him.

"Has he awakened?"

At Will's question, Natalie jumped. She'd been so lost in her thoughts, of him, that she hadn't heard him enter the room.

"I didn't mean to startle you."

"No problem," she assured. "No, he's not been awake since being transferred to my care."

"It's probably best for his recovery if he rests."

Natalie nodded. "It's almost time to let his family back for a few minutes. Do you want me to wait until after you've finished examining him?"

Will shook his head. "I met his wife earlier. Nice lady. Said they'd been married forty years and were high school sweethearts before that. She'll be anxious to see him."

Forty years. Natalie could only imagine the woman's anxiety at the day's events.

"If you don't need me, then I'll get her so she can spend a few minutes with him during visitation."

His mouth opened and for a moment she thought he was going to say something, but instead he turned his back to her, took out his stethoscope and placed the diaphragm against the man's chest without saying a word.

Natalie was still considering what Will had almost said when she returned to the CVICU room with their patient's wife. He was standing at the computer, logging in chart notes.

Rushing into the room, the woman took one look at her husband lying in the hospital bed with multiple tubes coming out of him and wires connected on various body parts and she crumpled. Natalie caught her, wrapping her arms around the woman, and trying to offer comfort where she could. In many ways, comforting family was the hardest part of her job.

"Mrs. Holland?" Will immediately came to her side. "We met earlier. I'm Dr. Forrest."

"I've met so many doctors today it's mostly a blur—" the woman blinked back tears "—but I do remember talking with you. You're the heart surgeon who operated on Jim."

Will nodded. "I know it's difficult seeing your husband this way, but he's fairly stable."

The woman's gaze bounced between Will and her husband.

"He's been through a lot today. It may be a few days before he wakes. I need you to be strong and encouraging because he may be aware of you being here despite his lack of consciousness."

The woman nodded as if she understood, but trembled against Natalie, who still held her, supporting a fair share of the woman's weight for fear she was going to topple.

"We'd been fighting earlier. I need to let him know how sorry I am for the things I said." The woman grimaced, then turned pleading eyes toward Will. "You think he knows I'm here?"

"Based upon how his blood pressure and heart rate sped up the moment you first spoke, I'd guarantee that on some level he's aware, and glad, you're here."

Natalie glanced at the monitor. Sure enough, the

man's heart rate had elevated from the baseline she'd previous recorded.

"As tempting as it may be, now isn't the time for re-hashing your argument," Will advised gently. "Let him know you're here for him. Reassuring him that he's going to push through this is what's important and what he needs to hear."

Amidst her tears, Mrs. Holland nodded. "I… I can do that. I will do that."

And she did. Stepping away from where she leaned against Natalie, she took her husband's hand and stood by his bed. Between sucking back a few sobs, she began telling him how their children and grandchildren were in the waiting area and were so concerned. She told him how loved he was by his family and by her. She continued talking and his heart rate and blood pressure leveled off to a steady state.

"Come on," Will murmured, motioning to Natalie. "Let's give her a moment."

Realizing she'd been staring as if frozen in place, Natalie glanced toward Will, nodded, then touched the woman's arm. "I'll be right outside his room. If you need anything hit the call button or poke your head out."

Without looking away from her husband or pausing in the things she was saying to him, Mrs. Holland nodded.

They left the room, but Natalie hesitated outside the door as the woman yet again broke down in tears. When she started to go back into the room to offer any comfort she could, Will placed his hand on her arm.

"Don't. She needs a moment and we'll give it to her."

"Upsetting him isn't good," she replied.

"No, but I'm leaning toward his needing to hear what she's going to say. She's known him over forty years. My guess is she knows what words to say to make him want to fight to get well much better than we do."

What Natalie was hearing from his distressed wife was mostly "I love you," "I'm sorry," and "Please don't do this" over and over.

"Give her five to ten minutes and then ask her if she wants to swap out and let one of their children come back," Will ordered.

"Okay." But her attention was back on the room. "Will, she's sobbing uncontrollably. You're sure about this?"

"Give her a few minutes," he repeated, his voice firm. Part of Natalie knew he was right and loved the way he was so sensitive to the emotional needs of their patient's wife. Another part worried the woman's tears might upset her patient and left Natalie feeling protective as her number one job was his physical health and well-being. But she also believed in the power of a hug and if ever a person needed a hug, Mrs. Holland did.

She glanced toward Will and her breath caught at the light in his eyes. His gaze was filled with kindness as he watched the woman holding her husband's hand and murmuring words of love. Kindness and something more that almost looked like envy, but that couldn't be right.

With mixed feelings Natalie stepped away from the doorway, planning to sanitize then go check on her other patient for a few minutes as she was struggling with her desire to console Mrs. Holland. But mostly, she just wanted to escape being with Will because seeing that raw look in his eyes made her want to hug him, too.

His tenderheartedness and desire to do good by people was one of the many things that had made her fall for him to begin with. One of the many things she missed as she'd not seen that particular emotion in his eyes directed at her for some time.

Mostly, these days, she felt the same withdrawal in attitude toward her that he'd shown at their lunch meeting and every time their paths had crossed since. The only positive being it might help her get over him sooner.

Was getting over Will even possible?

"Nurse!" Mrs. Holland shrieked.

"Yes?" Natalie asked, rushing into the room.

"He squeezed my hand!" the excited woman gushed, practically jumping up and down as she clung to her husband's hand still. "Oh, my goodness, he squeezed my hand."

Relief washed over Natalie. Heart thundering as she'd feared her patient's condition was changing detrimentally, she squirted disinfectant on her hands. Then, along with Will, who'd also heard her cries and come rushing into the room, rechecked their patient.

"Whatever you said to him seems to have helped," Natalie admitted, pleased that the man flinched when she tested his pain response. He hadn't opened his eyes or said a word, but he was responding to certain stimuli and that was more than could be said prior to Mrs. Holland's arrival.

The woman gave a wobbly smile and lifted her husband's hand to her lips to press a kiss there. "I just told him how much he means to me, to our family. It's what a woman should tell a man every single day of her life because one never knows when that opportunity will be snatched away."

Why did the woman's words strike so deeply into Natalie's heart? She *had* told Will she loved him. Just once, but she'd told him, and what had he done? Pretended to be asleep. He sure hadn't ever said the words back. Then again, she wouldn't have wanted him to say words he didn't mean.

"Wise words," Will said from where he stood next to the hospital bed, smiling at the couple.

"True," Natalie agreed, fighting to keep her tone from revealing the turbulent emotions bubbling within her. "And it's just as true that a man should tell a woman how he feels about her every single day." Then her gaze shooting to Will, she arched a brow and added, "Or maybe a man telling her one single day would suffice if he said the right things."

"Natalie, girl, I don't know what you did, but you're amazing."

Dumping her bag and light jacket onto the small table where she worked in Katrina's office, Natalie glanced toward her committee cochair. Katrina's smile was so big it looked as if it was about to split her face.

"We've sold out of tickets!"

Stunned and thinking that was the best news she'd heard all day, Natalie exclaimed, "Really? Wow. That's wonderful."

"It really is except we're having to turn people away. I'm keeping a cancellation list, but just wow." Katrina clapped her hands together in glee.

"I guess the board will consider this year's gala a success, after all," Natalie mused. At least, she'd accomplished something positive over the past few weeks.

Katrina grinned. "Are you kidding me? They may offer you a seat on the board after this."

"Because we sold out of tickets?" Natalie asked, confused, sitting down in the chair in front of her makeshift desk. "I seriously doubt that."

Katrina looked as if she were about to burst with excitement. "Okay, so probably not on the board seat offer, but a lifelong position on the committee. Selling out of tickets is wonderful, but it's the corporate donations pouring in that will tip the scale."

"You've heard back from some of the applications, then?" Natalie had assumed it would be a lengthy process and might take months, long after the gala, before they'd hear anything back. "That really is wonderful. I wondered if any would respond before the gala."

"Heard back and received the check from a couple of big ones."

That news was almost enough to dissipate her perpetually sour stomach.

"Oh, wow. That is wonderful."

"What's wonderful is the amounts Harroway Industries, the Harroway Foundation, and Stella Fashions contributed alone." Katrina named sums that would take Natalie years to earn. "Girl," she continued, looking impressed, "it's good to be friends with that family."

That Katrina lumped Stella in as part of the Forrest family knotted Natalie's stomach. She wanted to correct her cochair but didn't. She just smiled and told herself that it didn't matter. Will had implied that he and Stella were dating. Who knew? Maybe Rebecca would get her way and Stella would be family soon enough.

A knife jabbed her heart at the thought, but she kept a fake smile on her face.

It did surprise her that Harroway Industries had made a sizable donation since Rebecca would be aware that Natalie was cochairing the committee. It also surprised her that Katrina had insinuated that she was friends with the Forrests. Because of the awkwardness of their last meeting, she'd told her cochair about her relationship status change.

Natalie turned to pull her laptop from her bag, but at her movement an intense wave of sickness hit.

"Excuse me," she said, rushing to the bathroom to lose the crackers she'd eaten that morning. Eventually her nerves had to level out. If not, she was going to shrivel away because nothing tasted good and what she did manage to force down didn't want to stay down. It was going on two months since her birthday. Maybe she needed to arrange for counseling.

"You okay?" Katrina asked when Natalie returned to the woman's office and sat back down.

Natalie gave the woman an apologetic look. "Not really, but I'll eventually get there."

Katrina continued to stare with concern. "Your face went ghost white and you high-tailed it out of here."

"Just nerves getting the best of me," she admitted, hating the fact that her friend had noticed she wasn't feeling well. "Again. Between the breakup, working extra shifts, working on the gala and planning to move into my new apartment the day after the gala, I've a lot going on."

"That is a lot." Giving her an empathetic look, Katrina nodded, then laughed lightly. "Just so long as you're not pregnant, eh?"

Pregnant? Natalie's head spun to where she wondered if she might fall out of her chair.

She couldn't be pregnant.

She was on a twelve-week cycle low-dose oral birth control pill and hadn't missed any. Not even after she'd moved out of Will's apartment and no longer thought she'd have a need for birth control. She wasn't due her menstrual cycle for another week. She'd not even considered the possibility as a cause of her persistent upset stomach because she'd protected herself from pregnancy.

But medications weren't foolproof.

For the rest of the afternoon, her mind kept straying to Katrina's comment. What if that was why she'd been so emotional? So nauseated and ill at her stomach? What if pending motherhood had played a role in why she'd no longer been willing to let herself be on unequal footing with Will and had wanted to be included in his family life? Of why, instinctively, she'd known she had to try to make things right between them because their baby was growing inside her.

Feeling ridiculous and very self-conscious, she stopped by a discount drugstore on her walk home and purchased a pregnancy test.

It would be negative. She wasn't pregnant.

Only, when she got back to Callie's and ran the test, two blue lines appeared.

Two blue lines!

She sank to the floor, leaning against the bathroom cabinet, and stared in disbelief at the test.

She was pregnant.

CHAPTER SIX

"You have to tell Will," Callie insisted over dinner that night. Brent was pulling an extra shift at the hospital as one of the respiratory therapists had called out ill and Natalie was grateful for the alone time with her best friend. If ever she'd needed advice, it was now.

"Of course I'll tell Will. It wouldn't be right not to." Picking at her Alfredo noodles, Natalie winced. "I mean, if it's real, that is."

"Real?" Fork halfway to her mouth, Callie paused. "Why wouldn't it be real? You showed me the test. There's two lines, Natalie. Two. As in, you're pregnant."

"It could be wrong," she said. "I might not be pregnant. It was just a simple drugstore test."

"Which are pretty doggone accurate," Callie argued, then ate a bite of her pasta. "That second line doesn't just magically appear. Human growth hormone has to be present to trigger a positive result."

Natalie set her fork down on her plate. "Yes, but it could be a false positive." Rare, she knew. "I can't go to Will and announce I'm pregnant if I'm not really." Just the thought of doing so and then discovering she wasn't made her stomach heave. "Can you imagine how horrific that would be? He'd think I was trying to trap him into a relationship."

"I get that," Callie relented, wincing at the thought. "I'd like to think he knows you better than that, though, but just to be sure, let's go get another test."

Natalie was already sorry that she hadn't bought every test in the store just to make sure there was no doubt on the results, so she nodded.

"We could pick one up," or two or three or however many they had for sale, "and I'll do it first thing in the morning. That's supposed to be the most accurate time."

Callie clasped her hands together. "Perfect. We'll go as soon as we finish eating."

Natalie nodded. "If it's positive, then I'll call for an appointment with my ob-gyn and take the first available appointment. If she says I'm pregnant, then, and only then, after I definitely know, I'll tell Will."

If.

What if she was?

What if she wasn't?

Because as scary as she found the prospect of pregnancy, as untimely as it would be to have a baby, the idea that Will's child grew inside her brought along an excitement. An excitement so strong that she knew she'd be disappointed if the additional tests were negative or her gynecologist said the home tests had been wrong.

Before she'd first noticed Will withdrawing from her, she'd have been ecstatic to learn she was pregnant. Now, when their relationship was over, a baby would make things that much more complicated.

"Hello." Callie snapped her fingers in front of Natalie's face. "If you are pregnant, your baby would be the heir to the Harroway fortune. That's a big deal."

What would Will say if she was going to have his baby? Would he think she'd gotten pregnant on purpose? Would he believe all the things his mother had insinuated about her? That she was nothing more than a gold digger looking to latch on to the Harroway fortune?

"I don't want money from Will's family. I have a great job and make a decent living. I've saved my money while living with Will. I can take care of this baby."

Callie frowned. "Will would insist on taking care of you and his child. You know he would. He's too decent not to insist."

Natalie's hand dropped to her lower abdomen. "First, there's probably not a baby. Second, if there is, Will has never said anything about wanting children. Third, if he does want to be a part of this baby's life—" and she agreed with Callie that he would because he was a good man "—I'll encourage him for our child's sake, but I won't take money from him."

No way would she allow Rebecca to use that against her. No doubt Will's mother would accuse her of intentionally getting pregnant to try to hang on to her son. On more than one occasion she'd implied Natalie was nothing more than a gold digger. Ha. Rebecca might not have worried quite so much if only she'd realized Natalie had spent most of her time wishing Will had been ordinary and not mega-wealthy.

"Most likely, I'm not pregnant and all of this is for nothing," she spoke the words out loud for her own benefit as much as to say them to her best friend.

Callie's eyes held sympathy. "You don't really believe that, do you?"

The test had been positive. False negatives were much more common, but the test could have been wrong. The likelihood was slim, though.

Natalie closed her eyes. "I don't know what to believe anymore. My brain and emotions have been every which way for weeks. At least, being pregnant would explain that and my almost constant nausea."

Her friend leaned across the table to rub her shoulder. "Well, know that Brent and I are here for you. You are welcome to stay indefinitely if the new apartment doesn't work out."

Natalie gave a small derisive smile. "You think my new roommates are going to kick me to the curb if I'm a package deal?"

"Who knows?" She shrugged. "Regardless, we're here for you." Callie pointed at her barely touched food. "Now, eat something because you may be eating for two and if you hurry we can walk to the drugstore around the corner to buy another pregnancy test so I can know for sure whether or not I'm going to be an honorary aunt."

Natalie wasn't hungry, but the possibility that there was a tiny life within her needing nourishment prompted her to pick up her fork and take a bite.

If she was pregnant, she'd do everything within her power to make sure she and Will had a healthy baby.

The following morning, the CVICU was slammed and Natalie had been at a run all morning. For the first time, she didn't mind her nausea so much, though. Not if Will's baby was why she felt so bleh.

Her second test had been positive. And so had the third.

What were the odds of three tests taken on two different days being false positives? Low. Very low.

She'd been giddy when the second line had appeared almost immediately on the second test. Giddy and so light-headed she'd thought she might faint. She was going to have Will's baby. Her best guess was that she was somewhere around eleven weeks pregnant as her menstrual cycle had been normal between her twelve-week pill packs. How would Will react to their news? They weren't together anymore. She couldn't imagine that he'd be nearly as excited as Natalie was.

Funny, she'd not known she wanted a baby, to start a family of her own, but she now craved it. If this was how her mother had felt, no wonder Natalie had such a big family.

"Have you called your gynecologist yet? She is an obstetrician, too, right?" Callie whispered when they met up at the medication cart.

"Yes, and not yet," she admitted. She'd hoped to sneak away long enough for a five-minute bathroom break and make the call in private to avoid being overheard. With the flurry of activity on the unit, she hadn't been able to slip away.

"Go, call now," Callie insisted, smiling. "I'll watch your patients."

Natalie laughed. "What's your rush?"

Callie's grin widened. "I want to be able to tell the world I'm going to be an auntie."

"Shh!" Natalie shushed her, glancing around to make sure no one was within hearing range. No one was. Thank goodness. "Don't say things like that."

She was excited, but not ready to share her news with anyone other than her best friend.

"Sorry." Callie gave a sheepish look. "I shouldn't have said that here, I know, but I don't know how you can stand it. It's not even me and I want to scream it to the world."

Natalie did want to scream it to the world. She was pregnant. It was surreal. But part of her wanted to keep it quiet for a bit longer, too. She needed a little more time to get used to the idea herself before dealing with others' reactions. Admitting that she was pregnant with William

Harroway Forrest's baby came with a lot of fallout. Plus, the risk of miscarriage during the first trimester was high, especially with as stressed as she'd been,

"If I really am—" and, Lord, she was going to be devastated if she wasn't after a night of dreaming of having a baby and three positive home tests "—then we'll have plenty of time to celebrate." Natalie's gaze went to her best friend's, then she smiled softly again. "It's not something I'd given much thought to before yesterday. Just one of those things I expected to do someday. But now, I'll be disappointed if I'm not."

Callie gave a nod, then grabbing her meds, sighed. "Let me go administer these, and then hopefully, things will be settled down here to where you can sneak away long enough to make that phone call."

"Hopefully."

But Natalie was still at a run when Will arrived to do his rounds. He wore hospital issue scrubs so had probably been in the operating room that morning or would be heading there soon.

Seeing him took her breath away and made her want to leap into his arms and tell him their news. They were going to be parents.

Would her baby have his distinct Harroway green eyes or her brown ones? His dark hair or her red? Would Will insist upon using his family names if their baby was a boy? If he wanted another William, would they call him Billy or Liam or... Good grief. She needed to stop immediately. She shouldn't be picking out names.

"You okay?" he asked, making her realize she'd just been standing there gawking at him, analyzing his features and wondering which ones their baby would inherit. All of them, she hoped. She wanted their child to look just like him.

"Fine. Never better," she responded. She took a deep breath and told herself to calm down, which wasn't easy to do when seeing him made her want to burst with joy and tell him she thought they were going to be parents.

Just because she was overcome with joy didn't mean he would be. They weren't together. Even when they had been, he'd never told her that he loved her or wanted to spend his life with her. Once upon a time, she'd believed he did, but she'd been wrong.

He studied her, then said, "There's a sparkle in your eyes today."

She wasn't surprised she was glowing. She felt as if her very soul shined brighter than the sun.

"Life is good. I've found an apartment," she said, thinking he might be expecting an explanation for her smiley disposition. She'd tell him everything soon, but not at the hospital, and not until she'd seen her doctor for confirmation. "You know I love Cal and Brent. But it will be nice to have my own space again."

Her own space where she'd need to figure out where she'd set up a crib and put all the baby things she'd need in her bedroom so she wouldn't encroach on the shared living space with her new roommates. Her gaze met his and she couldn't hold back her happiness. *Oh, Will, we're going to have a baby.* No matter what had happened between them, what might happen in the future, he'd given her a precious gift, and she'd forever be grateful.

"Life is wonderful, actually. How about you?"

His brows formed a V, revealing his confusion. No wonder. She'd been trying to protect herself by avoiding him. She'd likely been walking around zombified from her aching heart.

For a moment she thought he wasn't going to answer, but then, he said, "Same. Fine. Never better."

His apartment was so close to Central Park. Would he take their child for long walks or to visit the zoo or— Looking at him, she knew he'd be a good dad. She'd seen how he interacted with the kids involved with the Children's Cancer Charity Gala, his patience and tender heart. Which reminded her...

"Thank you for the donation for the Children's Cancer Charity. Katrina told me what you did."

He shrugged as if it was no big deal that his efforts had raised the event's coffers by tens of thousands of dollars. "No problem. It's a great organization and I like kids."

There went her heart doing cartwheels.

"That's good. I've never heard you mention that before."

Staring at her oddly, and no wonder, his gaze narrowed. "You're chatty this morning. What's gotten into you?"

Your baby. Maybe. Probably. Three positive tests likely.

"I—nothing. Just making conversation."

Rather than comment, he sighed, then, looking uncharacteristically tired, he glanced down the hallway. "I'm booked in the OR again within the hour and need to check on my patients. Which room is Kevin Conaway in?"

Which told her he was done with their personal conversation and that the only interaction he wanted to have with her was on a professional level.

"Four. About the time I got Mrs. Johnson discharged— she was looking great, by the way—the operating room called to request a room. It's been nonstop all morning, as I guess you are aware."

Still giving her a confused look, he asked, "Any changes since Mr. Conaway arrived on the unit?"

"None." She'd gotten the sixty-one-year-old settled and he'd been resting comfortably when she'd left his room fifteen minutes before. His telemetry had remained stable. "His output has been minimal, but otherwise is as expected."

"His history is that he has pneumonia and went into renal failure with his respiratory distress," Will supplied, although Natalie was already aware of that from taking the report at the man's transfer to the unit. "When everything started shutting down, his heart couldn't take it and stopped. His son was able to do CPR until the paramedics arrived to take over. They got him here just in time."

"I'd heard his son saved his life but wasn't sure what the details were," she said, pleased that Will was at least making a little extra conversation with her even if it was work related.

"Lives alone with his adult son. Has been fighting a virus for a couple of weeks. Got a lot worse during the night and ended up here," Will said as they walked toward the room, pausing to disinfect and glove up. "I'm still not convinced he'll make it through the day and if he does that he won't have brain damage from how long he was hypoxic, but I did everything I could to save him. Only time will tell if it worked and to what extent."

All of their patients in CVICU were critical. Unfortunately, some of them not making it was something Natalie dealt with too often as it was the nature of working with such ill patients.

"You're a good doctor and man, Will." The praise slipped from her lips unbidden.

He paused outside Kevin's room. "Where did that come from?"

Natalie's cheeks heated. Ugh. What was wrong with her? She shook her head as if to clear it and replied,

"Sorry. Guess you're right—I am chatty this morning because that just popped into my head and out my mouth."

Donning his gloves and a mask, he glanced her way, curiosity shining in his eyes. "For whatever it's worth, I've always thought you an excellent nurse as well, Natalie. Seems professionally, we respect and admire each other. Too bad personally that doesn't hold true and we failed."

Stunned at both his compliment and his assessment of their relationship, she watched him go into the CVICU room to examine his patient. They had failed.

Both of them.

Because as much as she blamed him for the things that had led up to her moving out, she also shouldered that blame. Had pregnancy hormones clouded her mind and made her so moody she'd reacted in ways she typically wouldn't have?

She had been overemotional.

She shouldn't have moved out. She should have stayed and fought for what she wanted—for Will—rather than letting his mother's digs get to her. She'd thought she was taking a stand, protecting her pride, but instead she'd made matters worse.

She'd been sleeping in the love of her life's bed, and she'd left because his mother's disapproval had made her question everything. Mostly, her own self-worth in deserving a place in Will's life. He'd never said he loved her, but he had cared about her and invited her to share his home. She should have talked to him, told him how she felt, shared her fears and insecurities. Regardless of how he'd reacted, she should have told him she loved him more than just the one time.

Because she did love him. Always had. Always would.

Staring into the room, Natalie's heart swelled, and

she couldn't resist placing her hand over her belly. She'd made so many mistakes. They both had, but Lord willing, somehow, she'd make her wrongs right, become the confident woman he'd once fallen for before she'd let his world chip away at her self-worth.

She wanted Will. She always had. But she'd believed the act of leaving would somehow let him know what she wanted, what she needed. How foolish.

She'd use everything within her power to win him back.

Everything except the baby inside her.

Because if Will only returned to her after learning of the baby, then she'd always doubt his love for her and would spend the rest of her life feeling unworthy, and as much as she wanted Will, she wasn't willing to be second best.

Which meant she had to figure out how to win him back and soon before her pregnancy started showing.

Currently, though, she needed to check her patient with him.

Why was Natalie standing in the doorway watching him as if Will was doing something out of the ordinary? And what was up with her compliment? Where had that come from?

Had it been such a rough day with his mother going into surgery this morning that his brain was playing tricks on him?

Regardless, Natalie snapped out of whatever spell she was under, came into the room, checked the man's catheter bag and grimaced. "He's still not having any significant urine output."

"Get a basic metabolic profile on him. Let's make sure his glomerular filtration rate hasn't dropped further.

Consult Nephrology, as well. We'll get them on board in case he needs dialysis. I was hoping things would turn around once he was out of surgery, but apparently not."

Natalie nodded, watching as Will did a bedside ultrasound of the man's kidneys. It wasn't his specialty, but he knew the basics and wanted to make sure blood flow or obstruction to the organs wasn't an issue.

Will winced at what he saw on the screen.

"What's that?" Natalie asked, staring at the image on the monitor.

"Good question." Because Will wasn't positive what the mass on the man's left kidney was. "Possibly just an incidental finding, but he needs a CT of his abdomen and pelvis." He moved the transducer around, trying to get measurements on the mass. "I suspect his creatinine is still too high to risk contrast, so we'll make do without."

Natalie nodded, still staring at the screen. "Is it on the adrenal gland?"

"Appears to be just behind it but may be invasive of both the adrenal and his kidney," he answered. "Guess we'll know for sure after the CT."

"Poor guy can't get a break," Natalie mused as she ungloved, then punched orders into the computer while Will continued examining their patient.

Apart from how talkative she'd been, something was different about the way Natalie was looking at him. He'd swear he saw some of the old adoration on her face. Only, he didn't understand what had put it back there. Nor had he ever understood what had caused it to vanish to begin with.

That wasn't completely true, he admitted, wiping the conducting gel off the transducer. Her unfounded issues with his mother and his regrettable dance with Stella seemed to have triggered the avalanche that had buried their relationship. He didn't buy that his and his mother's generous donations to the Children's Cancer Charity had been enough to put the light back.

When she finished typing in the order, she turned to find him watching, and smiled. Smiled.

Confused, pulse pounding, he kept his gaze locked with hers. "Call me after Nephrology has checked him or any of his results are back."

"Will?" she asked just as he reached the doorway, causing him to turn around. "Would you want to go to dinner tonight after my shift ends?"

Something had definitely changed. He could see it in her eyes. Those big browns were filled with hope he'd say yes.

Will's throat tightened. "I can't."

"Oh." Her face flamed red and that light in her eyes dimmed. "I… Okay."

"I can't," he began, knowing he would be at his mother's bedside once she was out of surgery and no matter how curious he was about the reason behind Natalie's dinner invitation, he couldn't go.

"No problem. I understand." But her expression said she regretted asking and was more than a little mortified that she had.

That dejected look got to him. It shouldn't have since she'd sure rejected him often enough over the past few weeks. But he couldn't stand how she'd bitten into her lower lip and appeared ready to disappear. He had always been astounded that someone so amazing could ever doubt herself and it left him wanting to protect her from the world.

God help him at how this woman got to him.

"I already have plans, Natalie," he admitted, wondering why he was still making excuses. She'd left him.

He didn't owe her any explanations. Whatever had her reaching out to him didn't matter. At least, it shouldn't matter. Though, judging by how his heart raced, it did.

She nodded as if she understood, but he could tell she didn't and was slipping back into the defensive shell she'd been hiding behind for weeks.

Let her go, he told himself. Even if she wanted to go to dinner for all the right reasons, how could he ever trust in their relationship without wondering if she'd change her mind and leave again?

He couldn't.

Realizing he'd been holding his breath, Will exhaled and watched Natalie go to the nurses' station, say something to Callie, then disappear.

His heart squeezed. Although she'd refused to admit she was worried, he'd seen the fear in his mother's eyes that morning when he'd checked on her one last time before being wheeled back to surgery.

Although the contract had been signed the day before and was in the lawyers' hands, the stubborn woman still refused to risk anyone at Harroway Industries finding out she was having health issues, so she was claiming to be on a business trip. She had been admitted under an alias and was paying cash for all her medical care to keep it from showing on her company insurance. She had also ordered his father to stay away, as a senator being at the hospital would draw too much attention.

God, he prayed everything went according to plan, and that the doctor didn't find anything unexpected, and that his mother was soon back at the helm of her beloved company.

It was best that things had ended with Natalie.

If his mother's pathology report from her procedure today came back showing her cancer had spread into the lymph nodes, she would be needing him more than ever.

CHAPTER SEVEN

HOW STUPID WAS SHE? Natalie wondered. Had she really expected Will to jump for joy and say yes?

If only it were that simple.

But if she gave up at the first stumbling block, that didn't say much, either, did it? Wasn't that what she'd done in many ways when she'd left her birthday party?

No more. This was her future, her unborn child's future, at stake. Was she really just going to bow out again so easily?

Was she going to tuck her tail between her legs and let him spend the evening with another woman? If so, then she deserved to have lost him.

Sucking in a deep breath, she caught Will just as he was coming out of Kevin's room. Mustering up every bit of resolve within her, she pasted on what she hoped was a dazzling smile. "Is there anything I can say to convince you to change your plans tonight? To spend your evening w-with me instead?"

He grimaced and she knew there wasn't.

Oh, God. She'd asked Will to dinner and he'd grimaced. Had he just been being nice earlier when he'd said he already had plans?

Fine. What was a little wounded pride in the grand scheme of life? If she wanted Will—and hadn't she always?—then she was going to have to step outside her comfort zone.

Lifting her chin, she asked, "If not tonight, what about tomorrow night? I'll be here until end of shift, again, but could we go somewhere afterward?"

His gaze softened and her heart swelled. Maybe, just maybe, he was going to say yes.

"Things are complicated right now. I'm not sure what tomorrow is going to be like. It would be better if I say no, Natalie," he said instead, his tone gentle, as if he believed what he said, but didn't want to hurt her.

"Better for who?" Because she needed to know if it was already too late.

"Both of us." He sighed, stuck his stethoscope into his scrub pocket. "Everything I've said to you is true. I wasn't ready for us to end, but perhaps, in some ways, it's made things less complicated."

Less complicated? Ha. She was pregnant. How was that for complicated?

"I thought we had something special," he continued, his expression wistful. "I thought you felt the same, that, for the most part, you were happy." His eyes darkened to a deep green. "I know I was busy those last few weeks, but there were things going on." Glancing down the hallway as if he couldn't look at her a moment longer, he said, "The reality is, I need to focus on my family and work."

Telling him that his family was likely about to expand was on the tip of her tongue, but she couldn't do it.

If she and Will had any hope for the future, they needed to work things out before he knew about her pregnancy. Otherwise, no matter what happened or what he said, she'd never fully feel wanted. Since her self-doubts had played so much into her leaving, she couldn't risk telling him yet. If they were to work things out between them, it had to be because they both wanted their relationship to work, because they were both willing to put in the effort to make things good between them.

"Okay." Not that it was, but she smiled at him, hoping her uncertainty didn't shine in her eyes. "I'd hoped to talk to you about how the past few weeks have put things into perspective for me, too. Maybe if you have—" Her CVICU nurse manager stepped out of her office, catching Natalie's eye and frowning when she saw Natalie so close to Will. No doubt anyone looking their way could see that their conversation had nothing to do with patient care. Heat flushed Natalie's skin. She couldn't afford to lose her job. She needed it now more than ever. "Thanks for the update on Mr. Conaway," she said briskly. "I'll let you know the moment his CT scan results are available for your review. Have a good day, Dr. Forrest."

"Natalie?"

She paused but didn't turn to look back at him. If she did he might see the tears stinging her eyes. Tears she had no one to blame for except herself. Why had she wanted everything? Wanted him to love her and his family to accept her? Why couldn't she have been content with what she'd had? She'd had so much more than so many women ever experienced. Obviously, she had mush for brains. Only...

"You're an amazing woman. I'm sorry things didn't work between us." His soft words rammed a dagger through her chest, hitting its unintended target.

"Me, too," she replied because she truly was sorry, then took off toward her other patient's room as fast as she could go without appearing to be running away.

Once there, she drew the curtain, for once thankful her patient was unconscious. Then forcing herself to keep her tears silent, she gave in to them.

* * *

Natalie's words haunted Will, playing heavily on his mind, while he sat in his mother's hospital room. Natalie had looked so...different. She'd practically glowed when she'd asked him to dinner.

And had quickly dulled when he'd declined.

He hated that he'd caused that transformation, but what had she expected? That he would drop everything because she'd decided she wanted to go to dinner with him?

If not for his mother, he would have.

"William Harroway Forrest, have you heard a word I've said?"

Will blinked at his mother. Busted. She might have had surgery that morning, and still look frail with her monitors and lines, but she wasn't beyond calling him out.

"Sorry, Mother." He reached over and placed his hand over hers, not surprised when she ran her finger over the signet ring that had once been her father's and that she'd given to Will on his twenty-first birthday. "Can I get you anything?"

Resting against her pillow, she eyed him, then harrumphed. "The only thing I want you've already said I was banned from for the rest of the day."

He gave a wry smile. "You're right. No laptop. I promised your surgeon I wouldn't let you work for at least twenty-four hours."

He suspected that for all her huffing and puffing, she didn't really feel like working, anyway. Her normally vibrant skin was pallid, her eyes tired and a bit hazy from medications, and she'd been in and out of consciousness, mostly sleeping, since returning from the surgical recovery area to her private room. She grimaced with the slightest movement but hadn't uttered a word of complaint about her pain or loss of her breast—only showing frustration that everyone refused to let her work.

"Seems odd he's the one issuing all the orders when I'm the one footing the bill," she mumbled, then drowsily smiled as she curled her fingers around the tips of his. "Now, tell me that our Stella is what has you so distracted."

Stella? He frowned. He'd already told her that he didn't feel that way about Stella and their parting ways had been the right thing. Was she so medicated she'd forgotten?

"It was so good of her to drive me here this morning," she mused. Something Will had offered to do, but she'd insisted Stella would take care of. "I'm just so tickled she's back in your life."

Not wanting to upset her so quickly post-op when she already looked weak, Will considered letting her comment ride. Then again, maybe while she was trapped in a bed and had to listen would be the best time for him to reiterate what he'd been telling her for months.

"Stella isn't a distraction for me, Mother. I'm not sure she ever was. There's never going to be a romantic relationship between us again. It was a mistake the first time and a second time would just be tragic."

"Don't be so hasty, Will." His mother tsked. "Stella is a lovely girl who's bright, has a promising business and is from a good family. And she's my goddaughter, which is an added bonus."

"Not interested." Will was 99 percent positive Stella was no more interested in him than he was her. She did, however, adore his mother, and always had.

His mother sighed. "You need to get over the fact that she left. It was the right thing for her to do at the time."

Will's gaze cut to hers. "Stella or Natalie?"

They'd both left him. One had done him a favor by

doing so. The other…if she'd been destined to leave, then she'd done him a favor by not delaying further, too.

Surprise darkened his mother's eyes that were so similar to his own. "Why on earth would you think I meant Natalie or that you would want to get back together with her? You've nothing in common and it was obvious she didn't fit into our world."

Surprised, Will stared at his mother. "I'm not sure what you mean by 'our world,' but Natalie fit into my world. I liked her being in my world." He missed her being in his world. "I thought you liked Natalie."

Slowly lifting her hand, she brushed a short strand of hair back behind her ear. Will recognized the action as one she did when giving herself time to consider her response to something she found unpleasant. He'd never seen her use the gesture on him and supposed her medication dulled her senses. Interesting.

"Natalie was a nice enough girl, smart, pretty, and no doubt about it, you were the best thing to ever happen to her, but she was too different for your relationship to have worked out long term. She was just standing in the way of you finding real happiness."

It was only natural his mother would think the best of him. He was her only child. But hearing her assessment of his relationship with Natalie hit him hard. It had to be her post-surgery pain medications loosening her tongue, but negativity seeped into her tone and left an uneasy feeling in his stomach.

"I'm curious as to why you think I was the best thing that ever happened to Natalie?"

His mother was rarely caught off guard, and perhaps it was only the remnants of anesthesia and heavy doses of pain medication, but clearly his question surprised her. "Because you're you and she's…"

"An amazing woman who's an excellent nurse and a blessing to every patient in her care? A beautiful soul who put me and others before herself time and again?"

"Oh, God." His mother's gaze narrowed. "You fancied yourself in love with her, didn't you?"

Had he? Will shook his head. Natalie had said the words to him once. He'd been so caught off guard, so humbled and yet so exposed, that he'd pretended to be asleep rather than deal with his reaction. Her words had swelled his chest with pride that such a woman could care so much for him.

Which was why he'd been so devastated when she'd left him.

Her claim had lost all meaning.

"Answer me," his mother insisted in her boardroom tone, attempting to scoot up in her bed, but wincing and staying put instead.

Will shook his head but wasn't sure if he meant that he hadn't fancied himself in love with Natalie once upon a time, or if he didn't want to answer her question, or if he just didn't like seeing his mother in pain.

"I'm not even sure I know what being in love is," he finally said.

"I thought Natalie loved me, but she left." He took a deep breath. He'd always been close to his mother but hearing the hurt in his voice embarrassed him. She was so strong. Would she think him weak for the way he'd so misread his relationship with Natalie? "She wouldn't have done that if she loved me. If what she claimed to feel disappeared so easily, then how could I ever trust in love?"

When his eyes lifted to his mother's he was surprised by what he saw there. Guilt.

Her painkillers must be an especially high dosage, because Rebecca Harroway Forrest was known for her steely resolve and emotional restraint. No way would she normally show what her expression gave away.

"She wasn't what I wanted for you," she confessed, moving her hand to pat his with her fingertips carefully to avoid triggering pain. "I wanted so much more and felt she stood in the way of you finding that something more. I was surprised she was the one to end your relationship, but I wasn't disappointed that she did."

He knew his mother had always held out hope that he and Stella would someday reunite, but had she purposely tried to push Natalie out of his life in her desire for it to happen? Whether his mother had intentionally conveyed her disapproval or had just failed to hide it, Natalie had known.

He faced the truth: he hadn't believed Natalie's insistence that his mother was trying to drive a wedge between them. He should have.

He should have done a lot of things.

Taking a deep breath, frustrated at her interference, he met his mother's gaze. "Then you should be happy because you got what you wanted."

Will had purposely not scheduled any procedures or appointments the following day so he could sit with his mother.

Other than getting up every so often to stretch his legs, he'd been beside her hospital bed for almost as long as she'd been in the private room, including having spent the night with his feet dangling off the end of a rollaway cot. No matter what she'd done, how could he not be there when the strongest woman he'd ever known wavered between dozing off and frustration at thinking her well-orchestrated world would fall apart if she had to take a health leave? Until a couple of months ago when his mother had confessed that she'd found a lump in her breast, Will had never seen a chink in her armor. His mother had been invincible. A powerhouse willing to take on anyone who got in her way. Which, unfortunately, apparently included Natalie.

Natalie. Had she worked late? Gone to dinner by herself? Started moving her belongings to her new apartment?

What had she wanted to talk to him about when she'd asked him to dinner last night? No one knew why he'd blocked his surgery schedule. Did she miss seeing him at the hospital today or was she grateful she didn't have to face him?

Will's father refused to stay away any longer and had arrived incognito that evening, saying he should be there when Dr. Shasteen talked to them about the pathology results.

When Dr. Shasteen knocked on the door, then came into the room, Will tried to read the man's expression and was glad he got right to the point.

"The surgery margins were good. We got all the cancer."

Will, his father and especially his mother let out a sigh of relief.

"What about the lymph nodes?" Will asked. "Were they clear?"

Dr. Shasteen smiled. "They were cancer-free and there's no evidence the cancer has spread anywhere else in the body."

"So, I can go back to work tomorrow?"

The doctor laughed. "It's barely been twenty-four hours, Rebecca. Keep icing your breast per the instructions I gave yesterday and give your body time to heal."

"I suppose I have no choice. Everyone at the company

thinks I'm away on business for the rest of the week," she mused. "I need to get back soon or that Jasper Wilson who's in charge while I'm away will be trying to convince the board that he should run my company. I'm positive he wants my job." Her gaze narrowed. "If the man wasn't such a brilliant businessman, I'd show him the door."

"If you ask me, you should let him take over more of your duties, so we have more free time."

Will winced at the look his mother gave his father.

"As if you're going to have any time after you win another term on the Senate," she accused.

He shrugged. "Maybe I won't win this term."

His mother looked horrified that he'd even consider not winning. Losing just wasn't in her nature. "Of course you're going to win."

"I'm just saying it wouldn't be the end of the world if I didn't and we took time to travel and see the world. This breast cancer thing has me rethinking life. We need to enjoy it more."

Dr. Shasteen cleared his throat, calling their attention back to him. "I know you're anxious to get back to work, Rebecca, but the earliest I'll consider discharging you is tomorrow. Then, at home, you're going to need to take it easy for a few days. I'd say to give it at least until Monday, then start back slow."

Will could see the wheels turning in his mother's head. Apparently, her doctor could, too.

"Slow means no more than eight hours a day that first week back. I want to recheck your surgery site prior to you returning full speed."

The doctor spoke for a few more minutes, answering his parents' questions and the few Will had. After Dr. Shasteen finished with his consult and left the hospital room, Will's father hugged his mother gently, kissing her and whispering things Will couldn't make out and didn't want to. They weren't an overly PDA kind of couple and Will found himself looking away at their private moment. He was superfluous, and perhaps even forgotten.

Relief hit as his phone pinged. Maybe it was the hospital saying there was a dire emergency and he was desperately needed, so he'd have a great reason to give his parents alone time.

If by any chance you finish with your plans, it's a lovely evening and I decided to go sit in the bleachers on Times Square to people-watch. There's a decent street band I think you'd enjoy.

Natalie. His pulse sped up, sending his blood rushing through his body, which probably explained why he felt a little light-headed at seeing her name pop up on his watch face.

He pulled out his phone and texted back.

Times Square? Alone?

Her message came back immediately.

Is anyone ever really alone in Times Square?

Staring at his phone, he smiled at her question. Or maybe it was the smiley face emoji that had his lips curving upward. Or the fact that his mother's pathology results had been good news. Or all of the above.

Realizing he was grinning at his phone, he glanced up, but neither of his parents were paying the slightest attention to him.

You're welcome to join me.

His heart thundered.

He glanced toward his hugged-up parents. Although he'd planned to stay with his mother again, that had been prior to his father's arrival. Based upon the satchel he'd been carrying, he planned to stay. Will definitely wasn't needed. Wondering if he was crazy, he made a quick decision.

"That was someone from the CVICU," he said, standing. True enough. Natalie did work in the CVICU these days, and right or wrong, he didn't want to tell his parents where he was headed. "Mother, I'm so glad your pathology results came back as well as they did." He kissed her cheek. "Sorry to run, but I've got to go."

Also the truth because he'd seen how they were looking at each other. Maybe his dad had been serious about not caring whether he won or lost his reelection. He supposed his mother's cancer had made them both look at life differently. Although, recalling his mother's urgency to get back to the office, perhaps not so much in her case.

Either way, he said, "I'll check on you in the morning." Then turning to his father, he added, "Make her take it easy."

To which William Sr. laughed, his hand affectionately caressing his wife's. "Me and what army?"

Will grinned and took off. Best he figured he had about a fifteen-to-twenty-minute walk to Times Square if he hurried.

Natalie sat on the second from the top bleacher, the only open space when she'd arrived at Times Square. She'd opted to take the subway rather than walk the entire distance from Callie's alone.

Will's comment about her being alone had her closing her eyes.

She'd not been sure if he'd even text back, but she'd been so restless all evening, wondering where he was, who he was with, missing him, that she'd given in to the temptation.

Callie and Brent had plans with friends. They'd tried to get her to go, but Natalie had wanted to give them time without her. On a whim, she'd decided to visit the busy heart of the city.

For as long as she could remember, she'd enjoyed people-watching. Times Square offered a diverse viewing, from locals trying to turn a buck to visitors from all around the world and from all different walks of life there for the sights.

A trio of street musicians had the crowd singing along as the usual assortment of costumed characters posed for photos for a fee. Sitting with her feet propped on the tiny open spot on the bleacher in front of her, Natalie listened to the music, but caught her gaze drawn to a grinning older couple who were holding hands and looking super cute, making Natalie wonder at their history. Had they spent their lives together, raised a family and now looked back proudly on what they'd achieved? A few rows down from her, a young family were just getting started on their life together. The mom and dad were close to her age but had three small children with them. The oldest looked to be about five and the youngest couldn't be more than a few months.

Soon, that would be her holding a little one. Her hand went to her abdomen as she'd caught herself doing more and more. A baby was there. Her appointment with her gynecologist might not be for another couple of days, but she'd had her positive home tests.

And in her heart she knew.

The moment Katrina had said the word *pregnancy* the truth had clicked in Natalie's mind. Maybe on some level she'd already known but had been in denial.

Will's baby grew inside her.

If her loving him hadn't won his heart, if her leaving hadn't spurred him into action, was there anything she could do to make him love her?

And fast.

Because Will was a good man, an honorable man. He'd want to do what was right by his child. Natalie wasn't sure if that would mean marrying her, but she suspected so.

If Will didn't love her before knowing about their baby, she'd say no to marriage. She wouldn't tie him to her if she didn't have his heart. Not anymore than her having his baby already would bind them.

She glanced down at the phone she held. Fifteen minutes had passed without another reply from Will. Where was he? Who was he with? The possibilities made her head spin. He had every right to be with anyone he wanted to be with, she reminded herself.

Natalie swallowed, then told herself she was going to put all this out of her head and try to enjoy the music and the happy tourists around her. Forcing a smile to her face, she began singing along with them as they kept tune with the band.

That's when she saw him. There, just crossing the street to step onto the concrete pad of Duffy Square, was the most beautiful man she'd ever seen.

She'd told him where she was, invited him to join her, and he'd come.

That had to mean something.

"Will?" She stood, waved her hands in the air. "Will,"

she called louder, hoping he could hear her although she supposed it was impossible over the band and their singing fans.

But Will had been scanning the crowd for her and smiled when he spotted her.

Smiled.

At her.

Melting her heart.

She smiled back, then gave a little wave as if to say hi. He made his way up the bleachers, excusing himself as he weaved around others enjoying the nightlife entertainment.

"You're right," he said as he squeezed onto the bench next to her. "No one is truly alone in Times Square."

Soaking up the warmth of his body next to hers, Natalie nodded. "True, but there are definitely some things enjoyed best when someone is by your side."

Rather than comment, he looked toward the street musicians who were now belting out a hit from the nineties and grinned, "You thought I'd enjoy this?"

She knew he would. He was a big sucker for eighties and nineties tunes.

"They're not bad for free," she quipped, wondering if he could see her pulse hammering at her throat.

"There is that."

And then with all the noise around them, silence fell between them.

Rather than force conversation, Natalie sat next to him, acutely aware of the way their bodies pressed against each other.

Parts of her that had felt dead woke up, apparently surprised and thrilled by his nearness. Was he as aware of her body as she was of his? He hadn't jerked away or made any comment about her having told him to not touch her. Ha, if only he knew how much she wanted his touch. If only he would— She paused. There was no rule that said she had to wait for him to make a move. If she wanted to touch Will, she could touch him. He might tell her not to or pull away. But if she wanted him, she was going to have to show him.

Not that the truth in her eyes wasn't shining brighter than the lit-up signs on the buildings around them.

Natalie reached for Will's hand and laced her fingers with his. His hand was warm against hers, even his signet ring. Warm, strong, capable of such great things.

At first, she kept her eyes trained on the band, refusing to look his way to judge his reaction. But when he still hadn't pulled away after close to a minute, she cut her gaze his way.

He no longer watched the band but stared at their entwined hands. His expression was torn and Natalie's heart hurt.

"I'm sorry I left my birthday party."

His gaze shot to hers. This wasn't going to be easy. But emotion surged within her, bubbling over to where she had to tell him, even if it left her vulnerable. She wanted to tell him so much, about the life they'd created, but she had to make things right between them first. If that was even possible.

"Every insecurity I'd ever had about us hit me full force at that party." She took a deep breath. "Your mother was so thrilled at Stella being there, so approving of her." She could do this. She could tell Will everything. She had to. "It wasn't that I wanted a gift, per se, but it was the fact that a pretentious party your mother put together that included your ex was my birthday surprise, and it set the tone for an evening that just kept getting worse."

"It wasn't."

Not quite sure she'd understood his low comment with the music blaring around them, Natalie asked, "What?"

"Your party was only the first part of your gift, Natalie. You left before we ever got to the next part."

"Oh." If only she could go back to that night, not leave in a weepy mess and instead show gumption in claiming Will as her own when he'd been on the dance floor with Stella. Taking another deep breath, she asked, "What was the next part?"

He shook his head. "It doesn't matter now."

It mattered to Natalie a great deal.

"If I had it to do over, I wouldn't have left. Not because of a gift," she rushed on, afraid he'd think that's what she meant, "but because it was wrong to leave the way I did."

His eyes dropped to their held hands, again. "If you could go back to that moment in time, what would you have done?"

"When I stepped out of the bathroom and saw you dancing with another woman? With Stella?" She thought for a moment, then said, "I'd tap you on the shoulder and ask you to dance with me."

His gaze lifted, holding hers. "What's stopping you?"

"Now, you mean?" Left a bit in shock by his question, she glanced around the concrete pad full of people. There were a lot milling around, watching the band, a few swayed a little to the music. "No one's dancing."

His eyes still focused on her, he shrugged. "That's a shame."

"Do you want to dance with me?"

"Are you asking me to dance, Natalie, or asking if I want to dance with you?"

Her breath caught. Will was here, was giving her the opportunity to ask him to dance. They'd be the only couple in each other's arms, but someone had to be first, right?

She stood, tugged on his hand. "I'm asking you to dance with me, Will, because I want to dance with you."

He hesitated and Natalie thought he was going to decline, that he'd set her up to shoot her down. She probably deserved him to publicly say no. Publicly because a few of the other benchwarmers had started paying attention to them.

"Why do you want to dance with me?"

"That's easy," she admitted. "Dancing gives me a reason to be in your arms."

His brow arched. "You want my arms around you? For me to touch you?"

More than he'd believe.

"Yes."

I want to touch you, to be so close I can breathe the scent of you in and feel your heartbeat next to my cheek.

She wanted him to hold her forever.

His gaze darkening, Will stood. "Okay, but let's hope the band plays something better to dance to."

Natalie had been so caught up in Will that she hadn't paid attention that the band now played a fast electric number. She wasn't a great dancer under the best of circumstances, but at the moment, she didn't care. Maybe the band would see them, take mercy and play something slow.

Hand in hand, they made their way off the bleachers to a vacant spot on the concrete. Despite the fast pulsating beat, arms around his neck, Natalie laid her cheek against Will's chest, imagining that she could hear his heartbeat over the thrumming of the city and the music. In her mind, his heart raced along with hers in a rhythm that was all their own.

Around them the city thronged, the song played and tourists snapped photos. Natalie didn't even care if they'd figured out who Will was. This moment was hers and she was lost in it. There was nowhere else she'd rather be than in his arms.

At some point the music slowed. Whether in Natalie's head or for real, she wasn't sure. It didn't make a difference. They swayed together and nothing else mattered.

This was where she belonged. With Will. Forever.

She looked up at him to tell him how she felt. But when she did, his mouth covered hers in a kiss.

A kiss of possession and anger and passion and hurt and so many things she wasn't sure how to label. Rather than try, she put her soul into kissing him back, not trying to hide the emotion filling her that she was once again experiencing his kiss.

When he lifted his head, Natalie stared at him. Knowing her heart shone in her eyes anyway, she whispered, "I love you, Will. I never stopped loving you."

Not something she'd intended to say, and something she shouldn't have said as Will reeled back, and at the same moment, the song ended.

People around them clapped, including the band.

Realizing they were being applauded, Natalie's cheeks heated, but she held Will's gaze. What she needed to see in those beautiful green depths wasn't there. No joy at her admission of love. No return of her feelings. Just shock. And uncertainty. And anger. And a whole lot of fight or flight.

Her knees wobbled.

"It's easy to get caught up in the chemistry between us, to momentarily forget the things that have happened and say things that in the light of day, you don't mean," he finally said, pulling away.

She started to answer, but before she could a commotion to their left caught their attention.

"Somebody help my husband!" a curly haired woman in her seventies cried as she bent over where a man lay on the concrete.

Oh! The sweet couple she'd been watching earlier.

Natalie and Will rushed over to where the man lay, not moving, his wife frantic as she shook him.

"Sir, can you hear me?" Natalie asked, dialing for emergency assistance as Will put his fingers to the man's brachioradialis to check for a pulse, then checked for breathing status.

"We were listening to the band, watching you two dance, then decided we'd join you for the next song. Only, he grabbed my hand, then collapsed," the woman said in a panicky voice, continuing to shake her husband. "Is he okay?"

Even as the woman was asking her question, Natalie's eyes sought Will's and he shook his head. No pulse and the man wasn't breathing.

"I'm a nurse," Natalie told the woman, keeping her phone held between her shoulder and her head, hoping her voice sounded calmer than she felt as she quickly pulled her mouth guard out from her small shoulder bag. "And this is Dr. Forrest," she said as Will placed his hands over the man's sternum, then Natalie identified herself, gave her location and requested an ambulance to the emergency worker who'd answered her call.

"Oh, God, no." the woman gasped as she realized they were initiating CPR. "He's going to be okay, isn't he?"

Natalie's heart went out to the woman, but she'd leave it to someone in the crowd to try to calm her. Placing her phone on speaker and setting it on the concrete, she bent to give the man two breaths in rhythm with Will's thirty chest compressions.

One. Two. Natalie breathed, then kept count with Will pressing hard into the man's chest with the base of his locked hands. And again, one breath, two.

Noises around Natalie faded as they attempted to save the man's life. Time seemed to have stopped as they worked, but Natalie supposed it was mere seconds before she felt the faint flicker of a pulse.

"Will!" she exclaimed, checking to see if the man was breathing on his own prior to giving an additional two breaths.

Nothing, but after delivering the second breath, she felt a small swoosh of air from the man's nostril. Then, he took a deep inhalation, seeming to gasp and cough at the same time.

Yes!

Natalie moved back a bit in case the man became sick to his stomach.

"Oh, John," the man's wife cried, taking his hand and giving in to more tears.

When his eyes opened, the crowd that had gathered around them clapped and cheered.

Although they'd revived him, Natalie knew the man was far from out of trouble. Something had caused his heart to stop, most likely an acute myocardial infarction.

Sirens blared, cutting into Natalie's haze. The ambulance arrived, and the paramedics joined Natalie and Will in caring for the man. Within minutes, they had medication administered, an intravenous line going and the man on a stretcher to load him in the back of the emergency vehicle.

"You'll see to it that she gets to the hospital?" Will asked, his gaze meeting Natalie's.

Not surprised that he intended to go with the ambulance, Natalie nodded.

And then Will was gone.

CHAPTER EIGHT

NATALIE'S STOMACH KNOTTED as she hesitated outside the ballroom. She'd spent most of the day at the glitzy hotel with Katrina and a crew of volunteers making sure everything was perfect for the charity event.

She'd been so busy working she'd not let herself think about the last time she'd been inside the beautiful ballroom.

So much about her life had changed since her birthday.

She'd not seen Will since their dance in Times Square the week before. When she'd arrived with Mrs. Jones at the emergency department, Will was already prepping to go into surgery with her husband to stent a couple of blocked arteries. She'd hoped he'd call or text her to let her know how the man was, but she'd not heard from him. Nor had she seen him at the hospital, because Connie had returned to work and Natalie was back in the ICU.

During a rare break, she'd gone to the CVICU under the pretense of bringing Callie a drink after her friend texted her that she was thirsty, and oh, by the way, a certain doctor was making rounds. Unfortunately, by the time she got her patients covered, clocked out and arrived, Will had come and gone.

In the meantime, she'd seen her specialist, had her pregnancy confirmed and had an ultrasound scheduled for the following Monday. An ultrasound she desperately wanted Will at.

Had she not known she'd see him at the gala, she'd have messaged or called to see him prior to her test because he deserved to be there, to see their precious baby with her for the first time.

Which meant she had to tell him.

Would tonight be her last chance to see him before having to tell him? Her last hope of having him admit that what he felt for her was more than chemistry?

She'd told him she loved him, and yet again, he'd not expressed the sentiment back. Her heart twisted as she recalled his words. How could he think she hadn't meant her proclamation of love? If only he could see what was in her heart.

Had his comment meant that she was caught up in their chemistry or that he thought anything he felt for her was only due to physical attraction?

"A lot has changed since the last time we were here."

"Oh!" She jumped at Will's voice echoing her earlier thoughts. She hadn't heard him walk up next to her. "I was just thinking that."

"Any regrets?"

Why was he asking? She'd admitted to her regrets when they'd been in Times Square. Was he wanting to rub her face into her mistakes?

"You know I do." Forcing a smile, tight though it was, she asked, "Doesn't everyone have regrets, though?"

"I suppose."

"I heard Mr. Jones got to go home yesterday."

His gaze studying her, he nodded. "He's doing well."

Reaching up to touch his arm, she teased. "He's a lucky man that New York's finest cardiac surgeon was within feet of him when he had his heart attack."

"That's an exaggeration but I'd say the same regarding your nursing skills. I appreciate you seeing his wife to the hospital. She's a sweet lady, but I'm not sure she'd have done well traversing the city on her own."

"No. They were visiting from Missouri. It was their first time to visit the city."

"That's what they told me."

"Too bad I was no longer in CVICU. I'd have enjoyed taking care of them."

"You weren't glad to get back to ICU?"

Natalie bit into her lower lip. Here was her chance to let him know how she was feeling. "I enjoyed CVICU well enough. It was great to work with Carrie, but, mostly, I miss seeing you, Will."

His gaze softened and she felt her hope rising. He cared. She knew he did.

"Natalie—"

"Heavens, this place is hopping."

Natalie winced as Will's mother and Stella stepped out of the ladies' room. The young woman's blond hair was piled up on her head with tendrils dancing about her face and her lips shined with a fresh coat of candy apple red. She was stunning to say the least.

Natalie sucked in a breath and held it, hoping the oxygen dissipated the dizziness that hit at the realization that Will had arrived with Stella.

Yes, a lot had changed over the past two months.

"It's not what you're thinking."

Swallowing the lump in her throat, Natalie nodded. "Okay."

If he said it wasn't, she'd believe him. Only, her throat felt so tight that breathing was difficult.

"Stella's date for the evening ended up being called

out of the city last minute, and so Mother invited her to join us tonight."

Natalie glanced toward Rebecca, meeting the woman's shrewd green eyes and refusing to look away. She nodded, acknowledging the woman. Although perfectly made-up, something was different about Will's mother. Perhaps just that she'd lost a few pounds.

What would Rebecca say to Natalie being pregnant? It wouldn't be good.

But Natalie wouldn't let the woman rob her joy in the fact Will's baby grew inside of her. She just wouldn't. So, she focused on the fact that this dynamite petite woman was her baby's grandmother, and she pasted a smile on her face. "Hello, Rebecca."

Rebecca's gave a quick nod her way, then replied, "Natalie."

At her name, Stella's eyes met hers in the way that happens when two women who are in love with the same man come face-to-face for the first time.

"I'm Stella Von Bosche," she said, holding out her slim hand. "Cute dress."

Trying to decide if the upscale fashion designer was being facetious, Natalie gave a tight, polite smile. "Thank you. It's borrowed from a friend," she said proudly, grateful Callie wore the same size and had the blue number from a Christmas party the previous year. Funny how time changed things. Once upon a time she'd cringed at the thought of wearing someone else's clothes ever again. "I'm Natalie Gifford."

"Nice to meet you," the woman said, smiling in a friendly enough way that made Natalie momentarily question if the woman truly was in love with Will or if Natalie had imagined that earlier look.

What was she thinking? Of course the woman was in

love with Will. How could any sane woman who knew him not be head-over-heels in love with him?

"I appreciate your generous donations for the Children's Cancer Charity, and I know the families benefitting do. As you probably know, you'll have the opportunity to meet several of them tonight." Natalie gestured toward the front of the ballroom. "The table reserved for the Harroway Foundation and its guests is in the front just to the right of the stage."

Her gaze went back to Will's, hoping that he'd suggest they meet up later, something, anything, but the soft look that had been in his gaze earlier was gone, replaced by a stern expression as he eyed his mother and Stella.

Not sure what to think, Natalie eyed the group of guests coming into the room. Katrina was with them and pointing her way. "Now, if you'll excuse me, I'm sure Katrina has a lot of last-minute things she needs me to assist with," she murmured, planning to go help her cochair. But before stepping away, she met Will's gaze. "Talk with you later?"

Surprise lit in his eyes and, after a moment, he nodded.

Natalie's whole body felt lighter as she walked away.

She sat with several of the families being represented by the charity including two of the mothers, who served on the committee. Although she only picked at it, the meal was delicious. Everyone at her table was friendly and her nausea stayed at bay. If she could have kept her attention and off the neighboring table where Will sat, she might have followed her table's conversation better, though.

Will sat by his mother and, if anything, was even more doting than normal.

A quick auction was held for high-end donated items, a short keynote took place, then the dance floor was cleared.

Natalie made small talk with one of the parents, listening at all they'd been through with their son's non-Hodgkin's Lymphoma diagnosis the year before. Listening to their story helped keep things in perspective.

No matter what, the most important thing was that her and Will's baby was healthy.

Will's mother let out a long sigh, causing him to turn in his seat toward her.

"Everything okay?"

"No."

Concern filled him. She was less than two weeks out from her mastectomy. He'd tried to convince her to stay home, but as usual she'd done what she wanted. "You're in pain? Do we need to leave? I can go get Dad from where he's talking with the governor."

His mother's perfectly shaped brows drew together. "Don't do that. He'll start trying to drag me home, and I've been cooped inside those four walls long enough. Besides, I'm fine."

So, she kept saying. But, regardless of how subtle, Will could see the toll of her surgery on her face and in how she carried herself.

"It's you I'm worried about."

Will's gaze cut to his mother's. "Me?"

"You've not heard a word Stella and I have said for the past ten minutes, maybe longer."

He'd have sworn he'd responded at all the appropriate times, but there was no denying that he was distracted.

Even now he fought to keep from looking toward his distraction.

"She looks beautiful tonight, doesn't she?" his mother asked. He started to ask who, but her brow hiked up. "Don't you dare ask me to whom I'm referring."

"Okay, I won't. And, yes, she does. She always does."

"Which has me questioning a few things."

"Such as?"

"Why you are here rather than over at her table."

"Because you need me," he instantly replied.

His mother burst out laughing as much as someone who considered herself a true lady burst out. "Although the sentiment is appreciated," she patted his cheek, "it's quite unnecessary. I'm fine and if I need something, I have Stella."

Stella, who had been chatting with the couple to the opposite side of her, turned, smiled at them and answered, "Absolutely. You don't have to stick around here, Will. I'll stay with Rebecca."

His mother shook her head. "Listen to you two acting as if I need someone to babysit me. Both of you go, dance, be merry."

Will's gaze narrowed at her suggestion.

"Oh," his mother assured. "I didn't mean with each other. I know you aren't in love with each other."

Stella's cheeks flamed.

"You're not, are you?" Will asked.

Stella shook her head. "I love your family, Will, and you as a person, but no, I'm not in love with you." She cut her gaze to his mother. "Sorry, Rebecca. I know it's what you wanted."

"It was," his mother admitted, but kept her gaze averted from his. Shaking his head, he suspected that, even hearing that Stella and he were not interested in one another, his mother wouldn't give up on matchmaking if she thought there was any hope.

There wasn't.

Will's gaze went beyond his mother to where Natalie

chatted with a family. She smiled, brushed a stray hair back from her face, then laughed at something said.

He would never feel anything more for Stella because of the woman he watched.

She'd told him she loved him again, shocking him as he'd been telling himself for weeks that she didn't—couldn't—have really loved him. His defenses had gone up, trying to protect his heart from further disappointment, but had Mr. Jones not had his heart attack when he had, Will suspected he'd have made a confession. One that was long overdue and that had been on his mind almost constantly since that night, since seeing the Joneses together, his parents together, and realizing he did know what love was. What true love was.

He'd known for months, but hadn't given the emotion a label, possibly because of the tension between Natalie and his mother.

That tension shouldn't have kept him from admitting the truth, from saying the words and showing Natalie how much he cared about her.

"We don't always get what we want," he mused, eyeing his mother as a crazy idea hit him. "But maybe, sometimes, we can have a second chance to make things right." Hoping he wasn't making the biggest miscalculation of his life, Will stood, held his hand out to Stella. "Would you do me a favor and dance with me?"

"Will, I think you're making a mistake," his mother began, but he shook his head, ignoring her.

"Your mother is right, Will. I'm not in love with you."

"Which is wonderful, because I'm not in love with you, either," he said, "but I do need you to dance with me. It's important."

Because he and Natalie needed a do-over and, hopefully, this time they'd both get it right.

Curiosity lit her eyes. "Then, yes, let's dance, and you can explain to me why our dancing is important. Because I agree with Rebecca and think you're making a mistake since I'm not the person you want to be dancing with. You should be asking her, instead."

Natalie excused herself from the young family she'd been talking with at a buffet table and turned to see where she was most needed to help.

Her gaze lit on a beautiful couple on the dance floor and her world shifted.

Will and Stella were dancing. He'd said she was there with his mother. Had Rebecca pushed them into dancing again?

Oh, good grief. This was torture. She didn't want to watch them dance.

What she wanted to do was tap Will on the shoulder and ask to dance. What would he do if she did?

Don't be stupid, Natalie. You told him you loved him. He knows how you feel. Nothing has changed. So what if you interrupt and he dances with you?

Everything. That's what.

Body shaking on the inside if not the out, Natalie steeled herself for whatever happened because, before the song ended, she would be tapping on Will's shoulder.

Unfortunately, what she should have been preparing herself for was coming face-to-face with Rebecca Harroway Forrest.

"Natalie," the woman greeted, eyes so similar to Will's pinning her in place.

Natalie sighed. This was way too reminiscent of her birthday party where Will and Stella had danced and Rebecca had filled Natalie's head with doubts. Even if she was Will's mother, Natalie wouldn't let the woman do that. Not ever again. She loved Will, wanted peace with Rebecca, but she wouldn't let the woman emotionally abuse her.

"Hello, Rebecca. If you'll excuse me."

Rebecca ignored her, then gestured toward the dance floor. "They're a beautiful couple, aren't they?"

Ice picks jabbed into Natalie's heart, but she held the woman's gaze. "Have a good evening, Rebecca."

With that she lifted her head, kept her shoulders up and stepped away.

"He doesn't love her," came from behind her.

Natalie paused, closed her eyes, then told herself not to do it, not to take Rebecca's bait. Nothing the woman had to say to her could end well.

Just keep walking. You'll be glad you did, she told herself. Only her feet weren't moving.

"What Will does is no longer my business." Although, perhaps, in some ways, with the baby growing inside of her, that wasn't completely true.

Rebecca had the audacity to laugh. "That doesn't stop you from loving my son, though, does it?"

Natalie cringed, then turned toward the woman she'd let get under her skin too many times, the woman whose approval she'd craved but never had. "You're right. It doesn't."

But having to put up with the likes of you is enough to make me want to have a drink, she added in her head.

Not that she would. Not with the baby growing inside her.

The baby who was this woman's grandchild.

She needed to be nice, but Lord help her, she wanted to tell Rebecca to go fly a kite.

"I was wrong about you."

Not knowing where Will's mother was going with her comment, Natalie held her tongue and waited.

"I didn't think you were strong enough to hold my son's attention, but you did." Rebecca's gaze shifted toward where Will and Stella danced and she sighed. "Love is blind that way."

"No worries, Rebecca. Will doesn't love me," Natalie automatically countered, then wished she hadn't. Not that it mattered. Rebecca surely didn't believe he did.

But the woman's gaze moved back to her and studied her, then she shrugged. "That's not my place to say. But if I were you and there was any chance that a man as wonderful as my son loved me, I sure wouldn't just watch while he danced with another woman. I'd do something about it."

Natalie gawked at Will's mother. Was she encouraging her to interrupt the dance? Surely not. Rebecca wanted Natalie out of his life.

"What is it you'd do?" she heard herself ask even though she suspected she'd regret it.

Rebecca's expression bordered on *Duh*... "Tell him I love him, for starters."

"I've done that," she confessed, not quite believing she was having this conversation.

"And?"

"He pretended to be asleep the first time and the second—" Natalie winced. Why was she admitting these things?

"Go on."

"He told me he could never trust me not to leave again."

Rebecca's lips thinned, then she nodded. "Trust doesn't come easily when you're a Harroway or a Forrest. When you're both..." She gave a knowing look.

"Will's had a lot of women attempt to take advantage of him in the past. Although he'd never admit it, probably not even to himself, that was a big part of his attraction to Stella. As my goddaughter, she was safe—or so he thought until she left. Until recently, I didn't understand why she'd done that, but Will was never in love with her and for her to get over him she had to put distance between them. Lovely girl, so I'm glad she's found success and happiness with her business."

Was his mother suggesting Natalie needed to go far away to get over Will, too? That that would make her successful and happy? There was no distance far enough to get her over loving Will.

Will would never be out of her life. Never out of her heart. And not just because of the baby growing inside of her.

Natalie faced Rebecca. "Why are you doing this?"

"Because you were about to leave."

Confused, Natalie shook her head. "I'm not leaving. I'm the gala committee cochair. I'll be here until the very end. Besides, what do you care if I leave?"

"I love my son."

"I love him, too."

"I know."

Stunned that Rebecca's voice sounded approving rather than condescending, Natalie blinked.

"You do?"

Rebecca nodded, her gaze going to where Will danced with Stella. "He's easy to love but doesn't always make the wisest of choices."

Meaning Rebecca didn't want him dancing with Stella? Was this some type of trick? Some mind game to get inside Natalie's head yet again?

"For months I wanted your approval, would have done

anything to have you invite me to lunch or show even the slightest support of my relationship with Will. You never did." She eyed Will's mother suspiciously. "Why now?"

Had she somehow learned of Natalie's pregnancy?

Heart racing, she waited.

"Because I've been paying close attention to my son since you left him. Just this evening, I've caught him watching you a dozen times." Rebecca laughed. "But only when you're busy and he thinks no one is noticing."

Will had been watching her?

"I've monopolized my son's time the past few months. There were things going on that I won't bore you with, but that we can talk about one day over that lunch you mentioned. But I realize that in distracting him with my personal issues, and my beliefs in what was right and wrong for him, that I interfered in his life beyond what I should have." She gave a little shrug. "I'd always thought Stella would be his wife someday and was determined to see Will properly settled, just in case things didn't go well."

Although not fully understanding what Rebecca meant, Natalie just waited for her to continue. She was too shocked to find words, anyway.

"But what I thought really doesn't matter. What Will thinks and feels is what counts." Rebecca took a deep breath, then reached over and squeezed Natalie's hand reassuringly. "As I said, I want my son happy."

Eyeing Will and Stella on the dance floor and realizing she was rapidly running out of song to interrupt their dance, Natalie said, "I want him happy, too."

"Then do something about it."

Will skimmed the gala guests until he spotted a certain redhead.

When he did, and realized who she was with, he

missed his step, smashing Stella's toe and causing her to stumble.

"Ow!" she complained.

"Sorry," he apologized, steadying her, his gaze not leaving the two women across the ballroom, deep in conversation.

What was his mother doing? Natalie had told him given the chance to redo the events that had taken place at her birthday party, she'd have interrupted his dance with Stella. He was giving her that opportunity, offering that chance for them to start over.

Only, this time they'd do things right.

But his mother wasn't supposed to be interfering.

Turning to see what had distracted him, Stella asked, "Don't you wish you were a fly on the wall for that conversation?"

Yeah, Will did and considered charging over to find out, then stopped himself. Maybe it was more than just Natalie and him who needed a redo. Perhaps his mother needed the chance to make things right, as well.

"You think Rebecca is giving her hell for having left you? Or ordering her over here?"

"I trust her," he assured, his gaze briefly flickering Stella's way and hoping his trust wasn't misplaced. If she believed him wrong, would she think it her God-given right to intervene a second time?

Stella gestured toward Natalie. "If you'd ever looked at me the way you look at her, I wouldn't have left." She gave him a pouty smile. "You're such a great guy, I'd have ended up married to you and not even realized I'd settled."

Will frowned. "I'm not sure if you just complimented or insulted me."

"A compliment. Every woman deserves a man to look

at her the way you look at Natalie. Anything less is settling. You and I don't love each other so it would never have been that way between us."

What could he say? He'd never wanted Stella the way he wanted Natalie.

"The way I look at her didn't matter in the long run. She still left." For which he carried a great deal of blame. How could he have been so blind? So selfish for so long? "I plan to win her back."

Stella's brow arched. "Which is why you asked me to dance?"

"It's hard to explain, and I'm sorry to use you this way, but Natalie and I needed a redo of my last dance with you."

If this failed, he'd figure something out to let her know what a fool he'd been. Some other way to give them a chance to move on from the mistakes they'd both made.

"I'm still not sure I agree, but I hope it works out for you."

"Me, too." God, he hoped he wasn't wrong.

Her eyes full of approval, Stella smiled. "Well, it looks as if you're about to find out. She's on her way over here."

Natalie could do this. She could march up to Will, tap him on the shoulder and ask to cut into their dance. She didn't exactly have Rebecca's stamp of approval, but Will's mother didn't seem to disapprove. At least, Natalie thought that's what their conversation was about.

Even if she did, Natalie would be doing this. This dance, this moment, was her opportunity to correct the mistake she'd made on her birthday. She wouldn't be leaving tonight.

His back was to her when she reached him. Pulse pounding in her ears, she tapped his shoulder.

When he turned and her gaze met his vivid green one, she sucked in a deep breath and went for broke. "May I cut in?"

He didn't look surprised to see her or by her question, just stared at her a moment.

When he hesitated, Stella leaned over and hugged him, whispering, "Pride is nothing to a lonely heart. Don't forget that and good luck."

Natalie's knees wobbled a little at overhearing the woman's comment. Was Stella making a play for him?

Natalie had made so many mistakes in their relationship. She knew that. No doubt, if he gave her another chance, she'd make many more. But she'd love him through them all.

Invisible hands grasped her throat as the blonde kissed Will's cheek, then smiled at Natalie and stepped away.

When Natalie just stood staring at him, he cleared his throat. "You wanted to dance?"

She wanted him.

Nodding and still shaky, she moved into his arms just as the song ended and another began. As they slowly began to sway to the music, she laid her cheek against his chest. This was where she belonged. In Will's arms, listening to his heartbeat, breathing in his scent and marveling at how every fiber of her being yearned for him.

She needed to tell him everything in her heart but savored moving silently in his arms for a bit longer. She could feel his inner tension, his inner turmoil.

She knew he cared for her, but he obviously also cared for Stella. Natalie had already poured her heart out to him and he'd walked away. What did she really expect to be different tonight? If he was happy she was there, he wouldn't be so tense at their dance.

The song ended much too soon. Natalie didn't step

away from him, just held her breath and stayed close as the next melody began.

She didn't want this moment to ever end as she might never be in his arms again.

Only she knew the new song would soon finish, that she needed to use these precious seconds to convince him that they deserved a second chance, and a third, and a fourth, if that's what it took. What they had was rare and precious and deserved to be cherished. She'd poured her heart out in Times Square, but she'd do so again and again and again as long as there was hope.

She leaned her head back to stare up at him, searching for words to tell him that she regretted everything that led to their breakup.

Before she spoke, he lowered his forehead to hers. "I thought I had this clear in my head, what I'd say to you if you asked me to dance, but I've been trying to figure out what to say from the moment you tapped on my shoulder, Natalie."

Natalie gulped. "Tell me I haven't lost you forever," she suggested. Would he be able to forgive her? Could he ever understand her reasons?

"You never lost me, Natalie."

"It's felt that way, and it hurts because I never stopped wanting you." She took a deep breath. "But I also want your attention and to be a complete part of your life and for you to let the world know that I matter. It's what I always wanted. It was wrong to leave, but I wasn't wrong to want those things."

Will stared down at the woman in his arms. The woman who drove him crazy. Because he was crazy about her.

This wasn't easy for him, but then, he suspected it wasn't for her, either. And yet, she'd risked his turning her away, publicly, when he'd already done so once. "The world didn't matter, Natalie. Just you did. I'm sorry I made you feel left out." Will brushed his fingers along the side of her face. "I knew you felt uncomfortable, and was trying to protect you from that, Natalie. I'm sorry I didn't make sure you realized that."

At his words, a tear trickled down her cheek.

"My sweet Natalie, I was such a fool to not cherish every moment with you. I should have shown you how much you meant to me every single day that you were in my life."

Natalie inhaled sharply, but quickly came to his defense. "It's not all your fault. I didn't feel as if I was good enough to be in your life, Will."

"You were. You are." Here went everything. Will took her hands into his, raised her fingertips to his lips and pressed a kiss there. "Part of me regrets the past couple of months more than anything, but another is grateful they happened."

"Grateful?"

"We both had issues, Natalie. Things we needed to work through. It took you leaving to open my eyes." To make him realize what was so very obvious. "There's something I should have done a long time ago," he continued. "Something I need to make right."

Then, Will cupped her beautiful face and stared into her big brown eyes. Everything he needed to know shined there. How could he have ever risked losing her?

"I love you, Natalie. I have from the beginning and never stopped. I never will. Forgive me."

Natalie's knees had been wobbly for some time, but now they were water. Her entire body was water and her eyes had sprung leaks.

Never had she heard more beautiful words.

"I should have told you long ago. Maybe I was in denial about how much I needed you." He wiped away a tear running down her face.

"I love you, too. You know I do."

He wiped another tear. "I thought so right up until the moment you left me and nothing has been the same since."

Would he ever be able to forgive her? To understand how crazy her emotions had been? That had she not been so hormonal, she might never have left? "I'm sorry, Will. I let my self-doubt ruin what was between us. I should have told you how I felt instead of pretending everything was okay for so long."

"You should have felt as if you could tell me, but at the time, I'm not sure I would have heard you if you had," he admitted, knowing that soon he'd tell her all about what his mother had been through. Maybe it would help Natalie to forgive her. "I should have made you feel so loved that you didn't feel like you needed to pretend to be okay. I'm sorry I didn't, Natalie."

"How could you make me feel loved when I doubted myself so much?"

"I should have tried." He slipped his Harroway signet ring off his finger. "I don't want you to ever question how I feel about you or how important you are to me. Not ever again. And I don't ever want you to leave me again, even if I deserve it."

Oh. My. Goodness. Natalie couldn't believe what he was saying, what he was doing. Had she fallen and bumped her head and was dreaming?

She must be because what Will did next couldn't be happening.

He took her hand into his and dropped to one knee.

"Forgive me and marry me, Natalie. Be my wife, the mother of my children, grow old by my side and never leave me, because what we have deserves a second chance and I won't get it wrong this time."

Legs giving out completely, Natalie dropped to her knees and leaned into Will. "Yes."

"Yes? You'll marry me?"

Had he doubted her?

"Yes!" she repeated. "Oh, yes. To all of it. Your wife, growing old at your side, being the mother of your children."

Around them, having noticed Will on his knee, guests cheered and clapped, including his mother and father, but Natalie barely noticed as Will lifted her hand to slide his signet ring onto her left fourth finger.

"We'll replace this with whatever you want," he promised, clutching where the too big ring fit loosely over her finger as he stood and helped her to her feet. "Maybe my grandmother's sapphire. I'd meant to give you the matching earrings for your birthday."

But she'd left before he had.

"I don't need jewels. Just you," she whispered. She hugged him, then pulling back, looked up into his eyes, and wondered how he was going to take what she had to tell him. "Will, there's something else I need to tell you."

"Anything."

"Part of the reason I've been so emotional over the past couple of months is because of hormone fluctuations."

"Hormones?" he asked, not following what she meant, then his brows lifted as he realized. "Seriously? You are?"

She nodded. "I saw my obstetrician this past week and she confirmed it."

"Oh, Natalie." He wrapped his arms around her and lifted her off her feet.

"I take it you're happy?" she asked, laughing as he spun her, then dropped a kiss on her forehead.

"As long as I have you. Never leave me, Natalie. I'm lost without you."

"Never," she promised, and she never did.

EPILOGUE

THE CITY'S TALL buildings became suburbs, then homes
with big yards and gorgeous trees surrounded by acreage.

"Where are we going?" Natalie asked.

"It's a 'prise picnic, Mommy," three-year-old Willow
reminded her from her safety seat in the back of the
luxury SUV.

"You heard the boss," Will said, grinning as he kept
his eyes trained on the road. "It's a surprise picnic so no
more questions."

"Okay, sorry. No more questions." Wondering what
her dynamic duo were up to, Natalie laughed and settled
back into her seat to watch the vaguely familiar coun-
tryside pass.

Soon, they turned down a country road she recognized
from where they'd been touring homes. She'd scoured
the online virtual tours and they'd looked at several in
person over the past few months. He'd taken a different
route and she hadn't instantly recognized where they
were until he'd made that last turn.

She opened her mouth, then clamped it shut when she
remembered her husband, who was now singing along
with Willow's song about bus wheels, would only remind
her that she wasn't supposed to be asking questions.

She suddenly realized which house they'd toured was

located on this road. It was her favorite. She'd loved everything about the brick-and-siding house with its large front porch when they'd viewed it the previous month. She'd been disappointed when they'd learned it had sold earlier in the day. Will had made a significantly higher offer to the new buyers, but they hadn't been willing to let their find go. Natalie didn't blame them. She and Will looked at what felt like hundreds since, but none of them spoke to her the way the modernized farmhouse had, with its decent proximity to the train station to commute into the city.

"I recognize where we are."

"Do you?" he asked, still not taking his eyes off the road.

"Yes, we were here about six weeks ago."

"Hmm, maybe." But even as he said it the farmhouse came into view.

Natalie sighed. "It really is a gorgeous place. I wish the buyers had reconsidered your offer to buy out their contract. Has a similar home nearby come up for sale?"

"Not that I'm aware of. I wonder if the new owners are home?" he asked as he put his blinker on and turned into the driveway. "We could stop by and say hello, ask if they've changed their minds."

"Will!" Heart thumping, Natalie twisted in her seat to face him as he parked the car. "We can't bother them. I'm pretty sure your persistence in trying to change their minds semi-bordered on harassment as it is."

"We don't have to stay long. Just a quick hello. Besides, Willow needs some fresh air."

Giggles erupted from the back seat.

Rather than answer, Will came around and opened Natalie's door before freeing Willow from her car seat.

He set their daughter on the concrete drive but held

her hand. Immediately, she began squirming and dancing around.

Will and Natalie exchanged looks.

"Our princess needs a throne," he unnecessarily pointed out. "Sure hope someone is home."

Watching their daughter hop around, Natalie hoped so, too. The little girl had gone just prior to their leaving the apartment, but it was a long drive from the city.

They went to the front door, and Will rang the doorbell, but no one answered.

"It doesn't appear that anyone is here," Natalie mused.

"Willow isn't going to be able to hold it until we can make it back home." He reached for the door handle.

"Will!"

"What?" He grinned, feigning innocence. "Hey, it's unlocked."

"You're going to get us arrested," she warned.

He shook his head. "The owners will understand that a three-year-old couldn't hold it until she got back to the city."

"What if they have a dog? A big dog?"

He paused to listen. "I don't hear any barking."

Natalie didn't, either, but bit into her lower lip as Will opened the door, scooped Willow into his arms and stepped inside the house to head to the bathroom.

Should she stay on the porch in case the owners came home so she could try to explain?

"Mommy, I need you," Willow called.

Apparently she wouldn't be the lookout. Natalie stepped into the house.

"Surprise!"

Natalie's mouth fell open. To her left was a huge banner that read Happy Birthday.

In the dining room to the left of the entrance foyer,

her friends and family flanked a birthday themed table, complete with a large three-tiered cake. Her parents, her brothers and their families, Callie and Brent and their adorable two-year-old son, Will's father, and Rebecca, aka Grammy.

"My birthday isn't for another couple of weeks," Natalie pointed out, her gaze going back to her grinning husband.

"I didn't want you to wait that long for your present."

Realizing what he meant, what their being there meant, Natalie's eyes widened. "Really? The new owners agreed to sell?"

Looking quite pleased with himself, he nodded, reached into his pocket and pulled out a key with a ribbon tied around the opening. "I bought it fully furnished, but you're welcome to change out any of the furnishings to your taste. Happy birthday, honey."

"Oh, Will, it's perfect."

While Will took their daughter to the bathroom because she really did have to go apparently, Natalie hugged each one of their guests, saying how surprised she was and how wonderful it was that they were there.

"Will was right. This place suits you," Rebecca said, giving Natalie a kiss on her cheek. "Plus, it's got plenty of room to build a barn for Willow's pony."

"Willow has a pony?"

Rebecca smiled indulgently. "Will shouldn't have read her that horse story if he didn't want her to have a pony. It's all she's talked about since." At Natalie's wide eyes, she laughed. "Don't worry. I remember the rules on spoiling my granddaughter. I'll wait until her birthday."

Natalie laughed. "Because it'll take that long for us to have a barn built?"

Rebecca shrugged. "There is that."

When Will returned, Rebecca reached for Willow. "Come on, darling. Let's go outdoors with Grampy and see where we're going to have your playhouse built. For Christmas," she called over her shoulder.

Natalie and Will shook their heads.

"She has Mother wrapped around her finger."

"And she doesn't the rest of us?"

Will laughed. "You have a point. Now, come here so I can give you a birthday kiss."

Natalie wrapped her arms around him and kissed him.

"How did you know?" she whispered after their lips parted.

"That you loved this house and that I would move heaven and earth to give it to you?"

He would have, too. From the moment he'd professed his love at the charity gala, he'd set about showing her just how much every day since. She couldn't ask for a better husband or better father for Willow.

"That, but I meant that we needed more room for our family than we have at the apartment." She waited while her words registered, as his eyes widened, and his lips did the same.

"Really?"

She nodded.

He picked her up and spun her around, both of them laughing.

"This is your birthday party and I'm the one getting a gift. That doesn't seem fair."

"You can make it up to me later."

"Deal," he agreed, pressing his lips to hers again. "I love you, Natalie, and I always will."

Of that, and the fact she was always going to love him right back, she had no doubt.

* * * * *

THE
PAEDIATRICIAN'S
TWIN BOMBSHELL

JULIETTE HYLAND

MILLS & BOON

For Dot.
You're missed beyond measure.

CHAPTER ONE

DR. TESSA GARCIA leaned against the bar and slid the back of her heel out of the four-inch peep-toe shoes she'd crammed her feet into. The shoes had been uncomfortable when she'd purchased them three years ago, but she didn't remember them being such torture devices.

What had possessed her to wear them?

The same ridiculous urge that had driven her to give in to Lily's plea that she come tonight. Tessa had hoped that this outing might stem the loneliness that clawed at her when she collapsed into bed. At least for an hour.

She should have known better. But she'd wanted to believe she might still have a place with these people.

That she wasn't completely alone.

Tessa glared at the martini sign hanging from the bar. The former dive bar had been revamped over the last year. The pathetic-looking burned-out neon bar signs were now upscale artwork. But the worn bar and exposed brick walls were still the same. Likely a design aesthetic Tessa didn't understand—or maybe the new owners had run out of money during their revitalization effort.

Revitalization. Tessa hated that word. Out with the old, in with the new—the phrase applied to people, too, apparently.

A cackle went up from the patio, and Tessa hated the

heat coating her cheeks. She didn't belong here now. This had always been Max's place. His social circle, his night to shine. She'd been a girlfriend, and then a wife, but never a friend. That realization sent more regret washing through her.

They'd divorced a little over a year ago, though they'd inhabited the realm of uncomfortable roommates instead of spouses for far too long. She and Max might not have been able to save their union, but she hadn't thought the women she'd considered friends would also be casualties of their failed marriage.

But they were all married to Max's college buddies. God, Tessa wanted to slap herself. She should have been smart enough to make that connection.

Maybe if she had spoken to anyone outside the hospital in the last month besides food delivery people...

Tessa's eyes looked to the ceiling as her foolishness washed over her—again. The people in the corner had all stared when she'd popped in, the press of pity in their gazes as they tried to pretend it was fine that she'd stopped by. Even Lily's bright exclamations hadn't been able to cover the pink on her cheeks as her eyes darted between Tessa and her ex-husband's new bride.

Her divorce had been easy—at least on paper. Her lawyer had called it textbook. She and Max had divided their savings account, sold the starter home they'd purchased and said goodbye to their shared lives. It was the *after* that had rocked her.

In all her failed attempts to make him happy, Max's hobbies and dreams had taken precedent. When she'd suggested hiking or visiting the botanical gardens, or even hanging out in the backyard where she'd cultivated a relaxing green space, he'd balked. He'd point out that she was always asking him to do more than his share of things. That she should want to do what he wanted, since he was handling everything at home so she could advance at the hospital.

That hadn't been the full truth. He'd done slightly more than half the chores and complained every step of the way. But she'd given in every time. That still rankled.

Her father hadn't appreciated being asked to do anything for his family, either. Tessa's mom had always made excuses for him—just like Tessa had for Max. Tessa had watched her mom try everything to hold on to her marriage. Then she'd watched the catastrophic aftermath.

She'd witnessed all of it, and rather than protecting herself, Tessa had given in to a man's desires, too, hoping that by ceding her likes, her friends, *her dreams*, Max might look at her like he had when they first started dating, hoping that she could have the happy family she'd always craved.

As an only child, Tessa had longed for siblings. For a home life that didn't rock between stony silence and angry shouts. Tessa had wanted to believe her union would differ from her mother's. But life rarely produced fairy tales, and the Garcia women always seemed to end up alone.

At least she had a thriving career as a pediatric attending at Dallas Children's Hospital. Her ex-husband hadn't been able to strip that from her, though he had stolen the promotion they had offered her at Cincinnati Children's.

Maybe Tessa should have moved without him. But she hadn't been willing to admit what, deep down, she'd already known. Her marriage had been over long before they'd finalized the divorce decree.

She'd put so much of herself aside for Max, and what did she have? A closet full of colorful scrubs—and comfy shoes. And no one to grab drinks with. No one to see a movie or go to the botanical garden with. No one at the other end of the phone. *And no senior attending position.*

Hell, she'd even given up the garden she'd cultivated so carefully because Max had wanted to sell their home. Instead of fighting or making a sound argument for why she should purchase it, Tessa had just consented to the sale.

Her townhome didn't have a lot of extra space for a garden. Tessa harrumphed as she spun the ice around her cup. She'd been so focused on finding a spot close to work—and away from her ex—that she'd rushed the purchase. But she had her independence, and she would never let a man dictate her path again.

"I didn't think Max and Stephanie were coming." Lily's cheeks were red as she fanned herself and waved for another drink. "I swear, she's barely old enough to be in here." Lily dramatically rolled her eyes to the ceiling as she leaned against the bar.

"Mmm-hmm." Tessa kept her gaze focused on the ice melting in the glass that once held club soda. Lily might not be drunk…yet, but the wife of her ex-husband's oldest friend was tipsy enough to repeat anything Tessa might say.

At least the bubbly blonde had interrupted Tessa's pity party.

"It was nice to see you. Guess I probably shouldn't—"

She bit back the last part of that sentence, but Tessa had no problems filling in the silence. This would be the last time she was invited.

A martini appeared in front of them, and Lily sighed. "If I hear one more word about college sports…" Her first sip almost emptied the fancy glass. She laid her hand on Tessa's arm and then flounced back to the patio.

College athletics might not be interesting, but, apparently, neither was spending time with an ex-wife who didn't know her place. Lily clearly regretted the multiple texts she'd sent begging Tessa to show up tonight.

Not that it really mattered.

Over the years, girlfriends had come and gone, and now she was the first wife who was being booted from the group. It was past time for her to go home.

"Those heels look like hell."

She sighed. Flirting in a bar had never been her scene, but flirting in a bar where her ex-husband and all his friends were drinking felt like an extra level of desperation.

And she was not desperate. Lonely, but not desperate. *Never desperate.*

"I've already asked for the check and am going home to get out of these torture devi—" Her tongue froze as she met the honey eyes next to her.

God, he was gorgeous! His dark hair was trimmed, but a bit of a five o'clock shadow accented his firm jaw. His arms were muscular without looking like all he did was grunt in front of a gym mirror and drop weights on the floor.

Clearing her throat, she held up her empty glass and tried to push the unexpected arousal away. The man before her was extraordinary.

"Just let me strike out. Then I can tell my sister I tried and go home myself." He winked before waving over her shoulder. "If you want to throw the ice in my face to make it look really convincing, she will definitely let me off the hook."

Tessa laughed and had to stop herself from leaning closer. "I've never thrown anything in someone's face. But now I kind of want to."

"The option stands." Two dimples appeared in the Adonis's cheeks. "But if you keep laughing, it won't be believable—though I wouldn't complain. Even with the air-conditioning, this place still feels like an outer ring of—"

He caught the last word, and Tessa beamed. "Not from Texas, then?" The question slipped between them, and she gripped her glass. She hadn't meant to drag out this encounter, but she suddenly didn't want it to end.

She really needed to make some new friends...or set up a dating profile on one of the apps the single medical professionals were always discussing. *No.* She was not interested in that.

But what was five extra minutes in this hellhole, if it was with the dreamboat before her? At least he'd give her something delicious to think about in her lonely bed tonight.

"Originally, yes. But I've been out of the state for years. I forgot how hot it was in Dallas in June." He leaned over her shoulder, then shook his head. "She just gave me a thumbs-up. Ah, well, I can still tell her you told me to take a hike in a few minutes. I'm Gabe."

"Gabe?" The subtle shift in his voice tickled the back of her brain. Her gaze wandered his chiseled cheeks, and the bite of recognition stole through her. *It couldn't be...* "Gabe Davis?"

Tessa blinked as she tried to reconcile the stunning hunk before her with the teenager who'd spent a summer working with her in the Tinseltown theater. The honey eyes and smile were the same, and her mood lightened even further as he tilted his head and raised an eyebrow. He'd been cute then, and most of the staff had swooned over him.

Tessa had, too. They'd even shared an impromptu kiss late one night.

Then he'd disappeared.

She gave her best fake smile, "You forgot to tell me you'd like extra butter layered in your popcorn. *Of course* it's not too much trouble to get you a fresh one."

"Tessa Garcia!"

Gabe's deep chuckle rumbled through her, and this time Tessa didn't stop herself as she leaned closer. "I'd heard you left Texas. I assume it was for someplace cooler, given your hatred of this lovely June evening."

She bit the inside of her cheek as that piece of information floated out. She hadn't gone looking for him... not really. He'd been a recommended friend on social media, and she'd clicked on his profile once. Just for nostalgia's sake.

There'd been a picture of a lot of snow and a notice that he only shared his information with friends. She'd almost pushed the bright blue request button, but she'd resisted. Barely.

"I was in Maine. Just moved back." A shadow passed over Gabe's eyes as he signaled for the bartender, but it disappeared quickly.

If she'd had something other than club soda in her glass, she might be able to pretend the haunted gaze had never existed. But she was at a bar avoiding her ex-husband and his friends, so who was she to pass any judgment?

"Can I get a Coke and—" he turned to Tessa "—I owe you a drink for saving me from my sister's matchmaking schemes."

"Club soda with lime." Tessa pursed her lips as the barkeep barely kept the smile on his face. She'd worked in a bar through college and knew their tab wasn't enough to keep the great service coming. Still, she laid some extra on the counter as he put the two cups in front of them. "To cover the first club soda."

The man's shoulders relaxed a little, and he added an extra lime before passing them the drinks.

"If you're up for it, why don't we see if there are any seats on the patio? Get you off those dastardly high heels."

"My ex-husband is back there with his new wife." The words slipped from her lips, and Tessa could have throttled herself. The last person she wanted to talk about was her ex. But she also didn't want to sit back there talking to Gabe while all the people she'd thought were her friends either ignored her or studied this interaction.

"I really was getting ready to leave when you walked up. It wasn't a lie." She raised the drink to her lips, enjoying the bubbles tickling her nose. "Pathetic, I know."

"Nope." Gabe shook his head. "Plus, this saves me having to politely pretend I'm not sweltering back there while we nurse our nonalcoholic beverages and try to figure out how long we have to play catch-up."

He tilted his glass toward her, and his dimples sent another rush down her back. Pressing her fingers to her lips, she shook her head. How did this man make her swoon with just a few minutes of conversation?

"What if I want to catch up?" The question surprised her, but it was the sincerity behind it that nearly made her knees buckle. She wanted to catch up with Gabe. Wanted to know what the gorgeous, clever man—whose sister was thrilled he was talking to someone in a bar—had done for the last two decades.

Maybe discover why he'd disappeared after they'd kissed. *No.* That was not a question she was going to ask.

They'd had fun working behind the concession stand at the theater and goofed off more than they probably should when the theater was dead on the weeknights. But they hadn't gone to the same high school. Their final

flirtation, which had led to her first kiss, had felt like…
well, it had felt like the rush of first crushes that only
teenagers could experience.

She still remembered being hurt that he hadn't warned
her he was quitting. If it had been a few years later, cell
phones and social media could have transitioned their
flirtation into a more genuine connection. But those
things had still been just over the horizon.

"I wouldn't mind playing catch-up. Do you want to
down that drink, and we can head to another place?
Someplace where your ex isn't around?" The ridges of
his cheeks darkened as he made the offer.

Was he as out of practice at this as she was? Tessa
doubted anyone could be as rusty in the dating field as
her. She and Max had met in their freshman dorm and
dated all through college. They'd married just before she
started med school, and he'd gone to work in finance.
She'd been off the market for most of her adult life.

"My place is just around the corner. I have wine and a
patio that overlooks the community pond." Heat engulfed
her body as she met those sultry eyes again. "I… I… I
just meant that it's a good place for me to dump these
shoes. And then you can come back to your sister after
a drink on my patio."

Nope… There was definitely no one rustier than her
at this. And she wasn't even trying to flirt. Well, maybe
a little, but not like "invite a stranger back to your condo
fifteen minutes after he buys you a club soda."

He took a sip of his drink, and her breath caught as she
watched him mull the offer over. If he said no, it would
be fine. Better than fine—it would be the right answer.
But Tessa didn't want Gabe to say no. She wanted him
to want her—at least for a night of friendly conversation
on a condo porch.

How long had it been since someone outside the hospital wanted to spend time with her? Tessa didn't want to calculate that answer.

"Sure," Gabe finally stated. He looked over her shoulder again and smiled. "But just so you know, I'm telling my sister this went perfectly and counting it as a date. That will get her off my back for at least the next three days. Maybe even an entire week!"

Laughter again bubbled in Tessa's chest. How had he taken the most awkward moment ever and made it seem like she was helping him? And how was this gorgeous man still single?

He grinned, dimples deep in each cheek before heading to speak to his sister.

Another round of laughs echoed from the back corner, but most of its sting had evaporated. She laid another couple of dollars on the bar and spared one more glance at the over-the-top decor, then let her mind wander to Gabe's delicious dimples. She could get lost in that smile.

Maybe for more than one night.

That thought sent a cold bead of sweat down her back. She was not interested in dating anyone—even if she was more than a little tired of curling up with a pillow each night.

The position for senior emergency room attending was opening in a few weeks. Assuming the rumors were true.

And she'd learned the hard way that men did not appreciate a successful woman. Oh, they claimed to. Max had said he loved Tessa's drive for success. Asserted that her being so successful made them a power couple—a term Tessa hated.

Then his finance career had stagnated following several poor business decisions and the recession. When he was laid off, Max had grown increasingly agitated by his lack of job prospects. She'd understood, but after he accepted another position, their relationship had still raced toward its explosive end.

Particularly when she'd been offered the senior attending job at Cincinnati Children's. He'd refused to even consider moving for her job and suggested that it would be too much of a commitment if she wanted to start a family anytime soon.

So she'd stayed. Given up the promotion hoping that her sacrifice could repair the divide that had widened between her and her ex. Instead, he'd filed for divorce, claiming Tessa didn't need him for anything besides housework.

It had been a BS excuse—particularly considering he'd married again before the ink had dried on their divorce decree. But it was proof that many men couldn't handle being equal partners in a relationship. They always wanted to be more than their partner. And Tessa didn't have the time to wade through the dating landscape to figure out the good from the bad.

She licked her lips as she subtly checked out Gabe's beautiful derriere. If her heart thumped a bit as Gabe leaned over to tell his sister he was going to Tessa's place for a short while, that was just a symptom of loneliness and nostalgia for an old crush. A one-night escape.

Nothing more.

"I won't wait. You can just order an Uber." Isla's grin was too wide, but Gabe didn't want to disappoint his sister with the truth. He and Tessa were just catching up… which didn't explain the heat running through him, or his willingness to go back to her place.

She was uncomfortable at the bar. Her tanned skin had reddened after she'd invited him to have a drink on her patio, her gaze refusing to meet his. If any other person had made what sounded like such a bold request, he'd have found a polite way to demur. To redirect the conversation to something humorous, something that didn't sound like a direct refusal.

Gabe had only approached Tessa at the bar because he'd assumed the walled-off brunette would shut him down. She'd barely acknowledged the three men he'd watched confidently stride over to her. She'd raised her near-empty glass and waved them away.

He'd watched her lift her feet out of those absurd spikes and been certain she was about to call it a night. And the clock hadn't even struck eight. She'd been perfect.

All he'd needed was a refusal. Then he could pretend to be off his game for the rest of the night. That part would have been the truth.

Gabe Davis had been off his game for the last six years. If life had gone according to plan, he'd have been celebrating his fifth wedding anniversary to Olive this year. Maybe even have a toddler or two to keep their life busy.

But life hadn't followed the plan—it had shredded it. Something Gabe should have been used to. He'd learned at sixteen that the movie version of family and love was a fantasy.

A sitcom reality that drove advertisers to Saturday-morning cartoons and after-school specials. That laid the groundwork for kids to believe in happily-ever-after, leaving them vulnerable to the heartbreak that life seemed all too willing to deliver.

But instead of rejection at the bar, he'd found Tessa Garcia, the girl who could make a slow shift fly by in giggles and fun. Tessa had been a bright ray of sun at a dark time.

He'd applied for a job at the theater two weeks after his mother announced over pot roast that she'd finished her family experiment.

His mother had loved her career and the accolades that came as she climbed the corporate ladder more than she'd loved her children, and significantly more than she'd loved the man she'd married. But it was the word *experiment* that time hadn't driven from his mind. That still sent fury through him.

He'd shadowed his mom, always praying that he'd earn a bit of her praise. Of her love. Trying to earn things that other mothers gave so freely to their children. But his acts of service had earned him nothing when she'd packed her bags.

He should have quit almost as soon as he started. The theater had sent him home far too often on slow nights, and Gabe needed the money to help his dad. But he'd stayed because working with Tessa had made him happy. For a few hours he could forget the turmoil of his life at home.

He could still remember finally working up the courage to kiss her after they'd closed one night. It had been the highlight of his high school experience.

But the veterinary clinic had called the next day to offer him the afternoon and weekend front desk assistant position, starting immediately. He hadn't been able to turn that down.

His father had already been working two jobs and asking him to drive Gabe to the theater had seemed selfish, particularly when he didn't know her schedule. By the time he'd finally earned enough to buy a rusted-out car that barely ran, she'd left the theater, too.

He'd gone to the football game when her school played his—the only one he'd ever made it to—but if Tessa had been in the crowd, Gabe hadn't been able to find her. He'd left feeling defeated.

When she'd recognized him tonight, his lonely heart had lit up. The freckles on her cheeks had lifted as her lips turned up. The pretty young teenager had turned into a stunning woman. And a night of catching up was all his heart craved.

"Have fun." Isla's laughter was bright, but Gabe didn't turn around.

He could spend as much time as he wanted with his sister. Reconnecting with Tessa at a bar felt…well, he didn't know how to explain the emotions darting through him.

After the offer had spilled from her lips, Gabe had watched Tessa's eyes dart to the corner. He'd waited a moment, expecting her to withdraw the offer, disquieted by the twinge of longing rushing through him. When she hadn't, Gabe's heart had sped up—just a tick. He hadn't felt that brush of anticipation in so long.

He didn't want to let it go—at least not yet. "Ready?"

"To get out of these?" She gestured to her feet, where red spots were forming on the edges of her big toe, and the back of her heel had to be rubbed raw. "Absolutely!"

"Are you going to make it?"

Tessa sent one more glare south and then shrugged. "No other choice."

For a second Gabe considered offering her a piggy-back ride. It was something they'd done more than a few times on slow nights at the theater, racing down the halls, keeping their laughs as quiet as possible for the dozen people seeing movies on a random Tuesday.

He'd enjoyed every moment of her pressed against

him. The thrill of her cheek against his as they passed life-size movie cutouts.

Such an offer would be absurd now. They were adults, not goofy teens in the throes of first crushes. No matter how much the urge to help her pulsed through him.

That was just his nature. Gabe was a helper—all his siblings teased him about trying to do everything for everyone. Stacy often reminded him that he didn't have to do everything, but he enjoyed it. Gabe needed to be needed. And it had been so long since anyone had needed him.

It was just that side of him calling to Tessa, wanting to offer an old friend some comfort. If his heart yearned to see if her laughter still sounded the same or if her cheek pressed against his could bring joy back to his life, well, that was just a symptom of nostalgia. He didn't believe the lie his brain was feeding him, but it didn't matter. He would not do anything to break the evening's spell.

The walk to her condo lasted less than ten minutes, and he let out a breath as she stopped in front of the Boardwalk Complex. The most expensive condos in the Dallas area. The developer had bragged in more than one interview that he'd always dreamed of making a property worthy of the most expensive spot in the Monopoly game. It was exactly the type of place his mother would love.

What does Tessa do for a living to live here? He braced himself for opulence as he stepped through Tessa's heavy front door.

But the entry was bright and airy—nothing like his mother's upscale unit where she'd fretted over her breakable finery the few times he and his siblings had visited. A stack of gardening books was piled next to the gray couch, and a bright yellow blanket popped with color. The condo had a light floral scent that sent a thrill through Gabe. The home felt like home.

Which was impossible—and unsettling.

When was the last time he'd felt like anywhere was home? In the months before Olive's passing. Their apartment could have mostly fit in Tessa's spacious living room, but it had been a happy place.

Another wave of nostalgia rushed through him as Tessa grinned and pulled him toward her kitchen. The pinch of longing he hadn't felt in forever bloomed in his chest—again. He was lonelier than he'd realized.

"I have Diet Coke, water and wine." Tessa's voice was soft as her dark eyes held his.

What was he doing here? Gabe had never gone back to a woman's place right after meeting her. Except he knew Tessa, sort of…

But was the memory of teenage Tessa the only reason he was here?

Gabe didn't wish to investigate that question. Clearing his throat, he tried to ignore the flutters in his stomach. "Wine sounds great, but get out of those heels first. Point me in the direction of the bottle opener and glasses. Might as well let me earn my keep." Gabe's fingers brushed hers as she handed him the chilled bottle. Her warmth ran up her fingers to his. Such a minor touch that was over too soon.

Get it together. The innocent touch was nothing—really. This was a friendly catch-up session. A way for two lonely people to feel less alone for a few hours.

"Thank you." Tessa raised out of the heels as she pointed to a cabinet. "But these monstrosities—" she glared at the heels as she lifted them up "—are going directly in the trash! No woman should be subjected to such pain."

Gabe chuckled as he pulled two glasses down. "I think my sister Isla may have just shuddered." At Tessa's confused look, Gabe continued, "She's a buyer for a very fancy department store. She worked for years to become their main shoe buyer."

"Well, you are free to tell her that these are evil!" Tessa's laugh was deeper now, but it still had the lilting edge at the end he'd craved so long ago. The part of Gabe that had been mostly silent since Olive's departure burst open.

Handing her a wineglass, Gabe tipped his own up, trying to ignore the dangerous combination of ancient feelings and new desires. "To old friends and comfortable shoes."

Her dark eyes shimmered as she met his gaze and raised her glass to her lips. "The patio is this way." Her hand gripped his and her gaze floated across him again before she dropped it.

Did her palm tingle, too? The connection had been too brief and too long all at once.

"So, what brought you back to Dallas? Too much snow?" Tessa crossed her legs as she sat on the wicker love seat on her patio.

Gabe slipped in next to her, aware of how close the beauty by his side was. His neck burned. And he couldn't pretend it was the heat of the evening, particularly with the bright umbrella covering them with shade while the sun set. Her soft scent mixed with the evening breeze, calling to him. The intimacy of the setting was thrilling.

And terrifying.

Maine had been Olive's home. And he'd happily returned with her after they'd graduated from nursing school. But it hadn't felt like home with her gone. And after so many years, he'd finally felt ready to leave. The yearning to return to his home, to find a new life—whatever that meant now—had finally sent him back to the Texas heat. Swallowing the cascade of emotions floating through him, Gabe knew there was no way to articulate all those thoughts.

"The snow is not that bad." Gabe didn't directly answer her question, but the response was safer.

At least he thought it was, until Tessa playfully shivered and drew a millimeter closer to him. Her full lips were tinged with red wine, and the urge to dip his head to hers made it hard to breathe. Gabe lifted his glass, never taking his eyes from Tessa. "What is it with Texans and hating snow?"

"It's cold." Tessa held up a finger as she continued to tick off her reasons. "It's slushy. It makes driving difficult. It's cold."

"You already said that one."

"It bears repeating!"

Tessa's hand tapped his knee, and Gabe pinched his wineglass to keep from laying his hand over hers. What was wrong with him? He yearned to make her laugh, to see the hint of a dimple when her lips tipped up. To pull her close.

A small voice in the back of his brain wondered if he should take his leave—chalk the evening up to nostalgia and move on. But it was easy to ignore when Tessa smiled.

He leaned closer. "What Texans don't understand is that snowy weather just means you have to cuddle closer." The flirtation escaped his lips. Gabe watched an emotion he wanted to believe was desire flash in Tessa's eyes.

"I guess that could be true." Her tongue ran along the edge of her lip as she closed a bit more of the distance between them. "But the heat can be—" her gaze darted behind him before she pulled back "—sensual, too."

True… Gabe's tongue refused to form any more words as he stared at the woman across from him. This wasn't catching up, and discussing Maine's snow versus Texas's heat shouldn't make him want to kiss her. Shouldn't make him want to run his hand along her waist…shouldn't make him want so many things.

"I missed you when you left the theater. After we…" Her cheeks bloomed as she tilted her wineglass back. "You were my first kiss."

The words were so soft that Gabe wondered if Tessa had meant to say them out loud. "You were mine, too. I even went to the Trinity versus Bell football game senior year, hoping you'd be there. I wanted to apologize for vanishing. To explain that the job I got paid better and started immediately. To ask for your number." Gabe grinned. "If only every teen had had a cell then."

"If only…" Tessa took another sip of her wine, then set it on the table.

"If only…" Gabe repeated, setting his wineglass next to hers. Without the glass in his fingers, his palms itched to reach out to Tessa. The urge to follow a path that might lead somewhere ignited in him. Gabe crossed his arms, trying to redirect the desire.

It didn't work.

"So now, on to the major questions." Tessa's smile was infectious as she shifted beside him. "Why is your sister trying to set you up at a bar?" Her nose twitched. "You were cute when we worked together, but…" She gestured toward him. "I can't imagine you having trouble getting a date."

No. Gabe hadn't had any trouble getting a date, or he likely wouldn't have, if he'd had any interest in the dating scene. But his heart had gone dark after he'd lost Olive. An empty shell had occupied his chest for years. When it had finally started beating again, Gabe hadn't known what to do. But getting involved with someone new had held little appeal.

So what was he doing here?

"I was with someone for a long time." Gabe's heart hammered, but the sting of loss was muted now. Grief never vanished, but you learned to move around it. And with time, the memories, like Olive's bright laugh and her good heart, came easier. She would have loved Tessa's commentary on high heels. "She passed away."

Warm hands found his, and the cavity in his chest lit up again. Tessa's presence called to him in a way he'd never expected to feel again. His thumb rubbed along the edge of her wrist, just enjoying the connection.

"I'm so sorry, Gabe."

"Thanks. It's been over six years. The pain is distant now, but Isla wants to see me happy again. Of course, her idea of happy is me giving her more nieces and nephews to idolize. I guess Stacy's and Matt's kids aren't enough to sate the great Aunt Isla."

"You're an uncle!" Tessa squeezed his hand again.

Tessa's pressure was light, but it grounded him in a way that Gabe hadn't felt for years. *Six years.* The sensation was comforting—one more surprising element to add to tonight's growing list.

"Yes. My brother Matt has two young boys, and Stacy has two preteen girls and a three-year-old daughter who drives them all batty." Being nearby to help his siblings with their growing broods had been part of Texas's siren call, though Gabe wasn't needed for much.

"That's lovely," Tessa sighed.

"When you are goaded to approach a stranger in a bar, it doesn't feel that way. Though tonight worked out better than I could have hoped." That was the truth. Isla had probably texted everyone the moment he left. How would they feel when he told them that this was just catching up with an old friend?

Except it felt deeper.

That was a dangerous thought. And one that Gabe didn't wish to examine too closely. Everything had seemed easy from the moment he'd stepped up to Tessa at the bar. If he tried to unravel the mix of thoughts and emotions, it might get messy. At least for tonight, he just wanted to enjoy Tessa's company—for as long as she wanted him here.

"I meant the family meddling." Tessa sighed. "I'm an only child. I haven't seen my father since I was seven, and my mother passed when I was thirteen. They were both only children, too, so no cousins to speak of. I used to daydream about having a huge family." She grinned. "About sisters I could tell secrets to. Or a few brothers who might want to protect me."

Protect me. He felt his lips dip. Everyone should have someone to look out for them. Someone to run to when the world tilted unexpectedly.

"Children's imaginations are something, huh." Tessa rubbed her fingers on her lips and looked over his shoulder before meeting his gaze.

"I'm sure the Davis clan would adopt you." The offer hovered between them as Gabe smoothed his thumb along her wrist, again. The connection electrified him, and Gabe couldn't have dropped it even if he'd wanted to.

It wasn't an errant statement, either. He was sure that Stacy and Isla would willingly welcome the woman before him into their friendship group. If his sisters adopted Tessa, he'd get to see her often, too. That held so much appeal—and sent a thread of worry dancing through him.

Tonight felt like the perfect spell. But perfection was an illusion. If he fell for Tessa and lost on the gamble…

His heart constricted just at the thought. He wasn't sure it could survive another battering.

But he didn't withdraw the offer.

"The heat of the day is finally breaking." Tessa didn't address his suggestion, but she didn't let go of his hand, either.

"And at ten o'clock!" Gabe chuckled. *Somehow they were back to the weather.*

Tessa picked up her half-full wineglass and stared at the lukewarm contents. "Maybe we should have opted for the soda." She let go of his hand and uncurled her feet.

Gabe opened and closed his palm, trying to chase the sensation of emptiness away. The night was ending, as it should, but Gabe desperately wanted to pause time. To sit here with Tessa for hours, watch the sunrise and just be with her.

As she stood, her feet wobbled, and Gabe reached for her. She landed in his lap, her mouth falling open as she stared at him. "My feet fell asleep."

Gabe pushed a tight curl behind her ear. *God, she is gorgeous.* "It's okay."

Heat that had nothing to do with the Texas night crackled between them. When her lips met his, Gabe's body released tension he hadn't even realized he'd been holding. Tessa's fingers were heavy on his chest as she deepened the kiss.

The taste of wine lingered on her lips. This wasn't the innocent young kiss they'd shared as teens. This was deeper, electric, and the longing buried within it drove him close to the edge.

Tessa... All his senses lit with longing. *Tessa.*

She pulled back, and Gabe had to reach for all his control not to pull her close again.

"Do you want to go inside?" Tessa bit her lip as her fingers danced across his chest, each stroke sending another jolt through him.

"Yes." There was nowhere else he wanted to be tonight.

CHAPTER TWO

GABE'S WARMTH CARRIED through her as Tessa led them up the stairs. Her breath caught as she saw her bedroom door. She wanted Gabe, he wanted her, and they were single. She needed to lose herself, feel desired, cared for.

At least for one night.

His lips grazed the back of her neck, and the final flutters of nervousness floated away. Turning in his arms, Tessa locked her hands behind his neck and kissed him. His arms tightened around her as his mouth captured hers.

This wasn't a flirtatious test kiss. This was demanding and needy. It was everything, and her body reacted in ways she hadn't experienced in years—maybe ever. Her fingers caressed his back, loving the feel of his body as he molded against her.

They fit perfectly.

It was a ridiculous thought, but it sent shock waves through her as his fingers ran along her sides, each stroke growing bolder before he finally traced his thumb across her nipple. Even through her top, his touch burned. His lips trailed along her neck, and Tessa thought she might explode just from the heat of his lips. "Gabe…"

His name on her lips brought his honey gaze to hers.

"Tessa." He dropped a soft kiss along the edge of her jaw. "Do you want to stop?"

The safe answer was yes. She'd never gone to bed with a man on the first date. And this couldn't even qualify as that. But going to bed alone—again—had no appeal when there was such a stunning, sweet man before her. "No. Do you?"

His smile lit up the room. "No, I most certainly do not."

She slipped her hands under his shirt and lifted it over his head. Her breath caught as she stared at his chiseled abs and the dark hair that ran from just below his belly button under his jeans. He was amazing!

"You are beautiful." The compliment slipped between them, and Tessa wanted to slap herself. That wasn't a compliment for a man—was it? *Hot* or *handsome*—those were the words she should have used.

Nerves fluttered across her belly, and a heat that had nothing to do with Gabe's fingers stroking her arms cascaded across her. Max would have hated being called beautiful.

Striking was another word she could have used. Of course, now that the wrong word had slipped out, she could think of so many right ones. How could she be so out of practice at this?

"I mean—"

Gabe captured her lips before she could offer any explanation. When he pulled back, he ran a finger along her cheek. The gentle gesture made her bones melt.

"You're beautiful, too. So lovely."

The whispered words ignited deep inside her. It had been ages since anyone had called her beautiful.

Gabe's lips trailed along her neck. "I think we're both a little nervous."

"It's been a while," Tessa conceded.

"Well." His hands were warm as they slipped under her blouse. "What if we just go with what feels good?" His hand ran along the base of her bra, and Tessa's breath caught. "Does that feel good?"

"Yes." The breathy word echoed in the room, and Tessa let the worries slip away again. "But it's not enough." She yanked her shirt off and stood looking at Gabe, drinking in his admiration.

"Gorgeous." The tips of his lips curled up before he dipped his head to the top of her breast. "You are perfect, Tessa."

Perfect. That adjective had never been ascribed to her—at least not outside the hospital. But it pierced her, and a small part of her heart clasped it. Even if no one else ever said it again, she could treasure this one moment.

Her breath quickened and knees weakened as he dropped more kisses along the edge of her bra. The sensations scored across her as his fingers trailed ever closer to her nipple, but never quite close enough. Reaching behind her, Tessa unhooked her bra, reveling in Gabe's sigh as he gently sucked each of her nipples. The backs of her knees hit the bed, and she grinned as Gabe carefully laid her back.

His heated breath sent shivers along her skin as he slowly kissed his way down her stomach. He paused just above her waist and looked up. Their eyes connected. She unbuttoned the top of her skirt while he stared at her.

Was it possible to have such an instant connection with someone? To crave his touch?

His lips trailed fire as they traveled along the insides of her thighs. Her panties dropped to the floor, and she gripped the sheets.

"Tessa?"

When he lifted his head, Tessa sat up and grabbed the waistband of his pants. "It doesn't seem fair that I've lost all my clothes, and you haven't." His jeans slid to the floor, and she let her hands linger on his tight backside. He really was gorgeous.

As her fingers slid to the waistband of his boxers, Gabe gripped her wrist. "I want you, Tessa. Badly." He kissed the interruption from her lips. "But I still have plans."

"Plans?" Her heart skipped as she held his gaze.

His thumb grazed her nipple, and she shuddered. "I want to see you melt with pleasure." His fingers slid up her thigh, almost to her center but not quite. The heat scorched her, but it still wasn't enough. He licked each nipple before moving his way down her body—again.

Tessa arched as he drew closer to where she wanted him—needed him. "Gabe," she panted as he finally slipped a finger deep inside as his tongue teased her.

Dear God!

She wanted…needed more. "Gabe, please."

"Plans," the whispered word held so much promise as Gabe increased the pressure—barely.

Tessa arched again as waves of sensation crested over her. She lost herself in the feelings, the thrills his hands and mouth created as Gabe drove her closer and closer to the edge. "Gabe!"

Gripping his shoulders, she pulled him toward her and captured his mouth as she slipped his boxers down. Had she ever wanted someone so badly?

She rolled him to his back and reached into the side drawer. The condom box was stuffed in the back. She'd purchased them a few years ago and found them in the box she'd simply labeled "nightstand" after moving in.

It felt like forever, but when she finally slid down Gabe, her body took over.

His hands clasped her waist as he drove his hips toward her. Then he slipped his finger between them. The pressure made Tessa gasp.

"Tessa."

Her name on his lips was thrilling. "Gabe, Gabe... Gabe." His hips raised again, and Tessa crested into oblivion.

Tessa's breathing was light as he held her. Gabe pressed a soft kiss to her shoulder, simply relishing the feel of her next to him. He couldn't explain the rush of the connection between them, and he wasn't sure he wanted to.

Particularly after midnight. If he thought too much, he might rush from her bed. *Or get too comfortable.*

He ran his hand down her side. Her skin was so soft. The urge to touch her, to hold her, was burying itself deeper within him. Perhaps he should kiss her goodnight and slip out—but that held absolutely no appeal.

He'd tried dating a few times since Olive passed, but his ability to feel connected to another had felt broken. Because he'd been broken.

He'd accepted that belonging to another person had ended—before it had even started, at least for him. Tragedy ripped away part of your soul, but he still had so much to be happy for. He might not be complete anymore, but being Uncle Gabe, a skilled nurse, an excellent brother and a good son was enough.

It was.

But tonight, he'd wanted more. Craved more. With Tessa, he'd felt almost whole for the first time in forever.

For a few precious hours, laughter had come easy— and it had been real. Not the forced chuckles that he'd become so adept at. He hadn't had to remind himself to smile. He'd simply enjoyed each moment.

Because of the woman beside him.

What did that mean? Probably nothing.

Gabe's heart skipped in his chest. He should just enjoy this time by her side.

She let out a soft sigh, and his name followed. *His name...*

Gabe's heartbeat felt like it echoed in the dark room. His soul cried at the small connection. How did something so insignificant touch such a deep part of him?

"Tessa." His lips trailed along her neck.

Tessa moaned as his hand skimmed along her hip. She rolled over, and her dark gaze met his. Her eyes were hazy in the dim room, but the desire building there made him smile. *She* made him smile. *Tessa.*

"I didn't mean to wake you." The words were soft—and mostly true. He hadn't meant his touches to awaken her. But he wasn't sorry as her lips met his.

"I'm not sure I believe you." Tessa's long fingers stroked his chest, diving deeper with each exploration, "Did you want something?"

The question felt more profound than it should have, and Gabe's tongue was unable to form any reply. When her lips moved down his body, he let the question drift away in the fog of exultation.

Gabe's arm was heavy as Tessa slipped from the covers. His breath hitched, and all the flutters and questions she should have contemplated last night rushed toward her. The connection they'd had was electric, but she didn't know him. Not really.

They'd never even addressed the questions that one

usually answered on a first date. *What do you do for a living? Hobbies? Future plans?*

No, they'd flirted over the weather. *The weather!* How had such a superficial conversation led to explosions in her bed?

Whatever had pulled at them, she needed a few moments of distance. Even though her body wanted her to wake the gorgeous, kind Adonis with kisses. And more.

So much more!

Pulling on a pair of shorts and a tank top, she headed for the kitchen. She needed coffee and a bit of space. What did one do the next morning? She'd never had a one-night stand.

But what if she didn't want this to be a one-night stand?

That thought sent thrills and panic racing through her. She and Gabe had an easy connection and chemistry that ignited desires deep within her. But that didn't necessarily mean anything.

She rubbed her arms, hating the uncertainty warring within her. Emotions were dangerous, and getting hurt seemed to be the natural order of the world. At least for the women in her family.

She stopped at the base of the steps and listened for any sign that the striking man was awake. The memory of his fingers running down her skin sent longing and heat rushing through her. But instead of returning to him, Tessa started for the kitchen.

Love was a chemical reaction. A dopamine high that vanished with time. She hated that thought, but her father had abandoned her mother when the family life he had claimed to need no longer excited him. And the high had evaporated years before Max had demanded a divorce.

Even with the pain it had witnessed, her heart still

cried out for more. Maybe the organ was just a glutton for punishment as it whispered for her to consider that Gabe might be different?

Her phone buzzed, and Tessa frowned. She wasn't on call this weekend.

Dr. Lin told me he's retiring on our shift last night. His last day is in three months. His senior attending position should open in a few weeks. You're a shoo-in!

The text from Debra, the head nurse, made her smile. Tessa hopped from foot to foot. She wanted to burst with the news!

Now Tessa's heart was racing for another reason.

What would Gabe think?

She felt her lips tip down again. That errant thought was unacceptable. She'd known Gabe for six months when they were teens and now for one lovely night as adults. But she was not searching for the approval of any man regarding her career. *Not again.*

Tessa read the text again. *Senior attending...* Her skin bubbled with excitement. She wanted the promotion. It was the perfect chance to prove to herself that compromising her promotion in order to try to save her marriage hadn't dealt her career any setbacks.

She was the best choice, but that didn't always matter. She'd served as Dr. Lin's replacement when he'd had to have rotator cuff surgery last year, but she was younger than at least two other colleagues she knew would be interested.

And a woman.

Her gender shouldn't matter—but it did. She'd been asked questions throughout her career that her male colleagues had never faced. Particularly when it came to her plans to start a family.

People assumed her male colleagues had spouses, or ex-spouses, to look after their children. That they wouldn't need family leave. That they could operate at their best, even if they went home to a half a dozen children every night.

That wasn't an assumption that was granted to a woman of childbearing age. *No.* They had to prove that having a family wouldn't make them *less* of a physician.

For years, she'd said that she had no plans to start a family right away. There wouldn't be a need for maternity leave just yet. But she hated the answer. Hated being asked it. Hated answering it. Hated the emptiness that it always highlighted in her home.

She loved children. Tessa had never considered another specialty. Her mother had left med school after discovering she was pregnant with Tessa. Her dream had been permanently diverted, but she'd fostered Tessa's fascination with the human body and the healing arts.

Even as a teen, Tessa had known pediatrics was her calling. Taking care of children—big and little—made her happy. But it wasn't the same as coming home to a few of her own.

Rubbing her arms, Tessa tried to push away the pinch of unhappiness that always floated around her whenever she thought about how she had two extra rooms in this town house, and neither was a nursery or a playroom.

She'd always dreamed of having children. Of being the mom that hers hadn't gotten the chance to be. And she was sure she could be both an excellent mother *and* a wonderful doctor.

At least the question of a family was one she could

answer easily now. With her divorce behind her, she wouldn't be having children anytime soon.

Maybe at all.

Pain sank into the room, and Tessa had to force her lungs to expand. Biting her lip, Tessa closed her eyes and tried to focus on what she had. And how fulfilling those things were.

Her job. The prospect of a promotion. Her condo. Rediscovering herself after the divorce. She had more than many people. *Focus on the blessings you have*. Wallowing because everything she wanted hadn't come to fruition wouldn't make a family magically appear on her doorstep.

Her eyes wandered to the doorway. Last night's memory would always bring a smile to her lips. *Gabe*.

Tessa could fall for him, and that was terrifying. It would be nice to let the connection that had been so easy last night bloom. Get lost in his good heart and stunning dimples.

But there was always a cost to caring for someone. Her mother had paid the ultimate price for lost love. And if Tessa hadn't been so willing to make Max content, she would already be a senior attending.

No, Tessa wasn't prepared to pay for love and affection—not again. No matter how much a piece of her lonely heart cried out for it.

Dr. Killon is already talking about taking on extra shifts!

Debra's new text sent Tessa's eyes to the calendar. It was common for doctors to pad their résumés with extra shifts when coveted positions were opening. Luckily her calendar was completely clear. There was no one and nothing to stop her from working as much overtime as she could.

She looked at the empty last two weeks of the month and sighed. She should be excited that she didn't have to move anything around. That she could focus on this dream…but those blank dates highlighted a loneliness that cut deeper than she'd expected.

She lifted the page to look at the next month and stared at the block of leave she'd blotted out. She'd never worked on her birthday. Not out of any desire to celebrate the occasion; she hadn't celebrated the date since she was thirteen.

Tessa never did anything other than visit her mother's grave—which bore the date of Tessa's thirteenth birthday, too. But if the competition for the promotion was coming up, her mother would understand if Tessa broke that personal rule this year. After all, her mother hadn't gotten to chase her dreams—but Tessa could.

For both of them.

I can't wait to call you Boss!

That text forced away the pain.

Gripping the phone to her chest, Tessa spun around. She could do this. She could!

"Such a bright smile in the morning." Gabe grinned before his arms wrapped around her belly. Then he dropped a kiss to her cheek.

Maybe she didn't have to have an empty social life?

"A job that I have wanted for forever is finally coming open. My colleague was letting me know." Tessa brushed her lips against his.

"A job opportunity has you dancing around the kitchen

this morning?" Gabe's voice dipped. His hands loosened on her hips.

Tessa tried to ignore the pinch of anxiety that pulsed in her back. *It's early and he hasn't had coffee. That wasn't a frown.*

These were the excuses she had lived with for so long with her ex. And she was not going to pepper them in this morning.

"Yes." Tessa nodded. "It's the thing I want most." That wasn't exactly true, but her connection with Gabe was too fresh to mention that she also wanted a family. A few kids to call her Mom. A happy home. Those desires were buried deeper—and harder to achieve than a promotion.

"A job," Gabe repeated before he shook his head.

This time he definitely frowned.

"Last night was fun." Tessa hated the words as they tripped from her lips. Fun didn't describe last night—or at least not completely. Amazing, rejuvenating, exciting… the start of something.

Except something had shifted in the morning light. Did he regret their night together? Or had the fact that she was excited about a promotion changed everything?

Gabe's phone buzzed, and he smiled as he read the message. "My sisters are not so patiently wondering where I am. We usually meet up for breakfast on Saturday." He pushed his hand through his hair.

Tessa gulped down the desire to ask if she could come. She would not tie her friends to a man again—even if Gabe remembered his offer to let his sisters adopt her last night. "It was good to see you again." Those words felt wrong, but she didn't know the protocol for this.

She grabbed the notepad sitting on her counter and quickly jotted her number down. Gabe looked at the note and smiled before pulling the pad from her fingers.

His touch still sent fire licking up her arms, but she had a terrible feeling that he wouldn't call.

And that would be fine.

Her heart sighed as he passed the notepad back, his number scrawled across it. Then he pocketed her number. *Maybe he'll call after all.*

"I should probably get going." Gabe pursed his lips, looked at his phone, then back at her.

For a moment, she thought he might ask her to go. Instead, he dropped a light kiss to her cheek. After a night of passion, it crushed her.

But she was not going to let it show.

"It was good to see you, Gabe. Really." Tessa wrapped her arms around herself, the crumpled note with his number wrapped in her fist.

"It was good to see you too, Tessa." Gabe dropped another chaste kiss on her cheek, then he walked out.

CHAPTER THREE

PAPERWORK WAS NEVER-ENDING in the medical world. Tessa checked off another box on her tablet, trying to keep her mind from wandering to Gabe Davis. She'd alternately promised herself that she'd call him or throw his number away for the last two days. Not that throwing his number in the trash would offer her any relief.

She knew that number by heart now.

But every time her fingers hovered over the call button, the flicker of emotion he'd shown as she talked about the promotion stilled her fingers.

She'd seen a similar look before. Max had worn it for years. Before he'd given up the pretense that he didn't hate her success.

Gabe's face floated through her memory again, and Tessa wished, for the hundredth time, that that morning had gone differently. That he'd invited her to breakfast or asked when he could see her again instead of just exchanging numbers. That she hadn't witnessed the spark of uncertainty. That somehow their one night could transition to a fairy-tale story they'd tell their grandkids—minus a few details.

But life wasn't a fairy-tale. How often did she need to remind her heart of that?

Tessa's mother had married her father after a whirlwind romance. Less than four weeks after meeting her father, her mother had found out she was pregnant with Tessa. Her dreams of med school and becoming a surgeon had evaporated. But Tessa's father had immediately proposed and sworn he wanted to be a husband and father. That they could make it work.

He'd taken a promotion and moved their growing family from Houston to Dallas. Her mother's dreams had shifted from being a top physician to being the best wife and mother she could be. But it hadn't been easy. Tessa could still recall her practicing stitches on oranges—just for fun.

But they'd made do, and Tessa had never doubted that her mother loved her more than anything. Then her father had packed his bags to start a new business—one that he didn't want his wife or child to help him with. Last she'd heard, he was running a successful restaurant in upstate New York—with his fourth or fifth wife.

Her mother had believed in love. Even after setting aside her dream career to raise Tessa, and after her husband's abandonment. Even after taking on two jobs to make ends meet after her father's child support payments routinely failed to materialize. After watching her world implode, Tessa could still remember her mother saying that love was the most important thing. That it would all work out.

Except it hadn't.

Tessa had tried to take her mother's optimism into her own marriage, hopeful that she could have a love that lasted forever. But she hadn't gotten it, either.

Gabe wasn't Max or her father. At least, she was pretty sure he wasn't. But that dash of uncertainty she'd seen in his eyes had kept her from calling.

And he hadn't called, either. That stung.

"Dr. Garcia, have you met our newest pediatric nurse?" Debra, the head nurse on the unit, always walked the recent hires around, introducing them to their new colleagues. Most of the time, it didn't happen on their first day, and they already knew at least a few of their colleagues. But it was a Dallas Children's Hospital rite of passage. You weren't a full member of the staff until Debra had shown you off.

Tessa turned to smile at the new arrival, excited to focus on something besides paperwork or Gabe Davis. Her lips went numb. Gabe was standing next to Debra. She saw a glimmer of hesitation pass through his honey eyes before he offered a brilliant smile.

Had he missed her as much as she'd missed him? Why hadn't he called?

Neither of those were appropriate questions for the hospital.

"This is Dr. Tessa Garcia." Debra smiled at Gabe before turning her attention back to Tessa. "Nurse Gabe Davis."

"We met at a bar." The words blurted from her mouth. If there was a more embarrassing way for this reunion to go, she didn't want to find it.

Debra looked at her, and she saw the questions flickering in the woman's gaze. Tessa considered Debra a friend. She'd listened to her complaints when Max packed his bags and had declared him unworthy and suggested drinking away his memory. Tessa had thanked her, even enjoying the few jokes Debra had made. But lately, she'd been a little too interested in Tessa's lack of a dating life.

"What I mean—" Her cheeks were hot as she tried to find the right words, any words to follow her first statement as Debra cocked her eyebrow.

"We worked at a movie theater together in high school." Gabe turned the bright lights of his smile on Debra.

Tessa saw the happily married grandmother swoon.

"We ran into each other a few nights ago, and Tessa tried to convince me that the Dallas heat is preferable to the snowy locale I just came from."

"Snow!" Debra shook her head, horror drenching her features. "Not for me."

Tessa placed a hand against her cheek, grateful that it wasn't stinging with heat as she replayed where her last conversation about snow had led. Gabe's gaze met hers, and the draw she'd felt a few nights ago pulled at her. *He's here.*

"It's good to see you again, Tessa. I mean, Dr. Garcia. Always knew you were destined for great things!" His smile was deep as he nodded toward her.

His voice struck her, and Tessa barely kept from leaning toward him, her body aching with the memory of his touch. Her lips were desperate for one more kiss, even as her brain tried to remind her that he hadn't called.

"She *is* destined for great things!" Debra's voice echoed as she turned to lead Gabe away. "She's going to run this place someday—just wait and see." Debra looked over her shoulder and winked at Tessa.

Her stomach skittered and her body lit up as she let her gaze linger on him for a moment. How was she supposed to work with him?

By being a professional! Her brain screamed the command, but her heart wasn't sure. She'd certainly inherited her mother's romantic nature; unfortunately it hadn't earned either of them a happily-ever-after.

"I need help! Please!" The scream echoed from the room where a teenager was waiting on stitches following a skateboarding accident.

Gabe raced toward the room as the mother stepped out, carrying her younger daughter, his heavy footsteps pounding against the floor as he reached the mother.

"Please!" Her wail echoed down the halls.

Tessa saw several nurses motion for the other patients to stay in their areas—not an easy ask in a children's emergency room where little ones were already anxious and curious.

"Give her to me, please." Gabe's voice was firm as he reached for the young girl. His jaw tightened as he took the child. "Empty room?"

"Seven," a nurse from behind Tessa yelled.

Closing the distance between them, Gabe and Tessa quickly walked toward the empty room while another nurse tried to calm the mother enough to get details. "What do you think? I saw your face shift."

"Her breath is sweet. If she's in diabetic ketoacidosis, then we need—" Gabe dropped the statement as he laid the child in the bed. "Your orders, Doctor?"

Leaning over the small girl, Tessa could smell the sweetness of her breath, too. "Get me an IV line ready." She turned to the drawer and grabbed the blood-sugar-testing kit that was kept in each room. "Her blood glucose level is five-eight-six."

Any glucose level over four hundred was dangerous. But once you got over five hundred, you were dealing with a medical emergency. If they didn't get her sugar levels down, she could go into kidney failure or a diabetic coma.

Gabe nodded and immediately started working to secure a line in the girl's arm. A bag of fluids was hung on the hook. She looked so young and tiny in the bed as Tessa and Gabe worked to stabilize her.

"Her heart rate is steady." Tessa turned as Wendy, another nurse, walked in. "We need two units of insulin, and put another two on standby."

Wendy nodded and raced off.

The heart-rate monitor beeped, and Gabe looked over Tessa's shoulder. She knew he was making sure he knew exactly where the crash cart was. But they were not going to need that today. *Not today.*

A small sob echoed by the door, and Tessa turned. The girl's mom was standing just inside the threshold. "Do you have a history of diabetes in your family?" Her voice was steady but firm. People reacted to stress differently, but right now, they needed as many answers as possible.

The mother's eyes widened, and she shook her head. "No. No." She stifled another sob and squared her shoulders. Tessa had seen many parents do the same. Once the initial shock passed, they often fortified themselves to do whatever necessary for their children...and fell apart in the cafeteria when they were on a "coffee break" a few hours later.

"Okay," Tessa responded. Type one diabetes usually ran in families, but it could happen without any known genetic connection, too. "Has she been thirsty lately? Or complaining of headaches?"

Wendy stepped into the room and passed Gabe the insulin injections, then quietly took her place on the other side of the child's bed. A nurse's uncanny ability to enter the room silently or with as much ruckus as necessary depending on the situation never ceased to amaze Tessa.

"Rebecca is always thirsty. But the heat—" The woman's lip trembled. "I just thought—"

"This isn't your fault." Gabe's voice was firm as he triple-checked the line and readied the insulin injection that Tessa had ordered.

"Nurse Davis is right," Tessa agreed. "When you are

fortunate not to have a history of diabetes in your family, often you learn by having your child fall unconscious. Luckily, your son was here already."

The woman wrapped her arms around herself as she stepped closer to the bed where her daughter was resting. "Will she be okay?"

"We've given her rapid-acting insulin. It will take around thirty minutes to take effect, but it should stabilize her. Then we'll monitor her blood sugar and use regular insulin to keep her stable." Tessa nodded toward Wendy. "Nurse Hill will stay and monitor her insulin every fifteen minutes for me. We have extra shots ready if necessary."

Tessa waited until Rebecca's mother looked at her. "Once her insulin comes back up, she will regain consciousness and likely be scared."

Her mother swallowed and then looked toward the door. "My son—"

The poor woman had been through too much today. This was one area where Tessa could alleviate a few of her worries. "I'll make sure your son's stitches are done, and he's sent in here. Rebecca will need to spend at least tonight with us, and we'll arrange for you to start counseling with the diabetic specialist tomorrow, too."

"Thank you." The woman wiped a tear away and slipped her hand into her daughter's.

Once they were in the hall, Tessa turned to Gabe. "Nice work. You saved us valuable time."

Gabe's gaze fell on the door to Rebecca's room, and a small shudder rippled across his shoulders. Tessa ached to rub the worry lines from his forehead.

She needed to get control of herself. They were at work; she should not be concerned with the tension radiating from him. But something about Gabe called to her.

"My sister Isla is diabetic. A few weeks after my mom left, Isla started complaining of headaches. Dad was busy and…" His gaze flitted to the door as his voice died away.

"Anyway, we found out the same way they did—though we had to follow an ambulance and it took over an hour to figure out. She suffered permanent kidney damage. I will never forget the smell of ketoacidosis." He rocked back on his heels. "At least it saved us time today."

Tessa nodded, unsure what to say. The frown lines on his cheeks made her ache. As an only child, she couldn't really understand the closeness Gabe had with his siblings, but she knew what it was like to be scared for someone you loved and unable to change anything. At least individuals with well-managed diabetes could live close to a normal life, though Rebecca would always need to make sure she was monitoring her body.

"Want to help me stitch up a skateboarder?" Tessa tapped her shoulder against his. It was a small connection, but her body vibrated as she pulled away. Apparently, even that friendly gesture was too much. *And not nearly enough!*

"Of course." Gabe's dimples hit her again.

Tessa felt a warmth slip through her. Any of the nurses could help with stitches. But Tessa wasn't ready to give up the time with Gabe. That was dangerous, but she didn't care. She was glad he was here. She'd wrangle her heart later.

Gabe's skin was on fire, and his mind was racing. Tessa was here. Here! If he focused, he could still feel the ghost of her touch on his shoulder.

His brain tried to keep his sprinting heart in check. He'd spent the last two days hoping she'd call, but nervous about pressing Send himself. When he'd come down-stairs, he'd seen her do a little dance in the kitchen.

After their night together, Gabe's soul had soared that she might have enjoyed his presence as much as he'd enjoyed hers. That she might want to see what happened next.

And maybe she did!

But the excitement had been over a job—probably the senior attending position here. He'd worked two shifts and already heard multiple doctors and nurses discussing the potential opening.

His mother had danced in the kitchen like that once, too. He'd come down the morning before she packed her bags to see her swaying on the linoleum. She'd hugged him and told him that great things were coming. Except those things hadn't included her family.

She'd given him a list of things that needed done. And Gabe had done them. Hoping that he could earn a place in her new life.

Gabe was the only one who answered his mother's infrequent calls. She only ever called if she needed something, but Gabe hadn't given up hoping that she might want more of a relationship with him.

Tessa wasn't his mom—except she'd said this position was the thing she wanted most.

If Gabe was ranking his life goals, career progression would be on the list. Most people wanted to be successful. But it wouldn't be at the very top. Nothing would ever unseat his family.

But Gabe hadn't been able to drive away the longing to reach out to Tessa. He'd wanted to see if she might like to grab dinner, go hiking. He'd even wondered about the job she wanted. It had made her smile, a huge, warm smile, and he'd ached to know more.

He just longed to know Tessa. Gabe wasn't sure what to do with those feelings. But now wasn't the time to work through them.

"Ready?" Tessa's voice jolted him from his thoughts as she stopped in front of the door where he'd grabbed Rebecca.

"Is my sister going to be okay?" The boy's voice wavered, but he didn't break eye contact with Tessa as they stepped through the door. The teen's face had multiple abrasions, and his left arm was in a splint. He had to be in pain, but Gabe could see the worry coating him, too.

He'd worn that look often after his mom left. He'd worried over his father's exhausted features, over his siblings, over all the changes. It had taken him years to conquer the anxiety it created.

Then Olive had started complaining of headaches. She'd been so strong and independent. She'd blown it off as wedding and work stress, and he'd pushed away the worry that something was wrong, too.

Logically, Gabe knew that even if they'd discovered the aneurysm before it burst, there was little chance she'd have survived, given its location. But worry and guilt weren't things that you could easily wash away with logic.

And Gabe hated seeing it mirrored back to him with the young boy before him. There was nothing he could do for Olive now. But he could help the young man sitting on the exam table—after they addressed his visible wounds.

"Rebecca is going to be okay. But she's spending the night with the wonderful doctors and nurses upstairs."

Tessa's response released a bit of tension from the child's shoulders.

"Right now, though, Nurse Davis and I need to take care of you. Can you tell me your name?"

"Sam." The boy's lip trembled, but he stuck his chin out. "I want to see my sister."

"Not until we have you sewn up." Tessa smiled, but her voice was firm.

Even though the kid was still just a kid, he was at least three inches taller than Tessa and probably weighed at least fifty pounds more, too. But he looked so young as he glanced from Tessa to the door.

She examined his un-splinted arm before meeting the child's eyes. "I know you want to help your sister and your mom."

Tears welled in the boy's eyes, but he didn't drop his chin. "They need me. Dad's gone—" The statement was low and cut off by a sob he caught before it fully erupted.

"You can't help if you're not okay, Sam. Can't pour anything out of an empty cup." Tessa sat on the edge of the bed as she held up a light to examine the cut on his cheek. "I think we can just get by with a butterfly bandage on this one."

Gabe swallowed as she patted the boy's leg. The hospital was busy, but this was a child trying to be more than he was. Gabe understood that drive—and knew how tired Sam was. How tired he was going to continue to be. Tessa was taking extra time; making sure he knew that he mattered, too, was a balm that would soothe the boy for weeks, maybe even years to come.

Pediatric emergency room doctors were often judged on how quickly they fixed and released patients. And the metric was not weighted to give slow docs the advantage. At his last hospital a physician had been promoted because he was so efficient that his average time with a patient was less than twelve minutes.

It was not something Gabe thought should be rewarded. Stitches shouldn't take more than a few minutes. But Tessa was not rushing this simple interaction.

A lump formed in the back of his throat as Gabe pulled out the material for Tessa to stitch up the cuts on Sam's arm. That empty cup analogy was a line his sisters had repeated to him after Olive passed—when Gabe had tried to keep everything together while he was falling apart.

He'd been so used to helping others, to being needed, that he hadn't known how to ask for help—hadn't wanted it. Hadn't wanted to admit how lost he was.

That you can't keep trying to pour out of an empty cup was true. But following through with the sentiment was a lot harder for some people. And Gabe guessed Sam was like him. He would put everyone before himself and avoid his own wants—and needs—to make sure his mom and sister had as much as possible.

When Tessa stood to wash her hands, Gabe squatted, so he was looking Sam in the eye. "I know it feels selfish to put yourself first."

Gabe saw Tessa's head turn toward him out of the corner of his eye, but he kept his focus on Sam. "Anything you do for yourself, that makes you happy, takes time away from helping your mom and Rebecca, right?"

Sam sniffled and held up his splinted arm. "And it costs Mom money." He scowled at the appendage, and Gabe's heart broke. He'd crashed his skateboard. It was an accident, not a massive crime. But Gabe could see the loathing in the young man's eyes. That kind of thinking could worm its way deep inside and destroy so much.

"I've been there. I crashed my bike when I was seventeen. Ended up with a head injury, and it cost my dad almost a thousand dollars to make sure I hadn't cracked my skull." Gabe waited until Sam met his gaze before continuing, "But you're still a kid. A very helpful kid, I bet. But a kid. You aren't responsible for carrying everything. Dr. Garcia is right—you can't help if your well is completely drained. Trust me on that."

Pulling back, he watched Tessa stitch up Sam's arms. She talked in low tones about superhero movies and skateboards—two topics Gabe was stunned to realize she had so much knowledge of and was willing to spend time on. If metrics were being monitored for the senior attending position, too many extended interactions like this one could cost her. But she never cut off a question or rushed the stitches. They were going to heal with minimal scaring.

When the stitches were complete and she'd secured the bandage to his cheek, Tessa asked another nurse to walk Sam to his sister and mother.

"Gabe?"

He turned. Her dark eyes held such compassion *and* the emotions he'd seen the other night. Now was not the time to discuss what had happened between them, though. If Tessa wanted to talk, she had his number.

And he had hers.

"Do you think counseling would help Sam?"

Would it have helped you? That was the second question he saw dancing in her eyes. She might not realize the depth of his connection with the boy's circumstances—though maybe she did—but she'd seen it. The recognition of a soul trapped in the same cycle that caught many people in its lonely trap.

"I think so. But if money is tight—" Gabe shrugged. His father would have loved to have placed all his kids in counseling to deal with their mother's abandonment. Would have given them everything if he could have afforded it. "It will be the first thing to go if bills come due."

Tessa nodded and bit her lip. "I'll pull a favor from

Dr. Gendler. With Dr. Lin retiring, everyone is looking for a leg up. He'll probably want—" Her words drifted away. "It's important that Sam get help."

So there would be a high price for the favor. "But you want the job, too." Gabe's voice was low as he stared at the woman across from him.

"Not at the cost of my patients." Tessa's eyebrows rose as she clicked through the tablet, closing out the notes on Sam's case. "No job is worth that."

His heart sang at that simple phrase, and he wanted to pummel himself. He should have called. Should have invited her to breakfast. Should have taken a risk.

But maybe it wasn't too late.

"This is quite the change of venue from the Tinseltown theater, huh? But it's nice to be working with you again, Gabe."

"You too, Dr. Garcia." Gabe beamed. "Dr. Garcia. That has a very nice ring to it, you know. It suits you."

The look she gave him lit up the hallway. "Thank you." Tessa let out a soft laugh. "That means a lot." She started toward the nurses' station before turning. "It really is good to see you here, Gabe."

There was a touch of something in the way she'd said his name, a softness that warmed his heart. For an organ that had been silent for so long, he wasn't certain exactly how to proceed now. His gaze locked on her as she walked away. Dr. Tessa Garcia. He smiled. Gabe was excited to be working with her again, too.

CHAPTER FOUR

TESSA JIGGLED HER tray and looked over the heads of individuals in the cafeteria. Dallas Children's pancakes were fan favorites, always drawing a larger number of staff and patients. But there was only one person she was looking for this morning.

Gabe...

Her body still lit with excitement and more than a touch of need whenever she was with him. They'd settled into a pattern of friendly chats when their shifts were slow. But it didn't sate Tessa's need to be near him.

The night of passion they'd spent together seemed to have been a fleeting moment. They never discussed it, though its presence seemed to hover in the rare uncomfortable silences that dogged their talks. And as each day ended, it seemed harder and harder to bring up.

But avoiding Gabe wasn't an option, either—at least not one that Tessa planned to exercise. He'd burrowed deep inside her, and her heart refused to relinquish its quiet what-if questions. Though she tried to remind herself that she was done listening to that voice.

"You look deep in thought."

Gabe's warm tone ripped across her and she smiled. God, she had it bad.

"What are you so focused on this morning?"

You. Tessa set her tray across from him and slid into her seat, determined not to mention that truth.

"Just thinking about how Dr. Lin hasn't even officially put in for retirement, and Dr. Killon is already lobbying for the job. He certainly has a high opinion of himself." Tessa carefully monitored Gabe's features, but he just plopped another bite of pancake in his mouth.

Gabe seemed to be the only employee uninterested in discussing which physician was the most likely replacement for Dr. Lin. Despite attempting to keep away from most of the talks, Tessa had been locked into more than a few gossip sessions regarding the future competition. Gabe's refusal to engage in the discussion was usually refreshing, but sometimes she really wanted to know his thoughts. *And whether he thought she'd be a good choice after working with her for a few weeks.*

This was an easy topic, though. Dr. Killon was inexperienced and showed little care for his patients. Gabe was still in his first month of employment, but he'd worked several shifts with the man. He was the last person anyone should want to replace Dr. Lin.

"Really, Gabe? No thoughts?" Tessa raised an eyebrow, hoping to draw some commentary from him on the job opening, wishing there were a simple way to know if her reaction to it was why he hadn't called.

His honey eyes held her gaze, and Tessa had to remind herself to breathe.

"Tessa—"

Before he could finish that statement, something hot and sticky slid down Tessa's back. The heated syrup burned a line down her spine.

Then hands pushed into her, and a tray clacked to the floor. The owner of the liquid fell to the ground.

A cry of alarm echoed in the crowded cafeteria as Tessa turned to find a teen seizing.

She moved quickly. Pushing back at the curious on-lookers who were gathering, Tessa slipped next to the young man's side. She heard creaking and looked up to see Gabe climbing over the table to reach her and the patient. That was an effective way to get through a gathering crowd.

"Help me turn him on his side." Tessa nodded to Gabe as he helped shift the boy. Then her eyes went to her wrist. They needed as accurate a time count as possible.

"Make way!" a voice called.

Debra and Jackson stood by with the portable crash cart. Tessa turned so she could keep a better focus on her patient and her watch. The longer the seizure went on, the more likely the teen was to suffer long-term consequences.

Or need the crash cart.

The minute hand moved on her watch, and Tessa heard Gabe let out a soft sigh. She briefly looked to him. A bead of sweat coated his upper lip, and his shoulders were rocking. But he did not let his gaze leave their patient.

Blessedly, the boy started to release. *Thank goodness.*

"One minute, twenty-eight seconds." Gabe's voice was ragged as he sat back on his heels to let the gurney through.

"I got the same," Tessa stated. Gabe's hands were shaking. *What was going on?*

Something about this patient had impacted Gabe. There was too much for her to focus on. But as soon as she knew their patient was going to be all right, Tessa was going to find Gabe. Whatever memory this had dredged up, he needed someone. And that was something she could offer him.

* * *

Gabe's body swung between hot and cold flashes as he leaned against the wall in the employee lounge. He'd helped patch up a little girl who'd fallen from her bike and needed stitches, and delivered discharge papers to another, but his mind kept wandering to the closed doors where Tessa and others were dealing with the seizure patient.

The teen had briefly met his gaze before he dropped hot syrup down Tessa's back. The world had stopped, and his breath had caught in his throat. He hadn't even been able to find the words to call out a warning. His lips had been frozen as the past raced through him.

The unfocused eyes. The drifting step. The crash. Olive had experienced each of those symptoms in quick succession the morning he'd lost her.

The aneurysm that had plucked her away had bulged, pressing on a nerve, resulting in a seizure. Then it had ruptured.

Gabe knew the odds that a boy who couldn't be over seventeen was having a seizure because of an aneurysm were minuscule. Those types of clots almost always built up over a long lifetime. But Olive had been vibrant, independent and twenty-six when one had stolen her away. There were no guarantees in this world.

"Gabe."

Tessa's soft voice sent skitters across his raw nerves. The present overtook the past as he pushed away from the wall.

"He's all right." She didn't waste any words as she stepped toward him, her face open and concerned—for Gabe.

"Did he have an MRI?" Gabe's voice sounded off, and he crossed his arms. Olive had been fine for a precious hour after she'd seized. He'd sat next to her in the ER, trying to keep her spirits up as worries mounted. When she'd screamed from the pressure suddenly pressing through her skull, Gabe had known what it meant.

And been unable to do anything other than hold her hand as she slipped away.

Tessa's gaze flickered, and Gabe wondered if she could see the roller coaster rushing through him.

"No, I didn't order an MRI." She kept her voice calm as she carefully watched him. "You're so pale." She took a deep breath and placed a hand on his chest as she held his gaze. "Breathe with me." She inhaled, held it for a second, then waited for him to follow her.

Her soft scent chased through him as the present pushed the past's panic aside. His heart raced, but that was because of Tessa's light touch. When she stepped away, he hated the distance between them.

"He's an epileptic. The new medication his neurologist prescribed is not managing it as well as hoped. He was actually here under observation as they weaned him off it and restarted his old regimen. He got hungry and went for pancakes without asking.

"Teens, right?" She let out a soft laugh.

The sound sent a touch of longing through him. For the hundredth time, he wished he'd called her. That he hadn't let his fear still his fingers.

"I'm glad he's all right."

"Your girlfriend died of a seizure?" Tessa followed Gabe to the small window, her presence sending a wave of contentedness through him.

Gabe swallowed the twisting emotions as he stared out at the parking lot. He would always miss Olive. There was a hole in his heart that no one could fill. You learned to accept that a piece of you was gone, but grief transformed. It morphed. It became easier to hold others, to think about opening yourself up to another. At least that was what the books he'd been given following Olive's passing had said.

He hadn't felt that…until he met Tessa. Today the past had flitted into his future, and it hadn't been the debilitating pain of her loss that had driven his concern over the teenager. It was the aftermath that Gabe feared for another family.

As a pediatric nurse, he'd helped stabilize many seizure patients, but usually after the seizure started. Witnessing the start had thrown him because the teen had so perfectly mimicked her symptoms.

"Olive was my fiancée." Gabe let out a breath and squeezed Tessa's hand, grateful that she had seen how the episode had affected him. And sought him out.

"But I lost her to a brain aneurysm. She seized about two hours before. The symptoms were identical to the teen before…" He let the last words go unsaid. "I'm glad the patient is going to be all right."

"Winston. His name is Winston."

"Of course you know his name." Gabe forced himself to release the pocket of air he'd been holding.

A frown line creased Tessa's forehead. "Of course. I just left his room, Gabe."

"True." He offered a smile. "But not every doctor focuses so closely on their patient. I suspect if Dr. Killon had treated him, he wouldn't be able to tell me his name. He also wouldn't have noticed someone else's distress."

Gabe had heard all the rumors regarding Dr. Lin's position. The man hadn't even officially put in his retirement request, and people were acting as though his last day had already occurred. Gabe hadn't wanted to feed into that rumor mill but when Tessa had asked him about Dr. Killon this morning, he should have responded.

Should have joked that he didn't want to see the man running anything—anywhere. They were colleagues and friends now—a little workplace discussion about something Tessa cared about should have occurred.

The tips of her lips twisted up.

He enjoyed seeing her happy.

"That's true," she conceded, "but he would have correctly diagnosed his problems."

"Yes." Gabe took a deep breath and looked into the dark eyes that called to him. "But a senior attending should care about more than just the condition."

The look of joy that flitted across her face made Gabe wish he knew a way to bridge the gap that had opened since the night he'd spent at her place.

He wanted more than passing conversations in the hallway. More than the friendly waves and smiles. So what if she was interested in a promotion? That didn't mean that she'd choose it over everything else. She cared about her patients, and the staff.

His mother only cared about herself. She never looked at others as anything other than pawns to help drive her own desires. He'd let his fear keep him from seeking something that made him happy.

"How's your back?" It wasn't the question Gabe wished to ask, but he'd find a better place than the hospital break room to ask her out. *And soon.*

"Sticky." Tessa laughed as she stepped to her locker. "Very sticky!"

Tessa stepped into the elevator and leaned against the wall. Her day hadn't been terrible, but she'd run from patient to patient with no downtime. Her toes ached in her shoes. She was looking forward to comfy socks and an easy evening.

"Hold the elevator!"

Tessa put her hand to the door, stopping the sensor. Fingers grazed hers before pulling back, but her body lit with recognition. *Gabe.*

"Thanks." He grinned as he stepped into the elevator with her.

He leaned on the other wall, several feet from her, but Tessa's body called out at the close confines, aching to bridge the distance. To see what he'd do if she invited him to dinner.

It would be nice to have someone over to dinner. To have a house with noise that didn't just come from the television. To spend time with people outside the hospital. *To spend time with Gabe.*

Swallowing those desires, she shifted her messenger bag. "No problem. I know what it's like to want to get home. A little peace and quiet after the craziness here."

Gabe shrugged. "That might be nice, but I'm still couch surfing at my sister's place. Stacy's girls don't really do peace and quiet."

That would be nice to come home to, too. Sticky faces and loud noises. Belonging. *Family.* Tessa pushed that need away before she could mention that she'd love to come home to sticky faces and loud noises. No need to further embarrass herself.

"I'm constantly fending off her oldest's karate moves. She may be almost two feet shorter than me, but I am pretty sure Brett could pin me with ease!"

Tessa laughed as the elevator doors opened to the parking garage, wishing she could extend the interval with Gabe. He always found ways to make her smile. Real smiles, not the fake fixtures that had become her mask during the final years of her marriage.

"I'd love to watch you dodge her. I bet it's a sight to see." Tessa caught the desire to ask if she could come over sometime—but barely.

Get it together!

Her body heated as Gabe's dark gaze held hers. He cleared his throat and stepped from the elevator.

Gabe turned. "What are your evening plans?"

Her stomach flipped as she shrugged. "Reading up on hydroponic gardening." *Nothing that can't be rescheduled.*

His dimples appeared as he stared at her. Hope fluttered in the dimly lit garage.

Gabe put his hands into the front pocket of his backpack and pulled out a set of keys. "How—" His faced shifted as he looked away. "That sounds interesting. I'd like to hear more about it sometime."

An awkward pause erupted between them. Time extended as she looked at his chiseled features.

Why didn't you call? The question reverberated around her brain as they stood together.

The elevator dinged behind her and the spell binding them broke.

"Have a good night, Tessa and Gabe," Debra shouted as she walked toward her car.

"You, too!" Gabe called as Tessa waved.

"Enjoy your book." Gabe tipped his head as he spun his keys around his fingers.

"Watch your back around your niece." Tessa pulled her keys from her bag, too.

His deep chuckle sent need cascading through her.

"Always." He winked and walked away.

She let out a breath, trying to calm her heart rate.

Want to get dinner? See a movie? Why were those phrases so hard to utter? If he said no, Tessa would at least know.

But no also meant he really wasn't interested—and she wasn't ready to lose the bright bit of hope her heart was clinging to.

"I'm headed to the coffee shop. Do you want me to grab you something?" Tessa offered as she stepped out of a patient's room.

"I'd kill for an iced caramel macchiato!" Gabe's step picked up as he moved beside her. He still hadn't figured out the perfect way to ask her out. It should be simple. *Want to grab dinner?* But he wanted it to be…*epic.*

To be something she wouldn't turn down.

Tessa grinned, but her eyes weren't as bright as they normally were when she met his gaze before she offered a pretend shudder. "I asked if you wanted coffee. Not a cup of sugar."

He loved sweet drinks, but it was the company Gabe craved, not caffeine. He leaned as close as he could in the hospital and whispered, "You might like it if you tried it."

The twitch in her lips lifted his spirits even further. He was happy when he was with her.

"I think I'll stick to my regular."

Gabe shuddered as she winked, the playful exchange putting an extra bounce in his step. How Tessa gulped down cup after cup of black coffee was beyond him. He might like and sometimes need the caffeine boost, but it could be done with a little chocolate or caramel drizzle!

"Any word on the job?" Gabe tried to keep the question light. He'd never understand the craze this position was causing among the doctors. But he was trying to be supportive. It mattered to Tessa.

And she'd be great at it. Gabe knew that, but he was still concerned that she was pushing herself to the edge. Over the last few weeks, she'd been at the hospital during each of his shifts. And on most of the days he wasn't here, too, according to the other nurses.

It was one thing to love your job, to want the best for your patients—Gabe understood that drive because it rumbled through him, too—but living at your job, focusing only on it, was a recipe for disaster. But he wasn't sure how to bring up the worry—or if it was even his place.

But surely a friend could point out that Dallas Children's Hospital was not a person. That it couldn't love its employees. When one moved on, another would be hired. Even Dr. Lin, who'd been a senior attending for almost a decade and a half, could be replaced easily enough. Shoot, people were talking about his replacement before he'd officially announced his last day.

"No word." Tessa frowned as they reached the coffee shop.

The line was longer today than usual but Gabe didn't mind. A few extra minutes with the woman beside him was a joy.

"I'm worried they might look to an outside hire." She pressed her fingers to her lips.

Gabe bumped his shoulder against hers, hating the dip of concern he saw floating in her features. Dr. Lin had only told a few people he was retiring; he hadn't made anything official. There was nothing the hospital could do yet.

"Not that Human Resources will ask me, but I think hiring one of our doctors would be best."

"You'd be a good resource for them." Tessa looked at her hands before meeting his gaze. Emotion floated there that made his knees weak.

Did she feel the electricity that connected them, too? Did she still lie awake at night thinking of their time together?

Tessa leaned a little closer, and her scent made Gabe want something very different from caffeine.

"You notice things. You listen better than anyone I've ever met, and you genuinely care about the patients and staff. Actually, you probably care about everyone you meet."

"Life's too short not to make everyone feel special." Gabe grinned. A look passed over her face that he couldn't quite understand. Before he could ask, they'd reached the front of the line.

"Happy birthday, Dr. Garcia." A resident waved and raised his coffee toward them.

Birthday? Why hadn't she'd said something? The hollow in his belly expanded. He'd have gotten her a card.

Or used it as an excuse to plan a birthday dinner. It would have been the perfect opportunity to see if she wanted to test out the feelings that still seemed to crackle between them.

"Thanks." Tessa waved before staring at her shoes.

"Well, let me buy the coffee today. After all, I didn't realize we were celebrating." Gabe ached to throw an arm around her shoulder, but that was too much. *And yet not enough.*

"We aren't." Tessa's words were tight, and the flinch along her jaw nearly stilled his feet.

What had he said? Gabe hated the tension stringing through her. "Tessa?"

"Medium house blend, black." She held her badge up to the scanner and stepped aside to let him order his drink without looking at him.

"Large caramel macchiato with an extra shot of

espresso." Gabe pressed his badge to the scanner, too, before moving to her side. Her lips were pursed, and her gaze was far away. What was he missing?

Birthdays should be a day of celebration.

His father had always made a big deal of birthdays. Even when money had been tight, a birthday cake decorated in the birthday boy's or girl's favorite color always materialized on the hand-me-down kitchen table. Balloons purchased from the Dollar Store were taped to the wall, and the entire family sang to—or rather belted at—the newly aged member of the group.

Even now, his siblings had a tradition of trying to be the first to call on someone's birthday. The silly tradition had gotten so out of hand that a few years ago, a truce had been declared that no one could start the call until at least five in the morning in whatever time zone the birthday person was in. Only Gabe and Isla still competed to be first, but that was because Matt and Stacy preferred to sleep until a reasonable hour now that they were settling down with kids.

"So, you don't like your birthday?" Gabe grabbed his large drink and took a deep sip.

"No." Tessa lifted the coffee to her lips, but it didn't mask the subtle shake in her hands.

Most of the medical professionals Gabe knew didn't mind adding years. Once you saw how fragile life really was, you celebrated the additional laugh lines and crow's-feet that far too many people never got to earn.

"You want to talk about it?" He knew the answer before the question left his lips, but he didn't regret asking it. Gabe wanted to know about Tessa, and he wanted her to know that he wanted to know her.

"No." The word was clipped, but he saw the twitch of

her lips behind the cup. It wasn't much, but at least she knew he'd listen if she opened up about it.

She grimaced and ran a hand along her belly.

"Seriously, are you okay?" Gabe reached for her elbow as she shuddered. She had been working extra shifts; he knew how much exhaustion could bring emotions to the surface. What was going on?

"I think coffee in the afternoon just isn't sitting right with me." Her jaw clenched as she looked at the cup. "Maybe it's because I'm getting older." Tessa winked.

His chest seized as her dark eyes held his. This wasn't the place he'd planned or the perfect moment he wanted, but Gabe was done waiting. "How about we—"

"Code yellow! Code yellow!"

Tessa's eyes flew to the speaker on the wall before her feet took off.

Gabe dropped his full drink into the trash can beside the emergency room's side door. Adrenaline raced through him, but it didn't push away all the concern for the woman who hit the ER doors a second before he did.

"Seven-car pileup on I-635. At least four of the cars had families. We've got six patients incoming. More possible!" The call came up from the nurses' station, and Gabe saw the color drain from Tessa's face before she squared her shoulders.

They'd had a few bad days since he'd started working at Dallas Children's. It was always difficult when you had more than broken bones and stitches, but her panicked look as the nurse stated that the adults were heading to Presbyterian Hospital sent a chill down his spine. This was one of the worst ways to spend your birthday.

She hated this day! If there were happy memories tied to it, Tessa couldn't dredge them up.

"Where is my momma?"

The tiny voice belonged to Natalie Dreamer, the final patient on Tessa's long list of little ones who had been on Interstate 635. A church group had been carpooling to a campout. An elderly driver suffered a cardiac event and crossed three lanes of traffic. Seven of the fifteen cars in the caravan had been involved in the resulting pileup.

Bending to look at the dark-haired cutie, Tessa tried to keep her voice even. All she knew was that Natalie's father was on his way here, and her mother was at Presbyterian Hospital.

Please... Tessa sent the tiny plea into the universe, hoping that this might be the one time it listened to her entreaties. Tessa didn't want to add another tragedy to today's list of traumas. *Please...*

"Your dad will be here shortly, Natalie." Tessa smiled, hoping it seemed comforting. She'd been this child once, asked everyone where her mother was. All the smiles she'd been offered that day hadn't mattered as she'd sat in the waiting room with a tiny stuffed elephant that a nurse had procured from the gift shop. She'd clung to it, even though she'd sworn off stuffed animals as babyish in a fit of preteen drama the year she'd turned twelve.

It was the last birthday present she'd allowed herself to receive.

The door to the room opened and Gabe stepped in. His eyes were heavy with exhaustion, but he offered a bright smile to Natalie. Then he pulled a pink bunny from behind his back. Tessa couldn't quite control her recoil.

Gabe's gaze darted toward her before returning to Natalie. He was very perceptive, but Tessa hoped he'd just think she was tired. Which she was.

No matter how much sleep Tessa got lately, it was

never enough. But that was a problem for another day, too. *Focus!*

"Bunny!" Natalie grabbed the stuffed animal, snuggling it close with the arm that wasn't in a sling.

"I thought it might help to have a snuggle partner while Dr. Garcia puts your arm in a cast." Gabe made sure he was at Natalie's level as he addressed the child. It was a small thing, but children often felt more comfortable when an adult was at their level. Even after treating their share of the fifteen patients who had arrived from the car accident, Gabe didn't rush through his patient interactions.

He'd make an excellent partner and father.

The loose thought stunned Tessa as she prepared the material for Natalie's fiberglass cast. Mentally shaking herself, Tessa tried to focus on the task in front of her. But if you worked in a children's hospital, you saw more broken bones than probably any other medical professional, so she could do this routine in her sleep.

She should be thrilled that Gabe was such an excellent pediatric nurse—that he fit so well at Dallas Children's. Little boys needed to see men in caring roles—needed to know they could become nurses, too. That it wasn't just a girl job.

But Tessa wanted more than coffee runs and breakroom chats. There'd been a few times when she'd thought he was about to ask her out. Like that evening in the parking garage. But the topic always seemed to shift to something else.

Usually a question regarding Dr. Lin's position. Tessa felt her lips turn down and tried to wipe the emotion from her face. She'd been thrilled when Gabe had finally started talking with her about the job, but after previously ignoring the topic, he now broached it at least once every other shift.

Was that why he hadn't asked her out? Tessa didn't want to believe that. But she hadn't wanted to believe that her ex-husband was jealous of her, either.

She could ask him out. It was the twenty-first century. Women did that. But each time she'd considered it, her tongue had failed to deliver the words.

If he said no, she was afraid she'd lose what they had now. An easy work relationship wasn't all she wanted, but it was better than awkward silence. When he was around, Tessa didn't feel so unmoored in the world, a sensation she hadn't realized was so normal until Gabe's anchor had appeared.

Gabe's anchor? That was romantic fairy-tale stuff that rarely led to happily-ever-after. They'd had one perfect night, but that did not qualify as an anchor.

But as she looked over at him, Tessa's nerves and aching heart calmed slightly. Breathing through the pain of today was easier when he met her gaze.

"Will my cast be really pink?" Natalie's voice was soft, but it broke through Tessa's mental musings.

"Really, really pink—" Tessa grinned "—with sparkles." Having a broken bone wasn't a cause for celebration, but many kids got excited to have a fun color.

"Sparkles?" Gabe opened his mouth, pretending to be shocked by the revelation. Most of the girls who broke a limb asked for sparkle casts and many of the boys, too. Sparkles could make almost anything better. "Now I wish I had a sparkle cast."

"It hurts to get one." Natalie's eyes were damp with unshed tears as she looked toward Gabe. "I wish Momma was here."

A lump stuck in the back of Tessa's throat. Her gaze

flitted to Gabe, willing him to understand that she couldn't answer. She must be more exhausted than she'd realized. Tears threatened to spill into her eyes, too, as she looked at the young girl. She bore so many similarities to Tessa. What if today she joined the terrible club that no child should have a membership to?

Gabe sat on the table with Natalie and tapped the top of her bunny's ears to get her attention. "I called the other hospital before I came in. I have an old friend who works there. Your mommy is going to have to stay with them for a few days, but she is okay." He raised his eyes to meet Tessa's and repeated, "She's okay."

Tessa wasn't sure what strings he'd pulled to get that information, but she was grateful as she watched Natalie exhale. He'd given her the best gift possible. And a pink bunny, too!

"So, let's get your pink sparkle cast ready. That way, when your dad gets here, he can take you to see your mom." Tessa made the statement, then caught her breath. Gabe hadn't said what condition Natalie's mom was in, but she couldn't pull the words back now.

"That cast is a genuine work of beauty." Gabe grinned as Natalie held it up for inspection.

"Yes, it is," a man who looked strikingly like the little girl stated as he stepped through the door.

"Daddy!" Natalie hopped off the bed. "Look what Nurse Davis got for me!" She held the bunny next to her cast. "They're both pink."

"Imagine that." He bent and pulled his daughter close.

Tessa saw him tremble a little as he kissed the top of her head. The ache in her chest opened further as she watched Natalie's father hold her. Tessa's father had been gone for years when she'd lost her mother. She'd never gotten the hugs and comfort that Natalie's father could give her.

Tessa's grandmother had tried, but she'd been consumed with the grief of losing her only child and the added responsibilities of raising her granddaughter. She'd exited retired life, reentered the workforce and done her best for Tessa. But she hadn't been her mother.

The last person who'd held Tessa like that had been gone twenty-three years now. And this year, Tessa was officially older than her mother had ever gotten the chance to be.

"Her mom?"

Tessa felt the words leave her lips. There was no way to recapture them—but even if she could, she wanted to hear that the little girl's mom was all right. If it had been any other day, any other situation, she'd never have asked. But she wanted the confirmation that she'd never gotten as a child.

"Yes, where's Mommy?" Natalie bounced, trying to break the tight hold her father had. She was too little to understand how much he must need to touch her. To convince himself that his little girl was indeed all right—mostly.

"Mommy has broken bones like you. In her left leg. She's going to have to stay in the hospital for a few days, and she'll be in a bigger cast than you." Natalie's dad brushed a piece of hair from her cheek.

"Is hers pink, too?"

Her dad chuckled as he shook his head. "I bet she wishes it was. But nope. Just a plain white cast."

Gabe made a motion to Tessa, and she nodded to him. They needed to give this little family a few minutes together. Just before she closed the door, Tessa turned and looked at the father and daughter. Their embrace sent chills through her. How much she yearned for just the comfort of a hug. The comfort of knowing there was someone who noticed that she wasn't okay. A little wish that was so far out of reach.

CHAPTER FIVE

GABE STOOD IN front of Tessa's town house holding a box of cupcakes, hoping she wouldn't care that he'd just shown up. He'd tried to catch her after their shifts ended, but she'd vanished the second they could clock out. So he'd grabbed the box of cupcakes from a bakery by his sister's house, raced to Stacy's, showered and then come here.

He wasn't sure what was going on, but Gabe needed to see that she was okay. Something about the accident on the highway had touched Tessa more deeply than a stack of badly injured patients. That was not the memory that Gabe was going to let linger on her birthday.

Besides, even if they hated the day, no one should be alone on their birthday. Particularly after a day like today.

Medical professionals faced more bad days than most. It was a career field ripe with impressive highs. They occasionally got to witness miracles, but those highs came with devastating lows when the unthinkable occurred. Medical staffers were forced to develop coping mechanisms.

He always spent more time lifting weights when the weeks were going poorly. Not because lifting heavy things made him feel better, but because the pain in his aching muscles drowned out the other racing thoughts.

And pushing his body made him feel a little more invincible in a world where invincibility was a true illusion.

He didn't know Tessa's self-care routine, but whatever it was, she shouldn't do it alone. *Not today.*

The tears in Tessa's eyes as she watched Natalie hug her dad had cut across Gabe's heart. Tessa was hurting—aching—and he longed to reach out to her. But there wasn't an easy option at the hospital.

She needed someone. And he was done waiting for the perfect time. He was here for her—in any way she wanted.

Gabe was lucky. He had his family to walk beside him when the world turned upside down. She'd told him on the first night he'd seen her that there was no one in her life to protect her. No one to shoulder the trauma that a day like today would bring. It had troubled him then.

But it pulled at him now. If she'd let him, maybe Gabe could be that person.

Nerves chased up his spine as he made his way to her door. He wanted to be the shoulder she cried on, the one she danced in the kitchen with, the one who made her laugh and smile.

But if Tessa didn't want the same, he'd find a way to settle for being her friend. Tessa belonged in his life. He was certain of that.

The chime echoed through the door, and Gabe straightened his shoulders as his stomach flopped with nervous and excited energy.

"Just a moment." Tessa's voice sounded strange on the other side of the door, or maybe it was just the door making it sound like it was breaking up. His heart burned as he waited for her to open the barrier between them.

"Gabe?" Tessa's voice shook, and her cheeks were tearstained when her gaze met his. "What are you—"

Her gaze floated to the pink box in his hand. "Are those Maggie's cupcakes?"

"Yes." The tear streaks worried him. How long had she been crying? Maybe he shouldn't have taken the detour for pastries.

But her gaze brightened as she leaned toward the pink box. He flipped the lid open, and his soul eased as Tessa's body relaxed some.

He hadn't known which flavor was her favorite, so each of the cupcakes was different. They made a pretty display in the bubble gum–colored box. If the confectionery treats got him in the door to help her, he'd frequent Maggie's bakery more often. His nieces and nephews would love that!

"You didn't have to bring me cupcakes." Tessa offered a weak smile as she stepped back to let him in. "But I'm glad you're here."

"Today was rough." Gabe looked over his shoulder as he headed toward her kitchen. "You ran out before I could check on you. So..." He shrugged. "Figured a sweet treat might soothe away a few of the day's rough edges."

"So this isn't a birthday celebration?" Tessa cocked her head as she stared at him.

Raising his right hand, he grinned. "I promise these are only half birthday treats."

She let out a light chuckle as she grabbed the coffee cupcake and held it up. "Only half? So what's the other half?"

"You seemed upset earlier. So these are 'make sure Tessa is okay' treats." Gabe studied her as she sat across from him. Her eyes were red, and there were exhaustion pockets under them. She was tired and sad, and he was here to relieve as many burdens as she wanted to drop at his feet.

Tessa mattered to him. And he wanted her to know that. Needed her to know that.

"My mom died today." Tessa let out a soft sob as she pulled the wrapper off her cupcake. Her fingers trembled, and she set the cupcake down on its paper wrapper. Like she was afraid the confectionery wonder might tip out of her shaky grip.

Gabe's tongue was momentarily frozen as he tried to process that statement. What had she been doing at the hospital today?

"What can I do?" Gabe reached for her hand. His heartbeat steadied as her long fingers wrapped around his. He hoped he had the same calming effect on her that she had on him.

"Oh." Tessa squeezed his palm, and she didn't let go. "I meant this is the anniversary of her death. It's been twenty-three years. But this—"

She blew out a breath and stared at her ceiling for a second, trying to compose herself, like there was any shame in mourning someone years after they'd departed. He still took the day off on the anniversary of Olive's passing.

"It's okay." His thumb rubbed along the delicate skin just below her wrist. He knew what small connections to others meant. How it grounded you when it felt like everything else in the world was unhinged.

She ran her free hand under her nose and shook her head. "I'm not usually such a watering pot. I swear. I guess…" She shrugged and looked out the window. "I'm older than her today. Every birthday, starting with this one, marks a year she never saw. It feels weird. That probably sounds silly."

"No." Gabe let go of her hand and moved around the counter. He pulled her into his arms and just held her.

She let out another sob, and then another as he tightened his grip. She laid her head against his shoulder, and he felt the tension melt from her shoulders. He'd hold her for as long as she needed.

After several minutes, she let out a deep breath and pulled back. "Thanks. I needed that hug. But this is probably not what you expected when you brought cupcakes over." She tried to smile as she headed back to her seat, but only the tips of her lips moved. She reached for her cupcake and took a big bite.

"These are so good." She let out a sigh, but no tears hovered in her eyes.

"Happy to help. I'm here for you." Gabe waited until she met his gaze. "Any time you need it. I am here, hugs and all."

"Thank you." Tessa lifted the cake to her lips. "To sugar and—" her cheeks darkening "—friends."

Gabe swallowed the knot in his throat as he grabbed the double chocolate cupcake. That wasn't the term he wanted to use. But he wasn't going to push, at least not tonight.

She took a big bite of the pastry. "I love Maggie's!" She quickly finished the treat and looked at the box. "It's my birthday, and I am having another."

She sighed before grabbing the lemon cupcake. "I usually take the day off at the hospital. But with Dr. Lin's job potentially opening, everything gets monitored, discussed…dissected. I didn't want to take any unnecessary leave."

Unnecessary leave?

Recharging yourself on a difficult anniversary was not something he'd describe as unnecessary. He knew Tessa was interested in the job, but she still had years left at the hospital. If she didn't get the position, others would open. Why the focus on this one?

"Today is always difficult. But the accident—" Tessa's words drifted away as she met his gaze.

"You lost her in a car accident?"

Tessa spun the lemon cupcake around. Her gaze focused on the edible pearl beads decorating the light yellow frosting. Her mind seemed a million miles away, but Gabe wasn't going to draw her back. She'd tell him in her own time—or she wouldn't. Either way, he was here for her.

"She had two jobs, and she'd worked sixteen hours a day for almost two weeks. After my father left us, the bills were piled high and—" Another tear spilled down her cheek as she raised her eyes to meet his.

"Mom fell asleep. For just a minute, but that was enough. We drifted across two lanes of traffic. I screamed. She woke, but it was too late to course-correct. Twenty-three years ago, I waited at Dallas Children's with a broken arm, clutching a stuffed elephant that a nurse procured for me. Except when my grandma came to get me, my mom was gone." She hiccuped as she shook her head.

"I should have told Mom it was all right that I didn't have a birthday cake or present. That we didn't need to go get anything. Not that it would have mattered." Tessa hugged herself and sighed. "She didn't want her daughter to miss out on the birthday fun. She was a very determined woman. And caring."

"Just like her daughter." He was glad she had such fond memories of her mother. That the traits she used could so easily describe Tessa, too. "I'm sure she would be proud of everything you've done."

She pulled at the collar of her deep blue T-shirt before dipping her finger in the frosting and lifting it to her lips. "I like to think so. Mom was in her first year of med school when she found out she was pregnant with me. My parents married and followed my father's sales job to Dallas. She never got to be a surgeon, but I like to think my successes are both of ours.

"So how do you like to spend your birthday, Gabe?" Tessa held up the lemon cupcake. "I assume it's more celebratory than cupcakes and tears."

"Movie night." Gabe winked. "An enormous pile of popcorn and a list of streaming titles."

"Well, that sounds lovely." Her eyes met his, and he saw a touch of the sadness give way to something different.

"Name the time and place, Tessa. I'll bring the popcorn." He grabbed the mint cupcake and dipped his finger into the icing.

Tessa's eyes widened, and she wagged a finger. "You're going to regret that!"

"Did you want the mint cupcake?" Gabe playfully started to offer his finger full of icing to her before remembering that *that* was more flirtatious than the night's conversation allowed. Trying to ignore the heat in his face, Gabe devoured the icing.

Tessa grabbed his hand. The warmth from the connection burned as she held him. *Does she feel it, too?*

Her eyes sparkled as she held his fingers up. "See!" She pointed to his bright green finger and laughed as Gabe felt his mouth slide open.

"How?"

Tessa continued giggling; her laughs made his green finger completely worth it. She wiped a happy tear from her cheek and held up the cupcake. "It's called the Minty

Monster because they use so much food coloring in the icing that it stains anything it touches."

"The voice of experience?" Gabe leaned closer to her. Even with the tough conversations they'd had, the tears and green finger, there was no place Gabe would rather be tonight.

"The first time, my teeth were green for almost an entire day!" Tessa leaned closer, but still not near enough. Like they were magnets circling in an orbit, able to feel the pull of the other, but not close enough to get yanked together.

Yet.

"That cupcake is a kid and teenage favorite, so the bakery doesn't adjust the recipe. They make hundreds for Halloween. I always bring a dozen for the staff. The kids love our green mouths!"

She swallowed and met his gaze. "I really appreciate you coming tonight. It's been a long time since anyone noticed that I wasn't okay." She pushed a loose strand of hair behind her ear, and her gaze drifted to his lips just briefly. "And even longer since someone went out of their way to make me feel better."

"Any time." Gabe forced the words out. They were true. But he was in danger of getting lost in the depths of her eyes again.

Before he could follow up, Tessa reached for his hand. "You said today that life was too short not to make everyone feel special. Is that why you came tonight…to make a friend feel special?"

The air crackled around them as he searched for the right words. In the end, the words refused to materialize. So he just let his heart talk.

"Life is too short not to do your best to make others realize that they matter." Gabe rubbed the delicate skin along her wrist, grateful when she didn't pull back. "But no. That's not why I showed up on your doorstep with five gourmet cupcakes and one green icing bomb!"

She bit her lip as she waited for him to continue.

"I wanted to check on you. I *needed* to make sure you were okay." Gabe rested his head against hers, measuring the subtle changes in her breath. "You matter to me. I have wished a thousand times that I'd called you after we were together. That I'd invited you to breakfast with my family that morning. That I'd told you how much I enjoy just being near you. I've spent the last week trying to figure out the best way to ask you to dinner."

"Wow." Tessa sighed as she moved around the counter and slid next to him. "That was quite the pronouncement. I wish I'd called you, too. You matter to me, also."

His heart skipped a beat, not sure it could trust the statement. He wanted to pull her close, but there was a glint in her eye that stilled his hand.

"Can I ask you a question?" Tessa's voice was quiet as she crossed her arms.

Nerves raced around him, but Gabe nodded. "Anything."

"Did you not call because of my excitement over Dr. Lin's job?"

"Yes." Gabe let the truth rest between them. "And that wasn't fair to you. My mom left us like your father deserted you. Her career mattered more than her family. After our night together, seeing you dancing around the kitchen for a promotion made me nervous. And I'm sorry. That was wrong."

Tessa nodded, her lip twisting between her teeth. "I'm going for that position, Gabe." She pulled her arms tighter. "If that's a problem then we can just be friends. I won't hold it against you. I promise. But my ex demanded I refuse a similar position at a hospital in Ohio two years ago. I turned down that job for a man, and I won't do it again."

He blew out a breath as that truth sank between them. No wonder she hadn't called him! But he wasn't going to make the same mistake as her ex-husband. "It's not a problem." Gabe pushed a curl behind her ear. "And it shouldn't have been a problem then. I panicked."

Tessa let her fingers lace through his. "Life at the hospital is hectic, and my schedule is…" She squinted as she looked for a word.

"Jam-packed?" Gabe offered.

"Yes." She nodded. "But I want to give this a try. Give us a try."

The air rushed from his lungs and Gabe couldn't remember the last time he'd smiled so much. His heart rang with joy as his brain echoed tiny warning bells, but they were easy to ignore when Tessa was touching him.

He should reach for this. He wanted to grab this! Life was too short to wait for happiness.

"Are you free Friday night?" Gabe ached to kiss her, to taste her again, but he sensed hesitation in Tessa, and he wouldn't rush this. If he was going to risk his heart again, then he wasn't going to give Tessa any reason to doubt him.

"No." Her bottom lip pushed out as she looked at him. "But I'm free Sunday. Have you ever been to the Dallas Botanical Garden?"

"Not since I was in high school." Gabe smiled. "But I'd love to see it this weekend."

"Then it's a date." Tessa beamed as she leaned closer, her arms wrapped around his neck as she held him tight.

"Yes, it is," Gabe confirmed as he relished her body next to his. *Tessa.*

He ran a thumb along her cheek, grateful to get a second chance with this incredible woman.

When her lips met his, Gabe's body rejoiced. It wasn't the passionate need they'd experienced weeks ago. No, this kiss was comforting, and it spoke of tomorrow's promise.

It was perfect.

When she pulled back, he dropped a kiss along her cheek. "I'll see you at the hospital tomorrow."

Then he kissed the top of her head. "Happy birthday, Tessa."

CHAPTER SIX

"THIS PLACE IS bigger than I remember." Gabe's gaze wandered across the large parking lot.

Tessa bumped his hip with hers, enjoying the feel of his arm around her waist. They were on a date. Her heart felt like it might leap from her chest. She and Gabe were on a date.

"There are twenty-two gardens in all. At Christmas they set up twelve mock Victorian shops and houses to represent the twelve days of Christmas. The whole garden is sixty-six acres in total!" She bit back the other facts that wanted to pour from her lips.

This was one of her favorite places. She could recite as many facts as the volunteer tour guides who worked each of the gardens.

She'd wanted to be married here. But Max had balked at the notion. He wasn't going to contend with the garden's guests on their special day. Tessa had been hurt, but after her marriage had failed, she'd been grateful. At least she didn't have any poor memories here.

It felt right that she was here with Gabe. Tessa knew this was only their first date—their first real date, anyway—but she couldn't stop the smile spreading across her face as they crossed the threshold of the first garden.

"Sixty-six acres." Gabe squeezed her side as they wandered through the main entrance. "That's a lot of garden. So what other facts are popping around your brain, Tessa?"

"Am I that transparent?" She pulled him toward the Margaret Elizabeth Jonsson Color Garden.

"Transparent?" Gabe shook his head as he squeezed her waist. "You are basically bouncing. This is a place you have clearly been before—a lot, I'd wager."

Leaning her head against his shoulder, Tessa sighed as she drank in the peaceful settings. Even when the garden was full of families and picnic-goers, it always seemed like she was in her own bubble when she was here. Except now, Gabe was in her bubble, too. And that felt so right.

"I've been a member since I was a student in college. I used to come here to study on the grass yards. It's my happy place. Spring is my favorite. The tulips bloom for acres in the Color Garden. And you see everyone from brides-to-be, to girls celebrating their quinceañera, to moms and dads trying to snap the perfect picture of their rambling tots among the blossoms."

She used to dream of bringing her own small kids here. *But maybe...* Tessa pressed that bubble of hope away. This was their first date. It might feel like more because of their fiery first night, but she was not going to hope too much.

Clearing her throat, she pointed around the open space. "Right now it's got banana and tapioca plants in bloom. In a few weeks, it will be painted orange and purple with chrysanthemums."

"Really?" Gabe's gaze was focused on the field of colors before them.

Tessa swallowed the other plant information that was running through her brain. She'd had a thriving garden at the house she and Max sold. When she'd packed up her final things, she'd stood over the blooms she'd patiently coaxed from seedlings and cried. She'd driven by the house only once since her divorce and been horrified by the condition of her plants.

Except they weren't her plants anymore.

Her town house didn't really have the space for a large garden. She had a few ferns on her porch, but it wasn't the same. But she'd been doing some research on apartment gardens and she was pretty sure she could figure out a way to make a small green space happen.

"Sorry, I have a tendency to go overboard when talking plants." She pressed her free hand to her lips, willing all the things she wanted to say to stay buried.

"You don't need to apologize for being excited about something."

Gabe met her gaze and Tessa felt her spirit lift. It was such a small thing, to have someone willingly listen to her go on about the thing she enjoyed most. To care that she was excited.

"So, what's your favorite flower?"

"It's not here." Tessa leaned her head against his shoulder. Months ago, she'd come here on her own to see the tulips—and been painfully aware of how alone she was. This felt much more like an intimate day between long-term partners, and that should terrify her, but it was impossible to be worried when she was in her happy place... with Gabe.

"It's called Henry Duelberg salvia. It's drought-resistant and a deep bluish-purple. When you plant it in a bed, it will spread out, and—" Tessa watched Gabe's features shift. She always went overboard with plants. "Was that too much information?"

He chuckled and kissed her cheek. "Nope. But I was hunting for information on what types of blooms I might bring in the future that would make the smile you have right now appear."

"Oh." Tessa shook her head as they wandered towards the statues in A Woman's Garden. "I'm not sure there's a flower or plant you could bring me that wouldn't put a smile on my face. Though lantana does smell like gasoline if you brush against it, so maybe not that one."

Gabe pulled her into the shade and ran a hand along her cheek. "What if I leave it up to a florist to tell me which flowers will work, or maybe I'll grab some bundles at the grocery store? Those will look pretty enough on your table—at least until I learn the difference between lantana, salvia and roses, right?"

Learn the difference... Her eyes misted. She wasn't sure why she was so prone to waterworks these days, but she didn't care. She dropped a light kiss on his cheek. How had she gotten so lucky to be walking next to this man in her favorite place?

"Right," Tessa breathed out. But it wasn't Gabe's mention of a florist or his desire to make sure she had flowers that made joy race through her. It was his easy use of the word *future*. As though there would be more perfect moments like this to look forward to.

As a thrill rocketed through her, fear trickled behind it, too. Max had been interested early on, too. He'd never asked her favorite flower, but he'd been supportive of the garden she'd tended, helped her dig the beds and cooked dinner when she had to work late. She'd done her fair share, too, but when she'd gotten ahead, she'd asked him to take on a little more. And he'd hated her for it.

But as Gabe dropped his lips to hers, joy conquered fear—at least temporarily.

His touch was light, and Tessa craved more. Pulling him closer, she deepened the kiss. The gardens were lovely, romantic and the perfect place to kiss Gabe. Actually, the bar they'd reconnected in had felt perfect, too. She suspected every place might seem perfect when she was with him.

Gabe.

Her body molded to his as he stroked her back.

"Aren't they cute?"

Gabe pulled back and Tessa felt her cheeks heat as she caught a few knowing looks from others walking past them. She'd smiled at many lovers who'd worn expressions of contentedness, too—but never been caught kissing in the gardens herself. It was a memory she knew she'd treasure.

Before she or Gabe could say anything, Tessa's phone buzzed. "Sorry." She pulled it out of her pocket.

"No, it's fine." His voice was breathless as he turned to look at the flowers.

Knowing that she could make the handsome, sweet, generous man beside her swoon made her euphoric. She quickly glanced at the text and typed out a reply.

"Everything okay?" Gabe's fingers were warm as they ran along her side.

Slipping her phone back in her pocket, Tessa grinned. "One of the residents ran into a case today that they had some questions on. They want me to look over their notes tomorrow and give them some feedback."

An emotion played across his face that sent a bead of worry pulsing through her. Many people took work calls on their off day. "I'm always available to help."

His lips twitched before Gabe nodded. "That's nice." He kissed her cheek as they started down the walking path. His eyes were far away, though his gaze was focused on the flowers in front of them.

Another twinge of uncertainty washed through her. Was

he upset that so many people at the hospital relied on her? Had he not really meant it the other night when he said it shouldn't have mattered that she was so excited about the job opportunity? Max had done that—encouraged her to put in for promotions, then gotten upset when she got them.

No. Gabe was not Max. She would not let intrusive thoughts ruin this beautiful day and her time with Gabe.

She pointed out a few more of her beloved locations. Gabe nodded along and even asked questions. The disquiet that never quite left Tessa was silenced as they walked back to the car. Mostly.

"How did we manage to close the restaurant down?"

Tessa's laugh as they walked up to her town house door sent a thrill through him. After their day at the garden, Gabe had suggested they grab a quick dinner. *Quick.* He let out a soft chuckle, too.

"It really didn't feel like we'd been there for several hours." Gabe had made sure to leave the waiter a sizable tip for hogging the table for most of the evening. It had been unintentional, but he couldn't be sorry for it. Time just flew when he was with the woman beside him.

Tessa put her key in the door and turned the lock. Her dark eyes held his gaze as she leaned against the door. "I had the best time today, Gabe."

She leaned in, her soft kiss igniting flames of need through his body. Her fingers ran along his stomach, and Gabe ached with desire. *Tessa.*

She pulled back and let out a breath. "I…" Tessa bit her lip. Her cheeks flamed. "I know our first night…"

Gabe dropped another kiss on her lips, then he smiled. If she invited him inside, he'd gladly carry her to bed and worship each inch of her again. But there was no need to rush anything. Gabe wanted Tessa for more than a one-night fling; he'd wait however long she needed to advance their relationship. "I'm in no rush, sweetheart."

He pushed a curl behind her ear, enjoying the heat of her skin beneath his fingers. He'd wait a lifetime for the woman in front of him, though he hoped it wouldn't be that long.

Tessa laid her head against his chest and sighed. "I had the best time today. The best."

Her repetition made his insides melt. *Best.* "I did, too, Tessa."

Wrapping his arms around her waist, Gabe kissed the top of her head, enjoying the feel of her against him. Then the top of her pants vibrated.

Another text message from the hospital?

During their date, she'd gotten at least ten messages or calls from interns and residents. Gabe had worked in the medical field for years and he understood that it was a calling to many. But Tessa was so tied to Dallas Children's.

No. He was not going to tumble down the path of worry. Tessa was helping, not trying to advance herself on the backs of others. And she didn't reach for the phone as he held her.

But Gabe couldn't hold her on her porch all night. No matter how much he might want to. Running his hand along the edge of her jaw, Gabe waited until she looked at him, then he dropped another kiss to her lips.

He didn't rush the kiss or deepen it. It was soft, and comforting, and full of the promise of more. So much more.

Pulling away, Gabe forced himself to take a step back, otherwise he might never make it off her stoop. "I can't wait to see you again, Tessa."

Her face lit with excitement. "I can't wait either, Gabe. Good night."

* * *

Tessa spun the scrambled eggs around on her plate and tried to calm the tumble of her stomach. She forced herself to take another bite. Protein was important, and she was just starting her shift, but her stomach twisted again. Maybe the extra dessert she and Gabe had ordered during their extended dinner last night had been a mistake.

She enjoyed sweets, but her body was not as acclimated to the sugar as Gabe's. Electricity shot across her as she thought of him. Of their kisses on her porch.

Her body still ached with desire. Her dreams had all tumbled with images of him in her bed. Kisses and passion had lit through her sleep.

Until early this morning. After a peaceful night, she'd woken with a start from a nightmare. The remnants of the dream had faded quickly, but she remembered Gabe walking away from her after she received the promotion. It was just a product of an overactive subconscious. He'd said that he shouldn't have let the promotion keep him from asking her out. But the notch of uncertainty in the back of her mind refused to vanish.

The smell of the eggs made her queasy as she tossed her plate in the trash. Before she left the cafeteria, Tessa thought of grabbing a container of yogurt or a banana. But just looking at them made her stomach want to revolt. What was going on? Tessa rubbed her hand along her belly and started toward the nursing desk.

"Are you all right, Dr. Garcia?" Denise stared at her as Tessa reached for the thermometer.

Tessa's stomach lurched again, and she took a deep breath through her nose, trying to gather herself. "I'm not sure." She ran the thermometer along her forehead and sighed as it read ninety-eight point three. "No fever."

Her belly danced again, and she paged Dr. Killon.

He was on call today. Even with no fever, she wouldn't be able to stay if her stomach was going to betray her. Most rotaviruses didn't present with a fever, but they were highly contagious—and often carried by children.

"Maybe my stomach just really wasn't in the mood for omelets today, but I've paged Dr. Killon." Her brain felt foggy as she uttered the words. Her overactive dreams must have kept her from truly resting—though she was not sorry to have spent the night dreaming of Gabe.

Denise nodded but kept her distance. The cleaning schedule at Dallas Children's was intense, but hospitals were breeding grounds for germs. "Shame, I love omelets. I ate them every Saturday until I was pregnant with Ginger. That little one hated eggs, though you'd never know it now!"

She grabbed a chart tablet. "I hope you feel better soon, Dr. Garcia."

"Thank you." Tessa barely forced the words through her lips as Denise's statement registered. *Pregnant...that is not possible.*

Except it might be. Tessa's nails dug into her palms as she calculated her last period. Two weeks before she and Gabe had been together. They'd used protection, but the condoms had been older, and protection wasn't perfect. She'd been busy, focused on the upcoming job opportunity, but how had she not noticed that she was so late?

She pressed her hands into her side as she felt her entire body start to shake. She needed to get out of here. Needed to gain control of herself—needed to stop by a pharmacy. What was she going to do?

One foot in front of the other. The mantra did little to calm her racing heartbeat as she started toward the employee lounge. If she was pregnant, she'd be almost eight weeks along. Over halfway through her first trimester.

Her hands were clammy as she reached the lounge and pulled on her locker door.

Eight weeks along. That meant she'd spent most of her first trimester unaware of the little bean. She quickly racked her mind, trying to think through the last several weeks. She'd had alcohol the night she and Gabe… Her face heated at the memories.

Clearing her throat, she offered a short wave to a nurse as she headed for the parking garage. No alcohol since conception, but her caffeine habit had been maintained. Still, that wouldn't matter much at this early stage. And she hadn't been taking any prenatal vitamins.

Her chest tightened as she slid into the car. Prenatal vitamins were important, but many women started them after they discovered they were pregnant. The thought sent another wave of panic through her as she gripped her steering wheel. How was she calmly running through the checklist in her mind while her body was locked in terror?

She was probably overthinking this. In a few hours, she'd laugh at herself, order herself to look into stress relief tactics, and make an appointment with her gynecologist. It had been far too long since she'd seen Dr. Fillery anyway.

Her heart rocked a little at the idea that she might not be pregnant. She bit her lip as it started to tremble. That shouldn't make her upset—it shouldn't.

So why were tears coating her eyes?

Tessa forced air into her lungs as she tried to calm her aching heart. She'd wanted to be a mother for so long. To have a few little ones to come home to. But this wasn't the way she'd imagined it happening.

She and Gabe had decided to turn their one-night stand into something more. To see if the chemistry igniting them meant what they hoped. Yesterday had been so perfect, and Tessa was already looking forward to their next date. How might an unplanned pregnancy change the mixture?

And Dr. Lin was filing his retirement paperwork next week—or maybe the week after that. Though all those rumors had been false so far.

She was not prepared for a baby. This was not the right time. But her heart didn't seem to care.

Tessa rolled her free hand over the still-flat portion of her lower belly. She knew it was far too early to feel anything—assuming she even was pregnant. But she was protective of the potential life growing inside her.

Her child.

She could do this.

Whatever this might be.

The tile floor in her bathroom was cold and hard, but she didn't feel like moving. Not yet. In the two hours it had taken her to buy a pregnancy test—four pregnancy tests, actually—Tessa had managed to convince herself that she'd been overreacting. But the double blue line on three of the tests did not lie.

She stared at the unopened fourth box. The urge to open it and confirm what the other three had stated was almost overwhelming. Rolling her head from side to side, she pushed back at that desire. The fourth test would only confirm what the second and third had.

Her life was changing. *And Gabe's life is changing, too.*

As if just her thoughts were enough to summon him, her phone buzzed.

You okay? Dr. Killon said you were sick.

Her fingers shook as she laid the phone aside. She should respond, should say she was fine. But was she?

Yes. No. Yes. The words spiraled through her mind as she pulled her knees to her chest. Laying her head against them, Tessa stared at her phone as another message popped in.

Let me know if you need anything.

It was such a sweet offer. The kind Gabe made—and meant—without even thinking. What was he going to do? If they'd known each other longer, today's revelations wouldn't cause her such worry.

Gabe was going to be an amazing father. Tessa swallowed. Assuming this was an adventure he wanted to take, too.

Wrapping her hands around her waist, Tessa tried to ignore the worry rooting its way through her mind. She didn't think Gabe would step away from her and their unexpected family. But her father had told her mother that he wanted a family when she'd discovered she was pregnant with Tessa. He'd promised to take care of them both, had professed a desire to be a family man. Then he'd abandoned them. And her ex-husband had discarded Tessa with little thought, too.

And she'd survived that, she reminded herself. She was strong, independent and caring, just like her mother. This wasn't the path to motherhood that she'd expected, but Tessa was going to show her child that they could do it all. No matter what.

Her child would never question that they were loved, wanted and treasured. Tessa laid her hands over the stillness of her belly and sighed. "I will always protect you."

At least she knew why she'd been such an emotional

watering pot over the last few days. Taking a deep breath, Tessa tried to force her racing mind to focus. There were many things she needed to figure out. Things to do. Slapping her knees, she stood up.

Picking up her phone, she called her ob-gyn and walked to the kitchen. Pulling a glass down, she quickly swallowed her prenatal vitamin and started a small grocery list while she waited on hold. Then she texted Gabe and asked him to come over.

The text was vague; she didn't want to give too much away. Particularly since Tessa hadn't figured out the right words yet. But this was not news that she wanted to relay over text or phone. He deserved to hear that he was going to be a father in person.

They were going to be parents.

Parents.

Gabe spun his phone around as he waited at the traffic light six blocks from Tessa's townhome. He was barely holding to his pledge to ignore his cellular device while in the car but he'd already memorized Tessa's cryptic texts. All four sentences.

We need to talk. Can you please come over after your shift?

He'd sent her a text back saying that he wasn't off until ten, but she'd responded to that, too.

I know. It's not something I want to put off.

Are you all right?

She'd read his last message three hours ago, according to his phone, and not responded. His hands were clammy as he gripped the steering wheel.

They'd had an excellent time at the gardens. The daytime date had spilled into a lovely evening. He'd thought it was perfect. Surely this wasn't a maybe-we-really-should-just-be-friends talk?

Could she really be having second thoughts?

Please, his soul whispered. He didn't want to give up on the possibilities his heart was painting.

He pulled into the small alley and tried to ignore the blood pounding in his ears and the tightness in his chest. What was waiting for him in Tessa's home? Gabe wiped his hands along the jeans he'd changed into after his shift, then forced himself to head to her back door.

The deck furniture where they'd sat so many weeks ago made him smile. That memory would always be good. *No matter what happened now.*

Her back door flung open, and Tessa stood in the bright light. Her shoulders were stiff, but he saw her fingers flex slightly. Something was bothering her. What had happened in less than twenty-four hours to make her so stressed?

"How are you feeling?" he asked as she stepped back to let him in. Denise had mentioned that Tessa's stomach had been upset, but Tessa looked all right now—at least physically.

A little tired, maybe. Her dark eyes met his. Worry floated across her gaze, but hope was there, too. That eased part of his concern, but only a little.

"I'm better now. Thanks for coming."

"Anytime." He hoped she knew how much he meant that. If she needed him, he'd be there for her. Gabe reached for her hand, and his heart loosened as she let him hold it.

"I'm pregnant."

The world shifted under his feet as Gabe tried to process the words. "Pregnant." His voice was barely above a whisper. "Pregnant?" He repeated. He should have said something else. Anything else, but the word just kept bouncing through his brain.

Tessa let go of his hand and moved toward the living room. "I'm sorry. I had an entire speech planned. I should have asked you to sit down." She sat on the end of the couch and drew her knees under herself as she motioned for him to sit on the other end.

She wanted him to take a seat, but not too close to her. Gabe tried not to let that sting. He was dealing with the news, but Tessa had only known for a few hours, too. Their lives were changing, but it would be okay.

He was going to be a dad. A sense of peace washed through him. *I'm going to be a dad.*

Excitement bubbled within him until he looked at Tessa's pale face. Was she not excited? This was a big change for him, but an even bigger one for her. What if she didn't want to be a mom?

Before he could let that concern take root, he let out a deep breath.

"You don't have to be involved." Tessa's voice was soft, but the words cut him. "I've worked everything out. I'll—we'll—be okay if this isn't something you want." Her fingers shook as she gripped her knees. "I know we've not discussed the future too much."

"I am not going anywhere, Tessa." Gabe was stunned as she let out a deep sigh. They'd only known each other a few weeks, but surely she knew him well enough to know that he wouldn't turn away from his child. *From her.*

Tessa nodded and pulled her knees even farther up— which he hadn't thought possible. "I know this wasn't planned. I don't want you to feel trapped. Our first *real* date was yesterday. I know we talked about another—"

"Do you not want another date? Because this news does not change that for me." Gabe slid next to her on the couch. She might not be ready to relax yet, but Gabe was here whenever she un-cocooned herself.

Tessa looked at him, her eyes watering as she held his gaze. But the edge of a smile hovered on her lips.

"Are you okay? Denise said you looked positively green this morning."

"The baby doesn't like eggs." Tessa sent a small glare down to her belly, but it was followed by a brilliant smile. "Guess it's toast for right now."

"I bet the little bean will change his or her mind in a few years."

Tessa's bright grin sent a thrill through him.

"That's what I called the baby this morning. Little bean." She pulled her knees out from under herself but didn't slide any closer to Gabe. "I know I kind of sprang this on you. If you change your mind, I won't hold you to tonight's decisions. This certainly isn't how normal get-to-know-you dating starts."

Gabe couldn't argue with that, but he didn't care. He'd always wanted to be a father. This might not be the path he'd planned to walk, but he'd never turn his back on his child, or on Tessa. He hated the doubt he still saw floating in her expression.

"I won't change my mind, Tessa." Gabe laid his arm on the back of the couch, not touching her, but he hoped she viewed the open gesture as an invitation to move closer. "I've always wanted a family." It was the truth. He hadn't thought it was possible after he'd lost Olive, but staring at the woman across from him, Gabe couldn't be anything other than excited.

They were going to be parents. Parents!

He wanted, needed, her to know that he wasn't going

anywhere. This was where he wanted to be. "I was stunned when you first told me. I'll admit I came over here fully expecting you to tell me we were not going to have another date, and I already reserved tickets for the holiday festival at the botanical gardens."

"You did?" Her mouth slipped into the small O shape that he'd found so enticing a few weeks ago. "That's months away. What if something goes wrong?"

His hand reached for hers, and his body relaxed as she let him hold it. He'd never tire of touching her. "Yes. It is months away. But I purchased them from my phone as soon as I got to my car last night. I'm banking on the future, Tessa. I want many dates between now and then, but I can't wait to see the Christmas village set up in a few months. Spending time with you is my favorite thing."

Tessa's bottom lip trembled as she slid next to him and put her head against his shoulder.

"Actually, I was wrong. This is my favorite thing. You in my arms."

Her eyes were bright as she looked up at him. "This is my favorite thing, too. And the gardens are beautiful at Christmas. All the lights…"

His hand wrapped around her belly. Over the place where the child slept. They were going to be a family.

"I managed to get an appointment with Dr. Fillery tomorrow afternoon." Tessa looked up at him, and he saw her take a deep breath. "Her office had a last-minute cancellation. I know you're off tomorrow afternoon, too. Do you want to come?"

"Wild horses couldn't keep me away." Gabe sighed as she placed a light kiss on his cheek. Tonight was as close to perfection as he'd experienced in forever. "Want to try a movie night this weekend? See if the baby likes popcorn."

"That sounds lovely." Tessa closed her eyes, and her breathing slowed down as he held her.

"Then it's a date." Gabe kissed the top of her head and leaned his head back against the wall. Life had sent them a new twist, but it was going to be okay. Better than okay!

CHAPTER SEVEN

TESSA LET OUT a yawn and grinned. The smell of breakfast was one of the best things someone could wake to.

But she lived alone.

Her eyes flew open as she sat up. The room spun. Tessa held her head and groaned as her stomach lurched.

"Tessa?" Gabe's voice was strong but laced with worry as she felt him step beside her.

"Gabe?"

What time is it? What is he doing here? Will breakfast taste as good as it smells?

A piece of bread was pressed into her palm.

What is going on?

"Try a couple small bites. Stacy swore by a slice of toast first thing in the morning to curb some of her morning sickness."

Tessa took a bite out of the corner, then looked up. He was really here. "You didn't leave?" He hadn't left after she'd fallen asleep. Had he held her all night long?

They'd slept together again—except this time it had been on her couch. Nothing physical had happened between them, so why did this action feel so much more intimate? So much more permanent?

"I was surprised when I woke up, too." Gabe's lips turned up as he sat beside her. "Not sure how we slept so soundly on your couch, but I guess we were both past the point of exhaustion." His hand lay across her knee. The warmth it carried calmed her as much as the toast.

She let her gaze linger on his hand for a minute. So many things were running through her mind as she finished the piece of toast. He was right; her stomach felt infinitely more secure.

"I should have asked before I went rummaging through the kitchen, but you were still asleep. You barely noticed when I slipped away." He pulled on the back of his neck as he met her gaze. "And with the morning sickness yesterday, I figured—" He looked at her as his words died away.

She kissed his cheek, enjoying the fact that he'd stayed more than she probably should. "You figured you'd help." Tessa smiled.

"It's the thing I do best. Gotta earn my keep." Gabe offered a silly salute. "Do you want some ham? I fried up some in case your stomach was ready for something besides toast."

"Thanks," Tessa answered as she stood. Gabe was next to her, not touching but close.

Was he staying close in case she got dizzy again?

The gesture was sweet, but Tessa felt a touch of worry. They were going to be parents, but she didn't need him to watch her every step. Pregnancy wasn't a disease; it was something women had been doing since before the written word.

"It's nice that you like helping." She leaned against him, enjoying Gabe's strength. It balanced her before she started for the kitchen. She waved him away from the cupboard as she grabbed a few plates. She could fix her own breakfast plate.

"I'm the oldest, remember? I learned early on how to

earn my keep in my large family." His eyes were bright as he watched her grab her breakfast before fixing his own. "Even before my mother walked out, I was more of a third parent to Isla. I swear she's been getting into trouble since the moment she was born."

He let his gaze wander to her belly, and Tessa's cheeks heated. He was happy about this…he really was.

"Isla is going to be thrilled to be an aunt again. She loves to dote on little ones."

She could see the pride radiating off him. Their child would have cousins and aunts and uncles to watch them. A built-in extended family.

But what would *her* place be? She'd let herself be absorbed into Max's friendship group. And when the marriage failed, she'd been pushed out. She and Gabe would always be connected by their little one, but if they didn't work out…

Why was she plotting the worst-case scenario?

Because that was what always happened. Her heart ached at that truth. Just because her father had left her mother and Max had walked away, that didn't mean that her relationship with Gabe was doomed.

Particularly if she made sure that he never felt put upon like Max had.

"Coffee?" Gabe offered as he rummaged through her cabinet.

"I can do that." Tessa got off the stool.

"Just point me in the direction of the coffee filters. It's no big deal."

"What?"

Tessa's blood iced at Gabe's statement. It was the line Max had thrown around constantly when she'd asked him for help. *It's no big deal* had been the phrase she'd learned meant he was in a foul mood, resenting that she'd asked him for help.

"I said point me toward the coffee filters. Oh, never mind!" Gabe spun around holding the stack.

He laid a cup of coffee in front of her.

"Are you okay?" Gabe's gaze hovered on her. His eyes shone with worry.

"Does the little bean not like ham?" Worry lines pressed into the corners of his eyes as he started toward her.

"No." Tessa's voice was stronger than she'd expected. "I just don't gobble up my breakfast." She smiled, hoping it covered the anxiety coursing through her.

He playfully threw a hand across his chest.

The feigning-hurt gesture almost fully lifted her spirits.

"What time is the appointment this afternoon? Think they'll let us see the little one?"

"I hope so." Tessa grinned. She'd love to see the baby. And she couldn't wait to see Gabe's reaction to their child. He was going to love seeing the dancing bean.

At eight weeks there wouldn't be much definition, but she smiled knowing they might get a glimpse of their little one.

She stood and scooped the last bite of ham into her mouth before starting toward the sink.

"I can get that." Gabe held out his hand, waiting for her plate.

"It's fine, Gabe. I can do it." The worry lines reappeared, but he stepped away. She wasn't going to let him do everything for her. No matter how nice it might feel. She was pregnant, but that didn't mean that she needed help.

And she wouldn't risk his future resentment.

"My appointment is at three at the Plano office. Only

the nurse practitioner works in the Dallas office on Tuesday, and I didn't want to wait." Tessa dried the plate and put it back in the cupboard.

"Do you want me to pick you up? I need to at least swing by Stacy's to shower and change clothes." His face brightened as he mentioned his sister.

"I have a few errands beforehand. I'll just head to the doctor from there."

"I don't mind running errands." Gabe smiled.

She wanted to say yes. To ask him to come along. But she was only going to look at maternity clothes. It was still too early for her to need much, but with her hectic schedule, it would be good to have a few things on hand while she had a chance. But picking out stretchy pants was only going to be interesting or fun for her.

Her ex-husband had grumbled even when she'd wanted to make a quick stop, and Tessa suspected this wouldn't be a swift outing. No, she was going to enjoy each moment of this experience. This was an avenue where she could spare Gabe.

His gaze raked across her, but Gabe didn't press. "I'll see you at Dr. Fillery's at two fifty, then."

"Two forty." Her throat was tight as she explained, "I have to be there at two forty to fill out paperwork." She could fill out documents without him, but she didn't tell him that. It was a little thing, but she wanted him there when she walked into the office.

"Then I'll see you at two forty." He stepped next to her, his gaze holding her steady.

Her mind was racing with a million different excitements and more than a few worries, but as she slipped into his arms, her body quieted.

She wrapped her arms around his neck and kissed him, sighing as he pulled her tight. So much had changed over the last few weeks, but her body still reacted to Gabe the same. Still seemed to call out with joy and need as he touched her.

As he walked out, she hugged herself. Suddenly two forty seemed very far away.

Gabe hustled down the stairs of the parking garage. He hadn't expected there to be so much traffic between his sister's place and Plano. He'd been back in the Dallas area for over six months, but he still hadn't gotten used to the increased traffic. Normally, he gave himself extra time to get anywhere, but getting out of his sister's house had been a trial.

Stacy had peppered him with questions when he'd arrived home. She'd wanted to know all about the woman he'd spent the night with twice. And whether they were dating. He understood Stacy's questions and the concern he saw hovering in her eyes—to a point. She didn't want to see him hurt.

But there'd been no way to explain where he was going this afternoon without also saying he was going to be a father. And that conversation would have resulted in his phone blowing up with calls and texts. Secrets were not a thing in the Davis family.

He wasn't quite ready to subject Tessa to that. The Davis clan would love her and gladly initiate her into their crazy brood. But the Davis family was so many things.

Loud, intrusive and loving beyond measure. Overwhelming didn't begin to describe his family.

Tessa would fit in perfectly.

She was a strong, independent woman. But that didn't mean that she didn't need someone to care about her. He wanted to make things easier, particularly now that she was pregnant.

But that urge had been there before he'd found out about their impending bundle. Tessa made him happy. It was as simple—and as complicated—as that.

But what if she didn't want his help?

The worry tickled the back of his brain. That was the thing Gabe did best. He thrived on making sure those he cared about knew they could always ask him for anything. But Tessa had seemed unsettled by it this morning.

He tried to remind himself that she hadn't had someone to look after her. Maybe she just wasn't used to it. But the worry still bounced around his brain as he shuffled around a car in the parking garage.

Tessa could handle anything—Gabe would never doubt that—but it didn't mean she needed to shoulder all the burdens that were coming.

He was an expert at lightening the load. He'd just have to figure out a way to show her that she could rely on him for anything. *Always.*

"You still have a few minutes," Tessa's voice carried across the parking garage.

He spun and felt the small bead of warmth that had nothing to do with the afternoon heat spread through him as she started toward him.

She stepped next to him and hesitated only a minute before sliding her hand into his. "You ready for this?"

"I think so." Gabe matched her stride as they entered the building with at least a dozen different doctor's offices. The blast of air-conditioning sent a shiver through him, and he was glad that Tessa led the way. "I'm a little nervous."

"Me, too. This isn't the exact path I saw myself on to becoming a mom." Tessa's free hand rested over her belly. "But it's exciting." She let out a nervous laugh. "Everything is topsy-turvy, terrifying, happy, and I feel like I'm grasping at marbles as they all drop around me."

Squeezing her hand, he opened the office door she stopped in front of. "I think that's almost everyone's description of having a baby."

Tessa kissed his cheek. "I'm so glad you're here."

His heart sang as he followed her. *Here we go!*

Tessa's vitals were fine, and the nurse asked her the basic questions as Gabe hung to the side. Even though they were both medical professionals, he could see the bit of worry tracing across Tessa as she looked at the heartbeat monitor and gel on the counter. He'd glanced at them several times, too.

It was important for the nurse to get all the details, but waiting to hear the heartbeat was growing harder with each passing second. She was nearing her eighth week. The first trimester was always the riskiest for miscarriage. He knew that as many as 20 percent of known pregnancies ended in miscarriage. They were devastatingly common, which made the relative silence around them sadder.

But the metric also meant that nearly many pregnancies made it to delivery. At seven weeks, almost eight, their child's heartbeat should be strong and bright. But until they heard it, they'd each wonder—and worry.

"Can you lean back for me? This may be cool." The nurse smiled as Tessa lay back.

Gabe leaned closer, his eyes moving from Tessa's face to where their baby was growing. Her belly still betrayed no sign of their impending joy. When Tessa reached for his hand, he grabbed hers and squeezed. The nurse rolled the heartbeat monitor over Tessa's lower abdomen, and they each let out a sigh as a strong beat echoed through the monitor. Then the beat adjusted. The nurse's nose scrunched, and her forehead tightened for just a moment as she lifted the heartbeat monitor. She hid her reaction, but not quick enough.

Tessa's fingers clenched at her sides.

"What is it?" Gabe asked as the nurse lifted the monitor.

The nurse didn't glance at him as she asked Tessa, "How far along did you say you were?"

"Seven weeks—almost eight." Tessa's voice was tight as she stared at the nurse.

"Great." She tapped Tessa's hand. "Dr. Fillery will be in shortly."

It took all Gabe's restraint to keep his seat and not beg her to roll the heartbeat monitor back over Tessa's belly so he could try to catch what she had. As a nurse, he knew that it was the doctor's responsibility to pass along diagnoses, but he also knew that he often knew exactly what was wrong with a child, too. You didn't work in a specialized area without picking up the most common diagnosis capability—and even some less common ones.

He also knew from the look on the nurse's face as she patted Tessa's hand that she wouldn't tell them what was going on. That was the correct procedure, but when it was your baby, the emotions swirling around you felt so different.

He'd learned after losing Olive that life sometimes didn't let you protect those you loved. But Gabe would do everything in his power to protect Tessa and their child. *Anything.*

As soon as the door closed, Tessa's scared gaze met his. "Did you hear whatever made her demeanor shift?"

"No." Gabe shook his head and moved to her side.

Her fingers tightened in his as he squeezed his eyes shut and tried to think through what he'd heard. "I was so focused on the happy sound. The heartbeat sounded strong. Fast—but that's normal at this stage." He knew Tessa knew that, but he was just trying to figure out anything.

"When she rolled it closer to my belly button, it sounded a little slower. But that shouldn't matter. Should it?"

His top knuckle cracked as Tessa squeezed his hand even tighter.

"Sorry." She released him.

Gabe pulled her hand back. "Nothing to apologize for. That's just the result of me cracking my knuckles since I was ten." Lifting her fingers to his lips, Gabe placed a light kiss on her hand. "No matter what, I'm here for you. Okay?"

She nodded her head and stared at the door. "You never realize how long this feels from the other side— huh! We run from patient to patient—usually skipping meal breaks and living on caffeine. But now I want to run out that door and scream for Dr. Fillery to march in here."

Gabe chuckled as Tessa laid her free hand against her forehead. "I'm itching to rip the door open myself. But we are going to be patient, right?"

"I guess." Tessa laid a hand across her belly. "I'm just a ball of nerves."

"A gorgeous ball of nerves." Gabe kissed her fingers again, and a bit of the tension leaked from him. He loved touching Tessa, loved the feel of being near her. No matter what Dr. Fillery came in to discuss, Gabe knew they could handle it. Maybe that was naive given how long they'd known each other, but Gabe couldn't imagine it going any other way. He and Tessa were meant to be in each other's lives. They just were.

He wasn't sure where that certainty came from. But as she met his gaze, warmth burst through him again. She was his second chance. Gabe swallowed as that thought, that knowledge, settled around him.

The door opened and they both straightened. He'd have to work out exactly what that meant some other time.

"What did your nurse hear?" Tessa rushed the words out. "Sorry, she told me her name, but I'm panicking and can't recall."

Dr. Fillery offered a smile as she pulled the portable ultrasound machine toward Tessa. "Meghan thinks she heard two heartbeats."

"Two!" The word flew from Gabe's lips and heat flooded his body as Tessa looked from him to the ultrasound machine. "Sorry."

"It's fine," Dr. Fillery stated. "It may have just been that she caught the baby's heart rate shifting." She dropped more gel on Tessa's abdomen, then picked up the ultrasound wand. "Let's take a look."

Gabe doubted that the nurse had just heard the heartbeat shifting. He couldn't imagine a nurse working in obstetrics and not being able to identify multiple babies' heart rates. It would be like Gabe hesitating to differentiate between the chicken pox, rubella and measles rash. You just knew—even if the doctor passed along the actual notes and follow-up.

It took only a few seconds for the wand to find the sac. Gabe swallowed as he stared at the images on the screen. Two babies in one amniotic sac—identical twins. He was going to be a father...to two!

CHAPTER EIGHT

TWINS! TESSA'S FEET pounded on the tile of her kitchen floor. She hadn't stopped moving since she and Gabe had left the doctor's office.

She was pregnant with twins. *Identical twins.* All multiples carried risks, but identical twins were more likely to be born early and more likely to need the NICU. More likely to result in bed rest for the mother.

Her chest seized. She laid a hand across her belly; the babies were safe right now, and she needed to focus on that. Tessa squeezed her eyes shut and tried to force all the racing thoughts from her mind.

But they refused to vacate the premises.

How was she supposed to raise two at once? Her heart pressed against her chest. Tessa pushed a hand through her curls as she tried to rework everything she'd started.

She'd measured the room she was using as an office this afternoon. Two cribs could fit in there, but it would be tight. And she'd window-shopped for a crib, a high chair and clothes while grabbing a few maternity items, but she'd focused on the safety ratings, not the cost of outfitting two at once. The day care bills alone…

Her chest tightened again. She was not going to panic. At least not any more than she already was.

And the promotion? Her skin prickled as she tried to

remember the meditation tricks she'd learned during her residency. *Breathe...clear your mind.*

Would the human resources department even consider her a candidate now?

That thought wasn't helpful, but it refused to cede its place in her brain. Technically, it wasn't legal for them to discard her résumé due to pregnancy, but there would be no way to prove it.

No. She could be a twin mom and a senior attending in the emergency room. Her maternity leave might be longer than with a single pregnancy, and the possibility of bed rest was higher. The blood pounded in her ears, and Tessa ran her hands along her arms.

Breathe.

She'd just have to double her efforts at the hospital while she could. Her mother had lost her chance for the career she wanted because of an unplanned pregnancy. But it had been a different time, and they hadn't been able to afford day care and med school.

If she hadn't acquiesced to Max's demands, she'd already be a senior attending.

But then you wouldn't have met Gabe. Wouldn't be carrying twins. Wouldn't have this incredible chance at a family.

She couldn't wish that she was in Cincinnati now.

Tessa stroked her belly where two children—*her* children—were currently growing. She was going to take care of them. She could do this. All of it.

"Tessa." Gabe's voice sounded far away. His hand was warm as he grabbed her, and her heart slowed its racing pace. His anchor stabilized her.

"We need to figure this out." Tessa's voice was ragged as she stared at him. "How are you so calm?"

"That isn't an adjective I'd use to describe myself

right now. But I'm trying to think of it as an adventure."
His fingers brushed her cheek before he leaned his head
against hers. "With double the diapers!"

She laughed. It felt good to release some tension. His
rich scent sent a wave of solace through her. "I love how
you smell." The compliment slipped from her lips. She
knew that pregnancy heightened the senses, but it seemed
like such a silly thing to say when they were trying to
determine a path forward.

"That's good to know." Gabe pressed a kiss to her forehead. "I know there's a lot to do. And it seems scary, but
can we focus on the positives for a second?"

"The positives?" Tessa raised an eyebrow. They'd
gone from a one-night stand to parents-to-be, to parents-
of-twins-to-be, before they'd even made it to a second
date. The things that needed to be done looked more like
mountains than minor to-do lists. But as Gabe held her,
the panic that had been on a near-constant rise abated.

"You're healthy and our children are also healthy.
Those two things mean everything." Gabe smiled, his
dimples popping.

She hoped the babies inherited those!

She saw his gaze shift down her body. Tessa squeezed
his hand. Then she laid it over the place where their children were growing.

He dropped a light kiss to her lips. "It's going to be
okay. Our hands may be full, but we can do this—together.
Promise."

His hand sent sparks along her skin, even through the
light gray shirt she wore today. The connection between
them crackled as it had since that first night. He seemed
so certain, so sure that it was going to be all right. So
sure that they had a future. Why couldn't she focus on

that possibility? Maybe everything would work out for her—*finally*.

"So, what do we do first?" Tessa turned to grab a glass of water; she was still a little too keyed up to stay in one place.

"Well, we probably need to alert Human Resources."

"No." Tessa shook her head. "Dr. Lin's position is opening." She was so close to fulfilling her dream. To earning what her mother's unplanned pregnancy had stolen from her. Another chance might not open for several years. At least not at Dallas Children's. And she doubted Gabe would want to move. He was more tied to this area than Max was. Now was her best shot.

"Tessa." Gabe closed his eyes. His lips pursed.

He was frustrated—with her. A shiver of worry pressed against her spine. She wanted to keep this to themselves, at least for a few more weeks, but she hated upsetting Gabe.

She'd watched Max pull away from her whenever he was upset with her. Tessa had learned to control her emotions around her ex. But with pregnancy hormones racing through her, it was harder then ever.

Gabe hadn't reacted poorly to her tears when he'd brought over cupcakes. Hadn't gotten angry at the fear and panic she was displaying or told her to get a hold of herself. He seemed genuinely happy to help.

Maybe relying on him for something wouldn't lead to disaster? Surely he wouldn't blame you for his unhappiness? She felt her eyes widen at that thought. Gabe's eyes shifted, too—the man noticed everything.

"Tessa," Gabe's voice broke as he pulled her to him.

Before he could get any further, she offered, "I'm not through my first trimester. Dr. Fillery said everything was fine, but it's still early. I promise to alert Human Resources when I enter my second trimester."

Maybe by then a decision would have been made about Dr. Lin. She hated the thought. But she owed her mom. And she wanted to be a senior attending.

He pulled back a little and wiped a stray tear from her cheek. He smiled, "Okay. No telling HR until the second trimester."

He dropped a chaste kiss to her lips. "What if you help me look for an apartment? I can't really have the twins over to my sister's place when they're with me. Her couch was getting uncomfortable, anyway."

His statement struck her. *With him.* Tessa hadn't considered that her children would have two homes. The idea of her children being somewhere else brought tears to her eyes—again. *Hormones!*

It was ridiculous. Many people shared custody, but Tessa didn't want that—at least not when they were first born. "What if you moved in here?"

The question shot out, and there was no way to reel it back. Her heart rejoiced while her brain screamed. She had plenty of room in her town house. And the idea didn't seem so preposterous as she met Gabe's gaze.

She was on dangerous ground. It would be so easy to fall for him. *Fall for him more.*

But Tessa couldn't bring herself to retract the offer. Instead, she crossed her arms and dug in further. "I just mean, I have a spare bedroom. I was going to put the baby—babies," she corrected, "in the study since I never really use it. I want to breastfeed for at least the first few months, so they'd need to be here, anyway." The more she talked, the more this made sense.

And if he was willing to give the future a shot, she could, too.

"I know it's an unorthodox arrangement but…"

Tessa threw her hands in the air. She didn't want Gabe locked into a yearlong lease somewhere else. Didn't want her children split between homes from the second they were born. And she wanted Gabe close.

That was terrifying. But having him somewhere else made her heart ache more. Her palms were clammy as she waited for his answer.

"Why start with the traditional now? Whatever traditional means?" Gabe shrugged. "Are you sure, Tessa? If you want to take a few days to think it over…"

She didn't want to think it through. Gabe belonged here with their children. With her.

"No. I don't need a few days. We're a family now. Maybe an unusual one. But a family."

Family.

The word wrapped around her as she let Gabe pull her close again. Her heartbeat stabilized as she breathed in his scent. How long had it been since she'd belonged to a family? *A real one.* Not since the early days of her marriage to Max. As soon as he'd failed to advance at work, she'd become a competitor instead of his wife. An interloper in her own marriage.

But Gabe would never make her choose between her career and their relationship. He'd promised her.

"Family." Gabe brushed his lips against hers. Maybe this wasn't the usual path, the safe one, but for the first time in forever, Tessa's felt like her feet were on secure ground.

"We have one other thing we need to do." Gabe's grin was bright, but she thought she saw him hesitate a little.

He was always so sure of himself. The hesitation stunned her. "What?" Tessa put her hand on his chest and was surprised that it was thrumming. What was he so nervous about?

"We have to tell the Davis clan."

Tessa swallowed as she met his gaze. "Name a time and place." Then she raised her lips to his. Her life had shifted completely. But when she was with Gabe, those changes no longer seemed so frightening—in fact, they seemed perfect.

The alarm had gone off far too early for Tessa. Particularly now that she couldn't dose herself with a giant pot of caffeine fifteen minutes after her feet hit the ground. And waking alone no longer brought her any comfort either. Had it ever?

She didn't investigate that thought as she smiled at Gabe before he ducked into a patient's room. Gabe's family was helping him move in this weekend. He swore that it wouldn't take long. Apparently, even the stuff he'd moved into storage the first weeks he'd been here had only been a bedroom suite and a beat-up couch that he suggested they drop at the curb. The rental unit was close to Southern Methodist University. Gabe was confident that the battered but not broken piece would find a home in a college apartment.

"He *is* something!" Denise's statement broke through Tessa's mental wanderings as she handed her a tablet chart. "I know Gina and Rochelle are hoping that he might ask them out. I told them not to get their hopes up."

"You did?" Tessa tried to pretend that it wasn't jealousy racing up her spine. Gabe was kind, well-educated and stunning. Of course the single staff would be interested in him.

She winked at Tessa before leaning closer. "He only has eyes for you."

Tessa's cheeks heated as Denise leaned away. "Oh. Well. We're—" Her voice faltered as she tried to find the right words.

They were going to be parents and were moving in together, but they'd agreed it was too early to share a bedroom.

He promised they could move as slow or as fast as she wanted on this path they were traveling together. But that didn't leave a lot of standard definition for Tessa to fall back on in this situation.

"Don't worry." Denise grabbed another tablet chart. "Whatever it is, your secret is safe with me."

"Thank you." Tessa nodded. "I'll see to the little guy in room three."

"I know he's here for a stomach issue. But the little sister may have fifth disease." Denise swiped up on the chart she had in her hand and didn't catch the panic rippling through Tessa. "They noticed it in triage."

Fifth disease, also called erythema infectiosum, was a common childhood illness. Most kids had a low-grade fever and cold before a bright red rash spread across their cheeks, and occasionally their bodies. It was almost always mild. Except in pregnant women.

Her hands itched to stray to her belly, but they weren't discussing her pregnancy at the hospital. Fifth disease was most dangerous in the first half of pregnancy.

She'd likely had fifth disease, but she didn't know for sure. And it was nearly always asymptomatic in adults. Unless you miscarried. Tessa took a deep breath. She hadn't told anyone about her pregnancy, and the little boy had been ill for several days. She had to walk into the room. She'd take all the viral precautions she could.

"Hi." Tessa smiled through her fear as she stepped into the room. The small boy on the bed was lying on his side, holding his tummy. He looked miserable. The child's father was holding his little sister. Her cheeks were bright red, and he looked exhausted, too.

The door to the room opened, and Gabe stepped in. "Denise said you might need a hand." His nose scrunched as he met Tessa's gaze. She glanced toward the sister and saw Gabe follow her gaze.

"Hey, cutie."

Gabe bent to examine the sister while Tessa turned her attention to the little one on the table. "Can you tell me what's going on?"

The boy's eyes teared up, but he didn't say anything.

Tessa looked toward his father. "What can you tell me?"

The father looked from Tessa to Gabe, and she saw his shoulders sag even further as he looked at his child. "I don't know much. Ryan can't seem to keep food in. He doesn't throw up, but he's been in the bathroom for days. I've been working extra shifts this month." His voice wavered.

"My wife—ex-wife—might know, but she isn't returning my calls. She…" He let his words drift away.

"Okay." Tessa saw the desperation in the father's face. Heard it as he looked between his two kids. Her mother had worn the same expression in many of the memories Tessa could dredge from her mind. "What did you eat last?"

She moved to the sink and washed her hands as Ryan rubbed a tear from his cheek.

"Mac and cheese. It tasted good, but my belly hurt after. Now it feels like someone is jabbing it with knives. It's never been this bad before." Ryan clenched his teeth as he gripped his belly.

So Ryan had been experiencing the issues for a while.

"Does it hurt if you eat bread?" Tessa asked as she caught Gabe's gaze.

He held up a five as he headed for the sink, too. So he thought that Ryan's little sister had fifth disease, too. Nurses might not make official diagnoses, but every pediatric nurse could identify the different common childhood rashes. She'd double-check the rash, but if two of her nurses thought the rash looked like fifth disease, then she'd be shocked if it wasn't.

That was a worry for another hour.

Right now, Tessa was concerned that Ryan had celiac disease, or one of the other autoimmune diseases that attacked the intestinal tract.

"I don't eat bread. It makes me—" The boy's cheeks turned bright red.

"Fart?" Gabe smiled as he winked at the boy.

Ryan nodded but didn't say anything else. Most boys this age enjoyed talking about bodily functions. In fact, Tessa had participated in more conversations regarding gas with boys between the age of six and twelve than she had ever thought possible when she graduated from medical school.

If you were dealing with painful gas all the time, it could go from something silly to giggle about with friends to something you were embarrassed about really quickly. Unfortunately, there was no quick diagnosis for celiac disease. It would take a few weeks to confirm. But if they were right, then shifting his diet could bring him some instant relief.

"I think Ryan may have celiac disease. It means his body cannot process gluten. While he's here, I'm going to order a blood work panel. We'll also need to rule out a parasitic infection."

Moving around the table, Tessa squatted in front of

Ryan's little sister. "Hi, sweetheart." The little girl buried her head in her dad's chest, but she'd seen enough. Her cheeks looked like they'd been slapped, and there was a rash on her arms. Classic fifth disease presentation.

She met the exhausted father's gaze, "And your daughter has the symptoms of fifth disease."

Ryan's father blinked as his gaze shifted from his son to his daughter. "What?"

"The runny nose, pink cheeks and the rash on her arms." Tessa nodded. "The good news is that there really isn't anything to do for that except treat any symptoms if she gets uncomfortable."

"I am really failing at this single-parent thing, guys." Ryan's father kissed the top of his daughter's head.

"It's okay, Daddy." His daughter looked at him, her eyes so full of love that Tessa's heart nearly broke.

"Yes, it is," Tessa reiterated. "I need to talk to your dad real quick. But Nurse Gabe is going to stay with you guys."

"Yep." Gabe made a mock salute that caused Ryan and his little sister to grin.

The hallway was quiet as she stepped into it.

"I know I messed up," Ryan's dad started, and Tessa held up her hand.

"You didn't. You brought your son to the hospital, and kids get fifth disease all the time—literally! What's your name?"

"Adrian Farns." He wrapped his arms around himself and looked at the closed door where Gabe was probably starting to draw Ryan's blood for the autoimmune panel workup.

"I didn't bring you out here to discuss poor parenting. Negligent parents don't worry about their kids or bring them to the ER unless it's critical. You *are* doing a good job." Tessa offered what she hoped was a bright and comforting smile. "I wanted you to know that what your children need most is you."

Adrian blinked. "What?"

"You're exhausted, Adrian. That is a natural state for most parents, I know. But I think your exhaustion goes deeper."

His shoulders sagged even further. How heavy the weight of the world must seem to the man before her. "I came home to a note about four months ago. My wife— ex-wife—had left the kids with the neighbor, cleaned out the bank account and run off with her boyfriend. It's been a lot to handle."

"I bet." Tessa nodded. "I'm going to give you a list of dietary restrictions and recipes to try with Ryan to get him some relief. But I'm also going to include a list of services that can support your family through this. All the worldly goods don't matter if you're not there."

During her first year at Dallas Children's, she'd worked with their social worker to put together a solid list of contacts for services that could help parents. Whether they were struggling with financial issues, mental health issues or grief, Dallas Children's had a printout. The social worker made sure that the list of contacts was regularly updated.

If Tessa's mother had known who to ask for help, she might be celebrating becoming a grandparent now. She'd give as many people as possible the opportunities her family hadn't gotten.

Adrian nodded. "Thank you."

"You're welcome. Someone will be in with all those papers in a little while. If Ryan gets dehydrated, please bring him back. And introduce new foods slowly. His digestive system is at war."

Adrian mumbled a few words before heading back into the room with his kids. And Tessa headed toward the employee bathroom to scrub off the room's germs.

Tessa's hands were red by the time Gabe found her. He knew the odds of fifth disease transmission were minuscule. But in the 1 to 3 percent of pregnancies it affected, the consequences were catastrophic. And those numbers didn't seem so tiny when it was your children.

"I don't think any germs could have survived that scrubbing, Tessa." Gabe tried to keep his voice light as he reached for the taps and turned off the water. He hoped she hadn't burned her skin. Even if she hadn't, the vicious cleaning was going to leave them sore. Gabe made a mental note to make sure they had aloe vera or some other cooling lotion at home.

She held up her wrinkled digits and swallowed. "We have to tell Human Resources."

Gabe was stunned by the reaction. After her vehement refusal last night, he'd expected to argue the point with her. To have to address why they needed to be open about this.

When his mother had been pregnant with Isla, she'd been put on bed rest toward the end. Some of the worst fights between his parents had occurred during that period. His mother had been determined not to lose her position at the marketing firm where she worked. She'd only taken time off when the doctor had told her if she went into labor again, she'd have to be hospitalized until delivery.

There was no need to get into the actual details with everyone, but for Tessa's and the twins' safety, they needed to keep her from highly infectious rooms. There were only a handful of diseases that Tessa wouldn't be able to treat anyway. It was standard protocol for pregnant medical staff. She wasn't asking for any special treatment.

There would be some whispers, but at least a few of their colleagues already suspected that they were seeing each other. And hospital gossip shifted to new topics with lightning speed.

"I'm up-to-date on all my vaccinations. It should have a minor impact." Tessa voiced the thoughts that were rattling around in Gabe's mind. "And I'll let Patrick know that this will have no impact on my decision to apply for Dr. Lin's position."

And we're back to the promotion.

"Sure." His voice was more clipped than he'd meant it to be, but Tessa didn't seem to notice. Gabe understood wanting to advance at work. He understood Tessa's drive to be successful. But she was already incredibly successful.

What if, after this promotion, there was another and another? He'd watched medical professionals chase glory during his career. Higher pay and more prestige always came with trade-offs. And they were usually borne by the families.

Was that what Tessa wanted?

No, Gabe forced the thought to the back of his brain. If that was all Tessa wanted, he'd have already seen it by now. She loved their little ones, even though they were barely bigger than a cherry.

She'd scrubbed her skin raw out of fear of a disease that she'd almost certainly been exposed to dozens of times as a pediatric physician—even if she hadn't had it as a child. He'd heard her telling Ryan's father that he needed to take care of himself, too. And Gabe had seen the papers outlining how to deal with parental stress and divorce in the discharge notes he'd pulled up for Ryan. Those were not the actions of a woman who would put her work before everyone else.

Gripping her hands, Gabe wanted to make her smile. To lighten the day's heavy mood. "So, since we are having identical twins, there is one serious issue we need to consider." He tapped the edge of her nose as her eyes widened. "How do we keep from mixing them up?"

"What?" Tessa laughed.

The sound sent joy ping-ponging around his soul. Her smile lit up the room and his life. He'd do anything to make that smile remain forever. Of course, life wouldn't allow that. But as often as possible, Gabe was going to ensure that he made Tessa happy.

Gabe dipped his head. "I was surfing some online twin forums last night."

"Really?" Tessa grabbed a paper towel and gently dried her hands.

He shrugged. "My brain was a little too hyped up to sleep." In truth, the initial searches he'd done had nearly sent him spiraling. There was a reason that physicians always warned their patients not to go searching the web; you could find some truly terrifying statistics that would do nothing but worry you.

And there were more than enough medical horror stories about multiples pregnancy out there.

He'd finally found an identical twin forum and searched out funny stories to ease his tumbling brain. "I kept worrying that we might get them mixed up. Since, you know, identical!"

He made a silly face, enjoying the giggle that erupted from her. "Several parents recommended choosing a color or pattern for the little ones. One in yellow, the other in green. One twin in stripes and solids for the other bean.

So you don't confuse who is who when they're newborns, though their individual personalities shine through pretty quickly, according to most of the parents."

Gabe had only meant to look at a few things, but he'd loved searching through the forums. Finding out new things about the next step he was taking. *With Tessa.*

It was easy to care about Tessa. Easy to be around her. Easy to fall in love—

No. That had not happened. But even as Gabe stared at Tessa's wrinkled palms, which were blessedly less red now, he knew that was wrong. He was already half in love with her.

Emotions swirled through him, a mixture of excitement, joy and fear as he looked at her. She was his second chance. What if he lost her?

His mouth was dry as that thought tossed around his brain. Losing the person he cared most about had nearly destroyed him before, and now it wasn't just Tessa he might lose.

No. He could protect Tessa and the twins. Make sure that nothing bad happened to them. Make sure that he didn't face the bottomless pit of despair he'd known when Olive passed. He could make sure everything was fine. And it would be easier as Tessa's—

Boyfriend was the wrong word. *Roommate* made his skin crawl. The correct word refused to materialize. But Tessa's hand on his interrupted his mental wanderings.

"I said, I never even thought that I might not be able to tell them apart!" Tessa enunciated words that he'd missed while trying to work out ways to protect his family. At least she was unaware of all the thoughts racing through his mind.

"Sorry, I guess the day is longer than I thought." He stroked her palm, glad that twenty minutes under scorch-

ing water didn't seem to have injured her. "I read an ar-
ticle by a mom who swears she might have mixed her
boys up on the day they came home from the hospital."

"That sounds like the hook of a bad sitcom—and all
too possible!" Tessa's chuckle echoed in the small room.
"We should definitely have a plan!"

Gabe wrapped an arm around her shoulder. "That's
tomorrow's worry. Why don't I stop by Maggie's after
my shift and meet you after you've talked to Patrick?"

She cocked her head, "Expecting it to go poorly?"

"No." Gabe was almost certain that was the truth.
"Just looking for a reason to get some cupcakes."

"You don't need a reason, Gabe."

His heart burst as she winked and headed for the door.
"I cannot imagine a situation in which I would turn down
a coffee cupcake. I may drink nothing but decaf right
now, but I can at least enjoy that sweet treat!"

He offered another pretend salute and was rewarded
with a brilliant grin before she exited. He'd bring her
anything to make that smile appear. Seeing Tessa happy
was the best part of his day. She and their children made
him feel whole. It was as simple as that.

CHAPTER NINE

"I think it's time you got a new comforter for your bed!" Isla winked at Tessa as she followed Gabe up the stairs carrying a box of his belongings. "This one is not pretty. Maybe Tessa can help you pick another."

"It keeps me warm, Isla. It doesn't really have another purpose." Gabe took the lamp from Tessa's hands and kissed her cheek before setting it on his beat-up dresser.

Isla dumped what Tessa had to admit was an ugly comforter on the bed that Matt and Gabe had carried up an hour ago. "It's brown. And not a pretty warm coffee color. It looks more like…" Isla held her nose and smirked at her brother.

Tessa covered her lips to keep her grin from showing, but she caught Gabe's knowing look.

"This is the last one," Matt stated as he set another box on the bed. "And the comforter looks fine to me."

Gabe nodded to his brother before Matt headed down the stairs again. The nonverbal sibling communication made Tessa's heart race. Gabe's family interacted with one another just like she'd always dreamed of. They were a family—a real family.

"Two against one." Gabe laughed as he hung up a stack of shirts.

"Nuh-uh!" Isla slipped her hand through Tessa's. "Back me up, Tessa!"

She felt her eyes widen as her gaze shifted between Gabe and Isla.

Crossing his arms, Gabe leaned against the wall. The smile he offered her sent desire spilling through her. Those dimples were a work of art.

"Do you think it's ugly?"

"No using the dimples." Isla stomped her foot. "He knows they have power."

Gabe threw his arms in the air. "Guilty."

Tessa laughed at the fun exchange. She hoped her kids would have this type of relationship. The love was clear between them, even as Isla judged her brother's bad taste in bedroom decor. This was the life she'd yearned for. The life her kids would get.

"All right." Isla nodded before facing Tessa. "Honest answers only, Tessa."

Biting her lip, Tessa glanced at Gabe and shook her head, "Isla's right. It is ugly."

Gabe flung a hand over his chest and playfully threw his body against the wall. Tessa's and Isla's laughs echoed through the room.

"I guess the vote's tied then." Tessa shrugged.

"Oh, no, it's not. You count as three votes."

"Isla! My family would like me home for dinner. You coming?" Matt yelled from downstairs.

She offered Tessa a quick hug and high-fived her brother. "I'll find some suitable choices and email you, Tessa. The perks of being a department store buyer." She waved and disappeared.

"She never did play fair." Gabe laughed as he swung Tessa into his arms. "She means it, too. She'll send you a few choices and expect you to make me choose another comforter. Determined doesn't begin to describe Isla."

"They're wonderful." Tessa sighed before kissing Gabe's cheek. "Really, really wonderful." Tessa hadn't been sure how they'd react to Gabe moving in with her and becoming a dad, but the Davis clan had been nothing but loving.

"How about we get the bed cleared off so I can sleep in it tonight, then we can pop some popcorn and watch a movie? A nice night at home."

Tessa ran her hand along his chest. "That sounds lovely." And it did. Her heart swelled.

Such a simple word, with so much meaning. *Home.* Just replaying the sound of the word on his lips was enough to make Tessa's heart sing. Maybe this could work—truly work. Despite expecting twins and playing get-to-know-you—*really* get-to-know-you—at the same time, maybe everything would be all right. If she hadn't been nearly in love with him already, today would have sent her over the edge.

The words were on the tip of her tongue, but their unorthodox start had already gone through so many twists and turns. The last thing it needed was her confessing that she was falling in love with him the day he moved into her spare bedroom.

Telling him she loved him could wait. *But the timing is perfect*, her heart whined as her brain refused to operate her tongue. *Not today!*

Her phone buzzed, and she quickly glanced at the text. Dr. Lin was asking if she could cover a shift or three for him for the next few weeks. If she said yes, she'd be at the hospital nearly every day for a while. But if she said no—

No. That didn't seem like an option. In a few months, she might not feel like adding extra shifts.

Instead, she typed back a quick response and then grabbed Gabe's hand. "We'll have to make tonight count." She pressed her lips to his again.

"Oh?" Gabe wrapped his hand around her waist.

She leaned into him, enjoying the feel of him, the knowledge that he'd be here when she came home. It calmed her. "Dr. Lin needs me to take a few of his shifts. I guess he's finally getting his retirement paperwork filed and starting some retirement courses that the hospital mandates its staff take before they out-process."

"How many shifts?"

Gabe's tone was light, but his gaze flickered with a touch of worry. The look disappeared behind a smile, but Tessa was certain she'd seen it.

"I'll be at the hospital most days. But it will give me another leg up when they fill his position. Plus, it means Patrick believed me when I said that my pregnancy wouldn't impact my work. I know he told a few of the staff and asked them to be discreet."

"But nothing is discreet among hospital staff." He kissed the top of her head before moving to grab a stack of pants from a box on the bed.

She couldn't control the giggle. "I think that may be one of the biggest understatements of all time. But I'm happy that my colleagues aren't treating me differently. At least for now, I can still take on extra shifts."

"I'm glad." He dropped the pants into a drawer.

Is he frowning?

When he looked at her, Gabe's eyes were bright. He grabbed the few remaining boxes and set them next to the bed. "I can sleep in there now. Let's get our movie marathon going. I don't want to miss a single minute." He smiled again, but there was a flicker of something in his gaze.

Another uncertainty pushed through her. Was he upset that the hospital was still relying on her? Had he hoped she'd take a step back after they found out about the twins, even though he'd told her he'd support her?

"Rom-com or horror flick?" Gabe's grin chased away most of her worries.

But not all of them.

"Are those our only choices?" Tessa folded her arms.

"Nope. The choice is yours, my lady." He playfully bowed, and the final flutters of worry drifted to the back of her mind.

She was looking for ways to worry. Looking for reasons her world might implode. Just because it always had did not mean this was destined for failure. She was going to have a family—a real family.

After weeks of extra shifts, Tessa was reaching levels of exhaustion she hadn't experienced since she was a resident. It must be the pregnancy, because she'd kept long hours since she'd started at Dallas Children's. Often it had been easier to be at work than at home.

Following her divorce, she'd increased her hours even more. Anything to avoid the daily reminder that she had a job she loved but an empty house. A few days of double shifts were normal for her, but today, she was dragging.

Her stomach let out a growl as she started for the cafeteria. The granola bars she'd always kept in her pocket for between-meal snacks at work didn't come close to satisfying her. In fact, most days, she felt like she could eat her way through an entire grocery store and not burst!

"You look like you could use a strawberry smoothie." Gabe's voice was bright as he held up the cup. "Complete with a meal replacement supplement for hardworking doctors."

"You don't need to spoil me." She cocked her head and playfully folded her arms across her chest.

"So, you don't want it?" He smiled as he held the smoothie.

"Of course I do!" She grinned as her belly let out a growl loud enough for Gabe to hear.

"What would you do without me?" Gabe winked and took a big sip of his smoothie.

The smoothie stuck to the back of Tessa's throat. His tone was playful. He was kidding with her. There wasn't an underlying unhappiness. It didn't mean anything.

He leaned as close as was professionally responsible, and her heart jumped. "I also put a few snacks in the employee fridge for when I'm off in a few hours."

"Thank you." Tessa squeezed his hand quickly before dropping it. Gabe had made sure that she had a packed meal and several snacks to get her through the shifts. He'd been great and so reliable.

Too reliable. Tessa hated that niggling thought. Over the last week, he'd taken on so much at home. More than she'd ever expected.

It would be easy to rely on Gabe—to let him handle so many things. But hadn't that driven Max away?

Why wouldn't that thought disappear?

No, her heart screamed. Tessa could let Gabe handle little things. That's what partners did. They shared the load—without complaining.

Besides, if everything fell apart, she was more than capable of remembering to pack snacks. But what about protecting her heart?

"We've got a burn victim en route!" Fran, a triage nurse, called.

Tessa took another giant swallow of her smoothie before dropping it on the nurses' station. Gabe had made sure that her name was written in bold letters on both sides. Even if it was melted, it would provide the calories she and the twins needed. The man thought of everything.

His smoothie dropped beside hers, too, and they quickly made their way to the ER bay doors. Burns were common in the summer and fall. Children touched hot grills and burned themselves roasting marshmallows, but those emergencies usually resulted in a frantic parent bringing their child in. If an ambulance had been dispatched...

Her chest was tight. The waiting was the worst. Knowing that a seriously injured or ill child was incoming and needed support sent your adrenaline into overdrive. But the wait made your body doubt the reserves it was pouring forth. Tessa rocked on her heels and felt Gabe's strong body right behind her. He didn't touch her; he was prepping for the arrival, too. But just knowing he was there calmed the electricity racing along her skin. They made an excellent team—and could handle whatever was coming through the door now.

"Amy fell next to a pit where her family was roasting a pig. Caught herself with her hands in the coals," the paramedic called as he pulled the doors open. "Parents were distracted with a work call and left her in charge. Amy is eight."

Gabe heard the collective gasp of the staff that was waiting. It was impossible to work in a children's emergency room and not see unfit parents. Far too many individuals prioritized things that could be replaced over their children, which could not.

His mother's choices hadn't resulted in any of her kids taking a trip in an ambulance. But only because Gabe had become hypervigilant watching his younger siblings. If he'd been younger or less responsible, things could have been much worse when their father hadn't been around to act the way a parent was supposed to.

Anger, tension and a hint of fear raced along his spine. How could anyone do anything other than treasure their family? Prioritize anything over their children?

He forced his emotions into lockdown as the paramedics pulled the gurney down and passed the paperwork to the waiting admitting nurse. Being mad at her parents wouldn't help Amy. Hopefully, this would be a wake-up call for them.

"Hi, Amy. I'm Dr. Garcia, but you can call me Tessa. And this is Nurse Gabe. We're going to make sure you're all right." Tessa offered the child a smile, but her knuckles were white as she gripped Amy's gurney.

They treated so many things that resulted from accidents. Things that couldn't be helped. Kids flipped on their bikes and skateboards, trampoline injuries, but it was infuriating when it was the result of neglect.

"I didn't mean to mess up." Her whimper was so soft, and it broke Gabe's heart. "My hands hurt."

Tessa ran a hand along Amy's forehead. "This is *not* your fault."

He watched Tessa shake a bit of the fury away before she met Amy's gaze. "We're going to give you some medication to make it feel better."

Gabe saw Tessa swallow as they turned into the room. Burn patients were a medical professional's worst nightmare. The risks of infection and loss of use of an appendage were much higher than with other wounds. Plus, patients had a tendency toward shock within the first twenty-four hours of injury.

But it was a good sign that Amy's hands hurt. It meant

that the nerves were still intact. Unfortunately, it also meant that she would deal with a significant amount of pain while she healed.

"Pain management first, then initial debridement," Tessa stated as she put the orders into the computer tablet before turning to check the child's wounds.

The paramedics had loosely dressed her hands. When Tessa removed the dressings, Gabe saw her cheeks twitch. Second-degree burns covered both her palms and most of her fingers.

Amy sniffled. The child had to be in significant pain, but she was doing her best to hide it.

Gabe got down on her level. Maybe no one paid much attention to her at home, but here she was their primary focus. "What's your favorite color?" Tessa was going to need to clean the wounds, and even with the pain meds she'd ordered, it was going to hurt. Distracting Amy was the best thing he could do for her right now.

Where are the child's parents?

"Purple." Amy's voice was wobbly but strong. She wasn't in shock—at least not yet.

Denise entered with the pain meds Tessa had ordered and quickly administered them to Amy. The child didn't even flinch as Denise placed the needle into the meaty part of her arm.

"You're very brave." Gabe smiled. "Not many adults can just get a shot and not flinch. I cried the last time I got one."

Amy's eyes narrowed, but she offered him a tiny smile. "Really?"

"Cross my heart!" Gabe grinned. "I was hiking and fell on some rocks. I got a big cut on my leg that got infected. They gave me an antibiotic called Rocephin. It hurt bad."

"But you're okay now?" Amy's words were quiet, but he could hear the real question behind them.

His throat was tight, but he forced out, "Yep. Even the scar is less noticeable now. And *you* are going to be okay, too."

Amy's eyes teared up as she nodded.

As she exited the room, Denise looked over her shoulder. "Your mom is here. She'll be in as soon as she finishes her phone call."

"My parents are always on the phone."

The resignation in the little one's statement cut across him. The few times he'd visited his mom after the divorce, she'd always been on the phone, too. At least he'd had his dad to make sure he knew that he was important. But it hurt to know that something else mattered more than you. It was a cut that might heal, but the scar on your heart never disappeared.

His children would never believe that anything was more important than them. They wouldn't have to beg for attention like he had from his mom. Never wonder if he loved him.

"Gabe's right. You're going to be okay, but we have to make sure your hands are clean." Tessa smiled at Amy, but Gabe saw the subtle twitch in her hand. This was going to hurt, even as the pain meds took effect.

Amy swallowed and looked at Gabe. "You'll stay."

"You bet." Gabe patted the top of her head. "I'm here for you." He knew those words would comfort Amy, but he also glanced at Tessa. He was here for her, too—whatever she needed.

Gabe started from his bed. His brain thought he'd heard something, but the town house was silent. He rolled his head from side to side a few times, straining to hear any sound.

Nothing. He blinked and rolled over to look at his clock. He'd tried waiting up for Tessa. After taking care of Amy's burns, he'd thought she might need someone to talk to. Particularly since she'd been vibrating with anger as she talked to the child's parents, who'd seemed more concerned with their jewelry shipments than their daughter being admitted to the burn unit.

He'd waited after his shift ended, but Tessa had needed to handle one of her additional duties as the senior attending. He hoped she found the Thai food in the fridge and his good-night message.

It had been their routine since she'd started taking on additional shifts. The quick kisses as he passed her in the morning and the occasional stolen time for a smoothie at the hospital were so unsatisfying. At least she only had two more days of these nightmare long shifts before she rotated back to her regular schedule.

Was this really the position she wanted? And how much time would it steal from their family?

Gabe glared at his ceiling and threw an arm over his eyes. This wasn't Dr. Lin's shift. It was his and most of Tessa's shifts combined. She was working all the hours she could legally muster to prove herself to Human Resources, for a position that they hadn't even sent out an official announcement for.

What would their lives be like when the actual competition started? Gabe had watched doctors contend for positions before. He knew how cutthroat the healing professions could be when positions that rarely opened were competed for. It would have been daunting anytime—but she was pregnant. *With twins.*

"So, what else can I do to help?" The walls gave no

answer to his whispered question as he tried to calm his mind enough to drift back to sleep. He was off tomorrow. At least he could make sure Tessa had a solid meal before she headed back to the hospital.

Assuming she'd even come home. She'd slept in the employee suite a few nights ago and quipped about it reminding her of her residency days. Gabe had nodded as she talked about it, hating the circles under her eyes and worrying about her increasing focus on the hospital. He was doing his best not to voice his worry that she was operating on too little sleep for a physician and a pregnant woman. Tessa knew her limits.

But would she listen to them?

"Argh!"

The scream echoed down the hall from Tessa's room. Gabe's feet hit the floor.

He didn't stop until he was next to her bed.

"Gabe?" Tessa's eyes were open, but her voice was dreamy. He wasn't sure she was really awake. She couldn't have been home for long, and asleep for even less time. She had to be exhausted.

"I'm here." He sat on the bed and stroked her hair as she lay back down.

"I dreamed there was an accident." Her hands flew to her belly, and she sighed. "Dream…" Her voice was soft as she shifted her head on the pillow.

He dropped a kiss along her temple. "Pregnancy hormones can make dreams more vivid." Stacy had talked about how crazy her dreams had gotten after her first trimester. From birthing cats to her brain pulling the most horrific things from her subconscious.

Tessa's subconscious had more than enough material to make her dreams grim. Especially following a nightmare scenario at the hospital, and the fact that she was already running herself into the ground.

He stroked her back. She looked so beautiful in the moonlight as it streamed through the window. *And exhausted.*

When her breaths became even, he dropped another kiss to her temple and stood. They both had Monday off. And Tessa was going to do nothing but be pampered. She deserved to be taken care of for at least twenty-four hours.

He'd make sure they had plenty of popcorn for an epic movie marathon.

"Gabe?"

Would he ever tire of hearing her say his name? He hoped not. "I'm still here," he whispered.

"Stay with me." She pulled the covers to the side and slid over. "I don't want to be alone. Please."

The quiet plea nearly undid him. He joined her in bed and pulled her close. "I'm here." He kissed her shoulder as he wrapped his arm around her waist. She fit snuggling against him, and his heart soared as she sighed and slid back to sleep.

He tried to stay awake a few minutes to make sure that she was all right, but his eyelids kept drifting closed. Soon he gave up and let himself drift away, too.

Tessa rolled over and smiled as she stared at Gabe's lips. He'd come running last night. She couldn't remember the dream that had woken her so soon after she dropped into bed. But she could remember asking him to join her in bed. And how safe she'd felt as he slid his arms around her. How safe she felt lying in his arms now.

She ran a hand along his jaw, enjoying the feel of the bit of stubble under her fingers. They hadn't seen much of each other outside the hospital lately, and she was surprised by how much she hated that. It had been normal for her to basically live at the hospital before she met Gabe.

The employee suite, where staff routinely caught a few extra hours of sleep, was a regular overnight stay for Tessa. Gabe had looked so shocked when she'd slept there on Wednesday that she'd made up a story about it reminding her of her residency days—which it technically did—but also it wasn't uncommon for her.

But last night, she'd driven home rather than stay. Even if they weren't sharing a bed, she wanted to wake up in the same place as Gabe. Wanted to have breakfast with him.

And she'd asked Dr. Killon to cover the final two shifts for Dr. Lin. She wanted the senior attending position, but she was too tired. It wasn't safe for her patients or for the twins for Tessa to be so exhausted.

For the first time in years, she had three days off in a row. And Tessa planned to spend as much of it as possible in Gabe's arms. She dropped light kisses along his jaw, slowly working her way toward his lips.

He stirred as her lips met his. "Good morning." Gabe managed to get the words out between kisses.

"I missed you." Tessa ran her hand along his back, enjoying the feel of his skin beneath her fingers. She doubted there was a better place to wake than in Gabe Davis's arms.

"We live together, you know." Gabe's fingers traced up her thigh as he kissed her nose. "But I missed you, too. It would be nice to share more than just a few passing kisses and smoothies." His lips pressed against hers as he shifted his hips.

Tessa pulled him back. She wanted him—all of him—this morning. She let her lips trail along his shoulder as her fingers wandered farther south, and she enjoyed the hitch in Gabe's breath as they edged ever lower. "That isn't exactly what I meant." Tessa slipped a finger along the edge of his boxers.

Gabe gripped her hand, stilling its advance. "There is nothing I want more. Promise." He sucked in a deep breath. "But the next time I make love to you, I want to take my time."

He nodded toward her nightstand. "Your alarm should go off any second. I'm a little surprised it hasn't already."

"Dr. Killon is taking Dr. Lin's shifts for me today and tomorrow." Tessa pulled his face to her and kissed him—deeply. His hands trailed along her back, creating tiny bolts of electricity with each light stroke. "I have the next three days off."

Before Gabe could fully react, Tessa rolled him onto his back and started trailing her lips down his body.

In the morning light, he was stunning. And he was hers. That sent such a rush through her as she listened to his breathing increase.

Gabe's hands wrapped through her hair as she worked her mouth lower. When she slipped his briefs down, Tessa grinned.

She'd been wrong. There *was* a better way to wake up than in Gabe's arms.

CHAPTER TEN

"You have to be gentle with the seeds." Tessa pulled his hands out of the pot she'd handed him and gently rearranged the seeds he'd pushed into the soil before tossing dirt on top of them. Then she patted the soil and set the small pot to the side.

Gabe watched the process for the fourth time. He kissed her cheek as she laid another small pot in front of him and handed him more seeds. "I hate to break it to you, sweetheart, but that was *exactly* what I was doing."

Tessa's light chuckle made happiness burst through him as she stepped into his arms. Her hands wrapped around his neck before she kissed him. "I am patting the dirt, Gabe. You were mashing it."

He really didn't see the difference, but he'd stand next to Tessa all day while she worked with seeds. She'd decided last week that they should have a winter garden. Tessa was intent on trying the small garden ideas she'd found in the books she'd been leaving all over their living room. It would be nice to have fresh veggies, though Gabe believed she might have more fun growing the plants than anything else.

The bedroom he'd briefly called his own was now a veritable greenhouse. Grow lights were set up on a few small tables with labels announcing each pot's seeds and the watering schedule that needed to be handled for each grouping. This made Tessa happy, and that made Gabe happy.

Happy. Gabe stared at Tessa as she darted between her pots. His heart sighed at the image as he drank it in.

Life had dealt him an unimaginable loss. He'd never expected to feel this again. To relish the simple days at home. To be part of a family outside of the one he'd been raised in.

It was a gift. One he planned to hold on to tightly. To protect.

He'd do anything for Tessa and the twins. Anything to earn a permanent place next to her. *Forever.*

She planted another kiss on his cheek as she stepped beside him. Then her brow furrowed. "I got dirt on your chin." She held up her hands, staring at the dirt splatted on them. "And I've no way to wipe it off."

"You've had dirt on you since we stepped in here. It hasn't stopped me from wanting to kiss you yet." He shrugged. "What's a little dirt when you—" Gabe managed to pull back, barely.

Clearing his throat, he gestured to all the seeds. "When you're having such a good time."

Blood pounded in Gabe's ears as her beautiful brown eyes stared at him. The words *when you love someone* had nearly slipped into the space between them. His heart screamed for him to finish the statement. To declare what he wanted to believe was between them.

The last few weeks of living together, working together, watching her belly expand together had been some of Gabe's life's happiest. The hole in his chest that had refused to seal when he lost Olive had closed more the closer he got to Tessa.

He'd always miss Olive. But finding love again was a precious gift. And he was going to protect his family as much as possible.

"I was thinking about the nursery." Gabe pushed the seeds into the pot, barely controlling his grin as Tessa monitored his motions. When she accepted his pot and set it with the other spinach plants, Gabe thought his heart might shoot from his chest. *Success!*

"I know you wanted to wait a little while longer." He accepted another pack of seeds and a pot as Tessa started watering the plants on the far table. "But I think it's pretty obvious what theme we should go with."

"Theme?" Tessa raised an eyebrow as she looked over her shoulder at him. "I wasn't aware that we were actually going to have a theme. Is that a little overboard?"

Tessa's hands rested on her belly, and he knew that her shirt was going to have a dirt stain just over where their children were growing. It only cemented his idea. Gabe gestured to the seed pods around them. "Gardening! Picture it." He squeezed her shoulder tightly. "A room with images of flowers, green blankets, maybe even a few of their mother's plants in the corner."

He pulled the loose plan he'd sketched from his back pocket. "See."

Her dark eyes misted over as she ran a finger over the paper. "You did all this?"

"Of course. I love doing things for you and the babies. As much as you enjoy dirt and seed pods." He kissed the tip of her nose—one of the few spots that was dirt-free.

"That is a lot! Because I do love dirt and seeds." She giggled as she looked at her fingers. "I think cartoon characters and woodland creatures are more standard."

He shook his head as he pointed to the sketch he'd

made. "Standard is boring. Besides, I think we should lean into the twin parent thing. Two peas in a pod and all." He kissed the top of her head.

Touching Tessa, being with her, watching the small bump where the twins—his twins—were blooming, was exciting. He'd go all out at being a twin dad. Double strollers, minivan and all.

Tessa pulled one lip to the side as she looked at him. "I like this, but we have to make one change." She put a finger against the dirt, then added another thimbleful of water on the plant. "What if we find someone to paint a snowy mountain hiking path into a garden? A combination of us. And that is as close to a hiking trail we will be—at least until the twins are older."

Gabe hadn't realized it was possible for his heart to expand more. But his chest bloomed as she pointed to where the mural would be on the paper. "That would make this design perfect."

Tessa's grin lit up the room. "I never expected you to be so involved in the entire process. Max hated any decorating. I was all prepared to have to pick out all the colors and furniture on my own." She rocked back on her heels as she stared at him. "You are amazing. I lo—" Her eyes darted to the pots as she folded her arms. "I love the fact that you are so invested in our little family."

His ears burned as he stared at her. It felt like there was more to that statement. Or at least he wanted to believe there was. But Gabe didn't want to push—at least not yet.

Handing her another pot, he smiled. "I enjoy picking stuff out. Helping you, researching car seat standards, safety regulations—protecting our family in the cutest way possible." Gabe winked. "Besides, I'd do anything for our kids." *And you.*

Tessa started toward him and then abruptly stopped. "Oh!"

It took him three steps to reach her, but Gabe's heart felt like it was dropping from his chest. "What's wrong? Do I need to call the doctor? Or Emergen—?"

She grabbed his hand and placed it on her abdomen. "The babies are moving." Her smile was bright as she laughed. "Oh, it feels so funny! Like dancing gas. Wow. Not the cutest description I could have chosen. Though accurate."

His skin felt clammy as the adrenaline leaked from his body, and his stomach twisted. There was no danger here. *Nothing to worry about.* "You scared me." He hadn't meant to say that, and he saw compassion and concern float in Tessa's eyes.

Her fingers were soft as they touched his cheek. "You can't jump to the worst case." Tessa leaned her head against his chest. "I know you lost Olive, but you couldn't have known that she had an aneurysm. And Dr. Fillery said just two days ago that at seventeen weeks along, I am healthy, and the babies are doing great. Breathe with me."

Pulling in a few deep breaths, Gabe tried to remind his heart to slow. It was still too early for him to feel the twins twirling around her belly, but Gabe didn't remove his hand from Tessa. The connection grounded him.

His leap to calling the emergency line was too much for a light comment. But when you'd lost everything once, the urge to protect what you could engulfed you.

Letting the worries float away, Gabe enjoyed the feel of Tessa pressed against him. The feeling of rightness that echoed through him in these small moments. The movies made grand gestures seem like the epitome of romance. But they weren't.

It was these simple moments, with a hand on the belly where your children were growing, surrounded by spinach, lettuce and winter squash seeds, that made the best memories. "Sorry. I just…" He shrugged as the words and worries refused to materialize.

Her lips were warm as they pressed against his cheek. "I understand." Tessa trailed her fingers along his jawline. "We're fine. Promise."

He dropped a light kiss along her lips, sighing as she deepened it. "I also know you'll refuse to let me wrap you in Bubble Wrap for the rest of your pregnancy!"

"Nope. No Bubble Wrap. Too much to get done!" She held up a tiny pot containing a winter squash and marked the bottom.

She was always on the go. They'd yet to have another movie marathon or spend more than a few minutes relaxing on the couch since his first night here. The woman seemed incapable of slowing down.

"What are you thinking for dinner?"

"Oh!" Tessa held up her hand before reaching in her back pocket. "That 'oh' was because my butt was vibrating." She held up her phone. "Finally!"

Gabe playfully put his hands over his ears as her shout echoed in the room. "I'm scared to ask." Though he suspected only one thing would have sent such an excited yell through the small room. The job was finally open. The thing she wanted so badly.

He swallowed the touch of panic clawing at his throat. *It will be fine.*

Tessa danced like she had all those weeks ago before holding the phone to his face.

Gabe tried to put on a cheerful smile as he read the

confirmation of what he already knew. "So, Dr. Lin's position is open."

"Yep!" Her voice was an octave higher than normal. "I'll probably put in for a few extra shifts here and there. Pad my application and all." She smiled.

More shifts. Did she really have to take on more work? Spend more time away? Wasn't her expertise enough to speak on its own?

He bit back an objection as Tessa's eyes roamed his. He cared about her, loved her. He wouldn't dampen this moment with his own fears.

"I'll pace myself. Promise."

Gabe pulled her to him and rested his head on hers. "I'll do anything I can to make this easier." Tessa wanted this position, and he wanted her to succeed. He did.

His throat closed as he tried to stop the flutter of worry arching its way through his belly.

"Anything and anytime, right?" Tessa kissed the tip of his nose.

"Right," Gabe responded, hating the tingle in the back of his skull. There was nothing wrong with wanting a promotion, with wanting to reach for everything. *Nothing.*

Tessa wasn't his mother. She'd protect herself and the twins. All these fears were the past. If only he could get his heart to listen to his mind. Stop the bead of worry that lit up in his chest any time Tessa talked about the promotion.

She wasn't going to choose work over her family. She wasn't. Besides, Gabe was going to be the best partner he could be. He'd make sure she was as comfortable as possible at home.

If he did everything for her, she'd realize that being home with him and the twins was just as exciting as being at the hospital.

* * *

Tessa had never felt as exhausted and achy by the long shifts as she had over the last week. Just walking the floor was enough to make her yawn.

Growing children is hard work.

Her stomach grumbled again, and she popped a few blueberries that Gabe had packed into her mouth. Then she playfully glared at her expanding belly. "I am literally feeding you now!"

Or so it seemed. She smiled as she rubbed her belly.

Tessa had begun showing. She was enjoying each of these new steps. Though with as much as she was at the hospital, it felt like she was in danger of letting it fly by.

Stroking her belly, she grabbed another mouthful of berries. The selection process for the senior attending should be completed before Tessa hit her third trimester. She could dial it back a little then.

Or you could withdraw your name from consideration.

Her stomach lurched as the idea tossed around her brain. It was just the fatigue talking. She'd given up one senior attending position. She wasn't walking away from another.

The twins...

Tess quashed that thought before her exhausted brain could finish it. Her mother had lost her career because of an unplanned pregnancy. Tessa wasn't relinquishing this chance because her path to motherhood had been unexpected.

She was just tired. That was all.

The twins moved, and Tessa's nerves quieted a little. During her third trimester, she was sure she'd be uncomfortable as they danced and battled for the ever-decreasing space in her abdomen. But for now, it was the best feeling ever!

Hopefully, Gabe would feel it soon. She planned to memorize every moment of that event. He was going to light up, with that big grin that made his eyes nearly disappear. She loved that smile. Loved how much he'd taken on without her even asking.

Being protected by Gabe was a blessing she'd never counted on. He'd made life so much easier. She'd missed being taken care of.

Though a tiny kernel of worry still hid in the recesses of her mind. She never wanted Gabe to resent all his help. For him to wish that she hadn't taken advantage of the job opening. But it was easy to ignore the tiny voice when he held her in arms.

Her buzzer went off, and Tessa grabbed a final handful of blueberries before heading for the nurses' station.

"We've got twin boys in room four. One needs stitches in his arm and cheek. The other has an ankle the size of a baseball. Triage ordered an X-ray." Debra passed over the tablet chart.

Tessa looked over the triage report. A pair of seven-year-old boys had jumped out of a tree house.

"The mother is beside herself. Just so you know."

"I bet." Tessa tapped the chart. Children never calculated dangers into their adventures. She knew her own two were likely to send her into a panic many times before they hit their teens. And then a whole new host of worries would likely begin.

"Daddy!"

The stereo echo hit Tessa as she closed the door and turned to greet her patients. Identical pairs of watery eyes hit her, and her heart exploded as her own future stared back at her.

Offering a smile, Tessa stepped toward the table where the boys were huddled together. "Nope. I'm Dr. Garcia."

"I want Dad," the one that had a large gash on his right arm stated, before glaring at his mother.

"Dad will be here when he can. But I'm here, DeMarcus." The woman's dark gaze met Tessa's. "We're separated. He always handled everything. Never complained—" She caught a soft sob and forced a tight smile. "Collin said he'd be here soon."

Tessa nodded. She'd seen all sorts of family dynamics during her medical career. "It's all right. Can you tell me what happened?"

"We tried to fly," the little one with an ice pack on his ankle offered.

"And crashed," DeMarcus finished.

"But next time—"

"There will be no next time, Dameon." Their mother's lips pursed as the statement echoed off the walls. "Sorry."

The door opened and a tall man with the boys' curly hair stepped into the room.

Both the boys' eyes lit up.

"I thought I heard you, Eva."

The twins' mom shook her head and gestured toward the boys. "They're already plotting how to jump off the tree house again."

"Without crashing," Dameon added.

Both parents sent a look toward their son, dutifully ignoring looking at each other.

"We are going to X-ray Dameon's ankle." Tessa raised her voice, trying to regain some control of the room. The tension between the boys' parents vibrated, and she saw the twins squeeze each other's hands. It was always difficult when marriages ended, but when children were involved, the stakes changed.

She'd dealt with many struggling parents and all sorts of custody issues as a physician, but the focus had to be on the boys right now. "And DeMarcus is going to need stitches in his arm and cheek."

"Guess it's a good thing I remembered the insurance card and snacks." Collin's words were clipped as he passed a bag to his wife. "You need to do some of these things, Eva."

"I'm trying." Her words were tight as she looked from Collin to her boys. "There's just so much."

"Which I've always done."

Tessa crossed her arms as she stared at the warring pair. This was not helpful. "Why don't you two take this conversation to the hall while I start DeMarcus's stitches." Tessa smiled, hoping the oncoming quarrel could occur away from the boys.

The radiology tech stepped into the room and moved aside as Collin and Eva took their argument to the hallway. "Who am I taking for a ride to the X-ray machine?"

"Me!" Dameon shouted, but when he moved, the color drained from his young face.

"Careful, little guy. Let's get some pictures of that ankle." He nodded to Tessa as he took the child out.

"Let's see if we can't get you stitched up." Tessa smiled as DeMarcus stared at the closed door.

"I miss Daddy living at home."

The sadness in his childish voice caused a lump at the back of her throat. There was nothing she could say. His parents weren't divorced—yet—but it hadn't sounded promising.

"You might feel me pulling on your arm, but if you feel any pain, let me know and we'll make sure we give you some more numbing." Tessa hoped her smile was comforting, but DeMarcus's gaze never left the door.

"Dad makes better mac and cheese than Mommy. But

he was tired of doing everything while she was at work. They yelled a lot. But I miss the mac and cheese."

"I bet," Tessa conceded. Children missed a lot less than their parents thought. "You're a very brave little boy."

The door opened again, and Collin stepped through. "Sorry, Doctor."

Tessa nodded. She wouldn't say that arguing in front of your kids while they were waiting on stitches and X-rays was fine.

"Are you coming home?" The wistfulness in De-Marcus's voice hung in the room as his dad's shoulders slumped.

"I love you, buddy. And I love Mommy, too." He choked back a small sob. "But...not right now."

"He needs to keep these clean and dry for the next two weeks. After that, the stitches should be fully dissolved. One of the nurses will give you information on infection. And once we have X-rays back, we'll see what we need to do for Dameon."

He nodded. He still wore his wedding ring. Maybe their marriage wasn't completely over.

You need to do some of these things.

His words sent a shiver through Tessa as she left the room. She was still independent. Wasn't she? Sure, she liked Gabe taking care of her. She'd let him take over so much while she took on extra shifts. He hadn't complained, but Collin hadn't, either. And neither had Max at first.

Her lunch rolled in her stomach as Tessa tried to think of anything she'd contributed to the household over the last few weeks. Her mind produced very little. She'd ceded so much to him...

Was she setting herself up for another disaster?

Her phone buzzed, and she felt her frown deepen as she stared at Gabe's words.

Oil changed! And I got the grocery shopping done. Don't worry, I didn't touch the plants. How about we do takeout? I'm exhausted.

She'd told him she'd take the car to the mechanic this weekend. And she'd planned to do the grocery shopping on her way home. Though after a long shift, could she really be upset about this?

She bit her lip as the realization struck her. Tessa was independent—she was. But hearing the twins' parents' argument highlighted how much she'd changed over the last few weeks. She'd been relying on Gabe. For *everything*.

That would not do. She didn't want her twins to live DeMarcus and Dameon's reality. Hadn't she learned from her marriage that people didn't always mean it when they said they didn't mind? She loved Gabe. She never wanted to see him exhausted because she hadn't pulled her weight.

She could make a few changes. Ensure that Gabe didn't resent her like Max had.

"Ouch!"

Gabe started toward Tessa as she put her soapy finger to her lips. "That can't taste very good." He reached over and turned off the water, trying to control the frustration in his belly. He'd told her he'd clean up, but she'd insisted that she do the dishes since he'd cooked.

It was one of the many things she'd asserted control over this past week. The more he tried to assist at home, the more she insisted that she didn't need it. How was he supposed to help, to show how much he cared for her? No matter how he tried to lighten her load, she seemed intent on doing more than her share.

And she brushed off all his offers of help. That stung. He was happy to do things for her. Happy to make sure that she was taken care of. She'd told him the night they'd reconnected that no one had protected her—cared for her. He was here to do that.

If she'd only let him.

"I'll admit that a mouthful of soap is not appealing. But when I broke my nail, it was just an automatic reaction." Tessa looked down at her fingers. "That's the second one I've broken today. Guess I need to pay better attention, huh?"

"Second one today? Do you think your iron levels are okay?" Dr. Fillery had warned them that moms of multiples often ended up with vitamin deficiencies that weren't serious if they were caught early. Tessa had put the list of symptoms on the fridge, even though as a doctor she knew them. Just as a reminder.

Gabe passed her a glass of lemonade. "This should cut the taste of soap."

"You have a bank of knowledge on the taste of soap?" Tessa smiled before taking a few deep swallows.

"It was one of my mom's favorite punishments for saying curse words. I only got the punishment once, but Isla received it several times." Gabe frowned as he glanced at the list of low iron symptoms. Tessa had several. But it could just be that she was working so much.

His brain wrapped around the worries as he tried to shake himself. History was not going to repeat itself.

"Why don't I finish the dishes?" Gabe sighed as she held up the last dish.

"All done!" She yawned again and looked at her watch.

"Can we postpone movie night? I'll just fall asleep in your lap."

He'd be fine with that. Gabe would never tire of holding her, but it was probably better if they went straight to bed. Leaning over, he kissed her cheek. "Of course." This was at least the sixth movie night they'd tabled.

His gaze drifted to the list once again before he focused on the woman in front of him. He was worried about her and the twins. Sucking in a deep breath, Gabe raised his concern. "I know you've been tired lately, and brittle nails can be a sign of low iron. Maybe we should talk to Dr. Fillery at your next appointment." He nodded toward the sheet on the fridge, hoping she'd understand.

"No, we don't need to raise this with Dr. Fillery." Tessa pushed a hand through her curly hair before stepping into his arms. "Deep breaths, Gabe. This isn't a medical crisis. I am working more right now and growing not one, but two babies. A little tiredness is to be expected."

Except this didn't feel like a little tiredness. She yawned several times an hour, despite regular naps and falling asleep as soon as her head hit the pillow. "And the nails?"

Tessa sighed before she met his gaze. "I broke two nails, Gabe. Relax. Please." She squeezed his hand. "I'm fine. This is just what happens when you fail to keep your nails trimmed. The prenatal vitamins are making my nails grow faster than normal."

Her hand rested on his chest, and she grinned. "There isn't anything wrong with me, Gabe. Other than your two children are sucking up all my energy."

"What about cutting back at the hospital?" Gabe knew they were the wrong words as soon as they left his lips. But there was no way to reel them in—and this was a conversation they needed to have. He knew she wanted

Dr. Lin's position, and Tessa wasn't the only physician doing their best to prove themselves indispensable to the hospital.

And Dallas Children's was more than happy to take on their extra labor. It was a script he'd seen play out several times throughout his career. A hospital exploiting a cutthroat competition to get the most out of its workforce was standard. He'd participated in it at his hospital in Maine, too.

But a job was not worth hurting yourself or your family for.

"That's not an option, Gabe." Her hands slapped the counter before she crossed her arms. She was preparing for battle.

He didn't want to fight, but he was concerned. "It is," Gabe countered. Tessa was exhausted, and if her record and résumé didn't stand on its own, did she really want the position? "You are not required to burn yourself out for Dallas Children's. Doing everything is not possible."

He watched her take a deep breath and tension seeped from her shoulders. Tessa sighed. "I appreciate the concern." She stepped beside him. "I really do." Her lips were cool as they pressed against his cheek. "I'm a physician. I know all the signs for low iron and a multitude of other ailments. I'm fine. I promise. I don't need you to protect me."

The words cut as he held her gaze. There was so little he could do right now. She'd started packing her own lunches and insisted on dividing the chores equally. She got upset if he did something that she'd declared was her job. Protecting his family and those he loved brought him the most joy. Helping was how he showed his love.

But if the woman he loved didn't want his help...

His sister's text ringtone echoed in the kitchen, and

Gabe was grateful for the interruption. He needed a few minutes to gather his thoughts.

Barbecue Saturday. Three o'clock. You bring the chips and salsa.

"Everything okay?"

No. But Gabe didn't want to discuss the divide that he felt was opening between them. Tessa was stressed enough as it was. Part of Gabe was worried that she'd tell him she didn't need him at all if he pushed her to take it easier. And he wasn't sure he'd survive that.

"Stacy is having a barbecue Saturday. I know you're working the evening shift on Friday."

"But my Saturday is still free. Unless Dr. Lin or someone needs…" Tessa shook her head. "No. I am free, and I won't pick up another shift then. I promise."

She was choosing family time. Choosing *him*. The ball of tension in Gabe's chest relaxed a little on those words. It refused to dissipate completely, but at least it was easier to breathe. For now.

"I'm going to hold you to that. And I need to raid the cilantro plant—we are supposed to bring chips and salsa."

Tessa kissed his cheek, and more of his worry slid away. "I'll cut some. Just tell me how much you need."

Before she could walk away, Gabe pulled her into his arms. Her shoulders were tight, but they relaxed as he kissed the top of her head. A tiny thump got his attention, and he pulled back. "Was that…?"

Tessa's brilliant smile warmed his heart as she put his hands on her belly. "Yes!" She placed her hands on either side of his cheeks. Her face was bright with happiness as her gaze roamed him. "I promised myself that

I'd memorize every moment of you feeling the twins for the first time."

"You did?" Gabe laughed as a foot or elbow pushed at the hand he had on her belly.

"I knew it was a memory I would never want to forget." Joyful tears hovered in her eyes. "And I was so right. I can't wait to watch you be a dad."

She released her hold and laid her hands over his as the twins twisted in her belly.

His children...*their children*. Tears coated his eyes as Tessa leaned her head against his shoulder. Most of his final worries slid away as she let out a soft sigh, and their children kicked his hands.

CHAPTER ELEVEN

"How are you doing?" Isla handed Tessa a glass of punch.

Gabe was playing with his nieces and nephews on the lawn. He lifted a little girl high in the air, spinning around fast before collapsing with the child on the lawn. Peals of laughter rang across the patio.

Warmth and happiness bloomed in her chest. Tessa was watching a snapshot of the future—her future. Their children would never feel like they had lost their family. No matter what happened in their lives, they'd have a place here.

"I'm doing okay." It was the truth, mostly. She was tired, but that was the normal state for her now. No matter how many naps she took, she couldn't shake the exhaustion. But nothing was going to keep her from enjoying every moment today.

She loved watching Gabe with his family. He was going to be such a good father. And she was going to make sure that he never felt taken advantage of. *Ever*.

Her free hand rested on her belly as she took in the fun scene and sipped her punch.

"You know it's okay if you aren't." Isla laughed as a nephew jumped on Gabe's back and screamed for him to be a horsey.

Tessa barely controlled the yawn that pulled at the

back of her throat. She'd gotten eight solid hours of sleep last night and even taken a nap in the car on the ride over. There was no reason for her to be so tired. *Maybe you should talk to Dr. Fillery.*

"The Davis family can be a lot." Isla raised her glass to Stacy's husband as he carried their screaming toddler inside. "I swear I've lost a few girlfriends because I introduced them to my family. One didn't even make it to dinner before telling me that we had a nuthouse."

She wrapped an arm around Isla's shoulder and squeezed. "Your family *is* a lot. A lot of fun and love."

They cringed as a toddler, whose name Tessa hadn't learned, squealed. The sound echoed into the woods behind Stacy's house, and a group of birds took flight.

"And a lot of noise, too." Tessa winked at Isla. "Anyone who can't see the happiness here, and run toward it, isn't worthy."

This is what Tessa had always dreamed family was. The rowdy, joyful nature thrilled her. Her mother had done the best she could, but she couldn't magic a room of cousins for her to play with. No fun weekends with aunts or uncles. She sighed as she soaked it up.

Isla smiled as she raised her drink. "You're perfect for him. Even if you let him keep that ugly brown comforter."

Tessa laughed as Isla's pronouncement sent a thrill through her. Her eyes misted, and she ran a hand across them. *Hormones.*

The noisy Davis family was wonderful. And her children would be so loved here. With cousins galore!

"Thank you. I know this has been a different path." As the statement escaped her lips, Tessa wished she could withdraw it. Those words may have been right a few weeks ago—but they didn't feel accurate now. What did it matter how she and Gabe had gotten here?

"Your brother is special. He makes me happy." Those words brought another round of mist to Tessa's eyes. Second trimester waterworks were definitely stronger than first trimester ones. Her eyes might be constantly wet by the third trimester if this trend held.

"Yes." Isla leaned close. "Gabe is special, and *you* make him happy. I wasn't sure that was possible after—" Her voice died away.

"After Olive passed," Tessa finished for her. "You can say her name. It doesn't bother me. Gabe will always love her. I know that. But his heart is big enough for both of us."

Isla wiped a tear away from her cheek. "I'm so glad you're part of our family, Tessa. And you, too, little ones." She laid a hand on Tessa's lower belly. "Two more little girls!"

Tessa giggled. "I am delighted to be an honorary family member. But we decided not to find out what sex the babies are. Better to be surprised. Though I am wavering on that decision now."

Gabe had said it was her decision, and she'd wanted to be surprised. But she also wanted to know if Gabe was going to have two little girls to dote on or two boys they'd have to keep from trying to fly from tree houses. Though she'd patched up lots of little girls, too… They were going to be busy—and happy.

Isla shrugged as she looked back toward Gabe. "The twins are girls. I've guessed every one of my nieces and nephews correctly. Those are feisty little girls—*trust me.* And Tessa." Isla waited until she looked at her before continuing. "You aren't an honorary member of anything. The Davis clan is your family, too."

Her throat closed as she met Gabe's youngest sister's gaze. Isla really meant it. Before she could say anything, the babies twisted in her stomach, and suddenly she needed to find the restroom. "Thank you, Isla. You have no idea how much that means. But I need to find the bathroom. I think the twins have started playing hockey with my bladder!"

"Ahh, the joys of pregnancy!" Isla cooed. "At least, so they tell me." She winked again and quickly gave Tessa directions.

"I swear, you two need to find a better toy." Tessa joked while washing her hands. She knew that carrying twins meant even less space for the two of them to move around, but at twenty weeks along, she felt like she was constantly feeling them argue over who got to kick her kidneys.

She stepped into the hallway and yawned. This was out of control. She was *not* tired! At least not enough to yawn every thirty seconds.

"Isla has claimed Tessa as her new best friend. I think she plans to spoil your little ones to pieces. And she swears the twins are girls." The voice of Gabe's oldest sister, Stacy, was light as it traveled from the other room.

"Well, she's been right every other time." Gabe's laugh sent a small thrill through Tessa as she laid a hand over her stomach. If there were two girls in her belly, he'd be the perfect girl dad. But Tessa wasn't ready to buy girl dad stuff based on Isla's predictions.

"I don't care. As long as the twins and Tessa are healthy."

Tessa's heart expanded as the twins danced around her belly. Gabe had told her he didn't care what they were having, but hearing it repeated to his family was nice too. How had she gotten so lucky?

"I'm glad you found Tessa. She's perfect for you."

Tessa smiled. She really was part of the family. *Family.*

"She is. I just wish she'd relax some." Before Tessa could announce her presence, Gabe continued, "I'm worried about her getting this promotion."

Tessa's chest clenched and it felt like cold water was splashing across her dreams. *What?*

"Brett, stop practicing karate takedowns on your sister! I swear that girl needs constant attention." Dishes clinked, and Tessa heard Stacy turn the sink off. "I thought you said Tessa was really qualified."

She wasn't sure she wanted Gabe's explanation; eavesdropping wasn't a trait she wished to cultivate, but her feet refused to move. Maybe he was worried she'd be disappointed if the hospital hired someone else. Maybe it wasn't about Tessa getting the promotion.

Maybe this wasn't a repeat of Max. Gabe had said he was happy. Except he'd talked about her pulling back the other day. And he'd hesitated to date her because of the job.

Her brain rattled with worries as she twisted her palms together. *Please.*

"She's very qualified. That's the problem. If she gets it, well, I worry what that means for our family." His voice drifted away.

The happiness bubble in her chest burst. That Gabe could question her ability to be present for her family cut a deep wound across her heart.

Did he think her getting the promotion would make her less of a mother? She didn't want to answer that question. Tessa wasn't sure her heart was strong enough to handle it.

Squaring her shoulders, she rubbed away a tear before she stepped into the room. "Is there anything I can help with?" She hoped her smile looked real, even though it felt so false.

Gabe's gaze shot toward her. His jaw clenched, but he didn't ask if she'd overheard the conversation.

"Yes." Stacy smiled as she handed her a plate of cookies. "Can you put these out—but tell the kids they only get one!"

"Of course." Tessa's voice felt odd, and she couldn't quite bring herself to meet Gabe's gaze. Even as she felt it rake across her. If she looked back, Tessa feared she'd force him to explain his worry about the promotion now. This was not a conversation she wanted to have with an audience.

It wasn't a conversation she wanted to have at all. She loved him. Tessa was almost positive he loved her, too. But if her advancing at Dallas Children's was a problem—

She'd never live with someone who looked at her like Max had. She couldn't do that again.

"Oh, and we're doing ladies' night in two weeks. Friday night tacos while the boys watch the kids. It's not a late night anymore, just a few hours away from the madness. You should come." Stacy's smile made Tessa want to weep.

She wanted to go. Desperately. Wanted to belong to the Davis family. Fully. But this place would always be Gabe's. Their children would belong here, too. But if she got the promotion, and he left her…

Tessa barely controlled the sob clogging her throat. Her soul ached at the idea that she might not be welcome here someday. The Davis family felt like…like family. Her family.

Her heart screamed for her to say yes. To take the risk, to trust that Gabe hadn't really meant that it would be a problem if she got the job. But she would not make the mistake she'd made with Max's friends. If Gabe wasn't sure what would happen if Tessa got the promotion, she couldn't let herself get too close to them. No matter how much she might want to. "I have to work."

"The schedules aren't out yet," Gabe stated.

His eyes held a look that she couldn't quite read. But she already had a ready excuse.

"I promised Dr. Lin that I'd work a few final shifts with him." It was mostly the truth. Dr. Lin had asked, but she'd told him she had to think about it.

She saw Gabe's lips turn down, and her heart seized. How was she supposed to ask him about this? Until Tessa could find the right words, she was just going to pretend everything was fine. At least with the extra shifts, it would give her an excuse for putting it off.

Tessa smiled, and she caught Stacy's gaze. "Thank you for the invitation. It means a lot." *More than you could know.* She bit back that final statement as she lifted the plate of cookies.

Stacy smiled. "Don't let the kids talk you into more than one cookie. They are cute but diabolical!"

"I won't. Cross my heart." Tessa nodded to Stacy before she let her gaze drift to the man she loved. They'd never said that they loved each other, but her heart was his—completely. But if Gabe didn't feel the same way…

She forced those thoughts away. Now was not the right time or place. And the last thing she wanted to do was break down in front of Gabe's entire family. No, there'd be plenty of time to figure out what Gabe meant—and what it meant for their future.

"Cookies!" Her call was choked, but the kids came running. And Tessa let some of her fear go. Even if she wasn't destined to be part of this clan, at least her children would always have a place to call their own.

* * *

The sheets next to him were cold as he rolled over. Tessa hadn't come home—again. That made two nights in a row that she'd slept at Dallas Children's. Two nights she'd chosen an uncomfortable hospital sleeping room over their bed.

He flopped over and stared at the ceiling. His heart hammered as he tried to push at the doubt pooling in his belly. Something was wrong.

Tessa was putting distance between them, but Gabe didn't know how to draw her back. How to fix the situation. How he could help more when she seemed intent on proving that she didn't need it. Didn't want it.

Or maybe she was just too busy trying to ensure she got the promotion to notice the gulf between them. Maybe the promotion was more important than sleeping next to the man who loved her. His mother had felt that way.

Gabe pushed his palms into his eyes, willing the horrid thought away. But his brain refused to choose another track. What if this promotion wasn't enough? What if he wasn't?

He loved Tessa. Wanted to be with her. But waking up alone to cold sheets was not something he'd settle for. Being an afterthought to a parent left scars that never completely healed. He didn't want that for their children— or for himself.

He blew out a breath as he swung his feet from the bed. The few times he'd seen her this week had all been when they were on shifts together. There was no way to have a discussion during that time. No time to address whatever was bothering her.

And how could he help if he didn't know why she was avoiding him?

He started the coffeepot, adding an extra scoop of

grounds. He needed as much caffeine as the pot could create. Pulling open the fridge door, his heart squeezed as he looked at the meal he'd packed for Tessa. It was still sitting on the top shelf. It was ridiculous to get upset about a packed lunch. Particularly since he was sure she hadn't been home.

Maybe she didn't *need* his help, but why didn't she want it? It was a gesture of love; couldn't she see that? Didn't she want his love?

The garage door opened, and Gabe rubbed his palms on his blue jeans. She was home, and they needed to talk. But his fingers twitched as the worry ricocheted through him. What if he didn't want the answers?

So many thoughts and emotions chased through him. Ambushing Tessa as soon as she got home from the hospital wasn't ideal. But when else was he going to see her?

"You're awake." Her gaze hovered on the coffee cup in his hand.

The dark circles under her eyes were even deeper now than they'd been three days ago. *Is she okay?*

"I'm glad you're home." Gabe started toward her, but she barely paused long enough to let him kiss her cheek before she pulled open a cabinet and grabbed a granola bar and coffee mug. Gabe tried and failed to stop the pain that caused. When was the last time they'd kissed— really kissed, not just a peck on the cheek?

"That's not decaf," Gabe stated as Tessa poured the coffee and put a lid on it.

"It's okay." She sighed as she took a deep sip and ripped open the granola bar.

Having up to two hundred milligrams of caffeine a day was fine during pregnancy. But Tessa had refused to drink anything but decaf since finding out she was pregnant. He bit back his list of questions about her health and chose what he hoped was a safer topic.

"Rough night at the hospital?" He sipped his own drink as he slid next to her.

"Yes. Two car accidents and a trampoline injury that resulted in compound fractures of both tibias." She let out a sigh and took another sip of coffee before pouring the rest of it down the sink. "As much as I want to suck this down, I probably need a few hours of sleep first."

Yes! Gabe smiled and set his coffee mug next to hers. "Do you want me to tuck you in?"

Her gaze shifted as she stared at him. "I am working every day but Friday next week."

Her chin rose, and Gabe felt the air in the kitchen shift. There was a script—he was sure of it—but he didn't know which words she expected him to say. "I'm not sure what that has to do with my questions, but okay. Maybe after next week, you could take a day or two off."

"Why?" Her voice was tight, and there was a fire in her eyes that sent a shiver down his back.

She was exhausted, and there had to be a better time to discuss this. But he wasn't sure when the opportunity would show itself. "Because you will have been living at Dallas Children's for the better part of two weeks by the time those shifts are over."

"The other physicians are doing the same," Tessa countered, and straightened her shoulders. "Josh Killon has a newborn and two other little ones at home, and he is working similar hours."

"Working hours like that only proves that Josh Killon doesn't care about his wife or family. The man cares only about himself." Gabe wanted to kick himself as the words flew between them. That wasn't what he'd meant to say—though it was the truth.

Tessa looked like he'd slapped her. Gabe bit the inside of his cheek as he shook his head. "I know you aren't like Josh."

"Do you?" Tessa's eyes twitched as she met his gaze. *No. Yes.* That had been an unfair statement. Even if Tessa was spending more time at the hospital than home, even if he hadn't seen her in two days, she didn't see people as stepping stones like Dr. Killon did.

If he could have pulled his words back, he'd do it. Swallowing, he took a step toward her. "Yes. Dr. Killon only cares about himself."

He took a deep breath and pulled on all his reserves. He shouldn't have compared her to Dr. Killon, but there was a topic they needed to discuss. "But you should understand better than most that working to exhaustion is a recipe for disaster."

Tessa's eyes narrowed. "Meaning?"

"You have dark circles under your eyes. You're exhausted. What if you had fallen asleep on the drive home? Your mom was working so hard that she fell asleep behind the wheel."

Damn it! He hadn't meant to say that, either. *Why is your brain refusing to provide better words?*

"Sorry, Tessa. I'm messing all of this up."

"You're wrong."

The cool tone of her voice sent a wave of panic down Gabe's back.

Her eyes were clear, and her shoulders were firm as she met his gaze. "My mother didn't die because she was working too hard. She died because she left med school to have me. She died because my father got tired of supporting everyone and abandoned us."

Tessa hiccuped as she wrapped her arms tightly around herself.

"But would she have wanted you to push yourself to the edge for a job? A promotion isn't more important than family. It isn't worth injuring yourself or the babies." Gabe pushed his hands through his hair as he caught the final words.

Tessa's eyes widened and the final bit of color slipped from her face. "Do you want me to get this promotion, Gabe? Or are you hoping that Josh Killon or Mark Jackson gets it?"

"No one wants Josh to get it." The joke fell flat as Tessa raised an eyebrow and tapped her foot.

Swallowing the fear, Gabe shrugged. "I want so many things, Tessa. I want to protect you and the twins. I want to provide for you. I want you." He tried to say he wanted her to get the promotion. Those were the words she wanted to hear—but they refused to materialize.

She was exhausted. She looked sick. No job was worth that. Why couldn't she understand that?

"I'm here for you. Let me carry some of the load." The plea fell from his lips. *Please.*

Tessa's eyes flashed with tears, but they didn't spill down her cheeks. "We can share the load, but I don't *want* you to do everything. I don't *need* you."

Gabe blinked as her words pummeled him. "I see." Helping others, protecting them, was what Gabe did. All the things he offered to do for her, she didn't want him to do. Didn't need *him.*

At least not like he needed her. That was a painful truth. His heart cracked as he stood next to her. The walls felt like they were closing in as he tried to push back the hurt. What was his role if he couldn't help the woman he loved?

"I need to get some sleep, but Patrick talked to me today.

I have an interview for Dr. Lin's position next week." Tessa walked past him. "I thought you should know.

"And I heard you say at Stacy's barbecue that you were worried I'd get the position." Her voice cracked. "I can do this, Gabe."

Her shoulders slumped as she stood in the doorway. The final bit of fight draining from her. "I will be a great senior attending."

She would. Gabe offered a small smile. "I'm sure you will. But Tessa, you can't do it all." *At least not alone. And you don't have to.* But his tongue refused to say the words his heart cried out.

Pulling at the back of his neck, Gabe tried to find a path forward, anything that let him be in her life as more than just the father of their children.

How had the dream shattered so quickly? He'd watched his mother pull away from her family for years. Watched her put a little more distance between her and their father. Gabe wouldn't wait around to watch history repeat itself.

"Maybe I should stay at Stacy's for a little while." The words fell into the space between them. The obstacles this conversation had highlighted radiated around them.

Her bottom lip shook, and Gabe swallowed. If she asked him to stay, he would. He would do almost anything for the woman in front of him. *Just ask me to stay.*

"If you think that's best." Then she turned and left.

A hole opened in his chest as he stared at the empty doorway. How were they supposed to cross this chasm? The clock ticked away, and his heart cracked with each step he climbed.

Tessa was already fast asleep. She hadn't even pulled the covers down on the bed. Gabe grabbed a bag and threw in as many of his clothes as he could. Then he grabbed a blanket and pulled it over her.

Running his hand along her temple, Gabe didn't try to stop the tears falling down his cheeks. "I love you." At least he'd gotten to say the words once. Then he turned and fled the place he'd hoped would be his forever home.

CHAPTER TWELVE

TESSA WATCHED GABE walk to his car from the shadows of Dallas Children's parking garage. Her heart screamed for her to run to him. To yell for him to come home. To plead that three lonely nights was more than she could take.

To tell him she loved him and see if that could right the chasms between them.

She'd given up one career opportunity for a partner. And he'd left her anyway.

But Tessa hadn't expected Gabe to leave. That was the part that pummeled her. She'd been exhausted and had needed a nap to regroup. To find better words to explain.

When she'd woken she'd smiled at the blanket he'd thrown over her. She'd gone to find him, hoping to work through the divide that had opened between them. To apologize for her harsh words.

But his things had been gone. His bed was still in the room where they'd first put it. Still covered with plants. But his clothes were gone. The pictures of his family had been taken from the fridge.

When he'd offered to go to his sister's, she'd assumed it was only for a night. Just to give them each a day to cool off.

Not for good.

She hadn't even spoken to him in three days. Three

long days of silence. She'd drafted and discarded so many text messages in the last seventy-two hours. Tessa grabbed her phone and pulled up Gabe's number. *Again.* She'd never realized how difficult it was to press Send.

She yawned and slid her phone back into the pocket of her scrubs. Even if she'd known what to say—what the proper apology was—she didn't have time right now.

Closing her eyes, she sighed. She'd been at the hospital nearly every day this month. Even before he'd left, she'd packed her lunches, handled her share of the household chores—made sure that she was carrying her part of the load. And it still hadn't kept Gabe in her life.

It had driven him away.

What if Gabe really had enjoyed taking on so much? Enjoyed picking up extra chores so she could rest? Truly enjoyed helping her, instead of resenting her? What if she'd been so concerned with the past that she'd ruined her future?

His crushed face hovered in her memory. Her words had done that. She'd told him she didn't need him. *Didn't need him.*

That was the biggest falsehood she'd ever spoken. She needed Gabe more than she'd ever needed anyone. Not to help her around the house, but to love her. To believe in her—and that terrified her. Instead of clinging to that amazing gift, she'd let fear rule. And lost everything.

Her chest clenched as she started for the hospital entrance. Tessa put her hand to her heart as she tried to catch her breath. Spots dotted her vision as she tried to force her feet to move faster, but it felt like she was wading through quicksand.

Her skin was clammy, and panic raced across her spine. This wasn't a symptom of the brokenhearted. Her hand reached for her belly as she crossed Dallas Children's threshold.

"Dr. Garcia?" Denise's voice was far away.

"I…need…an ambulance." Tessa's chest clenched as she tried sucking in air. Blackness pulled at the edges of her vision, and she tried to keep it away.

Gabe… She tried to say his name. *Maybe she had.* But as the darkness took her, Tessa wasn't sure she'd managed to get it out. *Gabe…*

Dr. Fillery offered a nod as she walked into Tessa's room at Presbyterian Hospital. She didn't remember being transported here, but Tessa didn't care about how she'd landed here. She had only one concern.

"The babies."

"Are fine. My concern is about you." She strode to the bed. "Your iron levels were dangerously low, Tessa."

Dr. Fillery's voice carried an authority that she recognized. It was the *I am a doctor and I need you to follow the orders I am about to give* voice. Tessa had used it many times in her career.

She didn't care what Dr. Fillery said she needed to do. The twins were fine. She let out a soft sigh as she let that knowledge wrap around her. The babies were okay. A kick to her ribs sent a smile to her lips. Tessa rested her hand over where the twins were wrestling.

"You're staying here at least overnight, Tessa. You will need to take an iron supplement for the rest of your pregnancy and likely through at least the first few months postpartum." Dr. Fillery took a deep breath and then offered the final order. "And you need to take at least the next two weeks off at Dallas Children's. I know your patients are important, but your hemoglobin levels were at four point two grams per deciliter. I can't believe you were still standing."

"I'll take time off." She meant it. Tessa wouldn't fight the orders, but the forced time off carried other consequences. She bit her lips as the tears coated her eyes. It was fine. *It was fine.*

"If we can't get your levels regulated, I'll recommend bed rest. But right now, I'm just going to tell you to stay home, rest as much as possible, eat lots of leafy greens and lentils. I'll see you in my office at the end of next week, and we'll see if you're strong enough to go back to work then."

Tessa nodded, but the blood was pounding in her ears.

She'd have to cancel her interview—pull her name from consideration. She'd worked so hard for the senior attending position. She was the most qualified. It hurt to step away from it. But Tessa wouldn't risk the health of her children—or herself.

Still, she let a few tears fall for the lost opportunity. There'd be other job openings, she knew that. But that didn't fully chase away the pain.

Her throat was tight, but she pulled up her phone. It wouldn't take long for the gossip network at Dallas Children's to rehash one of their doctors collapsing as they started their shift. She didn't want Gabe to worry.

Besides, he deserved to know that their children were all right. She typed a few words, then hit Send. Then she gave in to the exhaustion chasing her.

"Brett didn't eat all her lunch today. Do you think she's feeling all right?" Gabe put the cheese stick and uneaten grapes back in Stacy's fridge.

His sister's scoff echoed in her kitchen as she passed him a plate and a towel. "She's almost thirteen, Gabe.

Lunchtime is more about socializing than it is about eating lunch. Besides, she told you that she only wants tuna and carrots. I know you're bored, but let the preteen pack her own lunch."

The statement sent a pain down his back. The fissure over not speaking to Tessa for the last three days was bursting at the seams. But he took a deep breath and forced the feelings back inside. He wasn't going to break down—at least not right at this moment.

It was a constant battle to just pretend to be normal when everything seemed lost. Colors no longer seemed as bright, and food—even the sugary treats he loved— had no flavor. Without Tessa, the world was bland.

Leaning against the counter, he tried to shake off the despair that had clung to him since he'd walked out of Tessa's town house. *Keep moving forward*; it was the mantra he'd used after Olive passed. The one that had eventually broken him. But Gabe wasn't going to let that happen—not again.

Besides, Tessa was still alive. Still at Dallas Children's. Still pregnant with their children. Still so many things—but not his.

He needed to get control of himself. "I'm just trying to earn my keep. Brett's barely been home between school, martial arts and dance. I swear that kid is always gone!"

The excuses fell from his lips as the truth ate through him. Tessa hadn't wanted his help, hadn't needed it. He was trying to ignore the hole their argument had torn through him. Who was he if he couldn't help the people he loved? If the woman he loved didn't want his help?

Stacy raised an eyebrow before dipping her hands into the soapy water again. "Help is appreciated, but Brett needs to do things for herself—it builds character."

"Mom! We're going to be late to weapons class." Brett's voice was high-pitched as she raced toward the garage.

"No running in the house!" Stacy dried her hands before putting her hand on his shoulder. "And Gabe—" his sister's smile was tinged with an emotion he feared was pity "—you don't have to do everything for everyone. There's no need to earn your keep with family."

Gabe didn't move as his sister grabbed her purse and rushed to the car. Crossing his arms, Gabe stared out the window of the back porch. Memories of Tessa laughing with his family played out before him, and pain raced through him.

There's no need to earn your keep.

His sister's words ate through his soul. He wasn't trying to. Not really.

Except...

He squeezed his eyes shut as the truth settled within him. After his mother's abandonment, Gabe had taken on more responsibilities. To help his dad and make sure everyone was cared for. To be enough...

Enough that a job wouldn't be worth more than him.

Tears blurred his vision when he opened his eyes. He'd tried for years to be "enough," so his mom would come home. To be more important than the career she'd given everything up for. But Gabe would never be enough for her—no one would.

But that wasn't because there was something wrong with him.

A weight he hadn't known he was carrying lifted off his chest. He was enough—just as he was.

But now he had to address how he'd let that fear destroy his family.

Rather than tell Tessa he loved her, he'd tried to earn his place in Tessa's life. Tried to be more important than her promotion. Because he was worried that she'd choose that over him. Like his mother had.

And she had.

The specter of hurt raced across his heart. But the truth cried out, too. She'd said they could carry the load. *Together.* That she didn't need him to do everything. She'd wanted a true partnership. And he'd wanted more. To be the protector who rode to the rescue.

She'd asked for a partner, and he'd walked away because she wasn't looking for a knight in shining armor.

The woman he loved had asked if he wanted her to get the thing she'd worked hard for. A job that she would excel at, and that would enable her to help others. She had a passion for serving others that their children would see and learn from. A true partner would have screamed, *Yes!* But he'd walked away—because he'd feared that one day she might choose it over him. Because leaving felt safer than getting left.

But Tessa was not his mother. He'd lost love once. But this time he'd thrown it away on the minuscule chance that he might get hurt.

How was he supposed to fix this? He banged his head against the kitchen cupboards, trying to force some idea to present itself. This couldn't be fixed with cupcakes or some other treat. He needed some grand gesture— something to prove...

No!

Gabe was done trying to prove that he was enough. But he needed to figure out a way to show Tessa how much he loved her. How lost he was without her. How much he wanted to stand beside her as she achieved her dreams. *All of them.*

His phone buzzed. His hands were clammy as he ripped the smartphone from his back pocket. He still

wasn't sure of the right words, but he didn't care. He
needed her.

Always.

The twins are fine. I don't know if you heard, but I passed
out at the start of my shift. I will be at Presbyterian overnight. Then two weeks of strict rest. I'm going to pull my
name from consideration for the job. You were right. I
can't do it all.

The words devastated him. She was brokenhearted
over the job—and he'd contributed to that. He'd made
her feel that she couldn't do it all. He could have tried
to be more understanding. Tried to see her asserting her
need to help him as wanting to be his partner.

Instead of seeing that as a blessing, he'd given in to
his own anxiety. And he'd shown her that she might have
to rely on herself in a world without him. Gabe slapped
the top of his head. *God, he was a fool.*

But Gabe could fix part of this. He made a quick call,
then grabbed his keys. There was one errand to run, and
then he was going to see Tessa. He was going to apologize, to confess his love, and to promise he'd stand by
her no matter what.

Presbyterian Hospital didn't have bright walls or pretty
murals to ease the hospital feel like Dallas Children's
did. As Gabe raced toward Tessa's room, his chest tightened. It had taken him almost two hours to get everything together.

A nurse brushed his shoulder, and his backpack
shifted. He'd grabbed the items he'd thought might make
her stay more comfortable. He didn't pause to make sure
the one breakable thing was fine. If he had to buy another

because her mouthwash leaked, Gabe would. He would not waste any more time getting to her side.

Her door was closed. Gabe took a deep breath to keep from rushing through. If Tessa was resting, he didn't want to wake her.

Only the small lamp was lit, but she turned as soon as he walked through the door. Her tentative grin sent a flash of hope through him. Even after everything that had happened, she'd reached out to him.

His heart leaped. He'd never walk away from her again. *Never.*

"You came."

Her whispered words cut across him. Gabe hated that she had doubted for even a second that he'd come to her. He never wanted her to worry about that again.

"I will always come. No matter what. Because I love you." The words fell from Gabe's lips as he slid in next to her bed. "I know there are a million other things that I need to say, apologies to make, but I need you to know that I love you, Tessa Garcia. All of you."

Her fingers wrapped through his, and tears coated her dark eyes.

Before she could say anything, Gabe rushed on. "I was trying to earn your love." He brushed his lips against her hand as the words rushed out. "All the chores, the dinners, the cupcakes—I needed to prove that I was worthy. But I never meant to make you feel like I didn't believe in you. Like I didn't think you could do it all, or that I wouldn't want to walk beside you from here to eternity. I am so sorry."

"Oh, Gabe." Tessa turned in the bed as much as the rails would allow. "You never need to earn my love. My whole heart is yours."

He thought his body might erupt from happiness as

she held his gaze. "I love you." He would never tire of saying those words.

Tessa bit her lip and squeezed his hand. "I was so concerned about making sure that you didn't feel like I was taking advantage of you that I pushed you away. Max may have hated when I leaned on him, but that was a fault in him, not me. I love you, Gabe Davis. What if we just promise to look forward now? Let the past stay where it belongs."

"That's the easiest promise I will ever make. I can't wait to spend each day with you, Tessa." Gabe ran his hand along her arm, unable to keep from touching her.

She wiped away a tear and gestured toward the room. "This isn't the best setting for a happily-ever-after, is it?"

The sterile room wasn't the location that he'd have chosen for this moment, either. Outside of their twins' birth, Gabe would be happy if he never had another night sitting next to Tessa in a hospital bed. But there was a bit he could do to brighten her room.

"I know you won't be here for more than a day or two—"

"One day, I hope." Tessa rubbed her belly as she interrupted him. "Though I'll stay as long as I have to."

How could he ever have doubted the woman he loved would choose anything over her family? If Gabe could kick his past self, he would. He knew the lifetime he planned to spend with Tessa was going to have valleys, but he was going to do everything in his power to make her happy every single day.

"I thought this might make it easier to stay overnight." Gabe pulled a small succulent from the front pocket of his backpack. "This was the smallest guy I could find— and you said they were hardy, so I figured a ride to the hospital wouldn't cause it too much worry."

Tessa grinned at the small plant. "You brought a plant. That's great. And it brightens the room."

"That isn't all I brought." Gabe took a deep breath and pulled out the router. He understood her raised eyebrow as she stared at the box. "It will make the internet at the house super strong. No dropped streaming videos."

"Oh." She nodded. "That will be helpful while I'm stuck at home. Lots of shows to catch up on. And movie marathons to enjoy."

"I can't wait for a movie marathon. I'm going to pop so much popcorn!" Gabe squeezed her hand and waited for her to meet his gaze before he continued, "Want some company in there?"

He sighed as she scooted over in the large maternity bed. When she curled into his chest, Gabe's world finally felt like it was nearly right. But it wouldn't be complete until Tessa had the chance to chase her dream. "But this isn't for movie marathons. At least, not completely. It's so there's no chance of your video freezing during your interview next week."

"Gabe." Her voice wobbled, but she sucked in a deep breath. "I'm not interviewing for the position."

"Why not?" He ran a hand along her side. "You're the best candidate, Tessa. Everyone knows it. I should have said it three days ago. I should have told you how great a senior attending I know you'll be. I should have encouraged you to get a little rest, but I should never have made you doubt yourself." He kissed her cheek as her lip trembled.

"I appreciate those kind words. I really do. And I'm not giving up on the dream. But there will be other positions. You and the twins come first. Always." She smiled, but he could see the hint of sadness still hovering in her eyes.

"Don't get mad." Gabe kissed the top of her head. "But I called Patrick before I went to get that router. There's no reason you can't do a video interview. They're even interviewing at least one outside hire that way."

"An outside hire!"

There was the fire he loved so much. "Yep. If you really want to pull your name from consideration, I will support you, whatever you want, but make sure it's because that's what you want, not because a crazy terrible week made you think you can't do it. Because you can."

"If I get the job, you'll have to take on more at home with the twins." Tessa looked at the router. "It won't be even."

The words were music to his ears. "No one's keeping score, Tessa. I promise."

"But I'll always handle the plants."

"Absolutely." Gabe ran a finger along her cheek and then bent his lips to hers.

The kiss was sweet and long. It spoke of all their hopes for the future. The years of love and happiness that spun out before them. *Together.*

EPILOGUE

"I'M HOME."

Gabe's deep voice echoed down the hallway, and Tessa smiled.

She would never tire of hearing him say that he was at home. However, today she was trying to surprise him. And she wasn't quite ready!

"Hold on!"

Tessa pulled the cake from the bakery box. It had flowers all over it—and Maggie's had promised that this green icing wouldn't leave stains on anyone's teeth. The sugary scent floated up as she set it in the middle of the small dining table, and one of the twins kicked.

Whoosh! At nearly thirty-two weeks along, they were almost out of room in her abdomen, but they still managed to level at least a few good jabs every day. But Tessa really didn't mind.

"Behave!" She glared playfully at her belly. "Or I might let Daddy eat all the cake."

Another rib shot.

"Tessa? Are you all right?"

"Fine," she called. Adjusting the silverware, she let her gaze wander to the decorations she hadn't had time to lay. *Oh, well.*

Swinging open the door, Tessa bowed as much as her belly would let her. "Dinner is served."

Gabe raised an eyebrow before dropping a kiss to her cheek. "This looks lovely. And that cake is making my mouth water. What's the occasion?"

She knocked his hip with hers as they walked to the table. "You pamper me. All the time!" After she'd taken over the role of senior attending, Tessa and Gabe had slipped into a routine that worked well, but he deserved some indulging, too.

"And you love it." Gabe's lips were soft as they brushed against hers.

Yes. She did.

"True." Tessa smiled. "But you deserve a night off, too. I'd have put up more decorations, but the delivery guy was running late."

"Decorations?"

She bit her lip as she gestured toward the cake. "Isla is driving me nuts with all the girl stuff. Figured we might want to know so we can get serious about choosing names! What better way than dinner and a gender-reveal cake."

The bristles on his cheek sent waves of need racing across her as Gabe pulled her close and kissed her. She leaned into him. Hope, excitement and love pulsed around them. And then the twins kicked.

"They're getting strong!" Gabe laughed.

"I know!" Tessa tapped his side as she gathered herself. "Do you want dinner or dessert first?"

"Like you even need to ask." Gabe ran a finger along her chin. His eyes held so much love that Tessa felt like she might take flight. "Cut the cake and tell me what we're having."

She quickly slid the knife through the frosting and smiled. *Pink.* "Isla's winning streak holds true. Girls!"

Turning, she barely managed to set the piece of cake on the table. Gabe was down on one knee. His smile was so big as he held the ring out to her.

"I love you so much."

"Yes!" Tessa yelled.

He shook his head, and a small chuckle escaped his lips. "I didn't even ask yet." He pulled the ring from the box and slid it on her finger.

"I love you." Tessa smiled at the ring, and then at him. "But if I don't feed your little girls, I think they might start rearranging my ribs."

He pulled her close as the twins kicked. "Definitely a dessert-before-dinner night!" He bent and kissed her belly. "But don't get used to it, girls."

* * * * *

MILLS & BOON

Coming next month

HOW TO WIN THE SURGEON'S HEART
Tina Beckett

"Okay. Nate…"

Except saying his given name…out loud…made whatever she'd been about to say vanish. So she just stood there, taking in his casual clothing, that was now rumpled in a way that was somehow wonderful. The hard lines of his body were more visible now, and she was having a difficult time looking away. Her gaze trailed up his face, noting there were dark circles under his eyes, probably from the stress of the day. She imagined he put in long hours most every day. A little far removed from the lap-of-luxury living she'd pictured him in over in this corner of the island.

"Not so hard, after all, was it?"

"W-what?" Had he read her thoughts?

"Saying my name."

Her senses went on high alert as an image of her whispering his name in an entirely different way scurried through her head, only to run away when she tried to catch it and banish it. Instead, the two beds in the room behind her seemed to taunt her, to remind her of how long it had been since she'd been with anyone.

She cleared her throat. "Maybe I was being a little silly when we met. I'd just heard stories…"

"Stories?" His frown was back. "Such as?"

Um, not happening. Because the words delectable and delicious had been interjected time and time again. "Nothing bad."

That line in his face played peekaboo. "I find that rather hard to believe."

"That nothing bad was said?"

He made a sound of assent. "Are you saying *you've* never had an unkind thing to say about me?"

Ugh. She'd had lots of unkind things to say. Patty had called her on it time and time again. But then again, her friend was a newlywed, still caught up in the early stages of love.

Her lips twitched. "Maybe you'll have to work on changing my mind."

"Is that a challenge…Sasha?"

The shock of hearing her name on his tongue washed over her like the waves of the sea. Warm. Sensual. Snaking up her calves, edging over her hips and making her nipples tighten.

Some dangerous part of her brain sent the word, "Maybe" from her mouth before she could stop it.

And when his hand moved from the railing and slid up her forearm, she was powerless to stop from leaning toward him, her eyes closing.

"That's one challenge I might have to accept."

Continue reading
HOW TO WIN THE SURGEON'S HEART
Tina Beckett

Available next month
www.millsandboon.co.uk

COMING SOON!

LET'S TALK
Romance

For exclusive extracts, competitions
and special offers, find us online:

 facebook.com/millsandboon

 @MillsandBoon

 @MillsandBoonUK

Get in touch on 01413 063232

For all the latest titles coming soon, visit
millsandboon.co.uk/nextmonth